House of Secrets
CLASH OF THE WORLDS

CLASH OF THE WORLDS

CHRIS COLUMBUS
NED VIZZINI
CHRIS RYLANDER

Illustrations by **GREG CALL**

BALZER + BRAY
An Imprint of HarperCollinsPublishers

Balzer + Bray is an imprint of HarperCollins Publishers.

House of Secrets: Clash of the Worlds
Text copyright © 2016 by Novel Approach LLC
Illustrations copyright © 2016 by Greg Call

ISBN 978-0-06-219251-6 (trade bdg.) — ISBN 978-0-06-244958-0 (int.)

Typography by Amy Ryan
16 17 18 19 20   PC/RRDH   10 9 8 7 6 5 4 3 2 1

First Edition

For Ned

House of Secrets
CLASH OF THE WORLDS

CHAPTER

1

Brendan Walker knew this story wasn't going to have a happy ending.

He stood on the beach near his home on Sea Cliff Avenue with his sisters, Cordelia and Eleanor, and stared out at San Francisco Bay. Not at the whole bay, but rather at the exact spot in the water where they had just seen their friend, a colossus named Fat Jagger, standing a few moments ago.

Cars were stopped on the Golden Gate Bridge. Several people peered over the edge, likely wondering if they had really just seen a massive, fifty-story tall, overweight version of Mick Jagger in the middle of San Francisco Bay, howling at the moon.

But it simply couldn't have been possible. Fat Jagger

wasn't *real*, at least not in the same way that Brendan and his sisters were. Fat Jagger was just a character in an old novel by Denver Kristoff. Or so Brendan had thought. Then again, the Walker children had witnessed enough "impossible" things in the past few months to convince them that literally *anything* was possible.

Most kids would probably run away screaming if they saw a huge colossus wearing a loincloth rise up out of the ocean. Or at the very least, call 911. They certainly wouldn't try to lure the massive giant even closer. But the three Walker children were definitely not like most kids. At least, not anymore. Not since they had moved into the Kristoff House and found themselves thrown into the magical world of his books—engaged in a seemingly endless battle with the evil Wind Witch, frost beasts, Nazi cyborgs, bloodthirsty pirates, and a variety of other horrors from the depths of the author's imagination.

"Well, now what?" Brendan asked. "We could call my English teacher, Ms. Krumbsly, to lure him out. She's still single and almost as big as Fat Jagger. They might make a cute couple?"

His younger sister, Eleanor, slapped his arm. "Bren!" she scolded. "Fat Jagger's our *friend*! You should be nicer to him; he did save our lives a couple times. Ms. Krumbsly is way too mean—I wouldn't even wish her on my worst enemies."

"Yeah, I know, Nell," Brendan said. "I guess what I'm

saying is that we don't exactly have a good plan."

"Since when have you ever worried about having a well-structured plan in place before acting?" Cordelia asked.

She was the oldest of the three Walker kids at nearly sixteen, although she tended to sometimes talk and act like she was at least twice her age.

"Hey, I can make plans and be the leader sometimes too," Brendan protested. His sisters just looked at him. They knew, as well as he did, that he was much better at making jokes.

The three Walker children were standing on the beach directly below the cliff upon which the Victorian, three-story Kristoff House was precariously perched—the same house that they would only be able to call home for one more night. Because after once again barely escaping from the fantastical book world with their lives, they had returned to a reality in which their father had managed to gamble away a ten-million-dollar fortune. And so the next morning they'd be moving back into a cramped apartment near Fisherman's Wharf.

"Come on," Cordelia said, pulling her coat closed to fend off the biting ocean breeze. "Let's at least try to get closer to the bridge, in the vicinity of where he surfaced. Standing around talking certainly isn't going to accomplish anything."

Brendan and Eleanor followed Cordelia along the beach toward the bridge. There was still no sign of Fat Jagger.

As the three Walkers moved farther along the beach, they passed a homeless man with a long gray beard sitting in the brush at the base of the cliff. He watched them walk by, but said nothing. The moonlight seemed to make his eyes shine like diamonds in the darkness of the shadows. For a split second, Brendan thought it was the Storm King, which was what Denver Kristoff had been calling himself ever since *The Book of Doom and Desire* had corrupted his soul years ago.

But that book was gone now; Eleanor had banished it forever, using its own magic against it. And so was the Storm King. The three Walker siblings had seen him get hit and killed by a city bus outside the Bohemian Club in downtown San Francisco—killed by his own daughter no less, Dahlia Kristoff, aka the Wind Witch. But in spite of the online news article claiming his body had been buried in a nearby mausoleum under an assumed identity, Brendan wasn't completely convinced that the crooked old wizard was actually dead.

"Fat Jagger!" Eleanor screamed, shaking Brendan from his thoughts.

For a moment, he thought the colossus must have reappeared. But Eleanor shouted his name again, calling out across the bay like she was looking for a lost dog.

"Fat Jagger, come out, we can help you!" Eleanor yelled.

Cordelia cupped her hands around her mouth and

joined in. "Fat Jagger, we're here now!"

"Come on out, Fat Jagger! It's us, the *Wallllk-errrrs!*" Eleanor shouted, drawing out the pronunciation of their last name the way he always did.

"Nice Fat Jagger impersonation," Brendan said as he looked around the beach. "Let me try."

Brendan stepped up to the water and began to sing,

"If you start me up, if you start me up I'll never stop . . ."

"Just because you were a rock star when we traveled to ancient Rome doesn't mean you're a great singer back in the real world," Eleanor said.

"You're just jealous of my sterling pipes, Nell."

Eleanor didn't bother responding.

A young couple jogging along the beach slowed and watched the three kids warily. They kept a safe distance from the Walkers as they passed.

The water lapped gently at the kids' feet as they continued to shout, but there was still no sign of their friend. Several other people taking an evening walk on the beach were now looking at them with a mixture of curiosity and confusion.

"Guys, let's take it easy with the shouting. People are going to think we're a few noodles short of a spaghetti dinner," Brendan said, borrowing one of his dad's favorite lame jokes.

The first few times Dr. Walker used that line, Brendan

had groaned. But after hearing it at every holiday and birthday party for so long, he had come to love it. Those had been simpler times back then, though. Back before the Walker family was in financial ruins, before they had gotten themselves tangled up in the dark magic and secrets surrounding Kristoff House. Back before the three kids had to spend their evenings on a beach trying to lure a fifty-story colossus named Fat Jagger out of San Francisco Bay.

"What are we going to do?" Cordelia asked. "Why won't Fat Jagger surface again?"

"Maybe he can't hear us?" Eleanor suggested, fighting tears. "Under all that water."

"Maybe we never even saw him at all?" Brendan said. "Did we just imagine him?"

"You're not helping," Cordelia scolded. "We all know what we saw. Even if *one* of us imagined it, there's no way we *all* did simultaneously. Three people don't just randomly have the same hallucination!"

Brendan sighed. She had a point.

"Well," he said, "we know Jagger can hold his breath for a really long time. So he probably won't drown."

"That's right," Cordelia said, turning toward Eleanor's panicked face. "Remember? The first time we were sent into Kristoff's books, Fat Jagger walked all the way across the huge sea to Tinz . . . just to save us."

Eleanor nodded and took a few deep breaths, still struggling to fight back her tears. She didn't quite know what it was about Fat Jagger that she connected with so much, but she had truly come to view him as one of her best friends, in spite of the fact that they'd never really had a conversation longer than one or two words.

"I mean, we could try to go fishing for him or something," Brendan suggested, only half kidding. "We could use one of Mrs. Deagle's cats as bait . . ."

"That's horrible!" Eleanor shouted.

"But she's got like twenty-seven cats," Brendan said. "She'll never miss one!"

"Not funny, Bren," Cordelia chided.

"Sorry, comedy is in my blood." Brendan shrugged. "I can't just switch it off."

"I would hardly call it comedy," Cordelia muttered.

Eleanor wasn't really listening to her older siblings squabble. She was lost in her own thoughts. And then the solution suddenly hit her—she knew how they could lure Fat Jagger out of the bay.

"I've got it!" Eleanor said. "I just need to get to a Safeway."

"Nell, we can eat later," Brendan said, but then put a hand on his stomach. "On second thought . . . now that you said it, I *could* go for a couple Lunchables."

Neither Cordelia nor Eleanor had the chance to respond,

because their mother's voice called out from behind them.

"Kids, there you are!" she called. "Don't sneak off like that; I've been looking everywhere for you three! Let's get back home. Our plans have changed."

"We can't yet!" Eleanor said. "We're, uh . . . not finished saying good-bye to the neighborhood!"

Eleanor knew she needed to buy more time to execute her plan to lure out Fat Jagger and get him away from the city, to head north up the coast where he'd be less likely to get spotted. She had seen enough movies to know that a colossus running loose in San Francisco would not end well. She could already envision Fat Jagger chained up and on display as a part of some sort of traveling freak show. Or even worse, swatting at fighter jets as they swooped in to destroy him.

"I'm sorry, sweetie, there's no time!" Mrs. Walker said, crushing Eleanor's hopes. "Things have changed and we need to move into the apartment tonight. The moving truck is waiting for us. We're leaving right now."

CHAPTER

2

The Walker kids looked at each other with expressions that ranged from complete despair to outright panic. Their looks said:

Now what would they do?

How could Fat Jagger possibly stay hidden throughout the night?

Man, I could really use a Lunchable.

But they had no choice. Mrs. Walker clearly wasn't going to allow any debate on the matter, and she already looked harried enough as it was. So they slowly followed their mother up the hill toward their street, Sea Cliff Avenue. Or, more accurately, their *former* street.

As they trudged up the steeply sloping hill, Eleanor took one last look back at the bay. That's when she saw a disturbance in the water out near the center of the bridge. At this distance, it looked like a small ripple, perhaps just a swirling current, or a seal or dolphin. But she knew better. To her, the ripple had looked more like a pair of pronounced colossus lips poking out of the water to get another breath of air.

As they followed Mrs. Walker back toward the Kristoff House, the three kids lagged a few feet behind. Brendan and Cordelia were surprised to see Eleanor smiling.

"I just saw Fat Jagger poke his lips out of the water to breathe," she whispered to them. "Which means I think he knows that he needs to stay hidden. If he can just stay out of sight until tomorrow morning, I have a plan to lure him out."

"But what are we going to do even *if* we get Fat Jagger to shore?" Brendan asked dubiously. "Invite him over for a slumber party? Play Twister, make microwave popcorn, and then spill our most embarrassing secrets?"

"We could bring him to school!" Eleanor said excitedly, totally missing her brother's sarcasm.

Brendan imagined Jagger rolling up the school bully, Scott Calurio, between his thumb and forefinger like a booger and then smashing him to the side of the school building.

"That *would* be pretty cool," Brendan admitted. "Plus, he would absolutely crush it in lacrosse."

Cordelia glared at Eleanor and Brendan, but before any of them could say anything else, their mom interrupted the conversation.

"Kids, there's something else I have to tell you," Mrs. Walker said, looking a bit nervous. "It's certainly not going to be easy—but it's for the best. It's the reason we need to move tonight instead of tomorrow."

The Walker kids stopped and waited anxiously for her to deliver the news.

"I know this will be hard for you, and it is for me too," Mrs. Walker said slowly, her eyes looking red and tired. "But tomorrow morning, your dad is going away for a few days, or maybe even a few weeks. To a gambling addiction treatment facility."

"Wait, Dad is a gambling addict?" Cordelia asked.

Guilt began to stir inside of her as she realized that her first thought was how this was going to affect her—what would people think? Would all the prestigious colleges she hoped to get into somehow find out that her dad spent time in treatment? Cordelia had always focused on her future, doing everything the "right" way and trying to be the best. But now she saw her dreams quickly fading in the face of this news. Did kids with addict fathers actually get into places like Harvard, Yale, and Stanford?

"Dad is going away?" Eleanor asked, her voice breaking. The thought of potentially losing Fat Jagger and her dad in one night was more than she could stomach.

"Don't worry, baby," Mrs. Walker said, pulling an arm around Eleanor and trying to force a smile. "It'll just be for a little bit, and we can visit him this weekend. And when he gets back, everything will be so much better. I promise. You kids are so strong and independent; you always have been. I know you'll . . . *we'll* get through this, together."

"But what will we do for money?" Brendan asked.

"*Brendan!*" Mrs. Walker said, glaring at her son. "Is that all you can think about right now?"

Brendan hesitated, perhaps a moment too long, before finally shaking his head *no*, feeling bad that he was more worried about family finances than his own dad's mental health.

Of course, there was always the Nazi treasure map they'd brought back from the book world. But that was a long shot. According to the red *X* on the map, the treasure was hidden somewhere in Europe. Which, the last time Brendan had checked, was a long way away from San Francisco. Plus, they still had no idea if the treasure would even be there in the real world at all. It might only exist inside one of Denver Kristoff's fictional books.

"In the meantime, I am more than capable of taking care of our family," Mrs. Walker continued, struggling to sound positive. "Which is why I will be starting a new job in the shoe department at Macy's tomorrow."

Just a few weeks ago the family lived in a beautiful Victorian home overlooking the Golden Gate Bridge and had a ten-million-dollar bankroll. Now they were moving into a tiny apartment with virtually nothing to their name. Well, except the embarrassment that their father, Dr. Walker, had brought by losing his medical license and then gambling away all their money in just a few short months. The family still had *that* to their name, of course.

Brendan suddenly felt horrible giving his mom such a hard time about money. None of this was her fault, after all. She was the one Walker who was probably *least* responsible for any of the family's recent and ongoing problems.

"Well," Brendan said, "if you need your first customer, I've got some birthday money saved up. I always wondered what I'd look like in a pair of red heels."

In spite of the somber mood, all the Walkers laughed. The sound of their laughter almost seemed to lift some of the darkness draped across Sea Cliff Avenue that evening. As if the moon had suddenly switched to a higher setting.

"I think I would actually pay to see Brendan in heels," Mrs. Walker laughed, hugging them all. "I love you guys, you know that? No matter how bad things get, you always find a way to make me smile. Anyway, you won't have time to shop for shoes tomorrow."

"Why not?" Cordelia asked.

Mrs. Walker then delivered what Brendan and Cordelia thought to be the worst news of the evening so far.

"Because you'll all be going back to your old schools tomorrow morning."

CHAPTER

3

Later that night, Eleanor tossed and turned in her tiny bed inside her tiny room that she shared with Cordelia in the tiny apartment they had moved into. Nightmares haunted her sleep. Nightmares of Fat Jagger fighting off massive great white sharks in the dark waters of San Francisco Bay. Nightmares of Fat Jagger getting caught up in a fishing net and drowning. Nightmares of Fat Jagger getting discovered and then hunted by men with giant harpoons in whaling ships. And in all her nightmares, there was nothing she could do to help him.

Brendan, however, was not even trying to sleep.

He was sitting at the small desk in his room with his head in his hands, thinking about having to go back to his old school and seeing all his old friends and teachers. They would all ask him why he had to transfer out of private school and come back. He'd have to tell them the truth. That his dad gambled away all their money and they got kicked out of their home. It'd be especially hard to face them after the way he'd left—admittedly (now) a little too cocky over how much better his new private school was going to be "than this dump."

This reality somehow filled Brendan with more fear than most of the crazy book adventures he had been on. He realized death was almost easier to face than total humiliation—which was a startling and sobering revelation.

Brendan distracted himself by switching on the fifty-five-inch TV that he'd brought with him from his not-quite-a-man cave in the Kristoff House attic. They could take away his cool attic bedroom and his old school and the money and his chauffer (which was probably his favorite part of their old life). But *nobody* was getting their hands on the TV he bought with some of the money Eleanor had wished for using *The Book of Doom and Desire*. He and the TV had been through a lot together already, including the Giants' most recent World Series victory. He'd been so excited on the final out, that he almost accidentally threw his half-full can of soda right through her beautiful and flawless screen.

Brendan flipped through the channels, looking for the

reruns of *Family Guy* or *South Park* that always seemed to be on late at night. He was just about ready to settle on ESPN as a consolation, when a headline on a news channel caught his eye. For a second, he figured maybe he was watching a parody news show, because there was no way the headline could be true.

But the channel was CNN. The news story Brendan watched play out on-screen was most definitely real. And it caused him to literally fall out of his bedroom chair and land on the floor with a sickening thud.

4

At the other end of the Walkers' apartment, Cordelia was in the middle of the strangest dream of her life. In fact, it didn't feel like a dream to her at all, but more like reality, with actual sounds and smells and textures. If it weren't for the fact that what was happening in her dream was impossible, she would have believed it was really happening.

Cordelia was back in the book world. She wasn't sure how she knew that, but she was certain of it. Perhaps it was partly because the sunshine seemed a little too bright as it poured through the narrow windows lining the walls of a huge castle. The slivers of sun lit up her feet as she moved through a long, vast stone hallway.

Except that her feet didn't look like *her* feet. They seemed . . . bigger, but also lighter somehow, almost as if they were capable of floating. But they *were* her feet; they had to be, since Cordelia could feel the coldness of the stone floors through strange, thin leather shoes.

She entered a large room at the end of the extensive hallway. It didn't take long to recognize the lush tapestries on the walls and large windows. The massive bone and amethyst throne at the end of the red silk carpet was the surest giveaway of all.

Cordelia was back at Castle Corroway from Denver Kristoff's book *Savage Warriors*. She was inside the evil Queen Daphne's throne room. Even as the royal guards knelt before her, Cordelia knew it couldn't be true. But yet, it clearly was. And somehow *she* was the new queen.

But still she pressed on, almost as if something was driving her besides her own free will. Cordelia marched up to her throne like she truly belonged there. She sat down and surveyed the room. She had guests, it seemed. But they were certainly not ordinary guests.

Before Cordelia's throne stood the most bizarre array of creatures and people that had likely ever assembled inside a castle, fictional or otherwise. Krom was there, from their first adventure, as the new leader of the band of Savage Warriors who carried out Queen Daphne's most vicious orders. Next to him stood a familiar German general who looked exactly like the only other German general Cordelia had ever met, the Nazi cyborg Heinrich Volnheim, *Generalleutnant* of the Fifteenth Panzergrenadier Division from Kristoff's book *Assault of the Nazi Cyborgs*. But it couldn't have been Volnheim himself, because she'd watched him get blown to bits on a snowy mountainside by a tank cannon. All the cyborg generals must look exactly alike.

Next to the Nazi cyborg stood a very stereotypical-looking vampire, complete with a pronounced widow's peak in his slicked black hair, pale skin, a black cape with a high collar, and protruding bloody fangs. There was also Ungil, the slave gladiator from Emperor Occipus's Roman Colosseum, German pilots most likely from the WWI adventure novel *The Fighting Ace*, a group of Prohibition-era mobsters, military officers from what looked like virtually every major war, a few hideous purple aliens with tentacles, and a vast array of other creatures and characters that Cordelia didn't recognize.

They were all staring at her expectantly. So Cordelia began to speak, surprising herself with the authority and confidence of her words.

"Welcome!" she said. "Thank you all for joining me. As you know, I've been trapped here for months. But now our time draws near. The worlds are ready to converge. As we speak, more of us are finding ways to break through, slipping past the barriers that separate us from the outside, from the place that is truly ours. And once we finally break through, nothing will be able to stop us."

The creatures and soldiers cheered. More words spilled from her mouth, almost of their own accord. Cordelia could feel that she meant what she was saying even though each word that came out shocked her. It was almost like talking on the phone with someone and hearing an echo of your own voice.

"The only person who could have stopped us is now dead!" Cordelia announced excitedly to the crowd. Except that by now she suspected she was not really herself, and she had a sinking feeling she knew precisely what was happening. "The old man's magic is broken, decaying like his rotting corpse inside the cold ground. So now the time has come for us to act. We must make our plans accordingly and prepare for the moment when . . ."

Suddenly Cordelia was torn violently from her dream. She was being shaken, and there were voices whispering harshly into her ear.

"Cordelia, wake up!" the voice said. "They're coming through! They're going to kill us all!"

CHAPTER

5

Cordelia Walker sat up quickly at the sound of Brendan's panicked voice, and her head slammed into the metal frame of the top bunk. She cried out in pain, suppressing the urge to curse loudly.

"Ouch! What's the matter with you, Bren?" Cordelia asked as she rubbed her aching forehead.

"Sorry about that," Brendan said. "I maybe got a little excited there, but I swear it's superimportant. You're gonna want to see this right away. Both of you."

Cordelia was used to having her own room and her own queen-size bed. But their apartment by Fisherman's Wharf only had two small bedrooms and a den. And so now Eleanor and Cordelia had to share a room. The movers had brought back their old bunk beds from storage that evening.

"Are you okay, Deal?" Eleanor whispered.

"Yeah, there's no blood," Cordelia said, still holding her sore forehead and trying not to take it out on her sister. She knew it wasn't Eleanor's fault that they had to move back into the bunk beds.

Eleanor climbed down the ladder from the top bunk as Cordelia groaned and dragged herself out of the lower bed.

"This better not be a collection of your toenail clippings again, Bren," Cordelia said. "That wasn't even funny the first time you did it!"

"No, this is for real," Brendan said. "And, by the way . . . that *was* hilarious."

A few years ago, Brendan had told Cordelia he had something extremely urgent and awesome to show her. He'd sold it so well he even managed to get her to pay a one-dollar entry fee to get into his room. Then he'd proudly shown her a collection of toenail clippings that he'd arranged into the phrase *Cordelia = Nerd* across his desk.

"Took me two years to collect enough toenails," Brendan said, smirking at the memory.

"Eww, Bren, let's just go see whatever it is you want to show us," Cordelia said, making a face.

They followed Brendan out into the dark hallway of the apartment. The door to their parents' room was closed and the light was off. The silence was broken only by the creaking of their footsteps down the hall toward Brendan's room at the front of the unit. His "bedroom" wasn't technically a bedroom at all. It was really a den that they had converted into a room for him.

Cordelia held her breath as she slowly pushed the door. The hinges creaked as it swung open. The room was dark, but a pale blue glow splashed across the bed like they were in a garishly lit horror movie.

It took Cordelia's eyes a few seconds to adjust to the light, and then she gasped in shock. She stared at Brendan's TV in silence. Her mouth hung open, her dream almost completely forgotten for the moment. Brendan pushed past her and sat down on the edge of his bed.

"Insane, right?" he said.

Eleanor shuffled around Cordelia so she could get a better look at the TV. This was another of those frequent moments when she hated being the youngest and smallest. She could never *see* anything!

She stepped into the center of the room and finally got a clear view. Eleanor gasped, just like Cordelia had.

How could this be possible?

Eleanor stood there shaking her head, as if it could make what she was seeing go away. It turned out that Fat Jagger wasn't the only character to cross over into the real world from one of Denver Kristoff's books.

A CNN headline scrolling across the bottom of Brendan's

TV read: "Real Abominable Snowman Gunned Down in Santa Rosa, CA"

Eleanor quickly recognized that the dead beast displayed on the screen wasn't merely an abominable snowman. It was one of the deadly frost beasts that she and the gladiator Felix had battled in Kristoff's book world alongside Wangchuk and his order of monks. One of the surviving frost beasts had not only crossed over into the real world . . . it had made its way to California!

CHAPTER

6

The three Walkers watched the TV in silence for several minutes. Grainy footage from someone's cell phone showed three local sheriffs posing next to the dead creature. One of them crouched on top of the massive, furry chest, holding an automatic rifle in his hand. Even with the poor video quality, the kids could clearly see a gaping bullet wound on top of the beast's head, right at its fontanel— which was the frost beasts' only weakness.

The news footage then cut to an interview with one of the sheriffs.

"Well, at first he wouldn't go down," the young deputy said into the camera, clearly struggling to keep a wide grin off his face. "But we just kept shooting, until the monster fell to its knees. Then I stepped up and put one right in his head and he dropped dead. Just like that."

Brendan hit the Mute button.

"What's going on?" Brendan asked. "Are we going to see Nazi cyborgs storming the White House next? Or giant dragonflies snatching up dogs off leashes in Central Park?"

"No!" Eleanor nearly shouted at the thought of poor dogs getting eaten by giant bugs. She clamped her hands over her mouth, worried that she might have accidentally woken her mom.

"My dream wasn't a dream at all," Cordelia said softly to herself. "It was . . . *real.*"

Eleanor and Brendan looked at each other and then turned their confused faces toward their older sister. Cordelia shook her head; her eyes were wide with a mixture of fear and disgust. It was the same look she had on her face when she'd discovered they were all direct descendants of the Wind Witch.

"What dream?" Eleanor asked.

"My dream, it was actually real," Cordelia repeated as if in a trance. "Which means all of this is really happening. And it's only going to get worse. The Wind Witch knows how to make it all worse somehow. . . ."

"Hello-ooo, *Deal?*" Brendan said, waving a hand in front of her face. "You want to clue us in on what you're talking about, please!"

Cordelia finally looked up and met Brendan's worried eyes. Then she glanced down at Eleanor, wondering briefly if her little sister could handle what she'd just figured out.

"Maybe you should go back to our bedroom while Bren and I talk?" Cordelia suggested gently.

Eleanor cocked her head indignantly, scowling.

"I'm not a baby," she said. "You don't have to protect me. Anything Bren can hear, so can I!"

Cordelia looked at Brendan, who merely shrugged. Perhaps she was right; somewhere along the way, they were going to have to stop treating Eleanor like a helpless toddler. Especially after everything they'd been through together.

"When you woke me up . . . I'd been having this dream," Cordelia began. "Except that it wasn't like any dream I've had before. It was like I was inside someone else's mind. And I think I *actually* was!"

She gestured toward the ongoing news story of the slain frost beast.

"Maybe you just banged your head a little too hard when you woke up," Brendan said. He held up two fingers in front of her face. "Maybe you got a concussion. How many fingers am I holding up?"

"*Two,*" Cordelia said, slapping Brendan's fingers away. "It was real! I'm linked to someone forever, remember? And when I was sleeping, I somehow became her, I saw what she saw, said what she said. I became another person."

"Who?" Eleanor asked, even though both she and Brendan feared they already knew.

"The Wind Witch," Cordelia said. "I *was* the Wind Witch."

CHAPTER

7

"How is that even possible?" Brendan asked.

"Remember back when I read our great-great-grandmother's journal?" Cordelia said. "The Wind Witch was somehow able to read it *through my eyes*. It must work both ways; sometimes she sees what I see, and I see what she sees."

"Great," Brendan muttered, "my sister is synched up to an evil she-devil like some sort of supernatural Wi-Fi network."

Cordelia shot him a look that could have killed someone less healthy.

"What happened in the dream?" Eleanor asked.

Eleanor and Brendan sat and listened quietly while

Cordelia explained what she'd experienced earlier that night. About seeing all the characters from Denver's different books gathered in one place: Castle Corroway.

"It's hard to remember which characters were all there, exactly," Cordelia said, frowning. "Even though it felt real, it's still like a dream in that I can't remember all the specific details."

"It sort of sounds like it was a gathering of the *Dark Avengers*," Brendan said. "Like an all-villain supergroup."

"Yeah, it almost would have been funny to see Dracula sitting between a Nazi cyborg and Krom if it weren't for the fact that they were definitely plotting something horrible," Cordelia explained. "I said . . . or, I mean, the *Wind Witch* told everyone that even though they thought they were trapped inside the book world . . . they really weren't. She said there was a way they could escape, a way they could *all* get out into the real world. She said the seams between the two worlds are frayed and getting worse with each passing day. Something about the magic being weakened. One of the last things she said before I woke up was that the only person who knew how to stop her was dead."

"Denver Kristoff!" Brendan said under his breath. "That old bag of rotting goat guts."

Cordelia nodded. "It makes perfect sense. After he died, we were able to bring an artifact from his books back with us into San Francisco—"

"The Nazi treasure map," Brendan said.

"And then Fat Jagger somehow crossed over," Eleanor said.

"And now a frost beast," Brendan added.

"It's only a matter of time before more characters get through," Cordelia agreed. "Or before the Wind Witch is able to pull off whatever it is she's planning and *all* of them get through."

"What do you think that is?" Eleanor asked.

"I'm not entirely sure," Cordelia admitted. "But whatever it is, it will let *everything* from the book world come through. I think she's amassing a whole army of evil book characters for an invasion."

"An invasion of our world?" Eleanor asked.

Cordelia nodded.

"You do have to admit, it *would* be kind of cool to see a T. rex tromping through downtown San Francisco," Brendan said. "Or a bridge troll escaping Alcatraz."

Cordelia and Eleanor both rolled their eyes.

"This is serious, Brendan," Cordelia snapped. "Thousands of people would die."

"I know that," he agreed miserably. "I just don't know what we're supposed to do about it. I mean, how could we stop something like that? It would take the Army, Navy, Air Force, all the cops in the city . . . and maybe that wouldn't even be enough!"

"The first thing we need to do is get to Fat Jagger," Eleanor said, not able to get the image of the dead frost beast from her head. She kept envisioning Fat Jagger on TV instead of the frost beast, his giant body riddled with bullet holes. "He's our friend, and we have to help him first. We need to make sure he knows that he needs to get away from the city and stay hidden until we figure this out."

"We will, Nell," Cordelia assured her.

But she also knew that would merely be treating one of the symptoms of the problem, not actually fixing the cause of the problem itself. Dr. Walker had explained the theory behind practicing medicine to Cordelia when she was ten years old and had spent the day at the hospital with him.

"The key to curing people," he'd explained, "is as simple as keeping your mind focused on the underlying cause. Don't try to fix the symptoms, instead fix the issue causing the symptoms. Sometimes they don't even seem related. Like, if your leg hurts all of the time, you can't just take aspirin every day for the rest of your life. Instead, you have to figure out what's causing the pain and fix that. Leg pain can be caused by a number of ailments not occurring in your leg at all, like back issues or a neurological disorder. That's why we strive to treat the underlying problem or cause, *not* just the symptoms themselves."

It was important to keep Fat Jagger safe, but Cordelia knew they couldn't merely ask him to hide in the ocean for the rest of his life. They would eventually need to find out how to get him back home. She knew nobody else was coming to help; the only other person alive who even knew the book world existed at all was the Wind Witch, which meant it was up to the three Walker children to somehow save the world.

"If only there was a way we could talk to dead people," Cordelia speculated aloud.

"What are you talking about?" Brendan asked, holding up three fingers in front of her face again. "Are you *sure* you don't have a concussion?"

"I'm talking about Denver Kristoff," Cordelia said, pushing his hand away again. "If he were alive, he might be able to tell us what to do. How to fix this."

"That old monster wouldn't help us even if we *could* somehow talk to his ghost," Brendan said. "He'd probably *want* his creations to exist in real life. What writer wouldn't?"

"Are you so sure about that?" Cordelia asked, pointing at the TV still showing images of the dead frost beast. "I mean, if his characters crossed over, many of them would probably end up getting killed. People shoot first and ask questions later. Would Kristoff really want to see his characters getting massacred? Or destroying the city he loved?"

"This is a ridiculous conversation," Brendan said. "Kristoff's dead. Unless you have a Ouija board and psychic abilities, we won't get a single word out of that stiff!"

"That's it!" Cordelia shouted. "You're brilliant, Bren!"

"Now you're calling me *brilliant?*" Brendan asked. "I think we need to get you a CAT scan."

"No, remember what happened at the Bohemian Club when we saw Aldrich Hayes and Denver raise the spirits of dead Lorekeepers with a simple spell?"

Brendan nodded, already not liking where this was headed.

"I don't see why their own spirits can't be summoned as well," Cordelia said.

"What are you saying?" Eleanor asked nervously.

"We're going to resurrect the spirit of the Storm King!"

CHAPTER

8

"But we have to help Fat Jagger first!" Eleanor nearly yelled. "I already have a plan and everything."

"We will help him, Nell. I promise," Cordelia assured her. "But we also need to find a way to fix this for good. And Denver Kristoff is probably the only one who can tell us how to do that. Brendan, do you still remember that spell?"

Brendan had an incredible memory. He could remember the smallest details years later after only having heard or seen something once—as long as it was something that interested him, like sports statistics, or cryptic spells that summoned real ghosts.

He nodded reluctantly—remembering that horrifying experience all too well.

"Good, so you get the job of trying to summon the Storm King's spirit," Cordelia said. "Nell and I will try to help Fat Jagger."

"This is never going to work," Brendan said.

"We have to try *something*," Cordelia said.

"Last time we snuck into the Bohemian Club we almost got killed," Brendan said. "So where exactly am I supposed to hold this charade of a séance? In our living room? Or how about a random street corner? Larkin and Bay sounds kind of magical. . . ."

"Start with the cemetery," Cordelia suggested, ignoring his sarcasm. "Where the old fart is buried. Use your brain, Bren. I can't always be the one with *all* of the ideas!"

Brendan didn't really have a strong desire to raise the dead alone in a cemetery. But it'd be in broad daylight. He could handle that. Plus, he didn't want to look like a complete wuss in front of his sisters. So he nodded, pretending it was no big deal.

"Yeah, cool," Brendan said, raising his chin to look confident. "But when are we going to do this? We have school tomorrow. Are we going to call in sick, or just wait until the bell rings?"

"We can't wait that long," Cordelia said, shaking her head. "Even as we speak, more creatures from Denver's books might be streaming into the real world! We have to do it now."

"Now?" Brendan asked, his voice cracking.

"Yes!" Eleanor said, her eyes glowing. "Poor Fat Jagger's probably getting tired of hanging out under all that water. He's all alone and scared!"

"*He's* all alone and scared?" Brendan asked, completely dropping his thin facade of bravery. "What about me? Your brother! I'm the one going to a cemetery alone in the middle of the night! The place is probably filled with San Francisco's weirdest creeps and lurkers. . . ."

"You've faced a lot tougher stuff than a graveyard at night," Cordelia said. "You can do this, Bren."

She put a reassuring hand on her brother's shoulder and smiled. Brendan turned to Eleanor. His little sister nodded at him, the look in her eyes reflecting back just how much she really did look up to him.

"We believe in you, Bren," she said.

Brendan couldn't back down now. His sisters could be a royal pain sometimes. But at moments like this, when he needed a burst of strength or confidence, they always provided it.

He smiled and nodded back.

"Okay," Brendan said. "Let's do this."

CHAPTER

9

To any regular bystander, Cordelia and Eleanor Walker must have looked completely insane. After all, it's hard to imagine why an eight- and a fifteen-year-old would be standing near the shore of the San Francisco Bay at two thirty a.m. throwing pounds and pounds of raw meat into a huge pile. They had created a meat tower of steaks, ground hamburger, pork shoulders, chicken thighs, and cheap fish fillets. The pile was almost as big as the two of them put together.

It had taken nearly all of the three Walker children's saved-up allowances and birthday and holiday money to amass such an impressive supply of meat. But Eleanor was still worried it wouldn't be enough. After all, even though the pile could feed a whole army of human beings, to Fat Jagger it was only the equivalent of a small chunk of beef jerky.

They'd all snuck out of the apartment and taken a late-night bus to a twenty-four-hour Safeway to get their stockpile. Brendan had helped them haul it out to Torpedo Wharf and then departed for Fernwood Cemetery, where Denver Kristoff was buried under a fake name.

It was three in the morning, cold, damp, and nearly pitch-black by the time the Walker sisters arrived at Torpedo Wharf, cut open all the packages of meat, and dumped them into a massive pile at the edge of the concrete pier. They shivered miserably while they stood and waited.

"Now what?" Cordelia asked her little sister. "We've been here almost twenty minutes."

"I don't know," Eleanor said. "This was the end of my plan. I guess I just thought he'd be hungry enough to smell the meat."

It definitely smelled. Cordelia held a hand over her nose to fight off the stench. But maybe the odor simply wasn't enough? The wind was blowing in from the bay, after all, carrying the shoreline scents away from where Fat Jagger lurked. And it would certainly be even more difficult, if not impossible, for him to smell anything underwater. There had to be something they could do to intensify the smell.

Cordelia was torn from her thoughts by a shrill squawk.

A white seagull plopped down on top of their four-hundred-dollar pile of meat and greedily gobbled up several chunks into its gullet.

"Shoo!" Cordelia yelled, swatting at the bird with her hand.

The seagull flapped its wings a few times and hovered above the meat for several seconds, before settling down again on the other side of the pile. Several other pilfering white birds descended out of nowhere, squawking greedily.

"Nell, I need your help here," Cordelia said desperately as she removed her jacket.

She swung it in wide circles near the growing group of seagulls feasting on the pile of meat. As the jacket neared them, they quickly hopped away or took flight. But each time it passed them by, they dove back in for another helping.

"Go away!" Eleanor yelled, charging in at the birds. "This is Fat Jagger's!"

The birds must have sensed her frantic energy, because they fled for cover as she neared. But then, one after another, they circled back hungrily.

Cordelia looked at Eleanor desperately.

"We need to do something fast," Cordelia said to her little sister. "Or else pretty soon there's not going to be anything left!"

CHAPTER

10

Meanwhile, seven miles away, across the Golden Gate Bridge, Brendan paid the cab driver and stepped out of the car into the dark night. He had no idea how he was going to get home. The number forty bus stopped running at eight p.m., and he'd had to spend all of his remaining money on the cab ride there. Thankfully, his driver didn't speak English very well, and didn't even bother asking why a twelve-year-old kid was taking a cab to a cemetery at two thirty in the morning on a school night. Brendan supposed this was a benefit of living in a big city like San Francisco. Nothing seemed weird there.

He was surprised to see that Fernwood Cemetery did not have a perimeter fence. He'd been fairly certain he was going to have to climb a ten-foot-tall iron fence with impaling spikes at the top. But the huge cemetery, surrounded by woods and built on a gently sloping hill, seemed almost welcoming to late-night trespassers.

It was dark; the only light was from several streetlights nearby and a few faded stars in the black sky.

Brendan braced himself with several deep breaths as he stared into the blackness of the cemetery, trying to tell himself that facing Savage Warriors, bloodthirsty pirates, Roman gladiators, hungry lions, and a vicious wolf the size of a horse had all been way more terrifying than this. There was no reason for him to be afraid.

His mind drifted toward the time when he was nine and had snuck into the living room late at night to watch *Night of the Living Dead* On Demand. He might as well have been a delicious brain sitting on a dinner platter. Brendan would have laughed at the image of his brain sitting neatly on a silver platter flanked by sides of braised kale and mashed potatoes if he were less petrified.

He tried to ignore his fear and instead focus on what he was there to do. First things first: he had to somehow find Denver Kristoff's tomb.

Brendan switched on his phone's flashlight and made his way into the cemetery, weaving past most of the headstones. It actually took far less time to find it than he'd suspected, given the cemetery's size. But his gut instinct to start by checking the larger, more expensive mausoleums paid off. After jogging to four or five of the newer-looking mausoleums, Brendan found the one labeled Houston, for Marlton Houston, the false name reported by the news in the days following Denver Kristoff and Aldrich Hayes being killed by a city bus downtown.

Kristoff's mausoleum was a grand affair. It was roughly the size of a large tool shed, but all similarities ended there. It was constructed of white marble and had three steps leading up to a set of bronze double doors covered in intricate carvings of hooded figures and mythical beasts. Two marble columns flanked the doors beneath a peaked roof containing a large carved symbol Brendan didn't recognize.

He stood in front of the steps and took a few deep breaths, cleared his throat, and thought back to the horrifying experience of watching Denver and Aldrich summon the spirits of past Lorekeepers inside the Bohemian Club with a simple spell.

"*Diablo tan-tun-ka,*" Brendan said, softly at first. "*Diablo tan-tun-ka.*" His voice grew louder as he chanted the spell several more times. "*Diablo TAN-tun-ka! Diablo tan-tun-KA!*"

Nothing seemed to be happening. Brendan continued anyway, recalling words the two Lorekeepers had spoken, but not quite remembering the inflections.

"*Diablo TAN-tun-ka, spirit of my . . . uh, great-great-great-grandfather,* um, I think," Brendan said. "*I summon you! I wish*

to speak to the one departed called Denver Kristoff!"

Brendan raised his arms toward the sky, as if he were literally trying to lift up the dead spirit of the Storm King from his resting place. He stopped and waited, his arms still raised into the air like he was signaling a touchdown.

Only silence greeted him. He lowered his arms and realized how ridiculous it was to think he could possibly raise the spirit of a dead Lorekeeper . . . or anyone for that matter.

A chill went up his spine as a breeze whipped across his neck and face.

Then a twig snapped behind him.

Brendan spun around, raised his phone's flashlight; his heart lodged firmly his throat. And then he screamed loud enough to wake the dead.

CHAPTER

11

B ack on Torpedo Wharf, Eleanor realized that Cordelia was right. They needed to do something fast or else the growing pack of seagulls would eat all of Fat Jagger's bait.

Eleanor looked around desperately. Her eyes rested on a nearby metal trash can full of newspapers and plastic bottles and Styrofoam coffee cups. A snoring homeless man in tattered clothing lay next to it. It was obvious he had just passed out because the still-smoldering butt of a cigarette dangled loosely from his fingers.

Eleanor glanced at Cordelia, who was still waving her jacket at the flock of seagulls. It was chaotic, and getting louder as more birds cawed along with Cordelia's screams.

Eleanor knew there was no time to waste. She didn't always need her older sister's approval or supervision; Cordelia wasn't the only smart one in the family!

So Eleanor pushed away the fear and marched right up to the man. She knelt down beside him and gently and carefully plucked the cigarette from his fingers. She stood up, a triumphant smile spread across her face.

A hand grabbed her leg.

"Gimme back my smoke!" the man growled.

She quickly shook the man's hand from her leg and ran around toward the other side of the trash can.

"Get back here you little brat!" he screamed, trying to get to his feet. But he wobbled unsteadily, having unusual difficulty standing up.

"Nell, what are you doing?" Cordelia yelled, swatting at several seagulls that were dive-bombing her, apparently tired of being hit by her jacket. "Stop torturing that poor man and help me!"

Eleanor didn't answer, carefully cradling the burning cigarette in her cupped hands so it wouldn't burn out. She knew that smoke and heat traveled upward. That's what the firefighter who came and spoke to her class about fire safety had said. She crouched down near the bottom of the mesh trash can.

"Get back here, kid!" shouted the man, who was finally on his feet and stumbling toward Eleanor.

"Nell, let go of that disgusting thing! What are you doing?" Cordelia asked as she swatted at another seagull.

"You'll see," Eleanor said as she touched the red ash of the cigarette to the bottom of the garbage.

She had no idea what the wadded-up newspapers at the bottom had been soaked in, but the whole thing ignited much quicker than she'd expected. After just a few seconds, the entire trash can was engulfed in flames that leaped several feet into the air, sending sparks floating into the night sky.

The vagrant grabbed Eleanor by the back of the collar and lifted her up.

"Gimme my smoke!" he shouted.

Eleanor held out the still-lit cigarette. He grabbed it and set her back down.

"Thanks, mister," she said.

"You really should respect other people's property, kid," he said, and then slumped back down to the ground.

"Nell, will you please tell me what's going on?" Cordelia shouted.

Eleanor ran toward the hungry seagulls, waved them off, and scooped up an entire armload of raw meat. She held her breath and reminded herself that she was doing this for Fat Jagger. She'd take an earthworm bath if that's what it took to save him.

She ran over and tossed the meat inside the blazing

trash can. The fire crackled and popped as the fat seared instantly in the heat. The aroma of cooking steaks and poultry was almost immediate and far more intense than the mound of raw meat.

Eleanor ran back for another armload.

Cordelia marveled at how clever Eleanor was as she grabbed an armload of meat herself. Fat Jagger would be much more likely to smell *cooking* meat the next time he resurfaced for air. Together, they ran back and forth, dumping loads of meat into the burning trash.

The smell of searing meats was so powerful that both Cordelia and Eleanor covered their faces with their shirts. They stood next to the makeshift barbecue and looked out into the dark bay. Cordelia draped an arm around her little sister's shoulders.

"Do you think he'll come up for air soon?" Eleanor asked.

"I hope so," Cordelia said. "But either way, I'm proud of you. That was really risky what you did, but it was a smart idea, Nell."

Eleanor responded by resting her head against Cordelia's side. They waited until the fire was nothing more than a smoldering pile of embers and roasted meat. The smell still wafted in the air even without active flames.

Ten minutes later, just as Eleanor began losing hope, a deep, rumbling *whoooosh* that almost sounded like wet thunder erupted from the darkness of San Francisco Bay.

Eleanor's hopeful smile slowly disappeared when she saw the massive tidal wave emerge from the blackness, coming right at them.

"Nell, duck!" Cordelia screamed, hugging her sister close.

But it was too late; the massive wave was upon them, drowning out their screams.

CHAPTER

12

The force of the water knocked both of the Walker sisters to the ground and pushed them thirty feet back, right off the walking path and onto the lawn of a nearby café and gift shop. It also scattered the cooked meat across the wharf.

Eleanor pushed herself to her feet and looked around frantically for Cordelia.

"Nell! Are you okay?" Cordelia asked, staggering to her feet a few yards away.

"I think so," Eleanor said, trying out her arms and legs, shocked that she didn't even feel bruised.

"That was close," Cordelia said. "We almost got—"

"Fat Jagger!" Eleanor screamed, cutting off her sister.

Fat Jagger, still submerged from the waist down, towered above the wharf, his hair stringy and sopping. Salty ocean water dripped off his hairy torso and splashed onto the concrete wharf like a torrential rainstorm. When the colossus saw the Walkers, he grinned.

"Waaalk-eers," he said.

"Fat Jagger!" Eleanor yelled again, running toward him. Cordelia followed her.

Fat Jagger turned his attention toward the wharf landing, where bits of meat were still scattered about. He reached down and began deftly plucking clumps of meat off the ground with his thumb and forefinger. He popped them into his mouth, a grin still plastered on his huge face.

"Fat Jagger, you need to listen to me," Cordelia shouted up at him. "You have to . . ."

But she didn't get to finish, because she was suddenly interrupted by the *whoop-whoop* of a cop-car siren behind her.

CHAPTER 13

Seven miles north, in the Fernwood Cemetery, near the expensive mausoleum for Mr. Marlton Houston, Brendan Walker's phone flashlight shone directly onto a man several feet away. He wore a gray security guard uniform and had his hand on the butt of a gun.

"What's going on here?" the security guard asked.

"Uh, nothing much," Brendan said. "You know, just visiting my uncle's grave. Yup. Definitely not performing magic spells to raise the spirits of the dead. No way."

The guard sighed.

"Come on, kid," he said. "Give me a break. I just wanted a quiet night. But now I've got to arrest you. There are signs everywhere that say no trespassing after visiting hours. Didn't you see them?"

"I guess not," Brendan said, already trying to plot his getaway.

He could not afford to get arrested.

"And where are your friends, kid?"

"Friends?" Brendan asked. "It's just me."

"Are you kidding me?" the security guard asked. "Nobody sneaks into a cemetery alone. Who would be that dumb? Unless you're some kind of weirdo. . . ."

"Now you sound like my sisters."

"Look," the guard said, "just tell me where your friends are hiding and I woooon-aaaAAAHHHHHH!"

Brendan stumbled backward a few steps as a pair of rotting gray arms emerged from the darkness and wrapped around the security guard's neck, turning his last sentence into a horrifying scream. The arms dragged the guard into the shadows. There was one final scream. And then silence.

"Mr. Security Guard?" Brendan called out. "This isn't funny, man. It's not cool to play sick jokes on kids."

From the darkness, the only reply was a deep, guttural groan. It sounded . . . *hungry.*

Brendan took a few more steps backward until his calves hit the cold marble steps of Kristoff's mausoleum. There was another groan, this time followed by the sound of shuffling footsteps. The groaning got closer as Brendan fumbled with his phone's flashlight. It felt like his heart had stopped beating, as if the pure terror of the situation had shut down all his bodily functions.

He pointed his flashlight up again and found himself face-to-face with a dead guy. Most of the corpse's flesh was gone. His face was basically a skeleton with a few scraps of skin stretched across it, covered by a mop of long gray hair in desperate need of a shampoo. The corpse's left eye was gone and an eye patch covered the right eye socket.

The zombie groaned again as it continued to shuffle toward Brendan.

"Um, hi," Brendan said, terror welling inside his chest. "We haven't met. I'm . . . Brendan. I should inform you that according to my sisters, and that security guard you just killed, I don't really possess a brain, so you're probably wasting your time."

The zombie stopped walking. It almost seemed to cock its head like a confused dog. And for a moment, Brendan thought he actually might have saved himself with his sense of humor for the first time ever.

But then the zombie suddenly lunged at Brendan and wrapped its bony fingers around his right arm. Before he could even scream in shock or terror, the zombie leaned forward and sank its teeth into Brendan's fleshy forearm.

CHAPTER 14

San Francisco Police Department Patrolman Nick Boyce was just three hours into his twelve-hour night shift, but he had already downed three coffees, a Red Bull, and one espresso. If it weren't for all the caffeine, it's possible that he wouldn't have believed what he was seeing when he pulled up to Torpedo Wharf.

It was a giant. Not a member of the three-time World-Champion San Francisco Giants out for late-night trouble, but an actual *giant*! Like from the beanstalk book he sometimes read to his nephew when babysitting.

Officer Boyce knew he couldn't just pull over a giant like he would pull over a vehicle in a routine traffic stop, so he got out of the car and took a few steps toward the monster, unsnapping the leather loop on his gun holster. In spite of his shock, he took a moment to marvel at how much the beast looked like Mick Jagger from the Rolling Stones. Well, if Mick Jagger were to go on a four-month diet of Big Macs and twenty-piece McNuggets, that is.

Officer Boyce grabbed his shoulder radio and clicked it on.

"Dispatch, this is unit fourteen-eleven."

"Go ahead fourteen-eleven."

"I'm down here at Torpedo Wharf," Nick said into his radio. "Requesting immediate backup. We have a . . . uh, a code four-two . . . no, um, we have a code . . . well, um, there's a giant, fat Mick Jagger down here, and he looks hostile. Send all available units. Send the chopper. Send SWAT! Send everyone!"

Officer Boyce was so transfixed by the colossus standing before him that he didn't even notice the two young girls next to the monster. He didn't hear them shouting in vain that the giant meant no harm. Instead, he pulled his service gun.

The giant was staring past Nick at his patrol car, seemingly transfixed by the lights. Then the beast reached out his massive hand, which was easily twice the size of the police cruiser.

Officer Boyce ducked instinctively, fearing he was about to become a midnight snack.

But the giant Mick Jagger reached past him and instead picked up the patrol car. It looked like a Hot Wheels car in the colossal hand. Fat Jagger held it up to his face, entranced by the flashing blue-and-red lights. This time, the caffeine and adrenaline backfired. Office Boyce felt the panic rise up into his throat. He was going die. He knew it.

And so, without considering the consequences of agitating a fifty-story colossus, Officer Nick Boyce raised his gun and fired.

CHAPTER

15

*C*ordelia and Eleanor were practically hoarse from shouting, but the cop didn't seem to hear them.

Cordelia barely had enough time to pull Eleanor back before the cop started shooting at Fat Jagger.

"Noooo!" Eleanor screamed as the gun cracked several times.

"It's okay, Nell," Cordelia reassured her as they huddled down on the concrete. "There's no way those small bullets can kill Fat Jagger. They're just like bee stings to him."

"Bee stings still hurt," Eleanor said, sniffling.

Fat Jagger was still holding the patrol car, his head tilted to the side when the cop fired. He seemed more confused by the onslaught of bullets than anything else. Several of the rounds struck him in the belly but he didn't even seem to notice. Several more ricocheted onto the concrete surprisingly close to where the Walker sisters were huddled.

Eleanor screamed.

Fat Jagger looked down at them, then back toward the cop, whose hands were shaking as he reloaded his gun. Jagger quickly tossed the cop car over his shoulder. It crashed into the San Francisco Bay with a massive splash at least a hundred yards behind him.

The cop readied his gun and pointed it back at the giant, his hands trembling so much that he likely couldn't even hit a target just two feet away.

The Walkers were in danger. Fat Jagger's eyes went wide with fear. He reached down, scooped Eleanor and Cordelia into the palm of his hand, and then popped them into his mouth like a pair of raisins.

The police officer began to scream.

CHAPTER

16

Officer Boyce grabbed his radio.

"Dispatch!" he screamed. "Where is my backup? The giant, he . . . he just . . . oh my God, it was horrible! He just ate two small kids! In one bite! Like popcorn! Please get me backup!"

On cue, several patrol cars pulled up alongside him. Four officers jumped out and gaped at the massive giant standing in the San Francisco Bay. The sound of an approaching helicopter whirred in the distance.

"At first we thought this was a joke, Boyce," his sergeant said. "But strange things have been happening everywhere! First, there were reports of a real yeti getting killed in Santa Rosa. And now this . . ."

"He just ate two kids," Officer Boyce mumbled, still in shock.

"What are we waiting for then?" the sergeant growled. "Let's take him down!"

All five of the SFPD officers drew their weapons and began shooting at a confused and panicked Fat Jagger. The bullets tore into his skin, not causing any real damage but still causing him to wince in pain.

Fat Jagger swatted his huge hands around his head like he was shooing away a swarm of gnats as more cops and a SWAT van pulled up to the wharf. They were armed with even heavier artillery. The sound of the police chopper drew closer.

Cordelia and Eleanor sloshed around inside Fat Jagger's mouth; his thick saliva was warm and gooey, but actually provided pretty decent cushioning to the constant movement of his head as the bullets pelted him on the outside. It felt like a bulletproof hot tub in desperate need of a whole dump truck of Listerine mouthwash.

They realized rather quickly that Fat Jagger had put them in his mouth to protect them.

"They're killing him!" Eleanor shouted.

"Not yet," Cordelia said. "But eventually they'll bring more weapons . . . bigger weapons . . . and he may not be able to survive that."

"We can't let that happen!" Eleanor said as the sound of

a police helicopter whirled around Fat Jagger's head.

"*This is the San Francisco Police Department,*" a voice echoed through a megaphone. "*Surrender yourself immediately, or we will begin using heavier force. We will not hesitate to take you down.*"

"Deal, this is horrible," Eleanor said, tears streaming down her cheeks. "We have to stop this!"

Her sister was right. Cordelia needed to *do* something.

"Fat Jagger," Cordelia shouted. "Can you hear us?"

They were suddenly swept off their feet by sloshing saliva as Fat Jagger nodded his head up and down. They heard the sound of machine gun fire outside and Fat Jagger winced in pain, sending them sprawling onto his slick tongue yet again.

"We need to get to Brendan!" Cordelia shouted, hoping that her brother had actually managed to summon the Storm King. It was their only chance now. "He can help us! Understand?"

Fat Jagger nodded again.

"Good!" Cordelia shouted. "Now take a deep breath and dive! Dive back into the water where they can't shoot you or find you! Swim along the huge red bridge toward the shore on the other side. Then I'll tell you how to find Brendan!"

Fat Jagger nodded one last time, and then suddenly Cordelia and Eleanor felt their stomachs drop as Jagger dove deep into the San Francisco Bay, essentially becoming a living submarine. The two girls hung on to Fat Jagger's huge molars for dear life as the colossus made a break for the Golden Gate Bridge.

CHAPTER

17

Deep within Fernwood Cemetery, Brendan Walker stumbled away from the zombie that had somehow managed to clamp its deadly jaws onto his forearm. Brendan yanked free from its clutches, and in the process tore off one of the zombie's arms. But the damage had been done.

Brendan slumped down into a sitting position and looked at the gory bite wound on his forearm. This was it; he was a goner. Everyone knew the first rule of zombies: If they bite you, then you will eventually turn into a zombie.

He swore to himself. He had always believed he would thrive in a zombie apocalypse. He'd read instructional books, had escape routes mapped out, and even had drawn up construction plans for a fortress on the cliffs of Battery

Crosby. Now here he was about to become the world's *second* zombie, literally the worst you could do in this situation.

He looked up and noticed more zombies stumbling toward him. Some of the walking corpses looked much fresher than others. A few looked old enough to have even fought in World War I.

They continued to advance on Brendan. Didn't they understand that he'd been bitten? He was already as good as dead.

He only had himself to blame. Not only had he failed to raise the spirit of Denver Kristoff, but he had somehow managed to accidently raise the dead! Brendan had just accidentally jump-started the end of the world with a zombie apocalypse.

But that didn't mean he'd go down without a fight. The knowledge of his own impending doom erased any fear and replaced it with pure rage and courage the likes of which he'd never experienced before. It was almost like drinking some sort of hero potion. It made him feel invincible—because, in a way, he sort of was.

Brendan leaped to his feet, still holding the zombie's severed left arm. He stepped forward and reared it back like a baseball bat. Then he swung at the nearest zombie like he was back in T-ball. The zombie arm connected with its head and it flew into the trees at least fifty feet away, still groaning the entire time.

"Home run!" Brendan screamed, before pivoting and taking another swing at a different zombie behind him.

He connected again. This time the zombie's head stayed attached to the neck but exploded on impact like an old rotting pumpkin. Bone and dirt and dust sprayed everywhere.

"Gross!" Brendan yelled.

He whirled around, swinging the severed zombie arm as fast as his injured arm would allow. Brendan stayed near the mausoleum, since it provided protection on at least one side, as more zombies began showing up.

Eventually, he climbed up the three stairs on the mausoleum. He looked around and then promptly dropped the zombie arm he'd been using as his weapon. From his new vantage point, he finally saw just how hopeless his situation had become.

The sea of zombies spread out around the mausoleum had grown to rock-concert proportions. If he weren't feeling so hopeless, he might have even performed the Bruce Springsteen song "Glory Days," which had saved him back in Emperor Occipus's Colosseum.

But, instead, he slumped against the ornate bronze doors and waited for the zombies to devour him.

CHAPTER

18

Fat Jagger came bounding into Fernwood Cemetery still dripping wet from the ocean water he'd been soaking in for the past ten hours. His mouth was open just enough for Cordelia and Eleanor to see outside so they could direct his movements. He'd been careful to avoid smashing any houses on the short walk there, just as Cordelia had instructed. But now, inside the cemetery, he was crushing people with each step.

"Oh no!" Eleanor gasped. "He's smooshing all those people! Wait . . . what are they all doing in a cemetery at three in the morning?"

"Those aren't ordinary people, Nell," Cordelia said,

straining to see over Fat Jagger's huge lower lip. "I think they're . . . *zombies*!"

"But zombies aren't real!" Eleanor said. "That's impossible."

"So is a colossus with two kids in his mouth walking around Mill Valley, California!" Cordelia reminded her.

Eleanor was about to admit that Cordelia made a good point, but was distracted by shouting somewhere far below them.

"Down here!" the tiny voice yelled. "Jagger, down here!"

"It's Brendan!" Eleanor yelled, pointing to their left. "Fat Jagger, can you see Brendan down there? He's in trouble! Save him!"

They saw Brendan on the landing of a white marble mausoleum, jumping up and down hysterically. There were hundreds of zombies closing in around him.

Fat Jagger closed his mouth to keep Cordelia and Eleanor from falling out and then reached down and pulled the entire mausoleum from the ground. Brendan clung desperately to one of the marble pillars. The bronze doors had burst off from the force of Jagger's grip. The roof of the mausoleum crumbled.

Fat Jagger opened his mouth wide and shook the mausoleum over it like a box of candy, dumping a screaming

Brendan inside. Then Jagger closed his mouth and turned back toward the ocean.

An SFPD helicopter suddenly hovered down into view from the clouds above the giant. A man in a blue SWAT uniform sat inside the open door of the chopper. He raised a huge rocket launcher, pointed it at Fat Jagger, and pulled the trigger.

CHAPTER

19

Brendan fell into Fat Jagger's mouth, not having any idea why his friend would eat him. Maybe Fat Jagger had become a colossus zombie himself?

In spite of the dizzying headache gnawing at the back of his skull, it didn't take Brendan long to figure out that Fat Jagger had never intended to *swallow* him, even. Part of it was the fact that he was still in the giant's mouth, sitting in a pool of gooey saliva on a massive tongue. The other clue was the arms of his sisters wrapped around him.

"Brendan, you're alive!" Eleanor said.

"Did it work? Did you manage to talk to Denver Kristoff?" Cordelia asked, getting right down to business.

Before Brendan could answer, the sound of a helicopter

outside interrupted their reunion. Brendan had never heard a real rocket launcher being fired before, but he'd played enough video games to recognize the sound right before they were all tossed around inside Fat Jagger's mouth from the impact, like toddlers in a bouncy castle.

Fat Jagger bellowed in pain. In the split second that his mouth was open, the Walkers saw a gaping and bloody hole in the colossus's left shoulder.

"They're going to kill him!" Eleanor shrieked. "Jagger, get back to the bay! You need to hide!"

Cordelia screamed, too, but for an entirely different reason. Rising up slowly behind Brendan . . . was the Storm King!

CHAPTER 20

It wasn't a spirit version of the Storm King. It was the real flesh-and-blood version. That much was obvious as they jostled and bounced inside Fat Jagger's mouth as he ran back toward the bay.

Brendan spun around, yelped, and then quickly scampered over to Cordelia and Eleanor.

Fat Jagger dove back into the water, shaking his four passengers together like dice in a cup. Once the colossus was smoothly swimming through the bay and his mouth was settled, the Storm King climbed slowly to his feet again with a loud groan.

The Walkers scrambled away from him, toward Fat Jagger's right molars. Their cell phone flashlights cast an eerie glow onto Denver Kristoff's rotting face.

"Denver?" Cordelia ventured. "I know we're not exactly best friends or anything . . . but we really need your help."

The Storm King had never looked worse. His normally putrid face was even more hideous than usual. If it weren't for a few greenish flaps of rancid flesh clinging to his head, he would have basically just been a skull with hair.

The Storm King finally opened his mouth to reply.

"Graaanghhhhh!" the Storm King moaned. "Brrrraaaaoooohhhhrrrr!"

"Um, what?" Cordelia said.

"Oh yeah, did I forget to mention that I accidently started the zombie apocalypse?" Brendan said.

"What are you talking about?" Cordelia asked.

"The spell *did* bring Kristoff back from the dead," Brendan explained. "But it also turned his corpse into a zombie, along with the rest of the cemetery's inhabitants. I must have used the wrong inflections or something. . . ."

"Are you kidding me? *Now* what are we going to do?" Cordelia asked, panicking. "He was our only way out of this!"

"Let's start by making sure no one else gets bit," Brendan said, standing up.

He'd watched enough zombie movies to know that they moved pretty slowly—plus, he'd already been bitten so he wasn't nearly as afraid to attack a zombie unarmed as he normally would have been.

Brendan charged at zombie Denver and slammed his shoulder into the old dead guy's chest. He wasn't sure what he expected to happen—he considered for a moment that the decrepit old man might simply explode from the force. But zombie Denver didn't explode. Instead, the old man went flying backward into a row of Fat Jagger's molars, a low moan escaping his green lips as he slammed into the teeth with enough force to cause Cordelia and Eleanor to look away.

Brendan tensed, waiting for the old man to get back up again. But he didn't. Zombie Denver just stayed there slumped against a pair of huge Fat Jagger teeth. Brendan took a few steps closer and then realized that the old man's arm was firmly wedged between the teeth. He was stuck.

"Well, I think we won't have to worry about him anymore," Brendan said, turning back toward his sisters with a satisfied grin.

"Nice check," Cordelia admitted, her voice wavering. "But why did you say 'no one else gets bit'?"

Brendan answered by showing them his infected and pulsating bite wound.

"I'm going to become a zombie," he said somberly. "There's nothing we can do to stop it. Pretty soon, I'll be trying to eat your giant brain, Deal."

CHAPTER

21

Instead of laughing at his joke, Cordelia choked out a sob.

Eleanor, meanwhile, seemed to not have heard Brendan at all. She just sat there staring at Denver Kristoff lazily struggling to free his trapped arm. He was more of a skeleton now than the rotting monstrosity he had been when he was still alive.

"I've got it!" Eleanor said suddenly. "I know how to fix this!"

"How?" Brendan asked. "It's too late to chop off my arm to slow the infection...."

"No, and that's disgusting, Bren!" Eleanor said. "I'm talking about the bigger problem."

"Geez, Nell," Brendan said. "Can't you at least pretend to be upset like Cordelia? Or say you'll miss me?"

"We have to get Fat Jagger back home!" Eleanor said, her words rushing out in a panic. "We have to somehow fix *all* of this! If not, more and more creatures and bad guys from the book world are going to come into our world and eventually destroy everything!"

"So what's your big plan then?" Cordelia asked her little sister with more edge in her voice than she'd intended.

"I'll explain later, there's no time right now," Eleanor said. "Fat Jagger!"

They felt him grunt in reply as he swam.

"Can you get to the surface and open your mouth?" Eleanor shouted.

Their ears popped as Fat Jagger ascended. They heard splashing as his head broke the surface of the water. His jaw hinged open slightly. A dolphin caught in Fat Jagger's hair dropped into the water and swam off to safety. Eleanor looked out of the giant's mouth and saw the pink haze of the sunrise on the ocean's horizon. They were currently headed west, out of the bay toward the open Pacific.

"Turn left slowly!" Eleanor screamed over the sound of an approaching police helicopter.

Fat Jagger spun slowly. As soon as Eleanor saw what she was looking for, she shouted for him to stop.

"Go back down and swim straight ahead!" Eleanor

screamed over the roar of the nearby helicopter. "When you get to shore, climb the cliff and look for our house."

"You remember what it looks like?" Brendan yelled. "You've held our house before, Jagguuhhhhhhnn . . ."

Brendan looked confused as he opened his mouth to speak again.

"Urhhhh," Brendan grunted, trying desperately to get the words out of his mouth. "Urgggghh?"

"You okay, Bren?" Eleanor asked.

Brendan lifted himself up slowly and Eleanor gasped. She wasn't sure if it was the Giant's saliva, the seawater, or something else entirely, but Brendan's face was now a pale shade of green.

"Cordelia?" Eleanor shouted frantically. "I think Brendan just turned into a zombie!"

CHAPTER

22

C ordelia instantly knew Eleanor was right; the pale twelve-year-old groaning in the center of Fat Jagger's mouth wasn't their brother anymore.

Brendan turned toward Eleanor and snarled, his jaw hanging open and his dead eyes unblinking. He limped forward, drool seeping out from between his teeth. His now-leathery grayish-green skin was filled with saggy wrinkles and festering welts, as if Brendan had aged a hundred years in a matter of seconds.

"It can't be," Cordelia pleaded desperately. "We were so close to the house. We were almost there!"

Eleanor ran into Cordelia's arms as they watched Brendan slouch down against the wall of Jagger's cheek. His skin seemed to tighten across his skull; he was looking more monstrous by the second. His head lolled to the side as a guttural groan escaped from his gray lips. Seeing their normally jovial brother just sitting there, looking so empty, gutted them both—it was almost worse than seeing him die. Their brother's eyes, which once gleamed with mischievous humor, now lolled vacantly from side to side, a shade of gray that was even more neutral than inexistence.

"Is there a cure for zombie-ism?" Cordelia asked frantically. "Holy water? Penicillin? Aspirin?"

Eleanor, having watched one too many scary movies with her older brother, shook her head dejectedly.

"The only way to stop a zombie is by destroying its brain," she said, fighting tears.

"I'm going to go try to talk to him," Cordelia said, unhooking Eleanor's arms from around her. "Maybe if we can get him to remember us, he can turn back? Maybe it's not too late?"

Brendan, still slumped against a pair of Fat Jagger's massive teeth, looked up as Cordelia approached.

"Hey, Bren," Cordelia spoke softly. "It's me, Cordelia. . . . Are you still in there, buddy?"

Eleanor peeked out from behind a molar, as Cordelia got even closer to their undead brother.

"Brendan, come on, I know you recognize me," Cordelia said, now just a few feet away from him. "We don't always get along . . . but it's me, your sister, Cordelia. Can you say *Cordelia?*"

The corners of Brendan's mouth slowly widened and his eyes glowed with life again, in what could have only been a sign of recognition. As Brendan's lips parted further, it was clear to Cordelia that he was trying to smile! She reached out to help him up, and his smile grew even wider.

"It's okay, Brendan," Cordelia spoke softly, offering her hand for support. "I knew you could fight through it!"

CRUNCH!

Brendan's teeth clamped down on Cordelia's hand before she even knew what was happening.

"Ouch! He bit me!" Cordelia shrieked.

CHAPTER 23

*C*ordelia screamed as she looked at the gruesome bite wound on her hand. She wondered if she might faint just from seeing it.

Eleanor joined in with Cordelia's screams until the colossus's mouth sounded like a haunted house. Cordelia looked up from her throbbing hand to see Brendan slowly chewing on his own arm like he was munching on a chicken tender.

"Don't eat yourself, you jerk!" Cordelia yelled, slapping Brendan across the face with her good hand.

Suddenly Jagger's mouth shook violently, sending all three Walker children flying.

"What happened?" Cordelia asked as she stood up

uneasily, still holding her injured hand.

Eleanor knocked twice on Fat Jagger's lower lip. He understood the signal and opened his mouth just enough for Eleanor to peek outside.

"We made it out of the bay!" Eleanor shouted excitedly.

But her excited expression instantly turned to one of horror. Coming right at them were helicopters, police boats, SWAT trucks, and patrol cars, all loaded to the brim with enough firepower to take out a whole family of Fat Jaggers.

24

Across the city of San Francisco, the residents feared that another Great Earthquake was upon them as the ground shook and rumbled. As cars rattled on their tires and antitheft security alarms blared. As windows shattered, causing sleeping children to scream out into the early-morning fog. As the entire city pounded to a steady beat like it was sitting atop a huge bass drum at a Rolling Stones concert.

But it was no earthquake.

Rather, it was a huge colossus named Fat Jagger bounding across the city in long loping steps. Crushing mailboxes, trees, and parked cars under his massive feet as he ran through streets.

Several helicopters were in close pursuit, including a small SFPD chopper and a dark green military helicopter manned by members of the U.S. National Guard. A stream of large-caliber bullets ripped across the sky and tore into the giant's back like a swarm of angry wasps.

A second later, a series of missiles erupted from the twin cannons mounted just below the whirring blades of the National Guard helicopter. They zipped across the faded pink sky and connected with the colossus. The colossus screamed in pain, his teeth gritted together to keep his mouth closed.

Inside Fat Jagger's mouth, the Walker kids screamed as pinholes of light started to appear in his cheeks from the machine gun fire. Cordelia pushed Eleanor down onto Fat Jagger's tongue, behind a row of molars, as blood pooled around their feet.

They peeked over the gumline and spotted their zombie brother. Not only had becoming a zombie robbed Brendan of his youthful looks, but also his sense of personal safety. He stumbled around Jagger's tongue, right in the middle of the firefight. Gun fire exploded all around him.

"We need to help Brendan!" Eleanor screamed over the deafening battle.

Cordelia was about to respond, but it was too late. The

National Guard helicopter let loose another burst of high-caliber rounds, sending Brendan sprawling onto Fat Jagger's tongue.

"Brendan, *noooo!*" Eleanor shrieked.

CHAPTER

25

Cordelia quickly hugged Eleanor, shielding her eyes. Brendan's body lay in the middle of Jagger's tongue, now with several bullet holes in his chest.

How could this have happened? Cordelia let her face fall into Eleanor's shoulder; she was too shocked to even cry. Cordelia thought she might never be able to move again. But then the sound of a low groan caused her to lift her head quickly.

Brendan's head rolled as if coming out of a very deep sleep. He slowly climbed to his feet to resume the search for a snack. He was much more interested in finding something to munch on than in the empty cavity where his lungs should have been.

"What?" Cordelia said.

She had just seen her only brother shot with enough force to stop an elephant, and now he was walking around like everything was fine.

"I told you! Zombies can only be stopped if their brains are destroyed," Eleanor explained. "You should put down *Pride and Prejudice* and read *The Zombie Survival Guide* sometime!"

The two sisters wanted to run and hug their brother, but didn't since it was likely that he would take a bite out of their faces if they tried.

Suddenly, Fat Jagger rocked violently to the right, sending the three Walkers sprawling once again. Every bullet, missile, and rocket impact could be felt inside Jagger's mouth and a gust of hot air rushed out of his lungs each time he winced in pain.

"I don't think Jagger can last much longer," Cordelia said, almost in tears. "We need to get to Kristoff House!"

They held on as Fat Jagger moaned in pain, which only made Eleanor sob more. Through her tears, she spotted Brendan fighting to keep his balance on the increasingly uneasy surface. Eleanor quickly bent down and unlaced her left shoe.

"Cordelia, I need a distraction," she said as she began working on her right shoelace. "Get Brendan's attention!"

Cordelia stood up and took a deep breath; her last

encounter with Brendan hadn't gone so well.

"Hey, Dawn of the Dork!" Cordelia yelled as she walked toward her zombified brother.

Brendan cocked his head in Cordelia's direction. He shuffled toward what he hoped would be his next meal, stopping to groan after each uneasy step—until suddenly his legs wouldn't move anymore. He groaned again before toppling over, a shoelace tied around his ankles.

"Nice one, Nell!" Cordelia said.

Eleanor grabbed Brendan's arms and tied his wrists together with her other shoelace, careful to avoid his snapping jaws. Even with the future of her family on the line, Eleanor's confidence surged through her. It felt good to know that she could actually help save her siblings—especially with a plan that was all her own.

Once Brendan was tied up, the two girls dragged him to the back of Fat Jagger's mouth and nestled him under the colossus's gigantic tongue for safety. Eleanor almost giggled at the image of zombie Brendan tucked under a giant's tongue like a pig in a blanket. But the reality of the situation quickly erased her smile.

"I hope your plan works once we get to Kristoff House, Eleanor, whatever it is," Cordelia said. "There are three lives on the line now."

"Who's the third?" Eleanor asked.

"Me," Cordelia said, holding up her wounded hand, already feeling a little woozy from the zombification process. "Brendan bit me. If my calculations are correct . . . I should start turning into a zombie in about twelve minutes."

CHAPTER

26

"How close are we?" Eleanor yelled as Fat Jagger stumbled again.

He opened his mouth just enough for Cordelia and Eleanor to peek outside. They saw Kristoff House sitting atop Sea Cliff Avenue a few more bounding steps away.

More rockets collided with Fat Jagger's back as he reached the house. He fell to his knees on the huge lawn next to Kristoff House, groaning in pain.

"Spit us into the attic, Fat Jagger!" Eleanor screamed, tears pouring down her face now.

She knew Fat Jagger was dying. Her only hope of saving him was if her plan worked. But the problem was, now that they were actually here, she was less convinced than ever that it actually would. It was a long shot, and she knew it.

Fat Jagger gently poked a hole into the peaked roof of Kristoff House with his massive index finger. He bent forward slightly and spit the contents of his mouth into the attic. Then he slumped backward into a cross-legged sitting position like a small child getting ready for story time, exhausted and breathing heavily and barely able to keep his eyes open. But he had done it; he'd finally saved the Walkers.

Fat Jagger smiled triumphantly, breathed his last breath, and then slumped forward onto the driveway, his face crushing a police cruiser like it was made of paper.

CHAPTER

27

The three Walker children and the Storm King spilled into the empty attic of Kristoff House, sloshing inside a tidal wave of warm and smelly Fat Jagger spit. They slid across the wooden floor like freshly caught fish being dumped onto a dock.

Eleanor climbed to her feet, slipped a few times, and then rushed over to the attic window. She watched in horror as Fat Jagger slumped over onto the driveway.

"He's dead!" Eleanor screamed. "They killed Fat Jagger!"

Guilt and grief ripped into her heart, as she realized that his death was on her hands. She was the one who insisted that they summon Fat Jagger that night. It was her idea to bring him to the surface. He had been safe and sound inside the bay, and now he was dead, and it was all her fault.

Her plan was mostly forgotten now, washed away by an overwhelming sense of sorrow. Eleanor fell to her knees and sobbed, crying harder than she had since she was two years old.

She looked over at Cordelia for support, but saw that her sister was just as distraught by the death of their friend as she was. Brendan, on the other hand, seemed perfectly content.

He was chewing on a pigeon.

"Brendan, get that out of your mouth," Cordelia commanded.

Zombie Brendan looked up, opened his mouth, and the pigeon escaped, flying away through the hole in the roof.

Eleanor probably would have stayed there crying, unable to move, right up until the moment the National Guard soldiers (who were currently breaking down the front door) rushed upstairs to find them. But her sister's chilling scream brought Eleanor rushing back to reality.

CHAPTER

28

Eleanor spun around to find herself face-to-face with the Storm King. Not a decomposing zombie version, but a very much *alive* Storm King. He rose up toward the ceiling, arms spread on either side of his body. His face was restored back to the ugly, sagging lump of gray that it had been on the day he died.

He grinned at her sickeningly. His teeth, yellow and crooked, gleamed in the morning sun that now streamed into the attic through the massive hole in the roof above him.

"Hello, my dear," he said. "Brendan's appearance certainly has changed. I actually prefer this new look. Ugliness creates fear in others. Fear creates power. My . . . shall we say, *unique* face has certainly opened many doors for me."

Instead of screaming in terror the way Cordelia had, or even backing away from the monster in front of her, Eleanor, amazingly, smiled.

"It worked," she said triumphantly. "My plan actually worked!"

Cordelia climbed to her feet, ready to tackle the Storm King before he could harm her sister. But now she stood there gaping at the smiling face of her younger sister. *Of course!* Cordelia wanted to kick herself for not thinking of it.

With the many rifts opening up between the book world and real world, some of the magic the Kristoff House possessed in the book world had crossed over. In the book world, skeletons brought into the attic came back to life. And the Storm King's body had pretty much been nothing but a skeleton covered in scraps of withered flesh.

Eleanor was a genius!

"We need your help!" Cordelia said to the Storm King, as the sounds of National Guard troops breaking down the front door reverberated through the floors below them.

The Storm King spun around, his eyes wide.

"I know precisely what is going on," he said, the usual menace in his voice surprisingly muted. "It's my magic. Since my rather *untimely* death, it has weakened. My book world and the real world are colliding. I never should have created it to begin with—there were better places to hide that wretched *Book of Doom and Desire*. Perhaps back where we found it in the first place . . ."

"We don't have time for this," Cordelia pleaded. "We all make mistakes, we get it. But now how do we fix it?"

"Fat Jagger is dead," Eleanor added, pointing across the attic. "Brendan's a zombie and he bit Deal, so she's about three minutes from joining him! Can we undo it all somehow? Please . . ."

Her plea came out as a whimper as her newfound confidence began to wane. After all, it was entirely conceivable that the Storm King would offer no answers. The death of Fat Jagger, Brendan's new hunger for flesh, Cordelia's eventual turning, all the destruction Fat Jagger had accidently caused trying to get them here . . . it was more than Eleanor could bear to think about.

"I *can* save them," the Storm King said, almost as if reading her mind. "*We* can save all of them. We can seal off the two worlds from each other forever, and undo the damage that's been caused. There is a magical fail-safe that I created when I made the book world. I always leave a way out, a way to undo the effects of any spells or magical constructs. That's the first rule of the Lorekeepers. No magic should ever be permanent."

As he spoke, he floated over to Brendan's body and easily hoisted him onto his shoulder, belying the appearance of his withered old frame. Draped across the Storm King's shoulder, Brendan tried to gnaw at the old man's back, his teeth clacking together viciously.

They heard the National Guard troops in the hallway below them, searching the rooms on the second floor of the house. It would only be a matter of minutes before they discovered the attic.

The Storm King carried Brendan over to the far side of the room, just past the folded-up attic stairs. He pressed his hand against the wall and muttered several words under his breath.

"In nomine Domini rex aperto tempestas."

A section of the wall suddenly vanished, opening a doorway into the secret passages that existed within Kristoff House. The Storm King turned back to face Cordelia and Eleanor. His eyes blazed as if they were on fire, the intensity causing both of the Walker sisters to look away.

"Follow me," he said, and then disappeared inside the dark passageway with Brendan still slung over his shoulder.

Eleanor and Cordelia met each other's stare before they cautiously followed the Storm King. As she entered the passageway, Cordelia looked down at her right arm. The skin up to her elbow was turning a pale shade of green and decaying. A growing headache pulsated at the back of her skull, making it increasingly difficult to focus on anything.

She clearly didn't have much longer.

CHAPTER

29

The Storm King spoke quickly as he led them through a maze of passageways lit by an eerie green glow.

"We don't have much time," he said. "If we don't get to the chamber soon, you and your brother will spend the rest of eternity as undead monsters. We need to get you three back into my books as soon as possible."

"Your books?" Cordelia said. "We have to go back?"

"Yes," The Storm King hissed, as he sped up through the interminably endless stone passages.

"But why?"

"There are three enchanted items hidden inside the book world, items called *Worldkeepers.*"

"What are Worldkeepers?" Eleanor asked.

"Merely objects," the Storm King said. "But objects that, when used together, act as a *key* between the two worlds. They must be retrieved and brought to my brother, Eugene, in Tinz. He can help you get them to the Door of Ways. If all three Worldkeepers pass through the Door of Ways at the *exact same time*, then they will act as a locking mechanism, permanently sealing off the worlds from each other."

"Wait, did you say your *brother*, Eugene?" Cordelia asked.

She never knew he had a brother. Surely he must be dead by now, in any case—only magic had kept Denver alive so much longer than he should have been.

"Yes, my brother has been in Tinz for decades now," the Storm King said. "There isn't time to explain further, but once you retrieve the Worldkeepers, you must bring them to Eugene. He will help you from there."

"Why can't you just come with us?" Eleanor asked.

"I can no longer go back," he said. "The same forces that trapped Dahlia inside the book world are keeping me out. It almost certainly has something to do with my death. Now enough jibber-jabber, we need to move!"

Eleanor and Cordelia glanced at each other, but didn't have time to question him further. They suddenly realized that they had entered a small chamber. Neither of them remembered going through any doorway, and the room appeared to be sealed off on all sides.

"How did we get in here?" Cordelia asked as she looked around the small room.

Denver Kristoff gave no response and uttered another low spell as several torches around the room ignited with flickering blue flames that almost looked like liquid. The chamber was the size of a large bedroom. Its walls seemed to be made of stone, in spite of supposedly existing within an old, wooden Victorian house. Bookshelves made of polished bone lined the walls, stacked two deep with old leather-bound tomes that looked far more ancient than Denver's rotting face. A small desk sat along the center wall, and this too was made of bones. But not just any bones; the entire desk appeared to have been constructed entirely from human skulls, the tops of dozens of craniums creating a surprisingly smooth surface.

"*Eeewww*," Eleanor said, shuddering.

"So . . . grotesque," Cordelia muttered.

"Not really," the Storm King said. "These are the heads of my old fraternity brothers. It always brings a tear to my eye when I see the grinning skulls of Winston, Charles, Xavier . . . and of course Henry, with that endearing gap in his front teeth. . . . Oh dear. Can't get emotional. There's work to be done!"

The Storm King flopped Brendan down onto the desk with surprisingly little care. Brendan groaned and gnashed his teeth.

"Be careful!" Cordelia said.

"He's already dead, my girl! A few more bruises won't do any harm—you can already see right through his torso!" The Storm King barked at her, his eyes still blazing.

Cordelia shrank back, not wanting to upset him further. Somehow this old, demented madman had become their only hope.

The Storm King grabbed the lower jaw of one of the skeletons that made up the desk. He pulled it down and a small drawer made entirely of mandibles slid open near the base of the desk.

"Take this," the Storm King said, spinning around.

He handed Cordelia a thin book. It was the size of a small novel, but was bound in some sort of strange light brown leather that felt rough and brittle. It had a surprisingly unsettling texture that she couldn't quite identify—but strongly suspected might be dried human skin. The cover of the book had a few words etched onto it by hand in a dark brown ink that looked suspiciously like dried blood:

Denver Kristoff's Journal of Magic and Technology.

"It's all explained inside," the Storm King said. "Every bit of my magic, every invention I created is documented within these pages. This will help you find the three World-keepers and bring them through the Door of Ways. It won't be easy. But if you are successful, it will undo all the damage that has been inflicted here, today. Do you understand?"

Cordelia nodded. She was scared, nervous, and full of questions. Eleanor looked at Brendan's dying body and nodded as well. She hated the idea of trusting the Storm King, but they had little choice at this point.

"You mustn't let Dahlia get her hands on the *Journal* or the Worldkeepers," the Storm King continued. "She will be there, lurking somewhere, full of tricks. She may not even appear as herself, so be extremely careful whom you trust. She doesn't know where the Worldkeepers are, but no doubt she can sense their power and could use them for great harm. If she gets her hands on any of the three Worldkeepers first, all will be lost. So guard them, and the *Journal*, with your lives. And stay away from Dahlia."

"Trust me, we don't wanna go anywhere near that horrible creature," Eleanor said.

Cordelia nodded. Brendan offered a few grunts and snapped his teeth with a low groan.

"Watch your tongue," the Storm King snapped defensively. "She's done many dreadful things, but she's still my daughter, my own flesh and blood."

"The old Dahlia is gone," Cordelia countered. "All that's left is the Wind Witch, the twisted, soulless monster that *killed you and then laughed about it*! How can you forget that?"

"You're not a parent," the Storm King said, tears forming at the corners of his saggy and yellow eyelids. "You can't understand. Dahlia wasn't always like this. She once was a gentle soul, so kind, so full of life. She loved nature and wildlife. At least once a month, she would come home carrying a pigeon or a robin, with a broken wing or foot, in the pocket of her favorite yellow dress. And she would nurse the poor creatures back to health. No matter how many times her mother told Dahlia to stop bringing home the birds, she never listened. Dahlia always did have a mind of her own, but she was generous and thoughtful; she always found and admired the beauty of this world—and the beauty in other living creatures."

"Big deal!" Cordelia shouted. "That's nothing compared to the pain and grief she's caused so many people."

"I know she's become a monster," the Storm King said. "But I believe that what was initially in her heart, in her soul, is still there somewhere. I know that little girl isn't completely dead. But enough of this. I'm starting to sound like a sentimental old fool. And it's time the three of you got back into the book world one last time."

Cordelia exchanged a glance with Eleanor. They never

thought they would have to go back there. The other two times, they had all barely escaped with their lives. And even the seemingly good things that happened in the book world only brought them more misery in their real lives. Going back was actually the last thing in the world either of them wanted to do—aside from maybe planting a kiss on the Storm King's withered old mug.

But they both knew they had no choice now. And so they slowly nodded, Eleanor fighting tears at the reality of having to go back. Cordelia clenched her jaw and told herself that she would do anything, *anything* to save Brendan and Fat Jagger and the rest of her family.

The Storm King grinned at them as he recited a spell.

Suddenly the chamber was spinning. It was spinning so fast that Cordelia could no longer make out the skull desk or bone bookshelves. She couldn't make out the faces of the Storm King or Eleanor, or Brendan's body crumpled on the desk. She couldn't see anything but the blurred streaks of blue flames and concrete walls.

Then it all faded away into darkness, and there were books all around her, books spinning with her, closing around her like some sort of coffin. They collided with her body and then stuck, as if coated in superglue.

More books piled on, emerging from the blackness around her. The books seemed to morph themselves into her skin, becoming a part of her.

Cordelia screamed out in pain, but no sounds came out. Sound didn't exist anymore, there were only books and pain and spinning in the dark. It was far worse than her two previous trips into Denver's book world. It was excruciating. But she could not even scream as she no longer had a mouth.

He had tricked them! Cordelia was sure of it. They had just willingly followed the Storm King to their own deaths.

Just as this horrible realization hit her, she was swallowed up completely by the darkness.

CHAPTER

30

The first thing Cordelia became aware of was light—light so bright that it seemed to pour right through her closed eyelids. She covered her face with her hands . . . and then grinned.

"Check it out, Eleanor!" Cordelia yelled excitedly, finally opening her eyes. "My hand's healed!"

They were still in the Kristoff House attic. Except the gaping hole in the ceiling was no longer there. Sunlight streamed in through the attic windows. It was quiet except for the chirping songs of several birds outside.

"Deal, we made it," Eleanor said, rushing over to hug her older sister. Then she stopped short. "Where's Bren?"

They both spun around and looked across the attic. In

the corner, Brendan was still hog-tied and rolling around trying to free himself.

"Why am I tied up with shoelaces?" he asked, spitting out a few pigeon feathers. "And how did we get back to Kristoff House?"

Cordelia marched up to Brendan and pointed an angry finger in his face.

"First of all, I want an apology," Cordelia commanded.

"For what?"

"You bit me!"

"Why would I do that?" Brendan asked.

"You became a zombie! Don't you remember?"

"Actually, no, I don't," Brendan said, suddenly fascinated. "But that is so cool! Did my eyes get all white and weird? Did my skin turn green? Was I really scary? Did I growl a lot?"

"Who cares! You wanted to eat us!"

Brendan gagged.

"Okay, that's pretty gross," he said.

Eleanor rushed over and gave her big brother a hug.

"I'm just happy you're not green anymore," she said. "It was really disgusting."

As Eleanor helped Brendan untie his feet, Cordelia explained what had happened after the zombie bite. When she told him about being shot three times in the chest by an attack helicopter, Brendan pumped his fist in the air.

"No way! People at school are going to freak when they hear about this," Brendan said. "So where are we, anyway? Transylvania? A volcano? What awful book did we end up in this time?"

He didn't wait for an answer, but instead ran to the nearest window to see for himself. Based on past experiences, he was nervous about what he would find. Seconds later, he spun around with a huge smile on his face.

"Guys, come check this out," Brendan said. "We totally scored. There are no forests teeming with Savage Warriors, giant insects, battling colossi, and bloodthirsty wolves; no Roman colosseums filled with lions and gladiators, nothing scary at all!"

Eleanor and Cordelia shared the same thought as they sprang to their feet and rushed over to the window: *It was too good to be true!*

But this time *was* totally different. As Cordelia and Eleanor peered outside, they both saw the same things: an open and vast prairie under a bright blue sky. The flat fields of grass and golden stalks of wild oats and weeds, spotted with patches of yellow and blue and purple wildflowers, seemed to stretch out before them forever. They'd never seen such a vast stretch of flat, grassy prairie before.

"Crazy, right?" Brendan said behind them. "I'm starting to wonder if Denver ever wrote a knockoff version of the *Little House on the Prairie* or something."

Cordelia tore herself away from the window.

"Denver never wrote about anything remotely pleasant," Cordelia said. "We'd better go downstairs and see what nasty things are lurking behind that beautiful landscape."

"So, you'd better tell me what happened after I turned into a zombie," Brendan said, leading the way back down the attic stairs. "Why *are* we back in the book world anyway?"

Cordelia remembered that Brendan had been out of commission during almost their entire ordeal. He didn't know that the Storm King had come back to life, or about their mission to find the three Worldkeepers, or any of it. So she explained what had transpired while he was a zombie as they continued down toward the foyer of Kristoff House.

"But the Storm King said we could save Fat Jagger?" Brendan asked as they arrived in the living room. "That by finding these Worldkeepers and bringing them through the Door of Ways . . . we would be able to undo all the terrible havoc the book world caused to the real world? And, um, you know, also undo the zombie apocalypse that I accidentally started?"

"Yeah, that's what he said," Cordelia answered, sounding unsure. "Supposedly everything we need to know is in here."

She held up the *Journal of Magic and Technology*. Brendan

reached out for it, but his sister pulled it back reflexively. She had already sort of assigned herself the role of official researcher and leader of the mission—she was the best at that stuff. That's the way it normally played out, anyway, even for smaller things like simply ordering pizzas for them all when their parents were out of town. She always took charge, and they never seemed to mind.

Instead of protesting, Brendan sighed. "What makes you think we can trust the Storm King?" he asked warily. "That old sack of donkey poop hasn't exactly been helpful ever before."

"I don't know that we *can* fully trust him," Cordelia said. "But we didn't have much choice. We still don't, especially now that we're back here."

"He said we could save Fat Jagger!" Eleanor chimed in.

"I really don't think Denver ever wanted the two worlds to coexist," Cordelia added. "Why would he? It would only result in a lot of destruction, especially for his beloved characters, his creations."

Brendan wasn't really sure he fully believed that argument. But even if the Storm King was lying, being here seemed to be a lot better than back in that mess at the moment. He had technically died in the real world, after all.

"Well, let's go outside and see where we are," he said, taking a deep breath as he reached for the front door.

But just before his hand touched the knob, someone

pounded the other side of the door so violently, it almost sounded like gunshots. Brendan flinched, his eyes wide.

"We know you're in there!" a voice shouted from the front porch as a fist pounded on the door again. "Now come on out or we're gonna start shooting!"

The three Walker children exchanged frightened glances, unsure of what to do.

"I knew it was too good to be true," Cordelia muttered.

CHAPTER

31

The sound of guns cocking just outside the front door pushed Cordelia into action. She crept forward, and gently pulled back the curtain.

Standing on the front porch were three men wearing cowboy hats and shiny gold badges. Two of the men had flannel shirts and held Winchester rifles. The man in the center wore a huge overcoat made of gray fur and held a Colt revolver with a smooth pearl handle in his right hand.

Cordelia turned back to Brendan.

"They look like lawmen, so I'm going to try to reason with them," she whispered. "You take Nell and go hide in the kitchen pantry. Just in case."

"No," Brendan protested. "You take Nell. I'm good at talking my way out of things."

"Those are cowboys out there," Cordelia said. "From the Old West. The men from that era were full of machismo, which meant other men threatened them. But they had a soft spot for girls and treating them properly . . . like ladies. I might have a better chance with them."

"But . . . ," Brendan started, not feeling comfortable with his sister playing the hero while he hid like a coward. Where was the glory in that? But even more than that, he simply couldn't stomach the thought of either of his sisters facing down armed gunmen alone.

"There's no time to argue," Cordelia cut him off. "Do it now!"

Brendan knew she was right. He grabbed Eleanor's hand and they headed toward the kitchen pantry. He heard Cordelia yelling at their unknown assailants just as he closed the pantry door.

"I'm going to open the door," she shouted. "Don't shoot, I'm an unarmed lady!"

Cordelia slowly opened the front door and then took several steps back. The men stormed inside with their guns ready. The man in the fur coat pointed his revolver right at Cordelia's face.

"Where is he?" he demanded.

"Who?" Cordelia asked, trying to keep her voice steady.

"The deadly outlaw that goes by the name Lefty Payne," the man said.

"Lefty Payne?" Cordelia repeated. "Never heard of him."

"He's called Lefty on account of him only having one arm, the right one," the man said. "But don't let that fool you, he's four times deadlier than most men are with two arms. He's a wanted outlaw guilty of at least fourteen unprovoked homicides. And we know he's hiding in here."

Cordelia did her best to look indignant. Like she belonged in this house in the middle of the prairie.

"Well, I certainly hope you catch him," she said. "But there's nobody here but me. And besides, you have no right to just barge into my house like this!"

"I have no right?" he said as if he was the King of the Prairie. "Don't you know who I am?"

"I'm afraid not," Cordelia said.

"Sheriff Burton Abernathy," the man said, and then paused as he pulled back his shoulders to make himself look more regal.

Cordelia's face remained blank. Sheriff Abernathy grew visually agitated.

"Well?" he finally shouted at her. "You ain't heard of me?"

Cordelia shook her head.

"They call me the Wolf Catcher," Sheriff Abernathy said. "You must know me by that name! I've caught over one hundred fifty wolves with my bare hands."

"How do you catch wolves with your bare hands?" Cordelia asked, not able to help herself. When some crazy guy in a fur coat says he's caught hundreds of wolves with his bare hands, further inquiry is required. It's an inescapable, proven law of science, like gravity or photosynthesis, or climate change or evolution.

The Wolf Catcher held up his right hand, allowing the sleeve of his coat to slide down, revealing a muscular forearm covered in hundreds of cuts and streaking scars.

"By jamming this arm down their throats!" he said triumphantly. "It keeps them from biting me."

"How . . . *macabre,*" Cordelia said, warily eyeing the old scars on the man's arm.

Even though he said he was a sheriff, and had the badge to back up his story, she was getting the sense that he was not to be trusted.

Sheriff Abernathy looked around the house for the first time. The relatively modern furniture and artwork and fixtures seemed to unsettle him. The odd setting of the house only seemed to make him more suspicious and angry than he'd been when he first arrived. He shoved the gun toward Cordelia's face again, practically jamming the barrel up her nostril.

"Mind if we look around some?" he asked.

"*No*, I want you out of here," Cordelia said, surprised by her own defiance in the face of this seeming madman.

The sound of a low cough drifted out into the foyer from the kitchen. The three lawmen's heads all snapped in that direction and then turned back toward Cordelia.

"I thought you said you was alone," one of the deputies said.

"You mean, *were* alone, Deputy Sturgis," Sheriff Abernathy corrected him.

"Yeah, whatever, she knows what I meant," Deputy Sturgis said with a menacing grin.

"You know, little lady," Sheriff Abernathy said to Cordelia. "Lying to an agent of the law is a felony offense. Punishable by death."

Cordelia was fairly certain that could not be true. But at the same time, Old West law was vastly different than the modern law she learned about in civics class last year, in the sense that the local sheriffs of counties in territories that weren't even states yet could virtually make up their own rules as they went along. There used to be judges known for that sort of thing in the Old West. Judges who acted as the sheriff, jury, and executioner all at once.

"I didn't lie," Cordelia said, her voice shaking. "There's nobody here but me."

"You're *lying* again," Sheriff Abernathy said with a nasty grin. "That's two offenses now. Which means we get to carry out your death sentence immediately and with extreme prejudice. Men, take aim. Fire on my command."

CHAPTER

32

"We ain't even gonna arrest her?" one of the deputies asked.

"No, Deputy McCoy," Sheriff Abernathy replied, "we *are not going* to arrest her. There's no time; we need to keep looking for Lefty Payne or else he'll get away again. Plus, arresting folks creates paperwork, and you know how much I hate paperwork. Now, reload your rifles if you need to. We'll fire on three."

All three lawmen raised their weapons and took aim at Cordelia. She couldn't believe it had devolved to this so quickly. She could only hope Eleanor and Brendan were busy making their getaway.

"One," Sheriff Abernathy started. "Two . . ."

"Hold up a sec," Deputy McCoy blurted out as he lowered his gun. "Shootin' an unarmed man is one thing, but shooting an unarmed female? Well, that just seems downright unhonorable. Plus, I'd be feeling mighty guilty about it for the rest of my days. Now, Sturgis and me is the same rank, why do I got to shoot this here little girl?"

"He makes a right good point," Deputy Sturgis said. "I don't want to shoot her neither. . . ."

"*Either*," corrected the sheriff.

"She reminds me of my own little girl," Sturgis said. "But one of us has to do the dirty deed, since the law is the law and all, and she done broke the law. Maybe we should vote on it?"

"That's a mighty swell idea!" Deputy McCoy said. "'Cause, you know, there's three of us, so we know it won't end in a gridlock tie or whatnot."

"We're not voting!" Sheriff Abernathy screamed, silencing them both. "It doesn't matter! I'll just do it myself!"

He raised his Colt and pointed it at Cordelia again. He pulled back the hammer. This time there would be no countdown. Cordelia closed her eyes and hoped it would go quickly.

"Hey, scumbags!" someone shouted behind them.

The three lawmen spun around to find themselves

face-to-face with two young kids. The smaller kid stepped forward. She couldn't have been more than eight or nine years old. She jabbed a small paring knife with a bright orange blade toward them.

"Drop your weapons," she sneered.

CHAPTER

33

*C*ordelia grinned at the sight of Brendan and Eleanor standing nearly shoulder-to-shoulder, brandishing their "weapons" as menacingly as possible. Their options had clearly been pretty limited, since the movers had taken most of the smaller household items to their new apartment the night before.

Eleanor held a small orange paring knife that had been forgotten, crammed in the back of the now-empty utensil drawer. And Brendan had a handheld vacuum. It had a big handle with a red trigger; a long, bright purple shaft with a corner attachment extended from the end. It almost looked like some sort of sci-fi laser rifle to Brendan. It was a strange-looking vacuum, even by modern standards, and so he'd hoped it might look more dangerous than it actually was.

The three men stared at the Walkers in shock for several moments with their mouths hanging open. A lump of gooey black chaw dripped from Deputy McCoy's lower lip and plopped onto the floor with a soft splat.

That's when Sheriff Abernathy began laughing. It was more of a hysterical series of high-pitched giggles than an actual laugh. Which caused the deputies to laugh as well. The three of them stood there and laughed at Brendan and Eleanor for an uncomfortable amount of time.

It caught Eleanor so off guard that she lowered her knife, momentarily forgetting the danger of the situation. Even though it was better than if the men had simply raised their weapons and shot at them, it was still humiliating to be laughed at so openly.

The Walkers couldn't have asked for a better distraction. But Brendan and Eleanor had been too surprised by the laughter to take advantage of it.

It was too late by the time the three lawmen finally came to their senses and raised their guns again.

"You can try to fight us all you want, little girl," Deputy McCoy said as he advanced on her, a streak of black spit from his fallen tobacco staining his chin. "But I bet you a nickel the bullet from this here rifle moves a lot faster than you do."

He raised his gun and pointed it right at Eleanor. She dropped her knife and took a step back. The deputy lowered the weapon slightly, seeming unsure if he really had the stomach to shoot an unarmed little girl.

That's when Brendan finally seized the moment. He hit the trigger on the vacuum and then pressed the Max button on the back of the handle.

The sound of the vacuum roaring to life actually elicited a startled yelp out of Deputy McCoy, causing him to drop the rifle to the ground with a clatter. The other two lawmen took an instinctive step back. Sheriff Abernathy's foot caught the edge of the entryway rug, and he went sprawling onto his butt with a grunt.

Brendan lunged forward and pressed the corner attachment to Deputy McCoy's cheek as the man reached for his fallen rifle. The vacuum attached itself to the baggy skin on his face with surprisingly powerful suction.

The deputy screamed in terror. He'd never heard or felt anything quite like it before, and was too scared to realize that it didn't actually hurt. Pure fear had taken over as he screamed uncontrollably.

Deputy Sturgis and Sheriff Abernathy watched in shock as the young boy inflicted unimaginable pain on Deputy McCoy with the strange torture device. They turned on their boot heels and dashed through the front door and back outside without a second thought.

Cordelia charged at McCoy, who was still screaming. She rammed her shoulder into his chest like she'd seen Brendan do before at countless lacrosse matches during the past few years. Deputy McCoy went sprawling backward onto the floor. He grabbed his gun, quickly scrambled to his feet, and ran out the front door after his two comrades.

Brendan rushed over and slammed it shut. He fastened all three locks and then peeked out the window. The three men were on their horses and galloping away from the house as if they were in a race with their own shadows.

He spun around and saw Cordelia practically smothering Eleanor with hugs.

"Thanks for saving me!" she gushed. "You were so brave!"

Brendan coughed loudly several times until Cordelia looked up at him.

"You know, I played a pretty big role in that whole thing, too," he said, puffing out his chest.

"Oh, Brenny, are you feeling left out?" Cordelia asked him in a baby voice. "Come on then, give sister a hug!"

She flung her arms open and charged at Brendan. He sidestepped and spun away from his sister with a grin.

"Just a simple thank-you will do," he said. "No need to get all mushy on me."

"Come on, give your sisters a hug!" Eleanor said, moving around to flank Brendan. "Walker Hugwich!"

Cordelia used to do this to him all the time when he

was five and she was eight. She would chase him all over their house threatening to give him hugs. He'd run, faking terror, but usually was laughing the whole time. Eleanor would be stumbling around clumsily after them, already feeling left out, even as a toddler. Once she was old enough to really join in, they would both go after Brendan, calling the maneuver a Walker Hugwich.

For a moment, the three Walker children stood there in the formal living room of Kristoff House in the middle of some fictional nineteenth-century prairie, grinning. They remembered simpler, happier times before they were always seemingly one second away from getting shot by a psychopathic cowboy sheriff, or vivisected by a psychopathic pirate captain, or fed to the lions by a psychopathic Roman emperor.

Things had definitely changed for the Walker family since those simpler times, back when the biggest thing to fear was a Walker Hugwich.

CHAPTER

34

"Well, now what?" Brendan asked as he plopped down onto the living room sofa a few minutes later.

"I'm hungry," Eleanor said, pulling her feet underneath her on the chair across from him. "And thirsty."

"Me too," Brendan said. "I really wish I'd eaten some of that meat we got for Fat Jagger."

At the mention of her dead best friend's name, Eleanor looked down into her lap and bit her lip to keep from crying. For a moment, her hunger was forgotten.

"Well, *I'm* going to start reading this," Cordelia said, holding up *Denver Kristoff's Journal of Magic and Technology*. "In case you forgot, we need to find the three Worldkeepers.

And as of now, we have no idea what they are, where they're at, or how to find them. Unless you have a better idea, Bren?"

Brendan shrugged. Of course he didn't. He was never the one with the good ideas. Pulling off impromptu comedy routines and legendary performances of eighties oldie classics? Sure, that was his territory. Knowing the perfect time to fart in public and then loudly blame it on Cordelia once other people smelled it? Brendan was pretty good at that too. But Cordelia was the one who was good at taking charge and making plans. So he wasn't going to stand in her way.

"Uh, Bren?" Cordelia said.

"What?" he asked. "I'm thinking, okay! You think vacuuming a deputy's face doesn't take a lot out of a guy?"

Cordelia grinned, rolled her eyes, and then began skimming through the pages of Denver's *Journal* as quickly as she could. Which proved far more difficult than she suspected. Denver's handwriting was narrow, cramped, and gratuitously elaborate. It made fast reading almost impossible.

But it slowly got easier as Cordelia began identifying the way Denver formed the more common letter and word combinations. And she eventually made several significant discoveries: For one thing, Denver created the magic realm of his book world specifically to hide *The Book of Doom and Desire*. He thought it would be as good as making it disappear entirely, while still allowing him to retrieve it should he ever need to again. Furthermore, Denver had always suspected that traveling frequently back and forth between the two worlds might start to corrupt the magic behind it all. The Walkers, Will Draper, the Wind Witch, and artifacts like the Nazi treasure map were never meant to go back and forth as many times as they had. Which was likely partly responsible for how Fat Jagger and the frost beast ended up in San Francisco.

Cordelia was only a few pages into the *Journal*; there was clearly so much more to learn, so much more inside the book that would help them with their current predicament. She had just found the section on the Worldkeepers, when Eleanor's horrified scream ripped her from the pages.

"Deal!" Eleanor gasped.

"Don't interrupt me," Cordelia said. "I'm trying to concentrate. . . ."

"Your eyes!" Eleanor yelled.

Cordelia looked up, confused. Her eyes felt just fine.

"What's wrong with my eyes?" she asked.

Brendan was staring at her now as well, the same horrified expression on his face. They both rose to their feet, and Cordelia's stomach dropped. She felt the panic rising in her throat.

"What is it?" she asked again. "Will someone please tell me?"

"Your eyes, Deal," Brendan said. "They're . . . *blue!*"

"Of course they're blue!" Cordelia said. "Has it really taken you twelve years to notice that?"

That's when Brendan walked over and put his hands on her shoulders.

"What are you doing?" she asked.

"Trust me," Brendan said softly. "You need to see this."

He steered her over to the large mirror with the ornate gold frame hanging on the wall by the fireplace. He positioned her right in front of it so she had to look at herself.

Cordelia screamed in terror.

CHAPTER

35

*C*ordelia's eyes were *completely* blue, from eyelid to eyelid. Not just blue, but almost translucent and sparkling like an ice-covered lake. It was almost as if her eyes had been frozen right inside her skull.

She stopped screaming abruptly, realizing exactly what was happening: The Wind Witch was possessing her right at that very moment!

She took several steps away from Brendan, who looked even more frightened and confused than ever.

"Stay back!" she shouted.

"Deal, we're just trying to help you," he said.

"Yeah, we don't want to hurt you," Eleanor pleaded. "We're just worried about you."

"It's not me I'm concerned about," Cordelia said. "It's *you!*"

"Huh?" Brendan said. "No offense, Deal, but even though I'm three years younger, two years of lacrosse have molded me into a compacted brute of pure strength. In fact, some would say I'm more muscle than man—"

Cordelia shook her head vigorously. The blue in her eyes began to fade, but her face was still contorted with panic. "You might be able to take *me* in a fight," she interrupted. "But not the *Wind Witch!*"

"She's inside of your head again?" Brendan asked.

Cordelia nodded, her eyes slowly recovering their natural color.

"Don't you remember?" Cordelia asked. "She and I are linked forever now. It's how I was able to see what she was seeing in my dream last night."

"So it's like having some disease that can just come back at any time?" Brendan ventured. "Like Uncle Frank's bad breath?"

"Unfortunately, it seems that way," Cordelia said.

"Well, you can relax for now," Brendan said. "Your normal, pretty blue eyes are back."

"Wait, did you just call my eyes pretty?" Cordelia asked, smiling in spite of the situation.

"No!" Brendan said hastily. "I said . . . I said . . . *creepy* blue eyes."

"Anyway, the Wind Witch isn't in your head anymore," Eleanor said.

"For now," Cordelia added bleakly. "But there's no way I can read this anymore." She thrust Denver's *Journal* toward Brendan. "Keep it far away from me. From now on, you're going to have to be the one to read it and take charge."

Brendan shook his head and refused to take the book at first. It wasn't that he didn't want to help, or was too lazy to read a book, but deep down he was simply afraid. He was afraid that if he were the one in charge, making all the decisions, then it would be his fault if his sisters were injured. He was worried he might lead them all right into danger, like he had done last time they were in the book world. His brief flirtation with power in ancient Rome had nearly gotten him eaten by a pair of angry lions. Which had only served to amplify his omnipresent self-doubt.

"Look, if I read this book, and I formulate the plans, then the Wind Witch might know what we're doing." Cordelia continued pleading her case. "She can see what I see. And she knows the book world better than the three of us combined. We'd always be one step behind her. She would surely find the Worldkeepers first and our mission would be over . . . and so would the world as we know it."

"Are you sure you want me to do this?" Brendan asked, still hoping for a way out. "What about Nell?"

"No, I don't think that's a good idea," Cordelia said, as if

Eleanor wasn't still sitting right there. "It's all on you, Bren. And if you see my eyes turn again, you can't even talk about what you've read or what you've found out. That goes for you too, Nell."

Eleanor nodded, but was feeling pretty hurt that Cordelia hadn't even considered giving the book to her. She wasn't as helpless as her older sister must have thought she was. She had been making a lot of progress with her reading lately.

Brendan looked at the old book uneasily, still tempted to pass it right back to Cordelia like a hot potato. But the look on her face told him to not even attempt it. He could see how much it bothered her to give up the responsibility of reading it. In fact, it was the last thing he ever suspected Cordelia would do.

Cordelia was almost in tears now. It was more than just being afraid that without her help and guidance they would fail—although certainly part of her believed that was true. She was always the leader; after all, she always took charge and Brendan and Eleanor simply weren't accustomed to the role. But what was truly bothering her, tearing her up inside, was the helplessness she suddenly felt, the sense that she was being forced to abandon her siblings. Because the truth was, she relished being the leader partly out of an innate sense of responsibility to protect her younger brother and sister, like a bear protecting its cubs. She had always felt that way—as the oldest, their safety was always in her hands—whether it was at the public pool when they were younger, or in a magical book world fighting off bloodthirsty villains. But now she felt completely helpless to protect them, and nothing had ever felt worse.

"It's okay, Deal," Brendan said, patting her shoulder awkwardly. "We got this! Don't we, Nell?"

Eleanor merely shrugged; still miffed.

"I believe in you, Bren," Cordelia said.

"You totally should," Brendan lied, trying desperately to muster up the same belief in himself. "There's no way we're going to let the Wind Witch stand in the way—"

But he didn't get to finish his sentence. Because a cold, evil voice behind them abruptly ended the conversation.

"Did someone just say my name?" the Wind Witch asked from the foyer.

36

The Wind Witch hovered behind them near the still-locked front door. Her face was as hideous as ever, the decaying skin stretched across her skull like an undercooked Thanksgiving turkey. She floated effortlessly, grinning at the Walker children as if she were trying to show off as many of her yellow and crooked teeth as she possibly could.

"No hugs and kisses for your dear old great-great-grandmother?" she asked, spreading her arms like she expected them to come running toward her.

"You're not welcome here," Cordelia said softly.

"Yeah," Brendan added. "Go back to your sad little pretend life in this pretend world where nothing is real."

"You see, that's where you're wrong, you ugly little boy," the Wind Witch said, still smirking. "If this place doesn't really matter, why did you three brats come back?"

The Walker kids exchanged a glance, not certain what lie to offer.

"No need to lie," the Wind Witch said, reading their

expression like a traffic sign. "I already *know* why you're here, why you have once again invaded *my* world. Cordelia was kind enough to *show* me, while reading that book."

Cordelia shook her head, close to tears. The guilt at having already given away important information to the Wind Witch ate at her conscience. How could she not have realized the danger sooner?

"Yes, I read many interesting things while seeing through Cordelia's eyes," the Wind Witch bragged. "But do you know the most fascinating thing I learned?"

"What's that?" Brendan asked.

"The *Worldkeepers*," the Wind Witch said calmly, still grinning.

"Worldkeepers?" Brendan repeated unconvincingly. "What's that? Like some kind of supergoalie?"

"*Don't* play dumb with me!" the Wind Witch hissed, and as she swooped in closer to the three Walker children, they all flinched. "I read the words myself, and they were written in my father's handwriting!"

"Then you know as much as we do," Cordelia said. "In case you forgot, my reading was rudely interrupted when I was possessed by an evil, soulless harpy."

The Wind Witch seemed amused by Cordelia's words. She floated down so her feet were nearly touching the floor.

"I also know that you resurrected my father and spoke with him," she finally said. Her voice turned earnest. "How else could you have gotten here? But do you really think you can trust him? After all, he's to blame for me turning into . . . *this*. It's his fault that all of this has happened. So whatever it is that he's told you, do you really think he actually wants to *help* you? He's *using* you to get the World-keepers for himself . . . as part of some terrible plan. My father cannot be trusted."

"Maybe that's true," Eleanor said, speaking for the first time. "But how can you expect us to trust you either? After everything you've done to us. You tried to kill us all last time we were here!"

"Valid point," the Wind Witch said. "But—and this is hard for me to admit—since then . . . you little brats have grown on me."

"She's lying," Cordelia said.

"Definitely," Brendan agreed.

"No, it's true," the Wind Witch insisted. "I'm very lonely here. And I've grown rather fond of you three. We are *family* after all. I'd hate to see you all perish, which is surely what will happen should you continue to let my father manipulate you. And that's why I'd like to offer you a deal."

"What kind of deal?" Eleanor asked.

"Nell, you can't be serious?" Cordelia shrieked. "There's no way we'd accept a deal from her, no matter what she offers."

"It doesn't hurt to at least listen!" Eleanor said back

defiantly. "I'm tired of being bossed around. I'm my own person, you know."

"Nell has a point," Brendan said.

Cordelia stood there and looked back and forth between her sister's and brother's faces, not believing what she was hearing. There was no way they would ever cut any kind of deal with the Wind Witch. Ever. So why bother even listening to her at all? But she also realized she had just been outvoted. So she crossed her arms and waited, still fuming inside.

"If you help me get to the Worldkeepers first, I can save your colossus friend," the Wind Witch said. "But beyond restoring his life, I can offer something even more remarkable."

"What's that?" Eleanor asked.

"I can turn him into a real human," the Wind Witch said. "He can come to your world and live with you and be your *real* friend."

"Really?" Eleanor's eyes seemed to light up in a way Brendan and Cordelia had never seen before and they found unsettling. "He can be . . . *real?* An actual friend?"

"And what would you do with the Worldkeepers?" Cordelia asked, trying to ignore Eleanor's hopeful enthusiasm.

"I want to put an end to the book world," the Wind Witch answered.

"Why?" Cordelia asked. "You have so much power here. . . . That's all you want after all, isn't it? More power?"

"No, I want to end it because we're all trapped in here like prisoners," the Wind Witch said, actual emotion creeping into her voice. "It's inhumane, really. Even your friends Felix and Will are not happy here. How could they be? Knowing that their entire *existence* is an illusion, that they are merely characters from my father's imagination. These character were never meant to *exist* like this. . . ."

"So what could you do for them?" Brendan asked. "You can't *make* them real."

"Oh, but I can," the Wind Witch said. "Just like Fat Jagger. I can make all the characters here *real*. Will and Felix and anyone else you'd like to be with . . . help me and you can be reunited with your best friends in the *real world*. It will be glorious."

Nobody spoke for several moments. Cordelia stood there shaking her head. Making Denver's characters real was a terrible idea. He wrote more villains and monsters into his books than he did courageous, good-hearted heroes like Will Draper. The bad guys always outnumbered the good guys in old, pulpy adventure books. Everyone knew that.

A tear ran down Eleanor's cheek. The memory of watching Fat Jagger die was still too fresh.

"You can really save Fat Jagger?" Eleanor asked.

"Of course I can, sweet child," the Wind Witch said.

Cordelia and Brendan exchanged a glance, both knowing this could be trouble.

"Nell!" Cordelia finally said, shaking her gently. "You can't seriously be considering what she's saying."

"Yeah, this is the Wind Witch!" Brendan added. "The same crooked old monster who stabbed me, your brother, in the heart! Doesn't that mean anything to you?"

Eleanor looked down and shook her head. She seemed to be coming to her senses. It was hard not to be tempted though.

"It means everything to me, Bren," Eleanor said, "I love you."

Then she turned and looked directly into the Wind Witch's cold eyes.

"We will never help you," Eleanor said. "I can't let you come between me and my family. My brother and sister are right. You're evil. That's all you are. Nothing but a twisted and sad old creature."

The Wind Witch lifted her chin defiantly and rose up toward the high ceiling of the grand Kristoff House living room. She sneered at them and her eyes glowed icy blue—just like Cordelia's when the Wind Witch was inside her head. The temperature in the room dropped noticeably, and Cordelia swore she could even see her own breath.

"Fine," the Wind Witch snarled. "I tried to make this

easy on you. But if you want to do this the hard way, it would be my pleasure. I'll simply take that book from your cold, dead hands!"

She raised her arms and swirls of wind developed inside the house, sending paintings flying until they smashed into the walls across the room from where they'd been hanging, shattering into a tangled mess of canvas and splintered frames. The large chair between Cordelia and Brendan slid across the floor and crashed into the fireplace hard enough to knock the decorative silver-and-brass clock off the mantel. It hit the floor and shattered, putting a softball-sized crater in the hardwood in the process.

Blue balls of light developed on the Wind Witch's palms. They glowed and crackled with energy as more swirls of wind developed around them. The balls of light grew and lit up the Wind Witch's face, which was grinning sickly, now a contorted mess of pure hatred and menace.

And then she descended on the three small Walker children with all her force. There was nothing they could do but cower together by the large sofa and hope that their impending death would be swift.

37

The Wind Witch dove toward the Walker children, bringing her powerful orbs of blue energy and winds strong enough to skin an alligator with ease. But as she neared, even as everything else in the room seemed to shred in the wake of this tornado tearing through Kristoff House, the children became aware of a growing sense of calm.

The spot where the three Walkers stood was somehow protected, almost as if they were in the eye of a storm.

And then, just as suddenly, the old crone was being blasted backward toward the fireplace by an unseen force. A look of shock on her face told the children that she had no idea what was happening.

She was sucked into the open fireplace and then whisked

up the chimney as if being shot from a cannon.

One last gust of wind whistled down through the chimney, carrying the fading voice of the Wind Witch with it.

"I will be back . . . and I will find a way to get my hands on the Worldkeepeeeeersss. . . ."

And then, all was quiet.

"What just happened?" Brendan finally asked. "I thought we were going to get vaporized!"

Cordelia stood there with a look of terror on her face for several seconds, as if she was still in shock, before finally shaking it away. Then relief flooded into her eyes as she hugged a dazed-looking Eleanor.

"I thought we were dead for sure," Cordelia said. "But . . . now that I think of it, we really had nothing to fear."

"What do you mean?" Brendan asked.

"She can't hurt us, remember?" Cordelia said.

"You think the family magic that protects us has gotten stronger?" Brendan asked.

"Possibly," Cordelia said. "But even more than that, some of the laws of science apply to magic. Based on the little bit I read in Denver's *Journal*, the Lorekeepers' magic was surprisingly rooted in the concepts and laws that govern science and quantum physics—"

"Can you maybe fast-forward to the point, Einstein?" Brendan interrupted.

"It's Newton's third law of motion!" Cordelia said, growing frustrated.

Brendan stared at her blankly. "That the raspberry Newtons are way better than the original flavor?" he ventured.

He may have had a flawless memory, but only for stuff that interested him. Physics was definitely not on that list.

Cordelia groaned and shook her head.

"Newton's third law of motion," she recited. "For every action, there is an equal and opposite reaction. It essentially means that all exerted energy has to go somewhere . . . it doesn't just disappear."

Brendan's eyes clicked on like a lightbulb. "So when she attacked us with her magic," he said, "since it couldn't harm us, then it backfired on her?"

Cordelia nodded. "It's the only logical explanation. Makes sense, right?"

"You're so boring I usually tune you out," Brendan said. "But this time I actually think your theory sounds pretty solid. Nell, what do you think?"

Eleanor, who hadn't been listening to them at all, looked up, startled. Her eyes were wide with fear and recognition. She knew what had just happened, but had been trying to convince herself that it couldn't be possible.

"Nell, what is it?" Cordelia asked.

"It was me," Eleanor said. "I did it. *I* was the one who saved us and made the Wind Witch go away."

CHAPTER

38

E leanor had expected her brother and sister to be shocked. Or confused.

But she certainly did not expect them to laugh in her face.

"What?" Eleanor asked as they giggled. "Why is that so hard to believe?"

"Because little girls don't just spontaneously develop magical powers," Brendan said, trying to reason with her.

"But it happened!" Eleanor nearly shouted. "I was standing there, watching her come at us . . . and I . . . I *felt* it. It was like, I knew I had the power to make her go away. Then I wished for it . . . and she went blasting out the chimney!"

"Nell, sweetie . . . ," Cordelia started.

"No!" Eleanor did actually shout this time. "I *felt* it. It was the same feeling that surged through me back when . . . well . . . the last two times I used *The Book of Doom and Desire!*"

Brendan and Cordelia exchanged uneasy and confused glances, all traces of laughter gone.

"Nell, that's impossible," Brendan said softly. "You know that. The book is gone."

"You made it disappear yourself, remember?" Cordelia said.

"Of course I remember!" Eleanor snapped. "Never mind . . . just forget it. You can believe whatever you want."

A long and awkward silence followed.

"Come on, let's go up to the attic and look out the window . . . see what's out there," Cordelia said suddenly, trying to change the subject and the mood. "The land here is so flat, I bet we can see for miles in all directions. There has to be a town around here somewhere."

Brendan followed Cordelia upstairs. Eleanor sighed and then followed as well. She felt like she couldn't be any help to them at all. She had just saved their lives, and they hadn't even bothered to thank her. Instead they had laughed at her! She knew she was being irrational, but there was something deep inside her that pushed all rationality away. It had been happening a lot lately; Eleanor had been finding it difficult to reason with herself anymore. Maybe it was simply that she was finally seeing the truth: Her older siblings truly didn't respect her the same way as they did each other, and she was just now learning to actually stand up for herself.

Once they were all in the attic, it didn't take long to spot a small town on the prairie horizon from one of the windows. It couldn't have contained more than a few hundred people, but they also saw dark lines that Cordelia recognized as train tracks passing through it.

"That's perfect," she said. "Since we likely will need a faster way out of this book when the time comes to leave and find the Worldkeepers. Speaking of, shouldn't you be reading?"

Brendan pulled the *Journal of Magic and Technology* from the back pocket of his jeans and looked down at it. It was still unopened. The truth was, he was sort of dreading having to read it. Reading was not his thing. Especially not reading Denver Kristoff's dry and boring musings on the origins of magic and science.

"But we're all starving," Brendan said. "Shouldn't we go into town first? Find some food?"

"Not a good idea. The sun is setting," Cordelia said. "We should wait until morning."

"Okay, fine." Brendan said. "Maybe I can fall asleep? After all, turning into a zombie, swimming in a giant saliva hot tub, getting shot, and then coming back to life only to get attacked by a psychotic sheriff and an evil witch make for a pretty exhausting day. At least as exhausting as a lacrosse match . . ."

CHAPTER

39

As they sat in the attic that night, an electric lantern from the kitchen pantry lighting up the room, Cordelia tried to distract Eleanor from their growing hunger by talking about Fat Jagger. About how amazing it was that he had saved them, withstanding so much pain in the process. It brought tears to Eleanor's eyes, but Cordelia reassured her again and again that they would be able to return the favor. That's what they were there to do, after all.

Brendan, meanwhile, was sitting in the corner of the room, trying to read the *Journal*. But he was getting frustrated. He finally slammed the book shut.

"It's hard to get through a single page of this garbage!" Brendan moaned. "It's like trying to read Sanskrit while getting your fingernails pulled out one by one."

"Do you even know what Sanskrit is?" Cordelia asked.

"That's sort of my point," he said.

"Just concentrate; take your time," Cordelia said. "Read carefully. The answers are in the details."

Brendan sighed and reopened the *Journal*. It wasn't a very thick book, but the pages were thin, almost like tissue paper. And Denver's handwriting was cramped and small, meaning he packed a lot of mindless rambling about a lot of pointless junk into the book. There were three whole pages just on the history of telephones. Apparently the "new" invention had fascinated Denver Kristoff enough to endlessly dissect and study telephones. Which sounded awfully boring in itself, yet had to be a lot more exciting than *reading* about someone dissecting old telephones:

This new mode of communication is truly astounding. To think one can pick up this device and speak to a colleague or family member hundreds of miles across this great country is truly a marvel. Perhaps someday we can even amend this sort of technology to be able to see the people as well!

Brendan stopped reading and shook his head slowly. That old goat was probably the first human being to have the idea for FaceTime! Brendan turned the page, and his mouth dropped open.

"Whoa!" he said, unfolding a huge, thick piece of paper wedged into the pages of the *Journal*.

"What is it?" Cordelia asked.

"It's like a huge map," Brendan said.

"A map of what?" Eleanor asked, sitting up and rubbing her eyes. She had just started to doze off in spite of her grumbling stomach.

"I think it's the book world," Brendan said, looking it over. "Or book *worlds*. Come over and check it out."

Eleanor scrambled over to join him.

"Deal?" Brendan said, looking at his older sister.

She looked at him expectantly.

"On second thought, you might want to leave," Brendan said nervously.

"It's my eyes isn't it?" Cordelia asked. "She's in my head right now?"

Eleanor and Brendan both nodded slowly.

"And frankly, it looks even creepier in the dark," Brendan said.

"I . . . I'd better get out of here then," Cordelia said reluctantly.

She marched down the attic stairs as if trying to punch a hole into the wood with each step. But even more than anger, she was mostly just feeling helpless and guilty that she couldn't *contribute* in any way. It suddenly came to her that maybe this was why Eleanor felt insecure so much of the time.

"It looks like all of Denver Kristoff's books are actually

connected," Brendan said to Eleanor up in the attic. "They're like one giant map and you can travel between them seamlessly. . . ."

"Cool," Eleanor said, looking over his shoulder. "But it's so huge, how will we get to all the places we need to go?"

Brendan hadn't considered that yet. Eleanor was right, though, and it was a real problem. He found the book world for *Savage Warriors*. And it was tiny; it took up just a small chunk of the map, barely the size of a quarter. It had seemed so huge while they had been inside of it. It had taken them almost two days to travel across a small section in a horse-drawn cart when they were Slayne's captives. And there were *hundreds* of book worlds, each roughly the same size. Some were in water, some on land, and some had water and land. The entire book world was truly massive. It'd probably take a few days to go all the way across it in an airplane. On foot or horseback, it would take *years*, if not decades.

The realization was a like a gut punch that just sucked all the air right out of him.

Once he discovered where the Worldkeepers were located, how would they ever get to them in a reasonable amount of time? Even if they could somehow get access to a jet or plane, it certainly wasn't going to be inside whatever book they were in now. They were in the middle of a prairie in the eighteen hundreds; he highly doubted there were any airplanes nearby.

He finally looked up at Eleanor, whose worried face matched his own.

"We're in trouble," he said.

Eleanor frowned. Usually, she had an answer to her brother's pessimism. There was no such thing as an unsolvable problem. At least, that's what Dr. Walker had always told them growing up. It's what had made him such an excellent surgeon. And Eleanor had always believed him.

But this time, she could think of nothing else to say. There was no positive spin. It seemed to her that their chances of succeeding looked bleaker than ever.

40

None of the Walker children slept well that night. In part, because their "beds" in the attic consisted mostly of bundled blankets collected from the furnished rooms within Kristoff House. And so all three of them were awake and ready to head to town at the first sign of sunlight on the eastern horizon.

"What about that psycho sheriff?" Brendan asked as he rooted around in the kitchen drawers, looking for any scraps of food the movers might have missed. "You think that's his town?"

"There's a good possibility," Cordelia admitted. "But we don't have much choice. We can't just stay out here forever."

"I did *not* like that man," Eleanor said, remembering his

fur coat. She despised anyone who wore another animal's skin as clothing.

"None of us do," Cordelia agreed. "But it's a chance we're going to have to take."

"We could wear disguises," Brendan said, pointing at his face. "Check it out!"

While they'd been talking, he'd found a black Sharpie marker in the kitchen drawer and had proceeded to draw a fake moustache on his face. And he'd actually done a pretty good job. Cordelia had to admit that for a second it *almost* looked real. Well, if it weren't for the fact that he still had the face of a twelve-year-old kid.

"That looks ridiculous," she said with a begrudging grin. "Now we'll definitely get noticed!"

Eleanor giggled.

"Okay, okay, I'll wash it off," Brendan said. He spun around and turned on the kitchen faucet. No water came out. "Uh-oh."

"Bren, you idiot!" Cordelia laughed. "We're in the middle of a prairie predating running water and modern plumbing. Duh!"

He wiped desperately at the fake mustache on his face. But his dry fingers didn't even so much as smudge the ink. Even after he licked his fingertips and tried again, the mustache remained.

"That's why they call it *permanent*," Cordelia said, still laughing.

"Come on, guys, I'm hungry," Eleanor pleaded.

"Fine," Brendan said, giving up. He glanced at himself in the mirror one last time. "At least it's a pretty sweet looking 'stache. All the hipsters in the Mission would be superjealous if they could see me now."

He tucked the *Journal* into his back jeans pocket. It was a tight squeeze, but it just fit. Then he headed toward the front door while pretending to stroke his fake mustache with his fingertips. Cordelia and Eleanor couldn't help themselves from cracking up as they followed him out into the cool morning air.

CHAPTER

41

The tall grass and wild grains growing across the prairie made for slow going. The morning dew practically soaked their jeans. But eventually they found a small horse path, just as the sun finally cleared the horizon.

Eleanor was in the lead, humming softly as she walked. She was at least ten or fifteen feet out in front. She couldn't stop thinking about the energy she had felt surge through her when she'd banished the Wind Witch. Even if her older siblings didn't believe her, she knew what had really happened. And deep down, all she could think about was just how much she'd been craving that feeling again. Even more, though, she was craving ice-cream cake or Cheetos, the thought of which was enough to nearly bring her to tears.

A few dozen paces behind Eleanor, Brendan pulled out Kristoff's *Journal* and paged through it as he walked, slowing him down even more.

"Why is it taking you so long to get through that?" Cordelia asked.

"I'm concentrating," Brendan said. "I don't want to miss anything. Maybe one of the Worldkeepers is in the town we're going to."

Brendan was at a section in the *Journal* where Denver was speculating on the true effects of using *The Book of Doom and Desire*, talking about how use of the book corrupted souls the way it had for him and his daughter. The Walkers already knew that, of course, which is partially why Eleanor had wished the book out of existence using its own power against it. But what Brendan read in that section of the *Journal* frightened him even more. Denver Kristoff's more detailed conclusions did not bode well for Eleanor. He looked up at his younger sister twenty yards in front of them.

"Hey, Deal?" he said softly.

"Yeah?"

"Have you noticed anything weird about Eleanor lately?"

"What do you mean?" Cordelia asked.

"I mean . . . well," Brendan started, not sure he could bring himself to say aloud what he'd just learned. "According to the *Journal*, here, it's . . . never mind . . ."

"What is it?" Cordelia asked.

"I can't tell you right now," he said.

Recognition spread across Cordelia's face. She frowned and then averted her icy blue and possessed eyes down toward the ground, hoping not give the Wind Witch any glimmer of what they were up to at the moment. She tried not to think about how helpless she felt. If she did, she might start crying, which would only make this whole situation even worse.

After over an hour of walking, they found themselves at the edge of a small, dusty town that consisted of two criss-crossing dirt roads and several dozen buildings. The path they were on connected to a wider, larger dirt road. Near the road was a small, wooden hand-painted sign: "Welcome to Van Hook, Dakota Territory."

A small girl, perhaps around Brendan's age, wearing a bright yellow dress, was picking wildflowers among the tall grass and weeds next to the road.

She looked up at the sounds of the approaching footsteps and smiled at them.

"I've never seen a boy with such a fine mustache before," she said, laughing.

Brendan covered his mouth instinctively with his hand. He had forgotten about his fake mustache.

"Uh, it's just a joke," he mumbled.

"I figured," the girl said, looking them up and down

slowly. "I'm Adlaih. My friends call me Adie. You three don't look like you're from around here. Are you lost?"

"Sort of," Cordelia said quickly. "But we're mostly just hungry and thirsty. . . ."

"Well, I've got some food and water," Adie said, pointing at a large picnic basket nearby. "My dad always makes me bring food when I go out picking flowers. Sometimes I end up staying out all afternoon and don't even realize it!"

The Walkers eyed the large basket greedily. Brendan licked his lips.

"Help yourselves!" Adie finally said. "We got plenty more back at home."

The Walkers hesitated again, but only for a second. The true nature of their hunger hadn't hit them until the offer of food and water materialized. They rushed forward and Brendan ripped open the top of the basket. Inside were stacks of warm biscuits and a little jar of freshly whipped butter. A canteen of water lay nestled next to them.

It took the three Walker children just a few short minutes to completely empty the picnic basket and drain the canteen.

Near the end of the feeding frenzy, Brendan let out a large belch. He smiled at first, taking satisfaction in Cordelia's disapproving and disgusted expression. But then Adie's soft giggle reminded him that there was a cute girl still watching, and he covered his mouth quickly.

"Sorry," he mumbled.

"You sure were hungry," Adie said, looking into her empty picnic basket like she was looking down into a dry well.

"Thank you so much," Cordelia said. "We haven't eaten in what feels like days."

"My pleasure," Adie said. "My dad always says it's our responsibility to help the less fortunate."

"I'm Cordelia. This is my brother, Brendan. And my sister, Eleanor."

"Nice to meet you," Adie said with a smile that Brendan already found impossible to look away from.

"Is there a train depot nearby?" Cordelia asked.

"Down the road a bit." Adie pointed toward a small, white building on the edge of town next to the tracks. "Where you headed?"

"Not quite sure," Cordelia said.

Adie nodded in spite of seeming a little confused by the response. She was about to ask another question, when she noticed something on the dirt road a few feet away. She quickly rushed forward and knelt down.

"Oh no!" Adie gasped, cupping something small in her hands.

Eleanor leaned in to get a better look and then covered her mouth in horror.

Adie stood up and spun around. A small robin with a

crooked and damaged wing lay in her small palms. The girl's smile was gone as she examined the little bird carefully.

"I hope you all find what you need," Adie said to the Walkers. "But I need to get home and care for this poor little fella."

The Walkers nodded and thanked Adie for the food one last time as she gently put the injured bird in the front pocket of her dress. She grabbed her picnic basket and hurried off toward the other end of town.

The Walkers trudged toward the train station, holding their overly stuffed stomachs.

"Exactly how do you think we're going to pay for train tickets?" Brendan asked.

"These are frontier times," Cordelia said. "Maybe the conductor's willing to take something as a trade. Like some of the books from Denver's library maybe?"

"Only if he wants to put himself to sleep," Brendan said, noticing the townsfolk stepping outside into the morning sun to stare at the newcomers with open mouths. The sight of three strange kids in odd clothes walking into town was apparently pretty out of the ordinary in Van Hook.

At the far end of the dirt road on the edge of town, they ascended a few steps leading to the train platform. They stepped up to the ticket window. The train station itself was the size of a large shed. A young man, maybe eighteen or nineteen years old, stood inside the small hole cut into the side of the building that served as the ticket booth. He had red hair, a lot of freckles, and sweat was dripping in streams down his face, despite the mild morning temperature.

"May I help you?" he asked. His voice cracked uneasily.

"Yes, sir," Cordelia said politely. "When does the next train depart and how much for three fares?"

"Um, well . . . ," the kid said nervously. He looked at something behind him and then fidgeted with a pen on his side of the counter. "Stay right here. I got to check on something. I'll be right back. Okay?"

Without waiting for an answer, he disappeared somewhere inside the small train depot.

"Why was he acting so weird?" Brendan asked.

"I don't know," Cordelia said.

She leaned against the wall of the depot, while Eleanor sat down next to her and closed her eyes as if taking a quick morning siesta. Brendan pulled out the *Journal* and unfolded the book world map. He might as well try to find out if this train could take them anywhere useful. But he barely had time to even glance at the map, before a loud voice shattered the silence of the small prairie town.

"Looks like we hit the jackpot, boys," a familiar voice shouted.

The Walkers looked up and found themselves staring

right at Sheriff Burton "Wolf Catcher" Abernathy and his two deputies, McCoy and Sturgis. They grinned at the children. Their yellow teeth gleamed in the morning sun almost as brightly as their shiny guns.

"Wait a second, Sheriff," Deputy McCoy said. "That ain't the same kid that used the strange torture contraption on me." He spat a huge stream of brown tobacco juice onto the dirt. "This one here's got hisself a mustache. A mighty fine mustache at that—even finer than Mustache Dan's . . ."

"That's not a real mustache, you jackass," Sheriff Abernathy said. "It's painted on."

"Kid's a mighty fine artist, though," Deputy Sturgis said with a low whistle.

"Don't matter," the sheriff said. "He and his burnt-boot-faced sisters broke the law, and we're gonna make sure we see that justice is served."

Cordelia noticed Eleanor balling up her fists, like she was ready to charge the lawmen. She put a hand on her younger sister's shoulder and held her back.

"Wait," Cordelia said. "Just let us take the next train out of here. Then we'll be gone and you'll never see us again."

"I'm afraid we can't let you do that," Deputy McCoy said. "You see, in addition to assaulting an officer of the law, you kids was aiding and abetting a known enemy of the state, the outlaw Lefty Payne. We caught him just an hour's ride south of your home. And according to the law of this great land, that makes you all . . . uh, uh, what's that make them again, Sheriff?"

"Accomplices," Sheriff Abernathy said.

"Yeah, accomplices," the deputy repeated. "And we ain't making good on the law if we knowingly let three outlaw accomplices go free, is we?"

This seemed like a rhetorical question to the Walkers and so none of them bothered to provide an answer.

"By the power instilled unto me as sheriff of Williams County, you three are hereby under arrest," Sheriff Abernathy said, drawing his pistol faster than the speed of sound. "Don't think about running or resisting, unless you want to suddenly find yourselves six ounces of lead heavier. Ain't nobody that can outrun a bullet, and that's the God's honest truth."

He grinned as the three Walkers raised their hands in defeat.

CHAPTER

42

"What are we going to do now?" Cordelia asked, pacing restlessly around inside the town jail's holding cell. "We have to find a way out of here!"

Brendan looked up from the *Journal*. His sister was clearly losing it. She was such a control freak that her complete loss of control as the de facto family leader was making her go insane.

"Calm down, Deal," Brendan said. "I'm *hoping* there's something in this book that will help us do that!"

"Don't tell me to calm down!" Cordelia shouted. "I'm sick and tired of you taking advantage of this situation!"

"What situation?" Brendan asked.

"Me not being able to read the *Journal*," Cordelia screamed.

"You just love the fact that you have more power than I do! And you're lording it over me!"

"I'm just trying to help," Brendan said.

The man in the corner of the cell raised his head slightly at the sound of their argument. His cowboy hat was pressed down so far that they couldn't see his face. He had been there when the three Walkers were tossed inside the cell like rag dolls. But he had barely moved and hadn't spoken at all since their arrival and so the Walkers had almost forgotten he was there altogether.

Eleanor stepped in between her two siblings.

"Guys! Stop fighting!"

But they didn't even acknowledge her. She gave up a few seconds later and sat next to the man in black. His arms were folded across his chest and he smelled faintly of tobacco and booze—a lot like their uncle Frank.

"No one *ever* listens to me," Eleanor said in defeat after slumping down onto the bench while her brother and sister continued to argue.

It wasn't like this last time. Last time they were here, they'd worked as a team. As a family. Eleanor hated what was happening to them.

"See?" Eleanor cried when she didn't get so much as a grunt of a reply from the stranger sharing their prison cell. "Even *you* don't listen to me, and you have no one else to talk to!"

The man in black's foot shifted slightly on the dirt floor. An intricate red pattern was stitched into the black leather on his boots.

"I like your boots," Eleanor said. "Are they custom-made? They look custom-made. Where does a guy get custom-made boots around here anyway?"

She thought she heard a soft sigh escape the shield that his hat brim formed over his face. But it was hard to tell with Cordelia and Brendan still bickering on the other side of the prison cell.

"What are you in for anyway?" Eleanor asked. "Train robbery? Jaywalking? Illegal miming?"

"There was a man," the man in black finally said without lifting his head. His voice was low and it sounded like the inside of his throat was coated in gravel. "He kept talking too much, and pestering me with silly questions. There was only one way to shut him up."

"What was that?" Eleanor asked uneasily.

"I cut out his tongue."

Eleanor recognized the words pretty clearly as a threat. She scooted back to the other side of the bench. The man still hadn't lifted his head. At the sound of his voice, Brendan and Cordelia had stopped arguing and now were standing in front of the stranger in black clothes.

"You can't talk to our little sister that way," Brendan said, but his voice cracked with fear.

"I can do whatever I please," the man said.

"Yeah, well . . . no . . . no, you really can't," Brendan said, struggling to come up with a better comeback. "Or *shouldn't*, anyway. I guess it *is* a free country and all that . . . but it's not nice to threaten little girls, you know. . . ."

"I'm not a little girl," Eleanor said. "I can defend my own honor!"

Brendan's words got stuck in his throat. Because the man had finally lifted his head so they could see his face. And Brendan was too busy staring at it to talk. The man's chin was covered in black stubble. A long, wicked scar cut right across his face from his left temple all the way down to his lower right jaw, scrambling his lips slightly along the way. He looked more like an impressionist's portrait than a real human being. But there was a dark edge to his face that sucked all the air right out of the room. His eyes were cold and hard as if they'd never seen a single second of happiness in their thirtyish years of existence.

"What honor?" the man said, uncrossing his arms. "You kids don't have any honor. All you've done is squabble over nothing. Where's the honor in petty arguments?"

Cordelia finally noticed that the man didn't have a left hand. His left arm had been severed at the elbow. His shirtsleeve was tucked into itself where the rest of his arm should have been.

"Lefty Payne," Cordelia said softy, recognizing that this had to be the deadly outlaw that Sheriff Abernathy had come to their house looking for the night before.

"You heard of me?" Lefty asked.

"We heard you're wanted for fourteen unprovoked murders," Brendan said, his eyes wide.

"You always believe everything people tell you?" Lefty asked.

"So, it's not true then?" Eleanor asked hopefully.

Lefty turned his head toward her.

"No," he said.

"That's a relief," Cordelia said.

"I've killed more like forty-six people, at my last count," Lefty added darkly. "Of course, I never was too good at counting. Just playing poker and killing people."

A long silence followed as the three Walkers struggled to swallow, their mouths suddenly drier than a hot desert. Lefty Payne looked from Eleanor to Cordelia and finally settled his sharp gaze on Brendan.

Brendan looked down like a scolded puppy.

"What happened to your left arm?" Eleanor asked.

"*Eleanor!*" Cordelia scolded in a harsh whisper. "That's a rude question."

But Lefty didn't seem to mind. Instead, he looked down

at the spot where his hand should have been and shook his head slowly. Then he paused for a long moment, and Cordelia was certain he wasn't going to answer.

"As a little boy, I went to see Thomas Cooke's traveling circus," Lefty said. "I reached out to pet a baby elephant . . . and the little monster bit off my arm."

The Walkers didn't get a chance to figure out if Lefty Payne was joking or not, because a shrill voice from the front of the jailhouse suddenly interrupted their conversation.

"Wooo-eeee!" Sheriff Abernathy shrieked as he walked through the front door of the jailhouse. "We've got some good news for you!"

His two deputies were with him. They walked over and stood in front of the iron bars. They were all grinning ear to ear as if they'd just won the lottery on a shared ticket.

"We just got a wire telegraph from Judge Bentley," Sheriff Abernathy said. "He gave us permission for a hangin'!"

"We ain't had a good hangin' in a while," Deputy McCoy said with a grin, eyeing the prisoners the way a chef picks out cuts of meat from the local butcher.

Cordelia stood up with panic on her face.

"Don't worry," Lefty said to her. "They mean to hang *me*, not you."

"Well, see, that's where you're wrong, Lefty," Sheriff Abernathy said with a sickening grin. "Per the good Judge Bentley's orders, at high noon we get to hang *all four of you!*"

CHAPTER

43

"No, that can't be right!" Cordelia said. "There's no way a judge would approve the execution of three children!"

"Children?" Deputy McCoy said. "Oh, are these outlaw accomplices *children*?"

"Well, let me think," Sherriff Abernathy said, putting a hand on his chin. "They sure look and act like children, but I don't seem to quite remember putting that little detail in our telegram to the judge. Did you put it in there, Deputy Sturgis?"

The third deputy pulled out a little slip of paper and pretended to read it with great care.

"Well, shoot, it does seem that we left that part out," he

finally said in mock surprise and outrage. "Our telegram just says 'Known wanted outlaw Lefty Payne and three accomplices.' Should we resend it to clarify?"

They were all grinning now, clearly enjoying their little charade, while Cordelia grew more nauseous by the second.

"Nah, I don't see the need to waste the good folks of Williams County's resources any further than is required," Sheriff Abernathy said.

"Lefty, help us," Cordelia pleaded with the outlaw. "Tell them you don't know us and we've never met before now."

Lefty Payne was still sitting on the bench in the jail cell. He looked undisturbed at the news of his own impending execution. In fact, he looked ready for another nap.

"Nah," he said. "I'd rather have some company up there on the gallows. No man wants to die alone."

The sheriff and his men laughed.

"Come on, man, tell them the truth," Brendan pleaded angrily. "We're just kids! You can't let them hang us for *your* crimes!"

"Wouldn't matter either way, kid," Lefty said, pulling the hat back down over his eyes.

Deputy McCoy fished out a pocket watch. His eyebrows rose and he smiled when he looked at it.

"We're just fourteen minutes from noon," he said. "We better start getting ready!"

All three of them turned toward the door, but stopped

at the sight of a small girl standing in the entryway of the county jailhouse. She was around twelve years old with shoulder-length brown hair, a slender and pretty face with a perfect smattering of light freckles. She wore a bright yellow dress. The girl smiled at the sight of the sheriff and deputies and held up a picnic basket covered by a cloth napkin.

"I brought y'all some fresh-baked biscuits!" Adie said brightly.

"Well, ain't that sweet!" Sheriff Abernathy said. "Look here, fellas, little Adlaih Stoffirk has brought us some biscuits. You know how I love biscuits. *But*, I got to go find us some rope, so you two enjoy. I'll have one when I get back. Excuse me, darlin'."

He stepped past Adie and then left the jailhouse. Meanwhile, the two deputies swarmed Adie like bees on honey. They dug their dirty hands into the basket and grabbed two biscuits each, shoving them into their mouths.

It sort of reminded Brendan of the national hot dog eating contest that aired on ESPN every Fourth of July. It was always disgusting to watch, yet impossible to look away for some reason. The two deputies jammed the biscuits down their gullets with speed that would have made the All-Time World Hot Dog–Eating Champion jealous.

The three Walkers watched in horror as the innocent-looking little girl who had fed them just a few hours earlier, now fed their soon-to-be executioners treats just minutes before the hanging. It somehow cemented the reality of their horrible situation in a way that hadn't quite sunk in before that.

Several minutes later, however, the two deputies slumped down on the floor as if they'd been clubbed on their noggins with tire irons.

"What just happened?" Eleanor asked.

Cordelia got to the point. "Did you just *poison* the deputies?"

"Not poisoned, exactly," Adie said cheerily as she unhooked keys from Deputy McCoy's belt. "My daddy's the county doctor. I just borrowed some medications that he uses to help patients sleep."

"Why are you helping us?" Brendan asked.

Adie hurried over to the cell with a key ring that held just four keys. "I saw what happened," she said, trying the first key. "How they arrested you for basically nothing. It's not right. Plus, I hate the sheriff. He murdered my dog, Duffy, in cold blood. One day I was walking through town with Duffy, and Sheriff Abernathy reached down to pet him and he growled. A tiny growl, nothing too threatening. He always could sense evil in people—which is why I suspect he growled in the first place. But the sheriff took offense . . . and shot poor Duffy right there in the street."

Eleanor's eyes widened.

"That's the most horrible story I've ever heard," she said as she rushed out of the cell. "Thank you for saving us."

She gave Adie a big hug, in spite of her being a relative stranger.

"I suspect you would have done the same for me," Adie said. "Now, we have to hurry; the sheriff will be back soon. Wait . . . is *he* with you too?"

She pointed at Lefty Payne.

He was still seated calmly on the bench as if nothing at all unusual were happening. But he did have his head up again and he looked at them intently.

"Not really?" Brendan said, unsure of what the truth was precisely.

Lefty stood up suddenly, causing all of them to flinch. He strode past them and out of the cell in four long, gliding strides. After retrieving his firearm and a wooden prosthetic forearm and hand from an evidence drawer, he headed toward the door of the jailhouse.

He stopped just before exiting and turned to face the Walkers and Adie.

"You may want to follow me if y'all want to survive," he said.

Then he stepped outside into the bright, high-noon sunshine.

CHAPTER 44

At first, they all just stood there staring at the doorway. Nobody said anything. Then the three Walker children looked at Adie, as if she could either confirm or refute what Lefty had just said.

"Guess we should follow him," she said with a shrug.

"But he's a murderer," Cordelia said. "He said he killed over forty men!"

"Maybe they deserved it," Adie suggested. "There's a lot of bad men around these parts. You met the sheriff and the deputies . . . and they're supposed to be the good guys!"

"You really think we can trust this Lefty guy?" Brendan asked.

"Seems like a man you can trust, to me," Adie said.

"Daddy always says that true honesty lies behind a man's eyes, not in his actions or words. I saw truth in that man's eyes."

"Yeah, well, I heard death in his words," Brendan said as he headed toward the door. "But . . . we've got no other option."

The truth was, Brendan knew the sheriff and his men would be coming after them with guns blazing. And Lefty was the only person here who could possibly stand up to them. His sisters and Adie followed, apparently seeing the same wisdom in his logic.

Lefty led them along the back of the northernmost rows of buildings in the town. As they passed several houses, they saw a young boy playing in his backyard. His eyes widened at the sight of them.

Lefty raised a single finger to his lips. The boy nodded slowly.

They eventually circled around to a small stable at the other edge of town. Lefty went straight toward a pair of large horses tied together near the back end of the stable. One was a huge black steed that looked more like a dragon than a horse. The other was deep brown with several white spots. Lefty retrieved two saddles and started strapping them onto the horses.

"He's beautiful," Eleanor said, running up to the black horse. It was so big it looked as if it could have gobbled her up in a few quick bites. "What's his name?"

She ran a hand along the horse's neck and then gave him an encouraging pat on the side. The youngest Walker loved horses so much that the prospect of getting to ride one completely erased the fear of the dangers surely ahead of them.

"I call him *Whoa!* because he was so hard to break," Lefty said, pointing at Brendan and Cordelia. "You two will ride him. He's normally my pack horse, but I can leave my supplies behind."

"Great," Brendan said, eyeing the huge steed warily.

"I think he's just joking with us about his name," Cordelia said, trying to comfort her younger brother.

Almost on cue, the huge black stallion reared back on its hind legs and let out a long whinny. It crashed back down and then snorted several times as if warning Cordelia and Brendan to keep away.

"On second thought," Lefty said as he continued to strap saddles onto the two horses, "perhaps me and the youngest will ride *Whoa!* You two can take Widowmaker." He pointed at the other horse, stamping his hooves on the dirt floor angrily. "He gets his name from—"

"Don't tell me," Brendan said. "I really don't want to know."

Lefty shrugged and hoisted Eleanor up onto *Whoa!*'s saddle. Then he climbed up onto the horse behind her.

"Why are you helping us?" Cordelia asked. "You don't

exactly seem like the charitable type. Especially if it means you'll have to leave all your supplies behind."

"Four children are a lot more useful to me getting away and past the Mexican border than all of this extra stuff." He pointed to the corner of the stable at the bundled packs that *Whoa!* usually carried. "Now stop yapping and get on your horse!"

"Are you coming with us?" Brendan asked Adie, his cheeks growing hot for some reason.

"Nah, my whole family's here," she said. "I just wanted to make sure you got away."

Brendan nodded as Cordelia pushed a small stepladder over to Widowmaker. They eyed the huge horse warily; neither of them had very much experience with horses at all. They were just about to start uneasily climbing aboard, when a sharp crack broke open the silence.

Specks of dirt exploded at their feet as a bullet smashed into the ground just a few yards away. Brendan, Adie, and Cordelia dove for cover behind a feeding trough as several more shots were fired and bullets zipped by them and smashed into the hitching post, spraying splinters everywhere.

Widowmaker and *Whoa!* whinnied nervously before bolting out of the stables at a Triple Crown pace, taking Lefty Payne and Eleanor with them.

"Gather your rifles, men!" Sheriff Abernathy shouted

from the center of town, as he reloaded his revolver. "We got fugitives on the run!"

"He's reloading," Adie said in a loud whisper. "Come on, now's our chance. Follow me!"

She began running away from the stables toward the train depot before Brendan or Cordelia could respond. They hesitated for a moment, worried about Eleanor riding off alone with an admitted mass murderer, but eventually dashed after her. After all, there was no way they could save Eleanor if they were dead.

As they approached the station, they saw a train just starting to pull away, and already knew what Adie had in mind.

The three fugitives ran onto the train platform and sprinted alongside the moving locomotive, which was gaining speed with each passing second. More gunshots rang out behind them, and Brendan was sure he was going to get hit at any moment.

Ahead of him, Adie caught the last car of the train and jumped up, snagging the railing. She pulled herself onto the back deck. Brendan caught up with the train a few seconds later. He ran alongside it for a few moments and then reached up and grabbed the railing on the back end of the caboose. His feet dangled for a few seconds and he had visions of getting sucked underneath the train by his shoelace. But Adie's small and surprisingly strong hands grabbed his shirt and pulled him aboard.

He spun around quickly and saw Cordelia struggling to keep up with the train as it gradually accelerated. Brendan held the railing and leaned off the side of the train car.

"You have to jump now!" he screamed at Cordelia. "Or you'll never catch it!"

Cordelia nodded determinedly and then took one more step and leaped forward into the air. But it was too late; Cordelia's outstretched hand fell just short of the railing.

She had just missed the last train out of town.

45

Brendan and Adie had been prepared for the possibility that Cordelia wasn't going to make it. They leaned off the back end of the train, holding the railing for support, and each snagged Cordelia's outstretched hand at the same time. As if they'd been working together as an action duo for years, they seamlessly pulled her aboard the train in one swift motion.

Cordelia collapsed to the deck on top of Brendan.

"I thought," she said, stopping for a moment to catch her breath. "I thought I was dead!"

"I knew we had you the whole time," Brendan lied with a grin. "Now, uh, you want to get off me?"

Cordelia climbed to her feet and then helped her brother

up. All three of them smiled in relief. But their smiles quickly disappeared when a bullet zinged past and lodged into the train's back door, right between Brendan's legs.

His eyes went wide and he thought for a second that his heart had literally stopped beating. But the sound of more gunfire snapped him back to life as more bullets peppered the rear of the train.

A dozen men on horses, led by Sheriff Abernathy in his wolf coat, rode up behind them, firing pistols and rifles at the passenger train with reckless abandon.

"He's insane!" Cordelia yelled, pointing at the passenger cars ahead of them. "There are innocent people in there."

Brendan grabbed the door handle to the train car and pulled. It didn't budge.

"It's locked!" he yelled, swaying slightly as the train rumbled on, picking up more speed.

The ground rushed dizzyingly past below their feet.

"Up here!" Adie yelled, already halfway up a ladder that led to the roof of the train car.

Brendan looked at Cordelia. From her expression, he could tell that she also didn't feel too excited about climbing onto the roof of a speeding locomotive. Especially with bullets whizzing past them. But then she shrugged.

"We can't just stay here like sitting ducks," she shouted, and jumped onto the ladder.

As if to drive home her point, a bullet smashed into the

wall right where her head had been just seconds before. Brendan started climbing up after them. He wasn't particularly fond of ladders, especially ladders attached to the back of a speeding train, but thankfully it was just nine quick rungs to the roof.

When Brendan got to the top, he stayed on his hands and knees. No way was he going to stand up on top of this thing. It was already hard enough to stay steady on his knees with the wind whipping into his body like a swarm of invisible hands trying to nudge him overboard.

Sheriff Abernathy and his men were still gaining on the train.

"Brendan!" Cordelia yelled over the sounds of the train's engine and the rushing wind. "We need to run toward the front! We're too exposed back here!"

She was on her feet, wobbling slightly with her arms raised like a tightrope walker. If she could do this, then so could he, Brendan told himself. *He* was usually the reckless one.

He grabbed Cordelia's hand, and she helped him to his feet. Brendan, Cordelia, and Adie began running on top of the passenger cars toward the front of the train. Once they got going, Brendan had to admit that it was slightly easier than he'd expected. The gaps between the cars were only a foot and a half, which was more like a long stride than an actual leap. And the rest of the train cars had slightly flatter

roofs, providing more stability. It was sort of like running on a turbocharged moving walkway at an airport.

They were six cars closer to the front of the train, when Brendan spotted Lefty Payne and Eleanor on horseback ahead of them to the right. Widowmaker and *Whoa!* were still tethered together.

Brendan waved his arms frantically. Eleanor saw them but had her arms firmly gripped to the saddle and couldn't wave back. Lefty looked back a moment later and then quickly motioned with a single sideways nod of his head for them to keep running toward the front of the train.

The guns continued to crack behind them, and every once in a while Brendan could hear a howling zip as a bullet whizzed past his head. He didn't need any more prodding than that. The three of them bounded across four more train cars until they were even with the horses.

"Jump!" Lefty shouted.

"Onto the horse?" Brendan shouted back, eyeing Widowmaker's empty back dubiously. It looked like it was forty feet down instead of just six or seven.

"Would you rather jump to the ground?" Lefty shouted.

Brendan glanced at the prairie rushing by in a blur of green and gold and brown. He definitely would not rather jump to the ground.

"Move, I'll go first," Cordelia said, stepping past him.

But once she was past him, she seemed entirely unsure

that she'd actually meant it. Cordelia stood at the edge of the roof and looked down at Widowmaker's back as if she were standing on the rim of an active volcano.

Before either of them could say or do anything more, Adie pushed past them both and hopped down easily onto Widowmaker's back as if she were simply slipping into a swimming pool. She grabbed the reins with one hand and held out her other hand.

"Come on, jump!" she yelled. "It's now or never, Brendan!"

He inched closer to the edge of the train car, until the back of the large brown horse was close enough that he maybe could have dipped down and touched it with his foot if they both weren't moving at least thirty miles per hour. He took a deep breath and hopped down onto the horse's back. He landed firmly on the saddle behind Adie, and for the next few minutes he writhed in pain and regretted not wearing his lacrosse gear—one specific item in particular.

Brendan was still howling in pain when he noticed that Cordelia was suddenly on the horse in front him, grasping at Adie's shoulders for dear life. He did his best to reach out and steady his sister. And then, just like that, they were all firmly on Widowmaker's back and veering away from the train behind *Whoa!* and Lefty Payne and Eleanor. The two tired horses sprinted up a gently sloping hill with a payload of five people on their backs.

The problem was the twelve or more heavily armed men still right behind them, still shooting. If it weren't for Denver Kristoff's attention to historical detail in making their old revolvers dreadfully inaccurate beyond twenty yards, all five of the fugitives would have been riddled with enough holes to be human water fountains.

But the sheriff and his men were getting closer. Nothing made this clearer than the bullet that slammed into Brendan's rear end just as they crested the low hill.

CHAPTER

46

"I've been shot!" Brendan screamed. "Oh, man, they shot me!" His panicked voice howled into Cordelia's right ear.

"We can't stop now!" Cordelia yelled back. "Is it bad? Where'd they hit you?"

"In the butt!" cried Brendan. "They shot me in the—"

And then he fell silent. His grip around Cordelia's midsection loosened. Panic rose up in her throat, making it hard to swallow or speak.

"Brendan?" Cordelia shouted. "*Brendan!*"

Could someone really die that quickly from getting shot in the butt? Cordelia wasn't sure, but was afraid to turn around and look.

"Is your brother all right?" Adie called out.

"I don't know, but we have to keep going!" Cordelia said, before finally looking back.

Brendan was writhing, his free hand on his butt. He faced Cordelia again, still wincing in pain, but clearly alive.

"I don't get it," he shouted over the tromping of horse hooves. "I felt it hit me, and it stings really bad, but there's no blood."

"We'll check it out when . . . *if* we ever get away from these psycho cowboys," Cordelia said, relief allowing her to finally breathe again.

Meanwhile, on the lead horse in front of them, Eleanor was completely unaware that Brendan had been shot. She was too busy looking across the endless horizon for somewhere, anywhere, to hide. And then she spotted the perfect place.

A few hundred yards away, tucked behind another hill, she saw the unmistakable peaked Victorian roof of Kristoff House. She pointed at it and shouted to Lefty.

"Head that way!" she shouted. "That's our house! It can save us!"

"How can a house save us?" Lefty asked.

"Trust me! Just go toward the house!"

Eleanor knew it wouldn't let them down. Somehow, whenever things seemed to be at their worst, Kristoff House always found a way to save them. It had been there to get them out of a pickle too many times to even count. Which is partially why it still felt so much like home to the Walker children, in spite of all the horrible things that had happened to them there.

Lefty pulled the reins and directed a fatigued *Whoa!* toward the house. The horses clearly didn't have much energy left. They couldn't flee forever. So this strange house that he could have sworn wasn't here a few days ago was as good a place to hole up as any.

Within a few minutes, the horses gratefully came to a stop at the front porch of Kristoff House. The five riders dismounted and rushed inside. Cordelia slammed the door shut and latched all three locks.

"Brendan!" she said. "Are you okay?"

He hobbled over to the couch, limping awkwardly due to the wound to his butt and the impact of the horse's saddle on his groin. He gingerly pulled something from his back jeans pocket. It was Kristoff's *Journal*. There was a smoking hole in the center, passing almost all the way through it. Brendan poked at it with his finger. A small black slug fell out and plopped onto the floor.

"I guess that's why there was no blood," he said, grinning. "That old crackpot's book just saved my butt. Literally."

Cordelia frowned in spite of her relief.

"I just hope that hole didn't erase anything important," she said.

"Seriously? That's all you care about?"

"Guys!" Eleanor shouted from the living-room bay window. "The men are still out there! They're heading toward the front door!"

"So it's at least twelve guns versus . . . ," Brendan said, trailing off as he looked toward the outlaw Lefty Payne. "One?"

Lefty nodded slowly, knowing that as good a gunman as he was, one six-shooter couldn't fend off a whole posse of armed men for very long.

"What are we going to do?" Cordelia asked.

"The Dyson?" Brendan suggested.

"That's not going to work again, especially against more than a dozen cowboys this time!" Eleanor said.

Loud pounding on the front door silenced them all.

"Come out of there," Sheriff Abernathy shouted. "Or we'll break down the door and shoot every last one of you!"

Lefty Payne stepped in front of the door and then looked at the three Walkers.

"The little one said this house can save us?" he asked with his eyebrows raised.

"Maybe," Brendan said, looking down at the *Journal* clutched in his hands. "I'll start reading. There's a section in here that had some technical sketches of the secret passageways and hidden features of the house."

"Make it fast, kid," Lefty said. "I can't buy us much more time."

Brendan opened the *Journal* toward the back and began skimming as fast as he could, looking for Denver's breakdown of all of the house's many secrets.

"I'll give you one last chance to open up or we're coming in," shouted Sheriff Abernathy as he continued pounding away.

Lefty pointed his gun at the center of the door and fired four rounds in quick succession. The bullets pierced the door. Several screams and a lot of loud cursing outside followed shortly after.

"They do got guns!" someone yelled.

"Fall back and take cover!" the sheriff shouted. "Those scoundrels just shot Deputy McCoy!"

Eleanor, Cordelia, and Brendan looked at one another in shock.

"Did you kill him?" Brendan asked.

"You're supposed to be reading," Lefty snapped.

Brendan forced himself to turn his attention back to the *Journal*.

Suddenly, a thunderstorm of gunfire erupted outside and bullets tore into the sides of the house like the walls were made of paper. Windows shattered and plaster and wood from the walls blanketed the living room. The occupants dove to the floor. The volley of bullets was continuous, as if there were now hundreds of men outside instead of just a handful.

"Upstairs!" Cordelia shouted. "The bathroom in the hallway on the second floor doesn't have any walls that face the outside!"

She led the way, as Adie, Eleanor, Brendan, and Lefty followed. They scrambled up the grand stairs in the foyer toward the second-floor hallway. Cordelia was sure somebody was going to get hit on the way up, but somehow they all made it into the bathroom uninjured.

Her instincts had been right; no bullets were penetrating the several walls surrounding the bathroom. Apparently, Denver Kristoff stayed pretty true to classic western tropes, because the men outside seemed to have an endless supply of ammunition and were content just unloading it into the sides of Kristoff House for the better part of fifteen full minutes. The house's occupants hunkered down and waited, Brendan reading the *Journal*, and the others trying to come up with some sort of backup plan.

Lefty was the first one to smell the smoke. Before long, they could all smell it. As soon as Cordelia cracked open the bathroom door to investigate they heard the crackling of fire downstairs and saw plumes of thick gray smoke drifting up into the hallway.

Cordelia slammed the door shut again and spun around to face the others with panicked eyes.

"They've set the house on fire!"

CHAPTER

47

"There has to be a way out!" Eleanor screamed.

Cordelia shook her head frantically as smoke trickled into the bathroom through the cracks in the doorframe.

"The lower stairs are already on fire," she said. "The only way we can go is up."

"Good!" Brendan shouted, leaping to his feet. "We need to get to the attic! I think I just found something that can help us."

They covered their faces with shirts, scarves, and bath towels before sprinting from the bathroom into the hallway. The smoke was already so thick they could barely make out the person in front of them. But with Brendan leading the way, they made it to the attic safely.

"What now, Bren?" Cordelia asked as she and Lefty pulled the stairs closed.

Brendan ignored her question; he was too busy running his hand along one of the wooden attic walls. He kept glancing down at the open *Journal* in his left hand while inspecting the wall with his right. Every few inches he would press hard and whisper to himself.

"What's he doing?" Eleanor asked, worried that her brother had inhaled too much smoke. Or maybe it was a lingering effect of becoming a zombie?

"Hopefully saving us all," Cordelia said, pushing her younger sister to the far corner of the attic away from the stairs. She could already hear the crackling of flames below them, even above the bullets and gunfire still raining down on the house from all sides, in addition to Lefty firing back at the men outside from the attic window.

Brendan was about ready to call it quits and just assume that what he'd discovered in Kristoff's *Journal* were plans that the old man had never gotten around to actually completing, when his hand suddenly passed over an unnatural seam in the wooden planks. He leaned in closer and examined a small fissure. It was nearly invisible, straight, and formed a small rectangle about the size of a notebook. He pressed down at the center and then pushed to the right. The wall didn't budge for a moment, but then something groaned and creaked and a false panel slid open.

The secret panel hid a small cubbyhole the size of a shoe box. Just large enough to house a steel handle covered in a red rubber grip with the words "Aerial Emergency Dispatch" stenciled across it.

Brendan grabbed the lever and pulled. The old metal creaked as the lever shifted into the up position. Nothing happened for a few seconds and then suddenly the whole house seemed to be vibrating. Several loud bangs and clanks thundered above them from the roof. The house shuddered and rattled as if it were about to disintegrate.

"*Bren-n-n-nd-d-a-a-a-a-n!*" Cordelia shouted, her words shaking as if someone were slapping her on the back rapidly with two open palms. "*Wha-att-t d-d-id-d-d yo-o-ou j-j-just d-d-do-oo?*"

He spun around just as something exploded above them. A huge shadow loomed over every window, blocking the sun entirely and plunging the attic into total darkness as the occupants screamed in terror.

CHAPTER
48

Outside, Sheriff Abernathy, his men, and several vigilante townsfolk of Van Hook stopped shooting at the house. Their smoking guns hung limply at their sides while they peered up at the sky.

The huge house was riddled with bullet holes. The bottom floor was on fire and black smoke poured from the broken windows. But nobody noticed either of those things in that moment.

Instead, they gaped at the massive balloon inflating itself above the house's roof. It was red with silver stripes, reflecting the sunshine so sharply that several of the deputies dropped their weapons to shield their eyes from the glare bouncing off the balloon.

It inflated so quickly that every single man on the ground would later swear it was either some sort of dark magic, or an act of God. And the balloon was so huge that none of the men would be able to accurately portray its size later.

The red-and-silver balloon dwarfed the house itself. It was at least fifteen times the size of the large home. It was attached to the house's roof, and as it fully inflated and rose up into the sky, it took the odd house right along with it, still ablaze and spewing smoke from every shattered window.

Sheriff Burton "Wolf Catcher" Abernathy clamped his open mouth shut and raised his pearl-gripped pistol again. He pulled back the hammer and resumed shooting at the house as it lifted higher into the sky above them.

"Whatcha y'all gaping at!" he screamed at his men while reloading his gun. "Keep firing! We're going to pop that balloon!"

"That ain't no balloon," said one of the townsfolk who'd ridden out to help apprehend the fugitives. "It's the hand of God, saving them kids from evil. I'm not taking part in this any longer."

Several of the other men agreed and followed the first man as he mounted his horse and started back toward town.

But the sheriff's remaining deputy and a few of the vigilantes followed orders and resumed firing at the house, the bottom floor still trailing smoke as it continued to climb.

They fired until their guns were empty. And by the time they had unloaded every last bullet they carried, not only was the massive balloon still intact, but it was now just a spot among the clouds, nearly smaller than even the largest star in a night sky.

"Ah, forget it," Sheriff Abernathy said, holstering his weapons. "Them kids and the outlaw Payne are as good as dead up there, anyway."

"You mean *those* kids," Deputy Sturgis said.

Sherriff Abernathy shot his deputy a stone-cold glare.

"What? You should be proud," Sturgis said. "We're starting to learn us some of that good language stuff!"

"Whatever, let's go," the Sheriff growled. "Like I said, they aren't long for this world. If the fire don't get 'em first, then the lack of oxygen will."

"Lack of oxygen?" Deputy Sturgis asked.

"Yeah, don't you ever read anything?" Sheriff Abernathy snapped. "Some Englishmen flew a balloon so high they nearly died. One of 'em passed out because there's no air to breathe up that high. That's a fact, God's honest truth." He took one last look up at the Kristoff House and grinned sickeningly. "They're all gonna suffocate up there."

CHAPTER

49

"We're actually flying!" Brendan screamed from the attic window.

Cordelia pressed her face against an adjacent window and peered down. The cowboys below them were still shooting. The little plumes of smoke coming from the ends of their guns grew smaller and smaller as the old house ascended. The men below looked like tiny action figures holding bouquets of ash-gray roses.

They *were* actually flying.

Adie had gone into a kind of silent shock when the house first began rising. She remained motionless with her eyes wide and mouth hanging open as the house continued its ascent.

Lefty sat down with his back to the wall, fear softening his normally steely eyes.

"What kind of dark magic is this?" he shouted.

Cordelia didn't answer him, but instead slid open the attic window. A gust of icy wind stung her face. She fought through it and stuck her head outside and peered up. A massive red-and-silver balloon was attached to the house by a series of cables. At the center of its base near the peak of the house's roof, a huge burner shot blue flames inside of it. She stared at the balloon for several seconds before realizing she could see her own breath. It was freezing up there.

Cordelia pulled herself back inside and closed the window.

"We're getting too high!" she yelled, cutting short Brendan and Eleanor's triumphant celebration. "We'll freeze to death up here, if we don't run out of oxygen first! There's not enough oxygen to survive past thirty thousand feet."

"How do you know that?" Brendan asked.

"Books," Cordelia said. "I read books."

"Well, so do I, Deal!" Brendan said "And according to the book I'm reading, Kristoff installed this balloon just in case the barrels under the house failed for some reason. Why would he even do that if it meant we'd float up into space to our deaths?"

"Maybe there's a way to control it," Cordelia suggested. "Keep reading."

Brendan started reading again, trying to ignore the black smoke drifting by the window reminding him that the house was also still on fire. But he pushed the thought away. He wasn't able to read Denver's nearly indecipherable handwriting without total focus.

Meanwhile, Lefty Payne stayed seated on the floor. His initial shock was gone, but he was still more confused and terrified than he'd ever been in his life, even though he'd never admit it. Being inside the floating house was like being at the peak of a moving mountain, except much higher. It made him very uneasy. There wasn't much that scared Lefty Payne. Heights was one of them. In fact, there were only three things in the world that scared him:

High Places

Imprisonment (he'd rather be hanged)

Circus Elephants

Adie, on the other hand, would have had to be pried away from the window. After her initial shock, she'd run to the window to see what the world looked like from so high in the air. She loved seeing everything below them looking so tiny. It was a marvel. But deep down, she was thinking about her dad and mom, how they would be worried sick about her. She was supposed to have been home over an hour ago. Plus, if she never went back home, who would finish nursing that poor injured robin back to health?

The temperature inside the attic of Kristoff House dropped quickly, alerting them as to just how little time they had left before they'd run out of air or freeze to death. Already, their breaths were growing more shallow and rapid and visible.

Brendan found it increasingly difficult to focus on the *Journal*. He'd found the right section; it was just a matter of deciphering the tiny print and faded drawings with an oxygen-deprived brain.

"I think we need to go back downstairs," he finally said, panting as if he were in the middle of a marathon.

"Are you insane?" Cordelia said. "It's on fire down there!"

"Not all the way downstairs," he said. "Just the second floor. The *Journal* says the controls are in the study."

Cordelia nodded and the two of them worked to lower the attic stairs. Plumes of smoke billowed into the attic, making it even harder to see and breathe. Adie coughed, and Eleanor pulled her down to the floor.

"Smoke always rises," Eleanor said, repeating what she'd learned in school. "That's why you're supposed to drop to the ground in fires."

"The fire is still only on the first floor!" Brendan shouted through his shirt, which was pulled up over his face like a bandit.

"We have to hurry!" Cordelia shouted back. "The smoke is so thick we'll be dead in minutes. You know, in fires, more people die from smoke inhalation than from—"

"We don't have time for a fire-safety speech!" Brendan cut her off. "Keep moving!"

He ran down the attic stairs, disappearing into the gray haze of smoke. Cordelia sighed and followed after him with Eleanor, Adie, and Lefty close behind. Brendan stayed low but moved fast, bear-crawling his way down the hall toward the study. The door was closed, which bought them more time since not as much smoke had drifted inside of it yet.

Brendan coughed as he ran into the room, waiting by the door for everyone else to get inside. Then he slammed it shut, removed his hooded sweatshirt and stuffed it into the crack underneath the door. The room was cold and hazy, like a movie flashback, but far from the impenetrable gray of the smoky hallway. The Kristoff House study was smaller and less grand than the massive library downstairs, but it still accommodated the five occupants comfortably, and the high ceilings helped distribute the accumulated smoke.

Cordelia headed over to the side window and quickly pushed it open. The cold air that rushed inside knocked the wind from her lungs like a sucker punch to her gut. But it also helped disperse the lingering smoke. She pushed the window closed again after several seconds, her hands growing numb from the cold. It had to be below zero at this height, which wasn't a good sign.

"Hurry, Brendan!" she shouted.

Brendan and Lefty hunched over the ledge in front of the large bay window across from the huge maple desk in the study. They pulled at one of the ledge's wooden planks. It groaned under the pressure, as if it were holding on for dear life. Then it cracked, and finally pulled free with a snap.

"Yes!" Brendan said, peering into the small hole left behind.

He reached inside the bay window ledge and pulled up a lever. The sound of ancient gears rotating rumbled below them. The squeal of old metal and rubber belt pulleys greeted them like a warning howl. Then the entire bay window's landing, roughly the size of a day bed, folded away and spun around on reinforced hinges. The bottom side rotated up, containing a wooden steering wheel with evenly spaced handles extending from the spoke, just like from an old pirate ship. Next to the steering wheel were several large levers, like oversize car stick shifters, and three glass-covered instrument dials.

Brendan referenced something inside the *Journal*, his teeth chattering and his shallow breaths bursting visibly in front of him like little puffs of smoke. Then he grabbed one of the levers and pulled it down.

The house stopped ascending almost immediately, the

sudden shift in direction causing the occupants to stumble slightly. Lefty clutched his stomach uneasily as the house began to descend.

"You did it!" Eleanor yelled, wrapping her arms around her brother's waist.

"We're not out of the woods yet," Brendan said. "The first floor is still on fire."

Cordelia jumped up onto the bay window, landing in front of the steering wheel, and pulled aside the curtains covering the three massive windowpanes. She peered outside. They were above a series of light and stringy clouds that looked like pulled cotton. Between the gaps she saw that the yellow-and-green plains that had been the landscape when they'd started their ascent were gone. Below them now was a deep-blue surface, sparkling in the sun as if it were coated in glitter.

"We're over an ocean!" Cordelia yelled. "Lower us more."

"And the Walker family finally catches a break," Brendan said, pulling the altitude lever back even farther.

He located the small altimeter and watched as the red needle swung to the right, back below twenty thousand feet. It moved slowly but steadily backward. Eighteen thousand. Seventeen thousand. He breathed out a sigh of relief. After a few more minutes it passed ten thousand. He looked out the window as his ears popped. The ocean was deep blue and dark. The ripples of waves were barely visible, like small cracks on the otherwise smooth surface of the sea.

Adie and Lefty and Eleanor huddled together near the desk. Lefty was too afraid to go anywhere near another window, and Adie was focused on trying to calm down a panicking Eleanor.

"We're moving too fast!" Brendan said. "At this speed the house will break apart when we hit the water!"

"We don't know that for sure," Cordelia said. "This house has already survived two major earthquakes."

Still, she didn't really believe her own words. She bit her lower lip and looked out the window again, filled with anxiety.

"I suppose we should all make peace with each other, before we die," Brendan said. "I'm gonna start now, because I've done a whole lot of bad things. . . ."

Cordelia glared at him.

"What?" Brendan said. "I'm just being honest."

"You really think we're going to die?" Eleanor asked, her voice shaking.

"Don't listen to him," Adie said, putting an arm around the youngest Walker. "Your brother sure has a way of seeing the most gloomy side of every situation. But we've made it this far; we aren't going to die now."

Brendan felt his face grow hot and then he looked away. He certainly didn't want to be known as the Debbie Downer of the bunch. Especially not by Adie.

"One thousand feet!" Cordelia interrupted. "Everybody brace for impact."

Adie and Eleanor ran toward the huge desk and scrambled under it. Lefty Payne clambered in after them.

"There's room for one more!" Eleanor yelled.

"You go." Brendan nodded at Cordelia, trying to be the brave one. "It'd be too ironic if one of these giant encyclopedias in here flew off the shelf and ended up knocking you out!"

His sister smiled at him. And he realized just then how difficult this trip to the book world had been on her. Brendan unexpectedly felt a lump in his throat.

"Brendan, listen to me. . . . You *have* to survive," Cordelia said. "Only you can read that *Journal* and find the Worldkeepers. Now get under that desk! I'll stay out here. Hurry up, we only have a couple seconds before we hit the water!"

Brendan realized he wasn't going to be able to argue with his older sister. Besides, she happened to be right, which was annoying to have to admit yet again. He ran toward the huge desk and squeezed under it with the others, sandwiching himself between the desk's right drawers and Lefty, who smelled like a mixture of pipe tobacco, whiskey, and a middle-school boys' locker room.

"Outlaws don't get to bathe much, huh?" Brendan asked.

Lefty's loud growl was the last thing any of them heard before the thunderous crash of Kristoff House impacting the sea. It slammed into the surface of the salty water with enough force to rattle their bones. And the truth suddenly became clear to Brendan: There was no way they, or the house, were going to survive.

CHAPTER 50

Brendan slowly opened his eyes, vaguely aware of a dull throbbing in his skull, as if tiny men were inside his head pounding away at his brains with their small hammers. He sat up, shielding his eyes. His vision was too blurry to make out anything aside from a bright light.

"Am I dead?" he asked.

"Unfortunately not," a voice answered.

"*Unfortunately?*"

"Yes, I only need a few of you to leverage as hostages once we get to the Mexican border," the voice said. "If you had died, I'd be spared your miserable jokes."

That's when Brendan realized he was talking to Lefty. He didn't bother to tell Lefty that of all the places they were likely drifting toward, Mexico was certainly not one of them. He started to climb to his feet, but swayed and then stumbled. Lefty's strong hand grabbed his shoulder and steadied him.

"Cordelia?" Brendan said, rubbing his eyes.

"I'm here," she said. "We're all okay."

A small pair of arms wrapped around Brendan's waist.

"I thought you were dead," Eleanor said.

"*Unfortunately* not," he said, hugging her back.

Slowly, his eyes adjusted to the light. They were still in the second-floor study. Bright sunshine poured in through the room's shattered windows. He shuffled over to the bay window, careful to avoid all the broken glass, and peered outside. They were back in the air now, the blue sea sparkling below them. He could see the distorted shadow of the house and balloon on the water's surface.

"The fire?" he asked.

"It's out," Cordelia said. "We hit hard enough to basically flood the entire first floor. In fact, we were actually sinking until I increased the balloon's flame to maximum power and lifted us back up again."

"The kitchen is all burned up," Eleanor said. "So is pretty much everything down there."

"At least we made it," Brendan said.

Adie stepped forward, looking guilty.

"I'm sorry about what I said before," she said. "About

you being so gloomy all the time. I'm glad you're not dead. You gave us all an awful fright."

Brendan felt his cheeks burning. He managed to throw an awkward grin her way and then turned back toward the bay window to hide his face.

"Well, I guess I should get started reading the *Journal* again," he said, trying to ignore his headache. "So we can figure out where we need to go next."

He plopped down on the floor and leaned back against the wall. He winced and then sat forward. There was a huge welt on the back of skull where it had hit the desk when they crashed. He did his best to ignore it and press on with the reading. At first everyone just stood there, watching him read. It was sort of distracting to have a reading audience.

But at the same time, part of him relished the attention. Being the one everyone was looking to for answers. It made him feel special and heroic. Not only would he get to be the savior of his own family, but also the savior of two entire universes! Even being the MVP of the lacrosse state title didn't come anywhere close to that. He continued reading, looking for some information about the Worldkeepers, while Kristoff House hovered among a few clouds and the sun over an open sea that stretched out in front of them and disappeared into the horizon.

The house was silent for the most part. Cordelia,

Eleanor, and Adie ventured downstairs into the partially flooded and mostly burned-out kitchen to see what was left of it. Lefty Payne stayed in the study with Brendan, plucking giant volumes of encyclopedias written decades after his time off the shelves, and paging through them with fascination.

Cordelia, Eleanor, and Adie were just about to give up on their search for rations when they heard Brendan shouting upstairs. They dashed out of the kitchen, their steps sluggish through several feet of seawater, and ran upstairs and into the study to find Brendan standing there with his chest puffed out like a superhero.

"I found it!" he said with an unabashed smile. "I know where we need to go to find the Worldkeepers!"

Before he could explain any further, a spine-shaking screech from outside forced them to cover their ears. Seconds later, a sleek head with a long, pointed beak poked into the study through the bay window.

Several rows of razor-sharp teeth inside a pair of wicked jaws clamped down onto Brendan and began pulling him out the window as he screamed for help.

CHAPTER

51

"Bren!" Cordelia screamed, running toward the window.

But Lefty got there first. He clubbed the monster's head with his right fist, hitting the giant beast's eye with enough force to knock it back out of the house entirely.

Brendan slumped forward to the floor and then scrambled quickly back to his feet.

"Are you okay?" Cordelia asked, distinctly remembering seeing teeth as big as her fist inside the monster's jaws.

"Yeah," Brendan said. "It just snagged the back of my shirt. I'm okay, thanks to Lefty. Wow, dude, you have one heck of a right hook. You could have knocked out Mike Tyson in his prime!"

"My left hook used to be even better," Lefty said, looking down at his prosthetic wooden hand.

"What *was* that thing?" Adie asked, her eyes open so wide that it seemed like she might never blink again.

"I think it may have been a—" Cordelia started, but was cut off by another horrible screech.

They all peered out the windows, careful not to get too close. Dozens of flying dinosaurs hovered around the house. Pterodactyls so massive that their wingspans were longer than a city bus. They screeched as they swarmed in looping, investigative patterns, their sleek, sharp heads swiveling on their long necks.

Off in the distance, Cordelia spotted a small island covered in bright vegetation.

"Over there!" she said, pointing. "Let's try to get to that island. It's covered with trees. . . . They won't be able to get close to us if we're on the ground."

Brendan nodded and then adjusted the levers and steering wheel until the gauges indicated they were heading straight ahead.

"Start bringing us down too," Cordelia said. "We don't want to overshoot it."

Brendan nodded, turning back to the control panel. He reached out for the altitude lever, but before he could grab it, a massive, yellowish-gray pterodactyl crashed into the house through the bay window, sending him sprawling

backward into Lefty Payne. They both fell to the floor as the dinosaur lunged toward Cordelia.

She dove left, barely escaping the creature's snapping jaws.

The dinosaur was so large that when it tried to flap its wings inside the study, it lost its balance and crashed into the desk, gnashing its beak around as it fell, nearly catching Eleanor's hair in its jaws.

The huge prehistoric bird was over eight feet tall with a beak large enough to skewer all three Walkers, Lefty, and Adie, and still have room for vegetables.

"Lefty, can't you shoot that thing?" Adie asked desperately.

"I'm out of ammo," he said, frowning at the empty bullet chambers on his pistol.

"We're going to be a Walker kebab!" Brendan yelled.

"Not if we get out of here," Cordelia said, grabbing Brendan's arm and pulling him to his feet. "Move it!"

"Back to the attic?" Lefty suggested, holstering his now-useless gun.

"Way ahead of you!" Eleanor shouted from the hallway, with Adie close behind her.

The five of them ran up into the attic. Brendan spun around, grabbed the stairs, and tried to pull them closed. They didn't budge.

"The stairs won't go up!" he said.

They could already hear the screeching pterodactyl making its way clumsily down the hallway in their direction.

Lefty came over and helped Brendan. The stairs wouldn't move even a centimeter. Cordelia knelt down and examined the folding stairs' hinges.

"It's stuck," she said. "The hinges must have warped when the house crashed into the sea."

The dinosaur appeared below them. It looked up, cocked its long head to the side, and then screeched so loudly that all of them cupped their hands over their ears. The pterodactyl started awkwardly climbing the stairs.

Brendan, Cordelia, and Lefty quickly shuffled backward toward the wall where Eleanor and Adie were already crouched with terrified expressions on their faces.

"Well, we've managed to trap ourselves," Brendan said. "Congratulations, everyone."

Nobody responded.

In the silence, they heard loud ripping noises above them, as if a giant had just torn a hole in the seat of his pants bending over to pick something up. There were more tearing noises, and seconds later it became clear that they were descending rather quickly—far too rapidly to survive the impact this time.

"The birds are ripping open the balloon!" Cordelia said.

Brendan spun around. Lefty, who had been standing right beside him a moment ago, was gone.

"Where did Lefty . . . ," Brendan started, but then stopped when he saw the outlaw on the other side of the room, behind the pterodactyl.

The dinosaur was completely inside the attic, walking toward them, its massive beak furiously snapping open and closed.

Brendan looked desperately at Lefty Payne, who walked slowly and quietly, just a few feet behind the dinosaur. The outlaw mimed a pushing motion and then nodded toward Brendan.

He spun around and saw a large window behind them.

"Guys!" Brendan shouted over Eleanor's and Adie's screams. "Stay right where you are, as still as you can. When I say *now*, everyone dive for cover. Okay?" They gave him confused looks. "Just trust me. Say *okay* if you understand!"

"Okay," Cordelia said, her voice shaking.

"Adie, Eleanor?" Brendan said.

They both nodded. Which was good enough for him.

Brendan turned to face the approaching dinosaur again. It was just ten feet away, almost close enough to extend its long beak and pluck out one of Brendan's eyeballs. He pushed this image out of his brain and instead focused on Lefty, still just a step behind the vicious dinosaur.

The pterodactyl reared back, getting ready to strike. From the corner of his eye, Brendan saw Eleanor flinch.

"Wait for the signal!" he said, his voice shaking.

The pterodactyl turned toward the sound of his shrill voice. It let out another horrible screech and charged, its beak aimed straight at Brendan's heart. He let out his own screech and dove to the right. Eleanor, Cordelia, and Adie followed Brendan's move, diving out of the dinosaur's path.

Lefty charged it from behind. He slammed into the pterodactyl with his shoulder, propelling the dinosaur into the wall of the attic, just below the window.

The huge bird crashed right through the thin wall, flying back outside and tearing open a gaping hole with jagged, splintered edges. Combined with the window, the hole was now large enough to drive a car through, and easily large enough to allow for a feeding frenzy, almost as if the doors to the pterodactyl's lunch buffet had just been opened.

Brendan scrambled to his feet.

"Sorry, I, um, hope you realized my screaming was the signal," he said.

Cordelia rolled her eyes as they climbed to their feet and gathered around the huge hole in the side of the house.

The five of them stood there and realized that one small pterodactyl had been the least of their problems. The balloon had been severely punctured. A wall of deep-blue ocean rushed up beneath them. Not only that, but even larger-winged dinosaurs were still circling the house. Several of them had spotted the huge hole in the attic and were dive-bombing right toward it.

Even if they all survived the fall, then there would still be the man-eating dinosaurs coming after them. There was really only one question facing them now.

"Well," Brendan said trying to force a nervous laugh. "Would you guys rather crash into the ocean, or get eaten by giant dinosaurs?"

CHAPTER

52

Nobody responded, because a crack of electricity ripped open the air, cutting out all other sounds. A flash of bright-blue light zigzagged across the sky like broken glass. There was a sickeningly wet explosion above them as one of the dive-bombing pterodactyls exploded into tiny red and gray pieces that sizzled as they fell toward the water, trailing tendrils of smoke.

The five occupants of the attic took a step back.

"What was that?" Eleanor yelled.

As if attempting to answer her, several more cracks tore open the sky and more blue lighting bolts discharged above them, incinerating three more pterodactyls.

Then a massive metal sphere floated down into view as

the remaining pterodactyls fled, scattering in all directions. The sphere was perfectly round and silver, reflecting the afternoon sun, the water, and a distorted Kristoff House with mirrored precision. Its surface rippled, almost as if it were made of liquid, or mercury, instead of solid metal. It hovered in front of them, and several more bolts of lightning erupted from it on all sides. They fired out and hit three more retreating dinosaurs, blasting them into zillions of smoking pieces.

"What is that thing?" Adie asked.

The Walkers seemed to know so much more about all the strange things she had seen that day, she expected them to know what this was as well. But her question was met with silence. The Walkers were too shocked and confused to even attempt to provide an answer that they didn't have anyway.

The sphere hovered in front of them for a few seconds, as the house continued its deadly plummet toward the ocean. And, just as suddenly as it had appeared, the sphere zoomed away below them and out of view.

They looked down, shocked to see that the house was just ten or fifteen seconds away from hitting the ocean. They were descending so quickly that their stomachs were in their throats and their ears popped.

They barely had time to cry out.

But then the house slowed. It was a jarring enough

transition to send all five of them stumbling to the attic floor and their stomachs plunging back down into their feet.

Cordelia became vaguely aware of light vibrations humming beneath them, as if there was a massive but silent engine running somewhere on the main floor of the house.

"That metal sphere," she said. "I think it's somehow slowing down our fall. . . ."

As if to put a period on her statement, the house hit the sea once again. But this time, it was gentler than even the best airplane landing. A small shudder rattled the floorboards already loosened from the first impact, but the five occupants barely shifted at all.

Cordelia climbed to her feet and ran over to the nearest window. She saw no sign of the strange sphere that had just saved their lives.

"Where did it go?" Brendan called out from the gaping hole that the pterodactyl had crashed through. "Do you guys see it?"

"No," Cordelia said, eyeing the huge hole in the wall warily. "But let's get out of here."

The five of them headed back downstairs into the second-floor study. From the bay window, they spotted the small island they had seen at the start of the pterodactyl attack. They were just a few hundred yards from shore and drifting right toward it.

"It's beautiful!" Eleanor said, amazed.

Indeed, the island was like none that any of them had ever seen. The sand at the water's edge was black and sparkling as if it were made of ash and gemstones. The plants and vegetation immediately behind the beach were a variety of bright colors and odd shapes that almost appeared to be backlit by neon. There were bright purple vines, psychedelic swirling green and yellow trees, and bright pink plants with gray flowers the size of houses on them. The whole island almost seemed to glow unnaturally.

Brendan pulled out the book world map and studied it intently. Now that he knew the location of the World-keepers, the next step was figuring out where on the map they were at this moment. His eyes scanned the three large oceans on the map. In the middle of one was a small island labeled Dinosaur Island, presumably also the name of one of Denver's many novels. Several inches away on the map was another, larger island with a name that terrified him. And it was almost certainly the island they were now headed directly toward.

He returned to the section in the *Journal* where Denver Kristoff described the three Worldkeepers and then cross-referenced it with the map. A short time later, there was a scraping beneath them as the house impacted the shore. The house tilted slightly, and the five of them stumbled back toward the same wall. Then, finally, it settled itself upon the black sand making up the island's shoreline and stopped moving completely.

"Let's go downstairs and see where we are," Cordelia said.

Brendan already knew where they were, and that knowledge almost tempted him to instead suggest that they run back up to the attic and hide like cowards. But he knew better. He knew that they would have to leave the house eventually in order to retrieve the Worldkeepers, and so they might as well not delay the inevitable.

They cautiously descended the rickety, blackened spiral staircase into the house's grand foyer and living room. Kristoff House had certainly seen better days. It was riddled with enough bullet holes to qualify it as a massive pasta strainer, the first floor was still flooded by a foot of water, it was tilting awkwardly, a ripped and wilted silver-and-red balloon draped over the broken windows on the left side of the house and trailed out into the sea like a massive tentacle, and the entire first floor looked like a crispy, burned marshmallow that fell off a stick and into a campfire. But somehow, amazingly, it still felt like home to the Walkers. It still carried with it the inherent safety that most homes do.

"Okay, I'll go first . . . ," Brendan said, stepping up to the front door. He didn't really want to, but felt it was his job as the new family leader.

He slowly opened the door and then stared in shock at what greeted him on the other side. It was . . . *himself.* An exact replica of Brendan Walker stood on the other side of the front door, gaping right back at him!

CHAPTER

53

Brendan leaned forward to get a closer look at his duplicate. Clone Brendan did the exact same thing at the same time. Which is precisely when Brendan realized he wasn't looking at a clone of himself, but rather a startlingly clear reflection.

"It's the sphere," Eleanor said softly.

She was right; the giant liquid-metal sphere had parked itself right outside the front door. They stared at it, growing collectively uneasy as they remembered how quickly and easily the sphere had vaporized half a dozen giant pterodactyls. The immense power of such a thing astonished and frightened them, even though it had saved their lives twice now.

Adie stepped forward, not having seen any science-fiction or horror movies in her life, and thus perhaps having the least reason to be afraid. She moved past Brendan and gazed at the strange sphere with a look of bewildered wonder on her face. She reached out a hand as if to touch the sphere, but then lowered it quickly.

"Thank you so much for saving our lives," Adie said.

"You are supremely welcome," the sphere said back.

The voice spoke English and sounded a lot more normal than any of them would have expected.

"It speaks," Eleanor said quietly.

The sphere began shifting, the liquid metal near the bottom rippled out in concentric circles until it grew and formed a small rectangular opening, just four feet tall. A small alien emerged from the sphere. It was no taller than three-and-a-half feet, and probably under sixty pounds. It had grayish-purple skin that seemed to shimmer and shift like a cheap hologram, or the inside of an oyster shell. It had two large black eyes, no visible nose, and a small opening at the base of its oval head that likely passed for a mouth. The alien had two legs, two arms, and two four-fingered hands, and a silver space suit with odd green-and-blue symbols all over it.

"Hello, unspecified organisms," the alien said, waving two of its arms. "My acoustic title is called Gilbert."

"Gilbert?" Brendan said. "What kind of name is Gilbert for an alien?"

"It is a seven-lettered title, meaning 'bright pledge' and derived from the Germanic elements *gisil* and *beraht*," Gilbert explained calmly. "The Normans of planet earth introduced this name to the nation labeled England, where it was common during the Middle Ages. It was borne by a twelfth-century British saint, the founder of the religious order known as the Gilbertines. It is also the name of Gilbert du Motier, one of the greatest war heroes, and also—"

"Never mind," Brendan said. "Forget I asked."

"Why would you provide inquiry if an answer is not desired?" Gilbert countered.

"It's called a rhetorical question," Brendan said.

"Be nice," Cordelia whispered. "This guy just saved us . . . twice."

"He's so pretentious," Brendan said. "Worse than you, even!"

"Just go with it," Cordelia said.

Brendan nodded and turned back to Gilbert.

"Okay, so you're obviously . . . you're an alien, right?"

Gilbert made a surprisingly human chortling noise as if this was the stupidest question he'd ever heard.

"I'm highly skeptical of the accuracy of such a conclusion," Gilbert said. "*You* are unmistakably the extraterrestrials here. Furthermore, I am copiously advanced beyond your own existences."

"Seriously?" Brendan whispered to Cordelia.

"I am at once *everything* and *nothing*," Gilbert continued, swinging his two right arms up dramatically, as if he were overacting in a bad high-school play. "I am the end of all existence and the definition of infinity. I go where nothing else can exist and exist where everything else begins. I am *All*."

Brendan stared at Gilbert as he made his flamboyant speech, unsure if it was supposed to be a joke or not.

The outlaw Lefty Payne seemed totally unimpressed. He crossed his arms and shook his head slowly.

"It takes just a few words to speak the truth, partner," Lefty said.

"But it necessitates sundry words to express all truths everywhere," Gilbert countered. "The burden of infinite knowledge is oppressive in a way none of you could possibly conceive."

"My sister Cordelia can," Brendan quipped.

Cordelia shook her head and scowled at Brendan.

"That is exceedingly implausible," Gilbert said, not getting that it was a joke.

For a being that claimed to know everything, he certainly had an odd understanding of humor. Or lack of understanding.

"So, you're really powerful and all-knowing . . . like some sort of supreme being?" Eleanor asked.

"I am beyond even the most supreme of beings," Gilbert said. "I am exceptionally more knowledgeable, extraordinarily more powerful. And more handsome."

"Don't forget more humble," Brendan added.

Cordelia shot Brendan a look. She figured he must have forgotten that Gilbert had just incinerated a dozen dinosaurs as if it were nothing. She didn't think mocking such a being was a particularly smart thing to do. Luckily for them all, the sarcasm was completely lost on the little alien.

"I am actually portraying my existence quite accurately," Gilbert said, a hint of concern detectable in his even voice. "I do not under- or overrepresent my qualities. However, I can translate the complete magnitude of my knowledge into a binary table, if that would prove more detailed and suitable for your analysis?"

"Never mind," Brendan said. "It was just a joke."

"So, with all of your great knowledge," Cordelia said, "that must mean you know who we are, where we're from, and why we're all here . . . right?"

Gilbert hesitated for several seconds before providing an answer.

"Correct," he finally said.

"Great!" Brendan said, grinning. "Because we need some help. I assume you can tell us what the three Worldkeepers are, and exactly where to find them?"

"Correct!" Gilbert said much more quickly this time. "But I cannot disclose their exact location."

"Why not?" Brendan asked, suspecting the arrogant little alien had no idea what the Worldkeepers were.

"Because it would then remove the inherent value of the ensuing exploration," Gilbert said. "The true significance of one human lifespan lies in the *excursion*, not the *endpoint*."

Cordelia groaned loudly. She hated the saying "it's about the journey, not the destination" more than anything else she'd ever heard, including the disgusting fact that the Wind Witch was her own relative. Of course life was about the *destination*, because where would anybody be without goals? Even still, Gilbert was clearly a being of immense power that could probably be extremely useful at some point—so she was going to be nice regardless.

"Well, then," Cordelia said. "Maybe you'd like to join us on our *excursion*? Even if you already know what's going to happen, it might be fun to be there to witness it firsthand."

"Precisely," Gilbert said. "I shall supplement you thusly."

"Great, welcome aboard!" Brendan said sarcastically.

"Welcome aboard what?" Gilbert replied, looking around Kristoff House. "This appears to be a domicile. Not an aquatic or intergalactic vessel of any sort."

"I meant welcome to the team, thanks for joining us, blah, blah, blah," Brendan said.

"What is this meaning . . . *blah blah blah*?" Gilbert asked.

"I'll explain it later," Brendan said with a sigh, and then turned back to the rest of the group. "Guys . . . I have some good news and some bad news."

"What's the good news?" Eleanor asked.

"Before the dinosaur attack, I found out where to find the three Worldkeepers."

"And the bad news?"

"The Worldkeepers are each in a completely different book, spread out across the book world map," Brendan said. "Which means we're going to have to split up in order to get them."

CHAPTER

54

"No," Eleanor pleaded.

"There's got to be another way, Bren," Cordelia said.

"I've been trying to think of something," Brendan said. "But it feels like the only solution."

"What about him?" Eleanor asked, pointing to the small alien.

"Gilbert?" Brendan asked. "How could he solve this problem?"

"Maybe he can fit all of us inside his sphere," Eleanor suggested. "I bet that thing can go, like, hyper-sonic-galactic-light-speed. . . . We'd probably be able to get all three Worldkeepers in no time."

"There is no such quantifiable rate as hyper-sonic-galactic-light-speed," Gilbert replied. "Also, my craft is only equipped to transport one passenger. Especially for beings of such substantial and considerable girth as yourselves."

"Did he just call us fat?" Cordelia asked, pulling down her shirt self-consciously.

"Don't worry about it," Adie assured her. "To him, everyone is fat."

"Do we really have to split up, Bren?" Eleanor asked.

"Unfortunately, I think so," Brendan said. "I really wish we didn't have to—I wish there was another way. But . . . um, Cordelia, you should probably wait in the other room while I explain . . ."

"Why?" Adie asked.

"Because she's linked to our mortal enemy, the Wind Witch," Brendan said. "We can't risk that old hag finding out any more information about our mission. . . . Look at my sister's eyes."

"I see they have transitioned into an unsettling shade of blue," Gilbert said. "But it is not wholly unattractive, even for creatures as amply constituted and unappealing as yourselves."

"When this happens," Brendan explained, "it means the Wind Witch can hear and see everything she does. So, Deal . . . you should probably leave now."

Cordelia hesitated before exiting, but then frowned and walked into the blackened library. Of course leaving was the right thing to do when the Wind Witch was in her head. But it still didn't make it sting any less. The worst part was knowing that it was her fault the link existed—since apparently her own mind was the worst place ever, which is precisely where Eleanor had banished the Wind Witch for using *The Book of Doom and Desire*.

Back in the living room, Brendan stood in front of Eleanor, Adie, Lefty, and Gilbert. He took a deep breath. There was a lot to explain. There was a lot he'd found out in that short ride to the island, but still a whole lot more they needed to figure out.

"The main problem is that I still don't know exactly *what* the three Worldkeepers are," Brendan began. "Denver's *Journal* is kind of . . . vague in that regard."

"What!?" Eleanor nearly shouted. "Then how are we supposed to find them?"

"The *Journal* does tell us which specific books the Worldkeepers are hidden in," Brendan said.

"Does it tell us *where* exactly we might be able to find them in the books?" Eleanor asked.

"Not really, but there are some clues," Brendan said.

"Now, wait just a second," Adie said loudly, her face contorted into a mixture of frustration and confusion. "What in the heck are these Worldkeepers . . . and being inside of books? This is getting awfully strange . . . and now I want some answers!"

Brendan had to admit that somehow, frustrated and angry Adie was even cuter than smiley, happy Adie. It was distracting.

"We're in the book world right now," Brendan said, choosing his words carefully.

"But what about *our* world?" Adie asked, motioning to her and Lefty. "Where we come from?"

"I also raise inquiry over this issue," Gilbert added. "By what mechanism did we voyage into the aforesaid 'book world'?"

"What have you kids gotten me into?" Lefty added darkly.

Brendan paused, debating how to proceed.

"Uh, well, it's complicated," he eventually said.

Brendan and Eleanor exchanged a glance. They remembered how hard it had been for other book characters, like Will and Felix, to take the news—and some were not able to comprehend it at all. Brendan studied Adie's distraught face, then glanced at Lefty and Gilbert, who were both watching him intently. And Brendan realized that he had to lie. There simply wasn't the time to try and explain to two people and an alien that they were all figments of some dead guy's imagination.

"This all has *nothing* to do with you—and we're so sorry we dragged you into our mess," Brendan said. "So trying to explain it would be a waste of time—something we don't have. But I promise if you help us find these Worldkeepers, then we will take you all back home very soon. Everything will be as it should again."

Eleanor looked surprised, but then she smiled thinly and nodded in agreement.

Adie hesitated, still frowning. Lefty stared at Brendan's face steadily with his slate-gray and hard eyes. As if he could see right through every single lie he'd ever been told. But eventually they both nodded too. Gilbert watched this all with interest, apparently ready to tackle anything, regardless of the how or why.

"I still don't think it's fair at all that you come to our homes and get us wrapped up in this mess," Adie finally said. "And then won't even explain what is going on. It ain't right. But if you need help and you're telling us it's important, and if it will get us home faster, then I'll do whatever I can."

"Lefty?" Brendan asked, turning toward the one-armed outlaw.

The man's eyes seemed to glow under the shadow of his wide hat brim. His fake hand was tucked into his shirt, which Brendan had noticed was where the man generally liked to keep it.

"Okay," Lefty growled. "I'll help you find these World-keeper things. But I'm only doing it to keep *myself* alive. I still think you kids are more valuable to me alive than dead."

"Noted," Brendan said. "Gilbert?"

"You will be supremely honored to have my company," Gilbert said.

"Love the modesty," Brendan said. "Okay then . . ."

Brendan cleared his throat, dying for just a simple drink of water. Something he hadn't had in almost twenty-four hours now. Then he held up the *Journal* and began reading the passage about the Worldkeepers.

"'The first Worldkeeper,'" Brendan read Denver's words, "'is hidden within my fantasy novel *The Lost City*. It rests deep inside the Eternal Abyss, in the Forbidden Zone.'"

"What's the Forbidden Zone?" Eleanor interrupted. "That doesn't sound like somewhere we should go."

"Supposedly, it's near the city of Atlantis in the book *The Lost City*," Brendan said as he referenced the pages of the *Journal* again. "The Forbidden Zone is a place that the citizens of Atlantis are terrified of. Kristoff created a 'fearsome and malevolent creature' called the Iku-Turso, which guards the Worldkeeper there."

"But it doesn't describe what this Worldkeeper is?" Eleanor asked.

"Unfortunately, no," Brendan said. "That's where old Denver gets a little confusing. He writes: 'This Worldkeeper is a talisman serving as one part of three—that when combined comprise a key between two worlds. But on its own, it is also a powerful emblem of truth. Those who wear the talisman as intended can see into the very souls of friends and foes alike.'"

Brendan stopped reading, allowing Eleanor, Adie, Lefty, and Gilbert time to take it in. He hoped they were less confused than he was. Although Denver called the item a talisman, Brendan had to admit that he didn't entirely know what that was. But at least there was a fairly detailed description of where to find it—inside the Eternal Abyss within the Forbidden Zone near the Lost City of Atlantis. Of course, they'd still have to get past the undoubtedly terrifying Iku-Turso.

A few moments later, Brendan cleared his throat again, and began reading Denver's description of the second item.

"'The second Worldkeeper lies within my science-fiction novel *The Terror on Planet 5X*. This particular Worldkeeper never rests. It is always on the move—it goes to places where it is most needed while keeping its vessel alive. However, once this Worldkeeper is freed from its armor, it gains even more power.'"

"Does it say what kind of power?" Eleanor asked.

"Supposedly, the person who 'releases' the Worldkeeper will be granted the opportunity to travel back in time once and reverse a terrible mistake," Brendan said.

His throat was growing scratchy, so he quickly moved

on to Denver Kristoff's description of the third and final Worldkeeper.

"'The last Worldkeeper is buried in my novel *Wazner's Revenge*,'" he read. "'Which is about an ancient Egyptian king who guards his most prized possessions, even in the afterlife. This particular item is the most powerful of all Worldkeepers. It can be used for incredible acts of both evil and righteousness. It is buried in a labyrinth of treacherous traps and secret passageways. Locating it will be impossible without the use of a secret map, designed by perhaps the most evil organization in the history of mankind in order to lead them back to their stolen bounties of war. This Worldkeeper is infinitely powerful. No mortally made substance can withstand its wicked edges.'"

"Now how in the heck are we supposed to get that one?" Lefty asked. "Unless you got one of these treasure maps it talked about."

Brendan eyed the outlaw warily. His eyes had gleamed unnaturally when he'd said the words "treasure maps." He remembered Cordelia telling him what the Storm King had said about not trusting anyone here and so he was suddenly regretting allowing three relative strangers into their group.

"I'm not sure," Brendan answered. "But we have to at least try."

"If I'm going to help you, then I get at least half of this war bounty you spoke of," Lefty said.

"Agreed," Brendan said.

Eleanor also noticed the greedy gleam in Lefty's eyes and remembered the Storm King's warning. Which is why she stayed silent, even though she was pretty sure she had already figured out how to get the third Worldkeeper. But she knew it would be safer to tell Brendan later, in private.

Brendan looked around the room. The group was silent and pensive, daunted by the seemingly impossible challenge of trying to obtain these three Worldkeepers. But he couldn't dwell on the negative. If they didn't decipher the cryptic hints about the Worldkeepers, locate them, and eventually bring them to the Door of Ways, they would never be able to seal off the book world from the real world. It was the only way to save San Francisco . . . and the rest of the real world.

"So what now?" Adie asked.

"Let's start by going to the library and getting the three novels Kristoff mentioned," Brendan said. "That will help us figure out how we'll need to split up. The good news is that we're already in one of these three books. I'm pretty sure this island we just washed ashore is *The Terror on Planet 5X.*"

Eleanor swallowed, not liking the sound of that.

They followed Brendan into the hollowed-out and blackened remainder of a library, where Cordelia was picking through the burned-up rubble. It was immediately obvious that the search for the three books was a complete waste of time. The entire library had been consumed by the fire. The few books that remained were little more than singed and tattered scraps of brownish yellow paper glued together at one end. *The Lost City* was the only one of the three novels that had survived the fire. And *survived* probably isn't the most accurate description. It was more that the book was the only one that wasn't completely destroyed. Only the spine remained, along with most of the front cover and about half of the pages, which were dark and mostly unreadable.

"Better than nothing," Brendan said, handing the book to Eleanor. "Now, let's figure out a plan. Quickly."

He knew the Walker kids couldn't stay together since they were the only three who had a true grasp on their circumstances. Each of the three search parties would need a Walker, further supporting the need for the three of them to split up.

"Adie and Cordelia, you guys will take *The Lost City*," Brendan finally said, plucking the novel from Eleanor's hands and giving the book to Adie. "Read as much of this as you can, and whatever you do, don't let Cordelia see it if her eyes turn icy blue."

"What if her eyes turn icy blue when I'm not reading?" Adie asked.

"What do you mean?" Brendan asked.

"Like, if we're in this Forbidden Zone," Adie said. "And we're just about to get the Worldkeeper, and her eyes turn blue. You wouldn't want the Wind Witch to see that either, right?"

"Good point," Brendan said. He turned and snatched the black scarf from around Lefty's neck.

"Hey," Lefty protested. "That was my grandpa's!"

"Just blindfold her with this," Brendan said, giving Adie the scarf.

Adie nodded.

"How will we get there?" Cordelia asked. "And where do we even go?"

"I'll draw you a map," Brendan said as he unfolded the book world map. "According to this, the Lost City is located entirely under the sea. . . . It's actually very close to where we are now. You guys could float there in the house."

"There's no way to steer a Victorian house floating on barrels, Bren," Cordelia said.

"Do not retain apprehension," Gilbert interrupted them. "I can assist."

"How?" Brendan asked.

"Let me exhibit my aptitudes for you," Gilbert said, closing all seven of his eyes. He slowly raised his hands in the air and within seconds, the sound of cracking and splintering wood came from the upper levels of Kristoff House.

The noises were rapid and fast, almost like a jackhammer

made solidly of wood slamming down on an even harder wood surface. There was a massive splash outside. Eleanor ran to the nearest living room window to investigate.

"No way!" she yelled.

The rest of them followed her to the window and looked outside.

Floating on the surface of the sea, tethered to the Kristoff House's front porch by a rope made from an upstairs curtain, was a small sailboat. The wood was unmistakably the same color as the wooden floors that lined the attic. Or *used* to make up the attic. The sail was constructed of more unburned curtains from various rooms throughout Kristoff House.

"You just telepathically built that sailboat out of the wood from our attic?" Brendan squeaked.

"Indeed," Gilbert said.

"I promise to never underestimate you again," Brendan said, patting the alien's tiny back. "You may be an egotistical blowhard, but you are one insanely powerful little dude."

"I will accept the flattery fragment of that testimonial and disregard the insulting segment," Gilbert said.

"Okay!" Brendan said. "So, Cordelia and Adie will take the boat to the Lost City to find the first Worldkeeper. The *Wazner's Revenge* book is the farthest away, so Gilbert and I will take his sphere ship there."

"Are you sure, Bren?" Eleanor asked. "That's where the

most powerful Worldkeeper is."

"It's also the most likely place for the Wind Witch to pop up again," Brendan said. "And Gilbert is our best chance at defeating her."

"I undoubtedly could destroy the being you reference," Gilbert said.

"What about Lefty and me?" Eleanor asked.

"You're staying here," Brendan said. "In *The Terror on Planet 5X*. You guys need to find the Worldkeeper that's here . . . the one that's always moving. Which sounds hard, I know, but this is the smallest of the book worlds, so it's only a matter of time before you eventually find it."

"Where will we meet back up?" Eleanor asked.

"Kristoff said we need to bring the Worldkeepers to his brother in Tinz," Cordelia reminded them.

Brendan studied the map for a moment longer and then nodded.

"Then we'll meet there," he said. "It's actually the closest-known spot to all three Worldkeepers, and the Door of Ways."

"That's probably not by accident," Cordelia said.

"How do we get there?" Eleanor asked, motioning toward herself and Lefty.

"Subsequent vessel presently completed," Gilbert said, just as another loud splash came from outside.

They peered out the window again and saw a small canoe with two oars moored next to the sailboat.

"You're awesome!" Eleanor said to the small alien, unable to mask her wonder.

"This is accurate," Gilbert said, nodding. "I do inspire awe."

"Okay, I need to go draw maps for all of you," Brendan said. "Do whatever you need to to get ready. We should head our separate ways as soon as I'm finished."

He didn't wait for a response as he walked upstairs toward the study to find some paper and a pen.

Eleanor and Cordelia turned to each other for a brief moment, before looking away quickly. Somehow, hearing Brendan say the words aloud one last time seemed to really cement the fact that they were all splitting up. They hugged each other, not wanting to let go. They both realized that this time, there would be no relying on each other.

This time, the three Walkers were going to have to do their parts to save the world on their own.

55

"Here you go," Brendan said, handing several sheets of paper to Cordelia.

It had taken him nearly an hour to transcribe the descriptions of the three Worldkeepers and draw a series of crude maps, showing how to get to Tinz and their respective book worlds.

"I can barely read this," Cordelia said. "Your handwriting is horrible."

"You're not supposed to see this stuff anyway," Brendan said, snatching the papers from her hands. "Never know when your eyes might turn blue!"

He handed them to Adie instead.

"Whatever," Cordelia said, tension creeping into her voice.

"Here's yours," Brendan said, handing a few sheets of paper to Eleanor.

"And this is for you," Eleanor said, pulling him to the side and handing a different piece of paper right back.

"What's this?" Brendan asked softly, understanding that she didn't want the rest of the group to hear.

"It's the Nazi treasure map," Eleanor said.

"You brought it with us?" Brendan asked.

"It was still in my pocket," Eleanor said. "I think you're going to need it."

"Why?"

"Because of what Denver Kristoff wrote about the third Worldkeeper," Eleanor said. "I thought about it while you were drawing the maps, and it just seems to make sense."

Brendan opened the *Journal* and reread the last passage about the third Worldkeeper in *Wazner's Revenge*. He stopped and reread a short selection several times:

Locating it will be impossible without the use of a secret map, designed by perhaps the most evil organization in the history of mankind in order to lead them back to their stolen bounties of war.

He looked back at Eleanor with an amazed expression.

"You're totally right!" he said. "I'm impressed, Nell."

"I'm not *always* just a little girl, you know," she said.

"I didn't mean that," he said. "I just—"

He didn't get to finish his sentence. A loud rumble

shook the ground violently enough to vibrate his brains like a blender.

"What was that?" Adie asked.

"Probably our cue to get the heck out of here," Brendan said, suddenly very worried about leaving Eleanor in this dangerous place.

He wrapped a protective arm around her. As much as she longed for independence, in that moment, she allowed herself to get lost in the comfort of her older brother's hug.

Lefty was a fearless and cunning man; Brendan just had to hope that the outlaw would protect her from whatever horrors they encountered.

The three Walkers embraced in an awkward group hug, with Eleanor getting smooshed in the middle. Cordelia had seen the sudden vulnerability in her little sister's face, and Brendan's protective hug, and it was all she could do to not burst into tears right then and there.

"Good luck, both of you," Cordelia said, straining to keep from crying. "And be careful, okay? I'll see you both at the Tinz marketplace very soon."

Eleanor nodded, wiping away at a tear.

"Unfortunately for you guys, I'll be there too," Brendan said, grinning in spite of his watering eyes. "And I'll already be two verses deep into my stunning rendition of another Springsteen classic."

This only made Eleanor cry more. But she still allowed

Lefty to pull her away from her siblings. They stood in the front doorway of Kristoff House, the night sky above them dotted with billions of stars, and watched as the rest of their friends departed.

Brendan crouched down and followed Gilbert into his odd sphere spaceship. The doorway collapsed on itself, disappearing into its shiny, liquid surface. It hovered for several seconds, rising slowly at first, and in the next blink of Eleanor's eyes it was gone, leaving behind just a single fading streak of silver across the black sky.

Cordelia and Adie pulled the sailboat closer to the half-submerged front porch and then climbed aboard. Cordelia untied the rope as Adie grabbed a paddle and pushed them away from the house. They floated slowly at first, the curtain sails hung limply. Then a light breeze caught the fabric, causing the sails to poof up and go taut. The boat drifted away with surprising speed. Cordelia raised a hand and waved good-bye. Eleanor responded in kind, wiping at her eyes with her other hand.

And just like that, Eleanor's brother and sister were gone. She took a deep breath and told herself to stop crying. A wooden prosthetic hand rested gently on her shoulder.

"Don't worry, kid," Lefty said reassuringly. "You got a real tough brother and sister. And they're smart too. I usually hate ankle biters. But the three of you have impressed me. Now c'mon, we got a job to do. Let's find that Worldkeeper.

Sooner we do that, sooner we can get off this strange island and get you back with your family. And me back to the stash of loot I buried in Texas."

Eleanor nodded, wiping her eyes as she followed Lefty back inside the house. She looked at the papers her brother had given her a few moments ago. Cordelia had been right; his handwriting was nearly as indecipherable as Denver Kristoff's ancient script. But she was his sister, and so was able to read his writing like she was breaking some sort of secret code.

Before she could finish even the first sentence, however, a massive, glowing, red circle appeared in the window beside them.

Eleanor and Lefty both took a step back as the huge red orb hovered, filling the entire bay window with menace. The red light felt intrusive to Eleanor, almost as if . . . right then she realized it was an eye. A huge, glowing, red eye, peering inside Kristoff House. Which meant that whatever it was attached to was massive, maybe even almost as big as Fat Jagger.

The eye disappeared, and a moment later, the whole wall crumbled as a huge metal claw ripped open Kristoff House like a can of beans. Splinters of wood sprayed across the night sky, revealing the true nature of their assailant.

Eleanor screamed.

56

Lefty grabbed Eleanor and pulled her toward the front door as her brain attempted to reconcile what she'd just seen.

It was a huge robot with long, metal legs that rose above the roof of the house. Its torso was short and boxy, with two arms extending on either side. One arm had a huge metal claw with seven sharp and devastating fingers. The other arm had a strange flamethrower for a hand, emitting an odd, wispy green flame that flickered in the night sky. The robot had an oval head with a single glowing red eye below a glass dome. Inside the dome sat the robot's pilot, a purple alien with at least seven or eight tentacles operating the controls.

Green fire erupted from the robot's right hand and engulfed Kristoff House. Lefty and Eleanor dove off the porch and into the cold sea. Eleanor surfaced, choking on salty seawater. Lefty grabbed her and threw her arms around his neck. She held on as he towed her to shore.

As they swam, Eleanor looked back and saw that the green flames weren't really flames at all. Kristoff House appeared to be *melting* amid the rolling plumes of green that streamed continuously from the huge robot's right hand.

Eleanor watched in horror as her home, their one oasis of safety through all their dangerous adventures, slowly sank into itself like a deflating balloon. Not only that, but the canoe Gilbert had built for them, their only means of escape, had also been engulfed by the green flames and was now nothing more than a miniature brown puddle.

They reached the shore, and Lefty hauled Eleanor to her feet. The sparkly black sand felt hot, even through her shoes. The combination of watching her brother and sister abandon her and seeing her house melt within minutes of each other had left her in an utter state of panic.

"Eleanor!" Lefty yelled as the robot spun around, its glowing red eye pointed right at them. "Eleanor, can you hear me?"

He gently shook her, snapping her out of a daze.

"We need to get out of here," he said, once he was sure he had her attention. "Follow me."

Lefty grabbed her hand and ran into the thick, colorful, strange vegetation that lined the shore of the island. Eleanor forced her legs to function as she ran after him. He pulled her along, pushing her legs faster than she thought they could go.

Suddenly Eleanor felt a hot blast as a wave of green flames melted a section of tree trunks directly behind her.

"Faster!" Lefty shouted. "Run faster!"

Lefty pulled her, forcing Eleanor to keep up with him. It felt like her arm was going to pop from her socket.

A wall of green flames blasted overhead, just inches from their heads. The top of Lefty's hat melted down onto the brim like candle wax. But they kept running.

After a short distance, Lefty let go of Eleanor's hand. She was still able to keep up, her relatively tiny size making it easier for her to weave through the thick foliage. If it could be called foliage at all, that is. To Eleanor, it was more like they were running through fields of giant psychedelic candies. There were yellow translucent tubes the size of an elevator, filled with bright red baseball-size fruits or seeds. There were massive orange flowers, some of which she swore she saw moving on their own as they passed by in a blur. The ground had changed and was now soft and spongy, like Styrofoam. And topping it all off were fluorescent purple-and-aqua vines stretched across everything in sight.

Lefty moved a few feet ahead of her, veering and running with a purpose, almost as if he actually knew where they were headed.

After running for what felt like miles, but couldn't have been more than a few times around a track, Eleanor became aware that she no longer heard the crashing footsteps of the giant robot behind them. Lefty finally slowed and stopped in a small clearing.

They were surrounded by dozens of tall plants that resembled cacti, except they were twice as tall, red, and instead of having rough skin covered in needles, were smooth and shiny like they were made of wet rubber.

"We lost it?" Eleanor asked Lefty hopefully.

"Not completely," he said. "I still hear footsteps over there." He pointed to the right. "We're behind it now, but it's only a matter of time before it finds us again. I think that metal beast's red eye can see through stuff."

Eleanor nodded. Even though Lefty clearly didn't comprehend the true scientific nature of a huge robot, he was perceptive enough to realize that it probably had some sort of high-tech tracking system. As if to make his point for him, the whirring of advanced hydraulics came from where he'd just pointed moments before. Then the crashing footsteps resumed. They had been detected once again.

"There's a cave," Lefty said, pointing through a small opening in the massive red cacti with his prosthetic left hand, "a couple hundred paces that way. I saw it when we doubled back to flank the machine. Go there and hide. Wait until I'm long gone, far away from here, then it'll be safe to come out. And you can go on with your quest."

"What are you going to do?" she whimpered.

"Distract that tin can so you can get to the cave," Lefty said.

Eleanor knew that Lefty couldn't distract the robot forever.

"No," she pleaded, terrified of being left completely alone. "Come with me. We can go together."

He shook his head and surprised her by smiling warmly.

"There isn't time; the two of us would never make it without a distraction," he said. "Now go!" He gave her a shove toward the cave.

Before Eleanor had a chance to respond, he was gone. He had turned and disappeared into the strange forest of overgrown red cacti.

And so in spite of her tears, Eleanor turned and ran in the direction Lefty had instructed. Behind her, the robot crashed through the alien jungle. It was moving away from her, in pursuit of the outlaw.

It didn't take long for Eleanor to find the small cave. It was less of a cave and more a sliver of a crack in the side of a wall made of smooth, polished black stone that glowed and swirled a rainbow of colors, as if it were alive.

Eleanor reached out and felt the surface; it was cold and hard and smooth. She crouched down and squeezed herself into the narrow fissure in the rock wall. Once she was through the opening, she discovered there was more room inside than she'd first suspected. Enough room for her to lie down if she curled up into a ball like a cat. She lay on the cold floor and looked out into the alien jungle through the small opening.

Above the tops of the nearest plants, off in the distance, the faint glow of the giant robot's red eye spun and swiveled in and out of Eleanor's view as it hunted for Lefty Payne. And then, several moments later, a flash of green flames erupted into the night sky.

Eleanor heard defiant shouting, full of curses.

It was Lefty.

His shouting was followed shortly by a sickening sizzle. Then everything was quiet.

Just like that, Eleanor knew that she was now truly alone.

CHAPTER

57

Meanwhile, several miles off the coast of the strange island where Eleanor was huddled in a cave—cold, alone, and terrified—Cordelia and Adie sat upright in their small sailboat and looked up into the surprisingly bright night sky.

They were both searching for the same constellation that Brendan instructed them to pick out before they departed. They had decided together on a formation of bright stars that created a partial circle, almost like a pie with one slice missing. Brendan had laughed and called it the Pac-Man constellation.

"Basically," Brendan had explained shortly before their departure, "the book world of *The Lost City* is huge. It almost takes up this entire ocean. So if you just stay on course and use Pac-Man as a guide, by morning, you'll be smack-dab in the middle of where you need to be. You almost can't go wrong."

Cordelia had to admit now, as they both spotted it again above them, that she was rather impressed with Brendan. She had no idea that he knew how to use stars to navigate on the high seas.

His reassuring words had been comforting at the time. But now that she and Adie were out here in a tiny boat in the middle of the night on a vast sea that housed who knew what kind of horrors, Cordelia was way more afraid than she'd expected. Not just of the dangers that may or may not lurk below the surface. But also that they might be drifting in completely the wrong direction. Using a constellation for navigation sounded easy enough in theory, but in actuality, she felt like she had no idea where they were going.

"Do you think we're still on track?" she asked Adie.

"I think so," Adie said. "I mean, your brother said we almost couldn't go wrong."

"Yeah, well, you don't know him like I do," Cordelia said. "Brendan isn't exactly known for being right all the time."

"You should go easy on him," Adie said. "He really cares about you. I'd eat fifty lizards to have a brother like him."

Cordelia laughed in spite of her growing anxiety. Then

something dawned on her. Something that had been obvious from the start.

"Oh. My. God!" Cordelia exclaimed. *"You have a crush on him, don't you?"*

"What?" Addie asked, confused. "Why would I want to crush him?"

"Sorry, *crush* is something we say where I'm from when you like someone," Cordelia explained.

"Of course I like him," Adie said. "He's a good person, a good brother to you . . ."

"No, it means you like him as more than just a friend," Cordelia said.

"You . . . you mean . . . *romantically?*" Adie asked, feigning horror at the thought.

Cordelia nodded.

"Brendan?" Adie said, turning away to hide her embarrassment. "He's not my type. You don't know what you're talking about."

"Whatever you say," Cordelia said, grinning.

A silence hung between them. The only noise was the light howl of the breeze and the lapping of small waves at the base of their boat.

It wasn't until an orange sliver of sun appeared on the purple-and-red horizon that either of them spoke again.

Cordelia sat up and rubbed her eyes as the sun continued to rise above the horizon at a seemingly impossible rate.

She could no longer see the island. Or the stars. Which meant Pac-Man was gone. The only indicators of their location were no longer visible. So now she simply had to hope that Brendan was right about how easy it would be to navigate the boat toward the Lost City.

"I think we're probably here," Adie announced.

"But how are we supposed to get from this tiny sailboat to a lost underwater city at the bottom of the ocean?" Cordelia asked.

"Clearly we haven't thought this through very well," Adie said, staring down into the mesmerizing depths of the clear ocean waters.

"What does the book say?"

Adie pulled out the charred remains of the novel *The Lost City*. She flipped through the pages slowly, as if she hadn't read many books in her life, which only made Cordelia want to do it for her. But, somehow, she made herself stay anchored to her seat. She knew better. They couldn't give the Wind Witch any more possible hints as to what they were up to than she already had. Even if her eyes weren't blue right at that moment, they could change at any time, and she couldn't risk being in the middle of reading something important when it happened.

"It says in the book," Adie said several moments later, "that the explorers used some kind of experimental sub . . . submarine to get to the Lost City. Do you know what a *submarine* is?"

Cordelia sighed and nodded. "Yeah," she said. "And it's something neither of us has. So, basically, we're out of luck."

Adie leaned over the side of the boat and stared down into the endless blue ocean in defeat. She let her fingertips trail lightly on the surface of the water, creating ripples around them. She was so caught up watching the little waves that it took her a while to notice the blue light beneath their boat.

"What's that?" she asked, sitting upright.

Cordelia came over to that side of the boat and peered down. The light was small, just a speck in the otherwise

dark blue depths of the sea. But it was growing. Almost as if it were an LED flashlight slowly floating toward the surface. Except, this blue light wasn't *slowly* floating toward them.

It was zooming upward like it had been shot from a gun.

"Oh no," Cordelia said as the light continued to grow.

The blue light spun and rotated as it ascended from the depths. It was now clear that whatever it was, it was at least as large as their sailboat, if not bigger. Cordelia stood up as it rushed toward them, unsure of what to do. Adie stood up next to her.

"What's going on?" Adie asked, panicking.

"Nothing good," Cordelia said.

"Maybe we should abandon ship," Adie suggested.

"No. That light is moving too fast," Cordelia said. "We couldn't swim fast enough to avoid whatever—"

But she never had a chance to finish her sentence.

The strange blue light hit the small sailboat, vaporizing it out of existence before either occupant managed to utter so much as a single cry for help.

CHAPTER

58

Several miles away, a strange metal sphere floated effortlessly through the sky, passing quickly over dozens of
worlds inhabited by characters of Denver Kristoff's novels.

Brendan wasn't sure how much more alone time he could
possibly handle with the strange alien known as Gilbert.
The little being simply never shut up. He talked continuously, as if talking were his species's form of breathing.

"Once, during a voyage," Gilbert said, right after finishing
a story about how he once caused a small moon to explode
with his mind, "I encountered a peculiar organism of a most
unusual composition and possessing a supremely foul dispo-
sition. It was constructed of a rotund, black-feathered torso
with two skinny and knobby orange legs with clawed feet.

Its wings were inexplicably slight and useless, despite the creature obviously being avian in nature. An elongated neck protruded from its spheroid plumage with a petite head and stout beak."

"That sounds like an ostrich," Brendan said.

"An ost-*rich?*" Gilbert repeated slowly, trying on the word for the first time. "Well, this *ostrich's* constitution was that of extreme displeasure and hostility and it pursued me aggressively until I eventually was forced to disintegrate it with my intellectual commands."

"Why does every story end with you telepathically blowing stuff up?" Brendan asked.

"It is a most natural progression of events when in danger, of course," Gilbert said. "Furthermore, I am not blowing up articles, but rather they are disintegrating through a process called vector-force implosion, which technically means—"

"Gilbert, do you ever have a thought you *don't* say aloud?" Brendan interrupted.

"Of course, many of them," Gilbert said calmly. "The average human brain processes fifty thousand thoughts per day, close to one per second. *My* brain processes fourteen billion thoughts per day, which is over one hundred fifty thousand per second. But I can only speak five words per second, even when not decelerating my speech pattern sufficiently for your comprehension. So, in fact, it is not even possible for me to speak every thought I have. It wouldn't even be possible for your inferior species, for that matter—"

"Okay, okay, I get it," Brendan said. "Sorry I asked."

"Apology accepted," Gilbert replied.

Gilbert's right arm reached out and pressed some buttons on the inside of his spaceship. Strange symbols and beeps flashed across an ancient-looking computer monitor. It was tan and boxy, like an old microwave oven. Brendan figured that Denver must have written the book Gilbert was from well before the invention of modern computers. The spaceship was unique and strange and cool on the outside, but on the inside it was surprisingly boring. Even though it was supposed to be futuristic, it felt like Brendan was inside a cheesy science-fiction movie from the seventies.

"According to my navigational calculations, we have arrived," Gilbert said, pressing another button on his instrument panel.

A viewport window slid open in front of them. They were still high in the air, as high as an airplane. But far below them stretched an endless tan desert, dotted with massive pyramids and one small city on the horizon.

"A Nazi treasure map for ancient Egypt?" Brendan said, looking at the map Eleanor had given him with his eyebrows raised.

"The Germans occupied parts of Africa during earth's Second World War," Gilbert said. "It is highly likely that some remnants of their presence endured years or decades subsequent to their withdrawal."

Brendan cocked his head at the small alien.

"How do you know so much about earth?" he asked.

"Because I—"

"Know all," Brendan said, finishing the alien's sentence. "Right."

Gilbert's mouth was small and didn't move much, even when he talked. But Brendan could have sworn the tiny alien was grinning at him. He looked back down at the Nazi treasure map. It was clearly a map of Europe, with the big red *X* resting somewhere near the heel of Italy. It just didn't make sense, unless Eleanor had been wrong about the Nazi treasure map being related to the third World-keeper, which was entirely possible.

"Are you sure this is the right area?" Brendan asked.

"Yes, we are presently hovering over the midpoint of the region labeled *Wazner's Revenge* on your book world map," Gilbert said, as he pressed a few dials and the sphere slowed to a stop, hovering in the air thousands of feet above a city in the middle of the desert. "Wazner was an ancient pharaoh entombed in one of the lost pyramids outside of Aswan, Egypt. Circa 3100 BC, Wazner arrived in—"

"I don't need his full history, thanks," Brendan interrupted, growing more anxious than ever to part ways with the alien.

"Technically, you do not *need* anything aside from the

organic supplemental materials that sustain your life energy," Gilbert said.

Brendan sighed and stuffed the Nazi treasure map into his back pocket with the *Journal*. He had concluded that it probably wasn't relevant after all, but that didn't mean he was going to throw it away just yet. After all, there's never a good reason to just discard a treasure map. Except, of course, after actually finding the treasure.

He was about to ask Gilbert to lower them into the city, when it occurred to him that the sight of a small alien flying inside a liquid metal sphere would probably upset the locals, to say the least. It might make it awfully hard for Brendan to poke around and try to find the Worldkeeper. He realized he'd probably be better off starting the search alone.

"Drop me off just outside of town," Brendan instructed.

"I can accompany you."

"It's probably not a good idea for me to be seen with you," Brendan said. "Most of the people down there look like me. Not you."

"Yes," agreed Gilbert. "They would also be supremely jealous of my handsomeness."

"Exactly," Brendan said, trying not to roll his eyes.

"But it is essential to caution you," Gilbert said. "Be wary of savage and ferocious local creatures known as camels. They can consume human persons in as little as eleven seconds."

"Wait, what?" Brendan sputtered. "I don't think camels eat meat."

"They do!" Gilbert said. "My internal databases are never erroneous."

That's when Brendan realized that Gilbert was legitimately scared. The tiny being's voice trembled slightly as he spoke and his hands seemed unsteady as they worked the controls of his spaceship. He was scared not just for himself, but also for Brendan. The little weirdo alien clearly didn't want anything bad to happen to him. He was surprised to feel a lump in his throat.

But ultimately Brendan supposed it was only natural for Gilbert to be scared. He was just a character in a book after all, one who had truly believed he was an all-knowing space explorer. And now that his world had just been turned upside down by their trip—he couldn't even feel sure about the veracity of his own existence.

"Look, I may need your help at some point," Brendan said. "How can I contact you?"

Gilbert held out a small device with one of his right hands, as the sphere slowly came to a stop on a dirt road a few hundred yards from the edge of the town. The device looked startlingly similar to the transponders from the old, original Star Trek movies.

"Just press the indicated button," Gilbert said. "I will arrive at your position within seconds."

"Thanks," Brendan said as a small doorway materialized behind him.

"I foresee this going very well for you," Gilbert said. "You will encounter no troubles at all . . . provided you avoid camels."

At that moment, Brendan truly wished that Gilbert really was an all-knowing being. It would have been extraordinarily helpful in finding the Worldkeeper. Still, he smiled at the small alien and nodded, pretending that he believed every word.

"See you soon," Brendan said, and then paused and added a genuine "thank you" before crawling out of the spaceship into the hot desert.

The heat hit him like a roundhouse kick to the face. It almost knocked him over. Brendan had never felt anything like it. His jeans stuck to his legs, and sweat dripped down his back after just seconds. He spun around to ask Gilbert if he had any canteens of water he could take with him, but the sphere was already ascending back into the sky.

Brendan turned to face the town. The road had twin ruts running parallel to each other, grooved out by car tires. He realized that he had no idea in what time period the book took place, or what it was about, aside from some vengeful pharaoh named Wazner. Which meant Brendan had no clue what exactly he was going to encounter.

The large city shimmered, the waves of heat making it

dance and ripple in the sun like an optical illusion. Brendan breathed in as if to sigh, but the hot air was so thick he gargled and coughed, the heat choking him.

He trudged along the road toward the town. As he approached, Brendan noticed a surprising amount of green for a desert. The city was built on a river, nestled in a shallow valley of low, tan hills. The flatlands on both banks of the river were covered in buildings and splotches of green palm trees and other plants. It gave Brendan hope of finding some fresh water there.

As he got closer to the city, he spotted a camel standing on the side of the road, tied to a fence. The animal looked content, even sleepy. Brendan grinned.

"Wow, Gilbert," Brendan said sarcastically. "These camels really are scary man-eaters!"

He reached out to pet the camel, when it suddenly opened its mouth, revealing two rows of razor-sharp teeth. The beast let out a roar that sounded more threatening than a mountain lion's. The camel's head shot forward to take a bite out of Brendan's arm, but he was tied securely to the fence and couldn't get close enough.

"Okay, I guess I owe you one after all, little dude," Brendan muttered to himself as he scampered away down the road. "You never know how twisted things are gonna get in Kristoff's books."

Tires crunched over gravel behind him, just before a

loud horn blared in his ears. Brendan spun around and found himself face-to-face with two bulbous headlights. A jeep barreled down the road right toward him at speeds better suited to a race track than a bumpy desert road. The horn blared again; the jeep wasn't slowing down, as dust and sand kicked up behind it like a trailing yellow cape.

Brendan just stood there and gaped at the car that was mere seconds away from turning him into human roadkill. He wondered briefly if some guy would come by later and scoop up his flattened carcass and dump it into a trash can on the back of a pickup. Maybe it was the heat, or his growing thirst, or maybe it was the same thing that caused deer to stop in the middle of roads when cars approached, but Brendan didn't and *couldn't* move.

It was like his feet were glued to the road.

Brendan stood there and watched as the jeep rumbled toward him at breakneck speed, still blaring its horn.

CHAPTER 59

In a small cave on a strange island that doubled as the planetary setting for Denver Kristoff's science-fiction novel *The Terror on Planet 5X*, Eleanor Walker huddled herself into a ball, cold and alone, and she cried. She cried for her dead friends, Lefty and Fat Jagger, and for her brother and sister who had abandoned her there.

Eventually, exhaustion took over and she drifted into an uneasy sleep. Eleanor dreamed of horrible monsters that melted her home and family and friends. She dreamed of Brendan and Cordelia having private conversations where they confessed to each other that Eleanor was really a hindrance on their mission and they wished they'd left her behind—back in San Francisco. She dreamed of all the things she still didn't have: a horse of her own, real human friends her own age, siblings who respected her, and a happy family with a big house and all the stuff they'd ever want.

At some point in her sleep, she became aware of voices speaking above her. Normal voices. *Human* voices.

"What is it?" a man said.

"What do you mean 'what is it?'" a crisp female voice replied. "It's a little girl."

"A little girl on Planet 5X?" the man said. "Impossible."

A third voice spoke, this one stilted and emotionless, as if it came from a machine instead of a person. "The probability of preexisting human life on Planet 5X is fourteen billion seventeen hundred million eight hundred seventy-six thousand six hundred five to one."

"I don't care what the probability is," the woman said again. "I trust my eyes, and my eyes are telling me that we're looking at a little girl sleeping in this cave."

"I think she's dead," the man said.

"According to my sensors, she is very much alive," the machine voice said. "Her heart rate has escalated to eighty-one beats per minute and she is severely dehydrated, but she is not deceased."

Eleanor groaned and rolled over. Two faces peered in at her from the narrow cave opening. A man and a woman. They took a step back as if the sight of a little nine-year-old girl was suddenly the scariest thing they had ever seen.

"Who are you?" Eleanor asked, also wondering where that third robotic voice had been coming from.

The woman took a gentle step toward Eleanor.

"Don't do it," the man said. "She could be armed."

"Armed?" the woman asked incredulously. "She's a little kid!"

"I still wouldn't go anywhere near her," the man said. "She could be carrying an infectious disease or some strange virus from her home planet. . . ."

"There's no need to be so cautious," the woman said.

"I'm just looking out for your well-being," the man said. "Like any good older brother should."

The woman rolled her eyes and took another step closer. She smiled at Eleanor as she reached her hand out. She had long, red hair that draped across her shoulders like fire and green eyes that burned so intensely Eleanor almost screamed, sure that they could shoot out the same green flames that had melted Kristoff House . . . and Lefty Payne. The woman's smiling lips were bright red and shiny with glossy lipstick.

"It's okay, little girl," the woman said. "What's your name?"

"Eleanor."

"How did you get here, Eleanor?" the woman asked.

"It's a long story," Eleanor said.

"Why don't you come with us," the woman said. "You

can tell us all about it."

"I don't think that's a good idea," the man said.

The robot voice suddenly chimed in, seeming to come from nowhere. "Maybe I should perform a routine examination scan before you—"

"Stop! Both of you," the woman said before turning back to Eleanor. "You'll be safe. We'll take good care of you, I promise."

Eleanor hesitated, but only for another second or two. The woman seemed nice. Eleanor already liked her. She was strong and didn't seem to let anyone push her around. Besides, anything was better than being alone. Eleanor had basically been ready to just give up and stay curled up inside this cave forever.

She reached out and took the woman's hand, which was covered in a gray-leather glove. The woman's grip was firm as she pulled Eleanor to her feet and then helped her squeeze out of the cave and back into the strange alien jungle. Once outside, Eleanor got a much better look at her new friends.

The woman was tall and wearing a skin-tight gray leather space suit that looked as if it did a much better job showing off her curves than actually functioning as a working space suit. Her matching gray boots had pointy heels almost as long as Eleanor's forearms, and she carried herself confidently, as if there was nothing she couldn't handle.

There was a bright yellow belt around her waist holding a small device and ray gun that both looked like they were from a fifties science-fiction film.

The man was just slightly taller than the woman, with the same deep red hair. His was buzzed on the sides and combed into a pompadour on the top that curled over his forehead like a red wave. He had a similarly tight gray space suit that showed off bulging muscles and a matching ray gun on his yellow belt. He gave a cautious grin when Eleanor looked at him, and his teeth were huge and white.

"Who are you guys?" Eleanor asked.

"I'm Zoe," the woman said. "The overly protective fellow here is my brother, Deke. And that voice you're hearing on our remote communication device is our spaceship's mother computer, Rodney."

"Rodney?" Eleanor said with a laugh. "That's kind of a silly name for a computer."

Suddenly, a deep whirring sound came from the speakers on the astronauts' belts. It sounded oddly like an electronic whimper. A low whistle followed it, sounding remarkably human and sad.

"Now look what you did, kid," Deke said. "You went and hurt Rodney's feelings."

Zoe leaned in closer to Eleanor and shielded her mouth

with the back of her hand. "You can't be too hard on Rodney," she whispered. "He's very sensitive . . . for a computer."

Eleanor nodded and then, in a soft voice, said, "I'm sorry, Rodney. I really like your name. It's very sweet."

"You really think so?" he asked. "I am quite fond of it as well."

More whirring sounds and several light beeps emitted from the speakers. They coursed with obvious mechanical delight.

"What are you guys doing out here anyway?" Eleanor asked.

"We're space rangers," Zoe said. "We're hot on the trail of an extraterrestrial we tracked to this planet, known as Planet 5X."

"Did this extraterrestrial do something wrong?" Eleanor asked. "Why are you after him?"

"*Him?*" Zoe said. "Why do you assume it's a man? It's an alien; it might not even have a gender. But girls can be on the run too, you know? What are you, from the Dark Ages?"

"Sorry, I didn't mean to assume anything," Eleanor said, worried that she'd just lost her one chance to make new friends so she wouldn't have to be alone anymore.

"Don't mind my sister," Deke said. "I keep telling her to lighten up on the whole strong-woman routine or she'll never find a good husband."

"Husband!" Zoe scoffed. "I don't need a husband. Maybe to do my laundry for me . . . but that's why we created robots! I'm perfectly fine being on my own. I can handle myself quite well, thank you."

"Right!" Eleanor ventured with a grin, assuming this was the response Zoe wanted.

"See?" Zoe said triumphantly. "She gets it! I think you and me are going to get along just fine, Eleanor."

"Me too," Eleanor said, smiling.

"But the real question is, what are *you* doing here all by yourself?" Zoe asked. "And how did you get here? This planet is supposedly unexplored."

"Like I said . . . it's a long and complicated story."

The sibling explorers looked at her as if they had all the time in the world.

"I hate to intercede," Rodney said in his monotone voice. "But my sensors have detected three more UWOs approaching your coordinates quickly."

"Don't you mean UFOs?" Eleanor said, as the ground began to rumble uneasily under her feet.

"Negative," Rodney said. "The acronym utilized stands for Unidentified *Walking* Objects."

"Oh," Eleanor said as the ground continued to shake. Then her eyes went wide with fear and understanding.

"OOOooh! You mean the giant robots that shoot melting green fire!"

"You've seen them?" Zoe asked.

Eleanor nodded. "They killed my friend and melted my house."

"You *live* here?" Zoe asked.

"We don't have time for this!" Deke yelled, drawing his ray gun from his belt. "Rodney, what's our best escape route?"

"Computing," Rodney said robotically. "Computing."

He computed for what felt like ages to Eleanor. On a smartphone she could have looked up driving directions from Fisherman's Wharf to Omaha, Nebraska, including traffic patterns and tolls in like two seconds.

"Escape route negative," Rodney finally said. "Window of evasion has expired. The UWOs have surrounded your position. The probability of survival is fourteen thousand—"

"No time for calculations now," Zoe shouted as she pulled Eleanor next to her.

The three of them huddled together with their backs to the cave wall as the massive, green-fire-spewing robots thundered through the tall trees and thick alien foliage. Three robots emerged simultaneously in a half circle around the smooth, black stone cliff, blocking any chance of escape. Then, as if they'd been practicing synchronization for weeks, the UWOs raised their green flamethrowing hands and pointed them at the explorers.

Eleanor's shrill screams pierced through everything else as the flames erupted from the robots' hands and turned her whole world bright green.

CHAPTER

60

Out in the sea, not too far from the "planet" desig-
nated 5X, Cordelia and Adie screamed in shock as
they both splashed into the cold ocean. When the bright
ball of light struck the bottom of the sailboat that Gilbert
had built for them, the boat had simply evaporated out of
existence, leaving the two occupants suspended several feet
in the air above the surface of the water for a split second.

It wasn't until Cordelia splashed down into the salty
ocean that she felt much of anything. The water was so cold
that it knocked the wind from her lungs, and she gasped for
air as she treaded water.

Adie splashed wildly next to Cordelia, screaming that
she couldn't swim. Cordelia swam over to her, glad to have

something distracting her from the temperature of the water. She looped her arm under Adie's armpit and pushed her up to keep her head above the surface.

"Stay calm, stay calm," Cordelia said slowly, trying to keep her own voice as steady as she could. She had done this before, back when she taught Eleanor how to swim a few years ago. "The more you thrash, the more you'll sink. Keep moving your feet in slow, steady circles."

Adie nodded and, slowly but surely, her flailing slowed so that she was nearly lifeless in the water. Cordelia saw her bare feet kicking beneath a billowing yellow dress in the water.

"I'm going to let go now," Cordelia said, struggling to keep afloat herself while holding Adie up.

"No!" Adie yelled, her eyes widening.

Cordelia told herself to be patient, remembering that there probably weren't a lot of swimming pools in the late 1800s Dakota prairie. Lakes, maybe, but traveling thirty miles away to a lake to go swimming wouldn't be particularly easy without cars.

"You'll be okay, I promise," Cordelia said. "I'm right here."

Adie nodded as she spat out some of the water she'd accidently gulped down while struggling.

"This water tastes awful," she said.

"Salt water," Cordelia said.

"I read about oceans being salty, but I never imagined this," Adie said. "I'm actually swimming in a real ocean!"

Cordelia nodded, glad that Adie's mood had shifted. But she was still worried about whatever had been the source of that blue light. It was incredible how Adie always looked at the bright side first. Cordelia wasn't sure she'd ever met someone so optimistic.

Cordelia treaded water and looked down into the deep, clear ocean. There didn't appear to be anything below them. But it was much harder to see with her face now just inches from the surface.

"Oh no," Adie said.

"What?"

"There's another light coming."

Cordelia spun around. Another blue light was coming up underneath them. But this one looked different. For one thing, it seemed to be slowing as it approached. Additionally, as it got closer, Cordelia could clearly see it was a larger object with a dark shape inside of it, and not just a ball of light.

They watched in awed silence as the light grew under their kicking feet. It was the size of a whole room. Cordelia realized then that it was a vessel of some sort. But like no vessel she'd ever seen. It was long and sleek, almost the length of a school bus, and entirely transparent, with just a few blue lights visible along the bottom. And there was a person clearly visible inside.

The vessel continued to rise, far more quickly than it had appeared to be moving when it was farther down, and for an instant Cordelia was sure it was going to break their ankles. So she closed her eyes and tensed for the impact. Except there wasn't one.

Instead, both Adie and Cordelia were suddenly sucked under the surface of the water and into the strange submarine, right through its exterior as if it were made of nothing.

They found themselves sprawled on a dry, hard floor. Cordelia shivered and looked up at the lone occupant of the vessel. The woman standing in front of them looked far more human than Cordelia had expected. She had a beautiful, striking face, with normal arms and legs. The only real difference was the color of her skin. It was tinted light blue and shimmered as if it were constantly changing colors. Her long, flowing hair was jet black. Her irises were red with pupils so tiny they looked like nothing more than a single drop of black in the center of her eyes.

She appeared to be ageless, and wore an iridescent pearl garment that looked more suitable for a runway than for piloting a submarine. The woman also wore a crown made of sparkling seashells and had an aura of royalty about her, as if she possessed more dignity and grace in one hand than one human could possibly ever hope to achieve in a lifetime.

The woman pressed a glowing symbol on an invisible inside wall of the strange vessel. The submarine had glass walls on every side, and it terrified Cordelia and Adie when it started descending into the depths again.

"Lucky I found you," the woman said. "It's nearly mating season for the nine-gill sharks. They are beautiful and wondrous creatures of the sea. But during mating season, they feast on just about everything and anything they can find. And that boat you were in wouldn't have done much to protect you."

Cordelia and Adie stared blankly at their rescuer. They were still too shocked to process much of what was happening, let alone offer any coherent replies.

"I'm sorry," the woman said after a few moments of silence. "Are you having difficulty understanding me? Do you speak a different language?"

She looked down at Adie and Cordelia still seated on the floor, shivering and wet. Her expression had shifted slightly. She was still smiling, but now it was tinged with pity, the way someone might look at a clumsy toddler struggling to take its first steps.

"We can understand you just fine," Adie said, finally climbing to her feet. "I'm Adie! And this is my friend Cordelia."

"How wonderful to meet you, Adie and Cordelia," the woman said. "You have beautiful names. I'm Grand Premier Annex Democritus, the humble elected servant of the people of Atlantis."

"The elected *leader* of Atlantis?" Cordelia asked. "Like, the president?"

"Why, yes," Democritus said politely. "You seem confused. Why does this unsettle you?"

"Well," Cordelia explained, "where I come from, it would be very strange to see an elected leader out and about all alone without a huge entourage and security detail."

"Why would I need security?" Democritus asked. "I should be free to explore my own world the same as any other citizen of our great city."

"Aren't you worried that someone could hurt you?" Cordelia asked.

"No, of course not!" Democritus said, horrified at the mere thought. "Why would I be?"

"Where I'm from, not everyone agrees with the elected leaders," Cordelia said. "So the presidents of countries never get to go anywhere without, like, at least two dozen bodyguards since there are a lot of people who would kill them if they got the chance."

Democritus's eyes went wide. "How awful!" she said. "The people were the ones who elected me. Why should they want to hurt me? Even the citizens who voted against me recognize that not accepting democratic results is not accepting democracy at all. Your world sounds *terrible!* In Atlantis, the only thing we truly fear is the Forbidden Zone, home of the dreaded Iku-Turso."

Adie and Cordelia both perked up at the mention of the Forbidden Zone. They knew that this was the place they needed to go in order to find the Worldkeeper. But Democritus spoke again before either of them had a chance to ask about it.

"But enough small talk; we are nearly home!" Democritus said, pointing through the clear walls of the submarine.

Cordelia had a hard time turning away from Democritus's huge smile. There was something about it that seemed almost too friendly. Why would the leader of Atlantis be so nice to complete strangers from another world? The politicians in Cordelia's time and place didn't trust anyone outside their inner circle. So Democritus's kindness didn't feel entirely real to Cordelia.

Eventually she managed to pry her eyes from the woman's smiling face, remembering that they were traveling into the depths of the ocean inside a 360-degree-view submarine. She'd probably already missed out on all kinds of awesome sights.

Cordelia looked down and gasped. Adie went rigid

beside her and grabbed Cordelia's hand. She squeezed it so hard, it almost hurt. But Cordelia was too awed to feel any pain; instead her eyes filled with the reflecting lights from the dazzling underwater city below them.

"Holy-moly," Adie said beside her.

Cordelia repeated the sentiment using a slightly different word selection.

The Lost City of Atlantis was both beautiful and haunting, a spectacular underwater world of unimaginable expanse and splendor. A hive of millions, perhaps even billions, of glowing multicolored bubbles was built into the side of an underwater mountain range covered with sea life and vegetation never seen before by human eyes. The intricate, glowing buildings each sparkled with their own magical illumination.

Some of the shimmering buildings underneath them were as small as a two-bedroom house. Others were several times larger than the huge sports domes that football teams like the Indianapolis Colts and New Orleans Saints called their home fields. Collectively, it was a nearly unimaginable sight—so spectacular that Cordelia's eyes darted around feverishly, almost incapable of taking it all in.

As the ship descended, the true scale of the city became even more apparent. It made Cordelia feel like a squished bug stuck to the bottom of someone's shoe.

"Well, this is definitely the most amazing thing I've ever seen," Adie said.

"And we've seen a lot of amazing things today," Cordelia reminded her.

"Welcome to our home," Democritus said, smiling. "The great city of Atlantis."

61

Somewhere, far away, just outside a fictional version of the city of Aswan, Egypt, Brendan Walker didn't feel all that surprised that he was going to finally meet his grisly end underneath an old, honking jeep on some dusty desert road. He'd been face-to-face with his own mortality enough times the past few days that he merely closed his eyes and waited for the impact.

Instead of blunt-force trauma, however, he received a mouthful of sand as the jeep swerved around him at the last moment. He opened his eyes, coughing, and spun around.

A middle-aged guy was behind the wheel, and next to him a small boy stood up in the passenger seat and looked back at Brendan. He shook his fist and screamed at him as the jeep sped away, the last of his shrill words faded away in the blowing sand.

"*. . . standing in the middle of the road, you idiot . . .*"

"I . . . was . . . try . . . ," Brendan said, unable to form a complete sentence, his throat filled with clumps of sand.

But they wouldn't have heard him even if he had been able to speak, since the jeep had already disappeared into town.

Brendan tried to breathe out but the sand in his throat made it nearly impossible. Water. That was his first priority. He'd already needed a drink in this insane heat, but now the mouthful of sand and dirt clinched it.

He trudged on, this time off to the side of the twin tire ruts that passed for a road. His steps were more sluggish in the loose sand, but it was probably better than getting run down by another car.

Brendan reached the city on the river desperate for water. He barely noticed the people wearing robes and headscarves staring at his odd clothes. Brendan didn't notice cars sputtering by on the cobbled roads, didn't notice that they were from the fifties or so. All he noticed was the small market near the riverbank. He saw people there in tents selling fruit and pottery and blankets. And best of all, he saw a massive canteen slung across a support post of the tent nearest to him.

He ran his sandpaper tongue across the cracked glass

that his lips had become. Everything else faded away. Even the intense sun and heat became secondary. It was just Brendan and that canteen, alone in a sandy, hot room. He stumbled toward it, not seeming to make any progress with each step.

But he was covering ground. And in just a matter of minutes he had reached the canteen. He grabbed the strap and pulled it off the post. He unscrewed the metal lid and started guzzling the contents without even stopping to sniff it. It was maybe not the cleanest, tastiest, coldest water, but at that moment Brendan didn't care. His lips and mouth soaked it up like a sponge. He had nearly drained the half-gallon canteen in a single chug, when a hand grabbed his wrist so hard he dropped it, spilling the last few drops onto the thirsty road.

"Thought you could steal my water, thief?" a gruff voice shouted.

Brendan locked eyes with his assailant. It was a middle-aged Egyptian man wearing traditional desert clothes. The man's eyes were on fire, and Brendan looked around nervously for help. A small crowd began to gather around the tent at the commotion.

"No, I wasn't trying to steal it," Brendan said. "I was dying of thirst. . . ."

"Thieves are not tolerated here!" the man screamed. "You must be punished severely!"

"No!" Brendan shouted. He tried to pull away, but the man's grip was like a cyborg's.

The man turned and addressed the growing mob.

"This boy stole my water!" he shouted. "He must pay for it the usual way!"

The angry mob cried out in approval. A small part appeared in the masses as a huge wooden box the size of a three-feet-deep kiddie pool was dragged into the clearing. It had a lid like a coffin.

"What is that?" Brendan asked.

Nobody replied. Instead, someone from the crowd shouted, "Throw him in the thief pit, Fadil!"

"No!" Brendan shouted, realizing that something called a *thief pit* coming from Denver Kristoff's demented imagination couldn't possibly be pleasant.

This was met with more cheers of approval from the gathered people. Two men stepped forward and pulled off the heavy wooden lid. Even amid the loud cheering of the crowd, Brendan heard hissing. Several black and brown snake heads poked up above the edge of the wooden box. The thief pit.

"Oh no, please!" Brendan screamed. "Please . . . I wasn't trying to steal. . . ."

Fadil grinned and dragged Brendan closer to the wooden box. He easily hoisted Brendan into the air, giving him a perfect view of at least a dozen snakes slithering around inside the box. It looked like a coffin because it clearly was going to become one for him very soon.

"Throw him in!" someone shouted.

"Thief!" cried another.

Fadil grinned at Brendan and held him out over the wooden pit. The snakes hissed and writhed in anticipation just several feet below.

"This is what happens to those who steal my things," Fadil said.

"Noooo!" Brendan screamed, but he knew it was too late as Fadil's grip on his shirt and pant leg loosened.

CHAPTER

62

"Fadil! *Stop!*" a voice from the crowd shouted.

"Why?" Fadil said, whirling around, still holding Brendan. "He's a thief! Why should he not be punished like all other thieves?"

"Because it was simply a misunderstanding," a man with a smooth British accent said, stepping forward.

He was around forty and had a thin, impeccably trimmed black mustache. He wore a black three-piece suit with a matching bowler hat. His black oxford dress shoes looked as if they alone cost more than Brendan's entire wardrobe. The man carried a leather messenger bag slung across his shoulder. If Brendan didn't know any better, he would have sworn the man was British royalty.

Brendan felt like he recognized him from somewhere. Then he saw the young boy standing next to him. He wore ratty canvas pants and a white shirt with dirt stains spread across the front. He held up his chin as if he were challenging everyone there to a fistfight, in spite of being almost a full foot shorter and at least two years younger than Brendan. He recognized the boy right away; he was the one from the jeep. These were the two jerks who'd almost run him over!

"Misunderstanding?" Fadil said, finally setting Brendan down, but still keeping a firm grip on his shirt collar. "The canteen was in his hand! He was drinking from it! I saw it with my own eyes!"

"He didn't know it was yours," the Englishman said. "Here, accept this as payment for your troubles. You can buy ten canteens with it. Just release the boy."

He tossed several gold coins at Fadil's feet.

"Why do you care so much about this ugly little boy?" Fadil asked.

"Hey . . . ," Brendan protested, but nobody paid any attention.

"He is my new assistant," the Englishman said. "He just arrived and clearly does not know the rules here."

"Very well, you have a deal," Fadil said, finally releasing his viselike grip from Brendan's shirt collar. "But I don't want to see this boy near my things again."

"I'd only go back there if I wanted to get cholera or listeria," Brendan said defiantly, straightening out his clothes.

Fadil ignored him as he bent down to scoop up the three gold coins on the dirt at his feet.

"Come along now, boy," the Englishman said to Brendan. "We have much work to do. Remember?" He motioned for Brendan to follow him.

Brendan nodded and followed the Englishman and young boy as they walked briskly out of the market, cutting through the dispersing crowd. Eventually, they stopped behind a building just up the hill from the riverbank market.

"Thank you for saving me," Brendan said. "Who are you, anyway?"

"My name is Sir Dr. Edwington Alistair Forthwithinshire III, Esquire," the Englishman said. "Professor of human studies and archaeology at Oxford."

"Sir, Doctor, Edward . . . wait, can you repeat that? I think I'm going to have to write it down," Brendan said, struggling to remember it all.

The man laughed. His laughter was somehow even

more charming than his accent.

"Such are the pitfalls of being a doctor, lawyer, *and* knight. You may simply call me Sir Ed if you wish," he said. "And this is my assistant."

"My name's Jumbo," the small boy said, eyeing Brendan suspiciously. He did not have an accent like the man. He looked Egyptian, but spoke perfect English.

"Okay, uh, Sir Ed and Jumbo, so why did you guys help me?" Brendan asked.

"Because I have a feeling we're both here for the same reason," Sir Ed said.

Brendan looked at him, not sure how to respond. Was he looking for a Worldkeeper as well?

"What makes you say that?" Brendan asked hesitantly.

"When Fadil dragged you into the middle of that crowd, something fell out of your pocket," Sir Ed explained, reaching into his bag.

Brendan's eyes went wide. The *Journal*! He was supposed to guard it with his life, it was their only hope of saving Fat Jagger and his own world from certain destruction at the hands of the Wind Witch. And he'd lost it taking a drink of water! Except, he hadn't. The *Journal* was still packed firmly into the back pocket of his jeans.

That's when Sir Ed pulled out Brendan's Nazi treasure map.

"I found it rather startling that you would possess such a thing," Sir Ed said, grinning.

"Oh, that? That's really no big deal," Brendan said quickly.

"But it *is* a big deal, a rather big deal indeed," Sir Ed said, reaching back into his bag. "Because how else would you explain this?"

Sir Ed pulled another folded sheet of paper from his bag, and Brendan's jaw dropped open. Sir Ed's copy was a little bit more tattered and worn, but the resemblance was unmistakable. Sir Dr. Edwington Alistair Forthwithinshire III, Esq. had an exact duplicate copy of the lost Nazi treasure map!

63

Hundreds of miles away, in an alien jungle on Planet 5X, three huge flamethrowing robots surrounded a duo of space rangers and Eleanor. Green flames burst from the robots' right arms and engulfed the trapped space explorers.

Eleanor Walker had never really wondered what it would feel like to be melted by strange green alien fire. But she was about to find out. Or, she would have, if the green flames spewing from the three UWOs' flamethrowing hands didn't pool off to the sides at the last second, melting the plants and trees all around her and her new friends.

"Force field has been activated," Rodney said calmly.

"Force field!" Eleanor shouted, even as the green flames continued to deflect away from them. "But you just said a second ago that we were all going die!"

"Had I finished my sentence," Rodney explained. "Then you would have heard that such fatal probabilities were calculated without the use of—"

"Not now, Rodney!" Zoe shouted as she pointed her ray gun at one of the massive UWOs and fired. Concentric rings of red laser beams blasted from the end of Zoe's weapon, expanding as they moved away. The beams hit the huge UWO and it shuddered and vibrated like it was going to explode. The robot went rigid and tipped over backward, crashing into the alien forest with enough force to knock Eleanor on her butt.

Zoe and Deke somehow stayed upright and continued firing their ray guns until all three UWO's were lying on several acres of crushed forest foliage, dead or disabled or whatever it was that their sci-fi laser pistols had done to them.

"Eleanor, let's go," Zoe said, holding out a hand. "We've gotta get out of here before more of them show up. Follow us."

Eleanor nodded and grabbed Zoe's hand without hesitation. She followed Zoe and Deke through the strange alien forest. After a few minutes, they finally emerged from the thick bed of odd plants into a rocky desert covered in craters and smooth black buttes and cliffs. It would have been terrifying if Eleanor were alone. The polished black formations were jagged and uninviting, as if she were stepping into the mouth of a carnivorous planet. But with her new friends at her side, the crater desert was actually sort of cool, almost beautiful.

They ran around the edge of a massive crater with pushed-up sides almost as tall as a small mountain. A spaceship with red fins and a huge jet engine sat just beyond a jagged outcropping. Several beeps and buzzes emitted from Zoe's intercom speaker, and a section of the spaceship opened up and stairs folded down.

Eleanor followed them inside. The interior of the ship was cold and futuristic in a way, but, like the rest of the space explorers' appearances, there was something gaudily vintage about the whole thing. It was covered in warm pastels and smooth, simple-looking computers with large, red-knobbed levers and bright, basic lights. This particular novel had clearly been written long before Eleanor's time.

"That was a close one, Zoe," Deke said as the door closed behind them. "I thought we were dead."

"But we still didn't get what we came for!" Zoe fired back. "We need to find that little alien."

"Why do you need to find him so badly?" Eleanor asked.

"He has something of value," Zoe said, cartoonishly throwing a finger into the air like she just had an amazing idea. "Something we desperately want."

"What's that?"

"His heart."

"His heart!"

"Yes," Zoe said. "His heart is a very special because he's the last of his kind. It's worth over a million InterGalactic credits on the Gray Space Market."

"And how will you . . . how do you get his heart?" Eleanor asked.

"We will slice it right out of his torso," Zoe said, making a cutting motion with her hand.

"Are you serious?" Eleanor asked, feeling a sick twinge in her stomach.

She had really liked Zoe, respected her strength and confidence. But being able to cut someone's heart out, even if it was an alien species, was not something a heroic or moral person would do. Zoe was obviously just a cold, heartless bounty hunter who only cared about money.

"And what does this alien look like?" Eleanor asked.

"He's very small, like a child," Zoe said. "He flies around in a metal sphere. Have you seen him?"

Eleanor was too shocked to respond at first. Zoe was

talking about Gilbert! The alien they were hunting was the same strange little being that had saved their lives twice. He was with Brendan, and now Zoe wanted to find him and cut out his heart!

CHAPTER

64

The vast underwater city of Atlantis was almost more breathtaking and beautiful from inside the strange bubble-shaped buildings that lined the walls of the deep ocean mountain range. They were so far beneath the surface of the water that the ocean outside the bubble was nothing but a wall of black. No light existed this deep, and so the other bubble buildings around them glowed in the darkness like giant stars in a night sky.

The resemblance made Cordelia and Adie both feel homesick.

"I'm sure you must be tired; you both should get some rest," Democritus said behind them.

"That'd be wonderful," Cordelia said with a smile.

Adie nodded in agreement.

"This way to your rooms," Democritus said, motioning down a long, narrow hallway leading into another bubble on the underwater mountainside.

As the three of them trekked down the empty hallway, Cordelia tried to find a way to bring up the Worldkeeper without giving away their intent to steal it.

"Have you ever heard of the Eternal Abyss?" Cordelia asked casually.

It was a question that changed the mood in an instant. Democritus's glaring eyes bore down on her as they stopped outside another of the glowing blue bubbles. All the niceties and smiles were suddenly gone.

"We do not speak of such things," Democritus said tersely. "Have a pleasant rest."

She hit a switch on the wall and a door to the adjacent bubble slid open. Democritus walked back down the hallway without another word, leaving Cordelia and Adie standing there at the entryway to their room alone. They entered, and the door slid shut behind them automatically.

The room itself was modest with clear walls, like seemingly every room and hallway in the city. It had two circular beds in the center. The bedding was deep blue and lustrous and soft, yet it was unlike any material either of them had ever felt before. Which made sense to Cordelia once she thought about it. . . . They likely had no access to cotton or silk or any of the usual textiles her clothes were made from. Instead, Atlantisan clothes and bedding were probably made of a combination of seaweed and various underwater organisms.

In between the beds were two tables covered with sleek pitchers of water and trays filled with food. Adie and Cordelia glanced at each other and huge smiles spread across their faces. They rushed forward at the same time and dug in.

The water was cold, clear, and maybe the best drink of *anything* they'd ever had. It was so pure it almost felt lighter than normal water. The food consisted, unsurprisingly, of seafood. There were huge crab legs, some as long as Cordelia's whole arm, a lobster nearly the size of a golden retriever, squid, fresh fish, clams, oysters, and a full array of sea greens that reminded Cordelia of sushi nori wrapping and seaweed salads, except they were much sweeter, saltier, fresher, and way better. The food was very lightly seasoned; it was essentially a feast of the freshest, sweetest seafood she'd ever had. Adie struggled at first, since it was clearly her first foray into seafood. But ten minutes in, she was cracking and devouring massive crab legs as if it were an eating competition.

After gorging for nearly an hour, they both crawled into their separate beds, feeling more content than they'd ever expected they would be when they set out on the high seas in a small makeshift sailboat just a few hours before.

As soon as their heads hit the strange, yet insanely comfortable pillows on their beds, they were both deep asleep. Cordelia was plunged instantly into an intense and vivid dream.

She was swimming deep in the ocean—zooming through it effortlessly without needing to breathe or even really swim at all. It was as if she were *flying* through the water. Deeper and deeper she descended, until there was only blackness. And then, gradually, a faint light formed beneath her. The pale lights from an ancient underwater city. And even before the lights became fully recognizable, Cordelia knew what was happening.

It was the Wind Witch. She had come for them. And even in the "dream," Cordelia could feel the old wretch's purpose. She was there to destroy them, to stop the mission, and she would leave the whole city in ruins if that's what it took.

CHAPTER 65

Back in the fictional version of Aswan, Egypt, circa 1955, a tall and lanky well-dressed Englishman stood in a dusty alley with two small children, grinning ear to ear as if he'd just won the lottery. Brendan was still staring at him in shock after finding out that his copy of the Nazi treasure map was apparently not one of a kind.

"We're clearly pursuing the same thing," Sir Ed said, putting his own copy of the Nazi treasure map back into his satchel. "How can that be possible?"

Brendan didn't really know how to respond, so he shook his head. How *could* it be possible? But then the obvious dawned on him: Both maps were fictional. They were just mutual parts of two separate books written by the same author. And so it was completely possible, likely even, that there was crossover stuff within Denver's books. Authors and movie directors did that kind of stuff all the time. There was even a name for it: *Easter eggs*. Like when Brendan saw a bunch of aliens from the movie *E.T.* in one of the prequel Star Wars movies.

"Are you listening to me, boy?" Sir Ed said, snapping Brendan from his thoughts. "If you could explain to me how you came by this map, it could be helpful to all of us."

"I got the map from . . ." Brendan hesitated.

He had been just about ready to tell the truth. That he'd gotten the map from a Nazi tank driven by a cyborg. But somehow Brendan didn't think that'd be such a good idea. Sir Ed from the 1950s probably didn't even know what a cyborg was.

"My dad is a professor of history at Stanford University in California," Brendan eventually said. "And he had it in his collection. . . ."

"Stanford, you say?" Sir Ed said. "I have many colleagues there. What's your father's name?"

"Um . . . well, it's, uh, Dr. Walker?" Brendan ventured.

Sir Ed studied him for a moment and then looked up at the bright blue sky. His blue eyes shone in the light.

"Ah yes!" he said suddenly. "I seem to remember meeting him once. A portly fellow, right? Walks with a limp and blinks quite a bit."

"Uh, yeah, that's him all right," Brendan said. "I stole his map and some money and bought myself a one-way ticket here to find the treasure."

"Well, nevertheless, this could potentially be very advantageous to both of us," Sir Ed said.

"How so?" Brendan asked.

"We can work *together* to find the Nazi treasure," Sir Ed said with a grin. "Two heads are superior to one, as you Americans say. There should be ample enough treasure to go around. No need to be greedy, right?"

Brendan realized, after several seconds, that it wasn't a rhetorical question. And so he nodded his head in agreement. After all, Brendan really didn't care about the Nazi treasure. Well, he did, sort of, because what kid didn't love the idea of finding lost treasure? But the reality of the situation was that he cared only about finding one item among the stolen treasure: the Worldkeeper. The most powerful Worldkeeper of them all, no less.

"Right," Brendan said, still nodding. "I can definitely share. I'm mostly here for the adventure, not the treasure."

"Splendid!" Sir Ed exclaimed with a smile. "So, the map's appearance is deceptive, as you've clearly figured out." Of course, Brendan hadn't figured that out yet, but he just nodded again. "It looks as though it's directing us to Italy. However, when held up to the sunlight . . ."

Sir Ed held up the map so it was between Brendan and

the bright sun. Through the now-translucent paper, Brendan saw a second set of lines.

A hidden map.

"The outer map is a very clever decoy," Sir Ed explained. "But when held up to the sun, the true map becomes visible."

Brendan examined the *real* map closely, following hidden lines that were clearly navigating their way through a labyrinth of pyramid passages as opposed to roads in Europe.

"And if you look closely," Sir Ed went on. "You can see where the treasure is located."

Brendan's eyes followed the map's trail to its end.

"The lost pyramid of Wazner's tomb," Brendan breathed.

"Yes," Sir Ed said. "As far as we know, nobody has entered it since the Nazis . . . just over a decade ago."

"Are you sure we want to bring him along?" Jumbo asked.

"Why shouldn't we?" Sir Ed asked his assistant. "Better to include him and work together than compete with each other, right?"

"He couldn't even jump out of the way of our jeep," Jumbo said. "If things get tough, he might choke. Could cost us our lives."

"I'm not going to choke," Brendan said. "I'm a lot smarter and tougher than you think."

"Oh yeah?" Jumbo asked, eyeing Brendan's hands suspiciously. "You ever been on a real adventure? Sure doesn't look like it. . . . It looks like you've been spending your life at some country club sipping lemonade and playing croquet with your grandma's friends."

"Believe me, I've been on more real adventures than you could imagine," Brendan said defensively.

"I don't believe you," Jumbo challenged. "So far you've only proven yourself to be a coward and a thief. If you're so tough . . . show me. . . ."

"How?" Brendan asked.

"Fight me," Jumbo said, raising his fists.

"Fight *you*?" Brendan asked, laughing nervously. "You're just a scrawny little kid. I'm not gonna fight—"

Brendan's sentence was rudely interrupted by Jumbo's small but powerful fist colliding squarely with his nose. Brendan stumbled back onto his butt, his nose burning and his eyes watering. He glared at Jumbo, who was now standing over him, fists upright.

"Come on," Jumbo snarled. "Get up! Show me what you got!"

Sir Ed just stepped back, crossed his arms, and smiled.

Furious, his nose on fire, Brendan leaped to his feet and started swinging wildly. The fight lasted a good five minutes with both boys missing more punches than they ultimately landed. But they connected just enough to be bruised, sore, and covered in dust and grime by the end. Panting and tired, both boys refused to back down.

Jumbo snarled at Brendan and lunged for one final attack. Brendan sidestepped him and threw out his leg, tripping the small boy and sending him sprawling to the ground. Jumbo was motionless for a few moments, but then stood up on shaky feet and glared at Brendan. Brendan tensed for another round, not sure if he had the stamina.

But that's when Jumbo did something completely unexpected. He smiled. It was warm and perhaps even reflected a little admiration.

"I've never, ever been knocked down before," Jumbo said. "Guys three times my size haven't been able to beat me. Except for you."

Brendan was brimming with pride, but tried not to let it show. This was, technically, his first fistfight. But he didn't want them to know that.

"Right then," Sir Ed said. "Now that you boys have solved your differences . . . are you ready to go find the treasure?"

Brendan and Jumbo looked at each other and gave a nod.

"Follow me then," Sir Ed said, handing Brendan's copy of the map back to him.

As they made their way down several deserted streets in the small Egyptian city, Jumbo walked right beside Brendan, barely looking away from him.

"Where'd you learn how to fight like that?" Jumbo asked.

"That's just how I roll," Brendan said, trying unsuccessfully to sound modest.

Jumbo laughed.

"You're as tough as I've met," Jumbo said. "I'll bet you're a real *hero* where you come from."

Brendan looked away, embarrassed, even though he suspected Jumbo was only kidding around. The hairs on his neck stood up. Something about Jumbo made Brendan uncomfortable, now that it was readily apparent that he had gone from distrusting him to admiring him like an idol in a matter of minutes.

"Believe it or not," Brendan said, not being able to help himself, "I've done the 'hero' thing a couple of times before . . . but now, it's about more than that. I just want to help people. You know, I just want to do the right thing when the right thing counts."

"Sounds admirable," Jumbo said. "Me, I just want to find some treasure!"

CHAPTER

66

Miles and miles away, on a craggy black wasteland of an island, Eleanor was still coming to terms with the fact that Gilbert was being hunted.

"You *have* seen him, haven't you?" Zoe asked.

Eleanor realized that her face must have given her away.

"Yeah, I saw him," Eleanor said cagily.

"Where?"

"First you have to answer a question for me," Eleanor said.

"Go on," Zoe said with a sly grin.

"Why is his heart so valuable?" Eleanor asked. "What could possibly make it worth cutting out?"

Deke and Zoe exchanged a look. But Rodney must have

completely missed the moment, or maybe his programming didn't allow him to pick up on subtle human social cues. Because he dove right into an answer before either of the sibling space explorers could stop him.

"The heart of the alien we seek is said to have powers than can disrupt the laws of nature, that can alter the space-time continuum," Rodney said. "It is said that whoever possesses the alien's heart can go backward in time and get *one opportunity* to fix their greatest mistake."

Eleanor stared at him with wide eyes. Something inside her brain clicked. She looked down again at the sheets of paper Brendan had given her before he left. She quickly reread the description of the Worldkeeper from Denver's *Journal*, her eyes stopping on several key phrases that supported her newly formed theory. But by now, she knew it wasn't a theory at all. It was the truth. The Worldkeeper she had stayed there to find was, in fact, Gilbert's heart! It was already with Brendan—which meant there was no longer any need for her to stay on this awful planet.

"I saw the alien," Eleanor finally said, realizing that these people might be her only way out of this terrible place. "And I can tell you exactly where to find him."

"Go on," Zoe said gently.

Zoe's smile was so caring that for a moment she reminded Eleanor of someone she knew. Was it her mother?

"He left with my brother," she said, hoping that by

332

telling them the truth, she could get off this island soon and be reunited with her siblings. "They left this world . . . *planet*, I mean. They're gone."

"What kind of brother would leave you on this terrible planet all alone?" Deke asked, horrified.

"I wasn't all alone," Eleanor said quickly. "He left me with a friend, Lefty Payne."

"And where is this friend now?" Zoe asked.

"He died," Eleanor said, tears stinging at her eyes. Not just for Lefty, but for the fresh reminder that she had been abandoned here. Deke was right, what kind of brother would do that?

"I'd never abandon my sister in a place like this," Deke said. "I don't care who was with her!"

Eleanor wanted to protest again. To assure them that Brendan wasn't as horrible as he sounded. She wanted to tell them about all the times he stayed up late watching Cartoon Network with her, about when he played lame board games with her for hours even though she could tell he didn't want to. She wanted to tell them how important their mission was and why they'd had to split up, but something stopped her. Perhaps they were right? How could her older siblings simply leave her in a book world called *The Terror on Planet 5X*? Did they somehow want to be rid of her?

"What was that?" Zoe asked suddenly as a screeching

noise pierced through the hull.

"More UWOs approaching," Rodney said. "Seven detected, closing in from all sides."

"Can we fly?" Zoe asked.

"Negative," Rodney replied calmly in his flat computer voice. "Thruster power cells are still recharging and are only at fourteen percent."

"Okay, you guys stay here and get this thing off the ground," Zoe said. "I'll take the rover and distract them."

"Take me with you," Eleanor said.

"It's too dangerous," Zoe said. "You'll be safer here. No sense in putting us both at risk."

"Please?" Eleanor begged; the desperation in her voice strained the word so it hung in the air. "I don't want to be left behind again."

Eleanor knew Zoe was the bait, that pretty soon all seven of the approaching UWOs would be chasing her through the alien wastelands. But she didn't care; for some reason she would still feel safer with her. There was something about Zoe that Eleanor connected with, something that comforted her beyond all reasonable logic.

"Okay, let's go," Zoe said. "Deke, pick us up on the beach as soon as you get this tin can airborne."

Eleanor followed her through a doorway and into a small hangar at the rear of the spaceship. The rover was a little vehicle that looked like a normal four-wheeler except that it had six wheels and an enclosed cabin that seated two people. And it also looked a lot more expensive than a normal four-wheeler.

"Climb aboard," Zoe said.

Eleanor clambered inside and took a seat next to Zoe. She strapped herself in with the shoulder-harness seat belt. A ramp lowered in front of them, and before Eleanor could even take her next breath, they were flying out of the hangar at close to sixty miles an hour. Her stomach dipped and churned as they zoomed down the ramp and out onto the black alien desert, bouncing on rocks and jumping over craters.

"It's okay, Eleanor, it's okay," Zoe said as she steered the incredibly fast little vehicle. "Calm down."

It was only then that Eleanor realized she had been screaming. She forced herself to stop, and watched as Zoe steered the rover right toward an approaching UWO. Green melting flames were already spewing from its right hand. But Zoe piloted around the flames easily and then zagged right back underneath the massive robot's legs.

She whipped them back and forth and toward and away from several more of the huge, alien-piloted robots, until five of them were in full pursuit. Their bounding steps rattled the equipment inside the rover. Zoe pressed a yellow button and the little vehicle rocketed forward even faster. It felt like the tiniest bump would send them flying up into space.

But somehow Zoe was able to maintain control while Eleanor grabbed the sides of her seat and held on for dear life.

"They're all after us now!" Zoe said with a gleeful grin. "Let's lead them into the jungle where we can lose them."

The rover hurtled toward the edge of the colorful alien jungle at close to 150 miles per hour. It felt like they were about to slam into it as if they were hitting a brick wall. But the vehicle ripped through the soft brush as if it were nothing. The speed and shape of the rover cut swaths through the jungle easily, the only obstacle being the trunks of the odd, bright orange trees that Zoe navigated around with ease.

And they suddenly came to an abrupt stop. Eleanor finally opened her eyes again. Zoe smiled at her.

"Fun ride, huh?" she said.

Eleanor nodded weakly. She looked around and realized they were back on the beach again. There was still a small, lingering puddle of what used to be Kristoff House. Seeing it made Eleanor want to cry. Or go back and somehow destroy the UWO that had melted her house.

"We lost them," Zoe said. "Now we just need to sit here and wait for Deke to pick us up."

She hit a switch, and the cockpit window flipped open. Zoe unbuckled her seat belt and then stood up on the seat. Eleanor did the same. From the higher vantage point, she could just barely see over the tall, alien foliage.

"There they are!" Eleanor said, pointing in the distance.

The ship was in the air and approaching them quickly.

"We'll be on board and out of here before you know it, kid," Zoe said.

Almost as soon as the words left her mouth, a stream of green flames fired up from the forest.

They engulfed the spaceship—melting it and its contents instantly.

Eleanor and Zoe could only watch in horror as what was left of Rodney, Deke, and the spaceship fell from the sky like a mercury rainstorm.

CHAPTER

67

Deep beneath the ocean, not far from where Eleanor had just witnessed her only possibility for a ride home getting melted right in front of her eyes, her older sister, Cordelia, could not keep the image of the Wind Witch zooming down toward Atlantis from her mind.

She and Adie had been woken from their sleep by a pleasant chime and a room-service breakfast of smoked fish and seaweed bread. Then Democritus ushered them out for a personal tour of the city.

But Cordelia knew they had to leave. She knew the dream had been no dream, but an actual vision into the Wind Witch's mind. She was there, now, somewhere in the city. And it wouldn't take long for her to find them.

Cordelia knew they needed to get out while they still could. They had to somehow get to the Eternal Abyss and retrieve what they came for before the Wind Witch got to them first. Not only that, but staying in the city much longer would endanger all the innocent inhabitants of Atlantis.

"This next building is the largest docking bay for Atlantis's fleet of vessels," Democritus said as they walked through another long, clear tunnel connecting the city's vast array of buildings.

They stepped into an especially cavernous building. Like the rest, it was essentially a massive, clear bubble built into the side of the underwater mountain. But this was by far the largest one yet. All along the outside walls were dozens of sleek ships like the one that had brought them there. In the center were hundreds of workers building or performing maintenance on several dozen more vessels.

"The city owns all of them?" Adie asked, barely above a whisper.

"Yes, and we allow every citizen to use them whenever they like," Democritus said. "After all, we can learn nothing new if we do not allow our citizens a means to travel and explore the world freely."

"Wow," Adie said.

It was a foreign concept for her. In Van Hook, Dakota Territory, and all the other towns across the prairie, every horse, carriage, or train was owned by someone looking to make a buck. It was even strange for Cordelia to consider. In San Francisco, the city had mass transit, sure, but it was still at least five dollars a ride.

"So if I wanted to take one of these ships to the Eternal Abyss, I could?" Cordelia asked.

She remembered very well what had happened last time she brought up the Abyss, but she had to keep pressing. The Wind Witch was after them; they had to hurry.

"No," Democritus said curtly. "These are only for *citizens*. Visitors may request transport to where they please, but never to the Eternal Abyss. It is in the Forbidden Zone. Why would you want to go there anyway? There is only death there."

"It's complicated," Cordelia said.

"Nobody who has traveled to the Eternal Abyss has ever returned alive," Democritus said. "The Iku-Turso consumes all life, all light, and shows no remorse or mercy."

"I'd take my chances," Cordelia muttered.

"You cannot go," Democritus said. "Do not speak of it again."

Cordelia sighed but nodded, and then followed silently once Democritus continued the tour. But she found herself continually looking at the sleek submarines lining the walls. Just sitting there, free for the taking. She knew she had to do something to get out of there. It was almost like the link between her and the Wind Witch was allowing her to *feel* the old crone's presence somewhere nearby.

Cordelia grabbed Adie's hand and began running toward the nearest Atlantisan submarine.

There were footsteps behind them, but she didn't stop or slow down. Instead, Cordelia ran even faster. Adie followed without questioning her. Once they got to the ship, she and Adie dove inside the already-open door. Cordelia remembered seeing Democritus press a small square of light on the clear wall when they'd first docked in the great city. She did the same and the door closed behind them.

Cordelia looked out and saw Democritus leading a group of alarmed Atlantisans toward her. They looked panicked, but still walked in a brisk yet dignified manner.

Cordelia stood at the front of the ship and studied the array of backlit controls and lights on the small console in front of her. It was covered in symbols she didn't recognize.

"Do you know how to fly this thing?" Adie asked.

"Of course not!" Cordelia shouted. "I'm just going to wing it. Pardon the pun."

"The pun?" Adie asked.

"Wing it. . . . Fly. . . . Never mind. Let's go!"

Cordelia pressed a button. Nothing happened. Then she pressed several more. Again, nothing. Democritus was standing just outside the ship now. She looked upset, but more worried than angry.

"If you go to the Forbidden Zone, you will die," she said

calmly. She didn't need to shout; even through the ship's walls, Cordelia heard her clearly.

"I have no other choice," Cordelia said. "Trust me, I'm going there for your own protection, for the safety of all Atlantisans."

Democritus frowned, but said nothing more.

Cordelia ran her hand along the console, pressing all the buttons until finally the ship slowly started moving forward, toward the outer shell of the huge bubble. It reached the edge and simply passed right through it as if there was nothing there.

And then, they were out in the dark ocean, slowly drifting away from the huge and bright hanger. Cordelia saw Democritus still standing there looking up at their vessel with disappointment and maybe even a little pity on her face. No ships were dispatched after them. They were not prisoners after all, but guests.

"Now what?" Adie asked as they drifted farther away from Atlantis and into the dark ocean behind them.

"I wish I knew," Cordelia said. "But at least we're hopefully getting away from the Wind Witch."

She turned around to face the black wall of deep sea.

Cordelia wasn't sure she had done the right thing. The Wind Witch was a terrifying creature, but because they were related, she couldn't actually kill Cordelia. She had tried before and failed. The dark ocean, housing deadly creatures like the Iku-Turso, however, followed no such rules. And to top it off, they were drifting aimlessly in a ship she didn't know how to pilot.

The truth was, Cordelia had probably just taken the two of them from a bad situation to an even worse one.

CHAPTER

68

The entrance to the pyramid containing Wazner's tomb was nothing more than an excavated opening in the side of a nearby hill just outside of Aswan.

"I thought you said we were going inside a pyramid?" Brendan said as he looked at the small opening in the hill-side dubiously.

"It's one of the *lost* pyramids," Sir Ed said.

"So . . . it's buried underground?" Brendan asked.

"Yes," Sir Ed said as he lit a torch. "If we spent years chipping away at the rock and dirt and sand and rubbish on the side of this hill, you'd eventually see the pyramid. But that's rather meaningless to us. All we care about is what lies inside, right?"

"Right," Brendan agreed.

"Let's get on with it, then," Sir Ed said, as he led them into the small opening of the lost pyramid.

Once inside, his lone torch was bright enough to illuminate the narrow tunnel at least ten yards ahead of them. The walls were lined with hieroglyphics and other drawings. Sir Ed moved cautiously in the lead, with Brendan behind him and Jumbo right on his heels.

"Careful," Sir Ed whispered. "The pyramid is rumored to be rigged with all sorts of deadly booby traps. It's doubtful any of them still work, but it's best to be cautious just the same."

Brendan was suddenly aware of every single step as they slowly crept deeper into the pyramid. After thirty or forty yards, they reached a fork that split into three alternate paths. Sir Ed pulled out his copy of the Nazi treasure map, holding it closer to the torch.

Brendan noticed that Sir Ed had drawn over the secret, hidden lines on the map with a pencil so they were more visible. The Englishman led them down the left branch.

A few steps down the passageway, Brendan's foot landed on a loose stone tile in the floor and sunk down several inches. The stone block crunched as it slid into the floor. He was about to take another step, when Sir Ed stopped him.

"Don't take another step!" Sir Ed shouted, his eyes wide with fear.

"Why?" Brendan asked.

"Do you hear that?" Sir Ed asked.

Brendan listened carefully. From within the walls echoed the sound of ancient mechanics and grinding stone gears.

"You just activated a booby trap," Sir Ed said. "Take one more step and it will surely be your last."

CHAPTER

69

"What do I do?" Brendan asked, panic causing him to wobble unsteadily.

His foot was on top of a stone block that had depressed four inches into the floor.

"Stay calm, for one thing, boy!" Sir Ed said, grabbing his shoulder to steady him. "We'll figure this out. Nobody is getting left behind."

He crouched down near Brendan's foot and examined the stone block. Then he passed the torch along the nearby walls. There were holes near the ceiling all along the corridor with drawings underneath them. He examined the symbols carefully and then faced Brendan and Jumbo again with a worried look on his face.

"Oh dear, this is much worse than I thought," he said.

"What do you mean?" Brendan asked.

"It's so sad," Jumbo sighed. "I feel like I had so much to learn from you."

"Hey, try to be a little more positive!" Brendan said.

Sir Ed ignored them and instead walked several more paces down the corridor, holding the torch up near the ceiling. He came back a short time later and referred to his map again briefly.

"We may be able to make a slight detour up ahead before it consumes us," Sir Ed murmured to himself.

"Before *what* consumes us?" Brendan asked.

"This chamber is going to flood with liquid death," Sir Ed said.

"Liquid death?" Brendan cried.

"Well, the translation may be a little wonky, but yes, I'm afraid so," Sir Ed said. "However, we do have a slim chance of escaping alive. On the count of three, start running. Follow me, follow my every move. There is a passage up ahead that will take us up and away from this level . . . and hopefully to safety. Ready?"

Brendan and Jumbo both nodded.

"Okay," Sir Ed said. "One, two . . . three!"

He began sprinting down the corridor with Jumbo right behind him. Brendan stepped off the trigger stone and followed. The walls creaked and moaned. A thick, smoking black liquid, almost like tar, began oozing down the walls all around them from the small holes near the ceiling.

"Don't let it touch you!" Sir Ed shouted back.

Brendan took bounding leaps over the growing puddles of black ooze that pooled on the floor around them. He glanced back. A huge wave of liquid death had formed, bubbling and churning as if it were alive, racing after them like a black tsunami.

"It's gaining on us!" Brendan shouted.

But when he looked ahead again, the corridor was empty. Sir Ed and Jumbo had disappeared! He was about to give up and let the growing flood of black gunk overtake him, when a hand fired out from a narrow passage to his left and grabbed his shirt, pulling him into another corridor. The wave of black poison missed Brendan by inches.

"You need to move faster, boy," Sir Ed shouted, his face inches away. "Now come along then!"

Brendan followed Sir Ed and Jumbo up a narrow set of stairs that wound their way slowly up in a loose spiral. All Brendan saw were orange flames from the torch, stone steps, and shadows. He wasn't sure how high they'd gone, when suddenly they emerged into a cavernous chamber, breathing hard and sweating.

Human-shaped sarcophaguses lined the walls around them. Pottery and jewels were scattered across the chamber floor and along built-in stone shelves. In the center of the chamber lay a massive, sealed tomb—carved, painted, and decorated with great care and precision.

Sir Ed panted as he ran his hand along the top of it.

"Wazner's tomb," he said.

Brendan, Jumbo, and Sir Ed stared in awe at the ancient tomb.

"Shall we open it?" Sir Ed asked as he handed Jumbo the torch. He opened his backpack and pulled out a crowbar. He wedged it under the tomb's lid and began to pry it open. There was a loud, painful creak as it started to give.

Just then, a pair of bony arms wrapped around Brendan's torso.

"Look, Jumbo," Brendan sighed. "I'm still tired from the fistfight. . . . I'm not sure we need to have a wrestling match as well."

Brendan turned and saw Jumbo a few feet away from him, still holding the torch with both hands. Sir Ed was beside his young assistant, prying open the lid of Wazner's sarcophagus.

"Wait . . . if this isn't Jumbo . . . then who . . . ," Brendan said, his voice rising.

Jumbo screamed, and Sir Ed's eyes widened with fear in the glow of the torch's flames.

"Oh dear God!" Sir Ed cried, staring at Brendan in terror.

Brendan slowly turned his head back as the arms

tightened, and he struggled to breathe. He saw the empty sarcophagus first. And then he found himself face-to-face with a head wrapped entirely in browned linen.

It was a mummy. And it was literally squeezing the life right out of him.

CHAPTER 70

Inside the book world of *The Terror on Planet 5X*, the last of the liquefied remains of Zoe's ship fell from the sky. Eleanor's scream faded as her last hope of escape vanished right before her eyes.

She expected Zoe to break down completely. After all, she had just watched her own brother and spaceship get destroyed.

But Zoe did not do that. Instead, she shook her head slowly from side to side as if she were mildly disappointed and nothing more.

"I always told him he flew that thing too low," Zoe said quietly.

"What are we going to do?" Eleanor asked weakly, still

panicking. "How will we ever get out of here? I need to get to Tinz to meet up with my brother and sister again."

Zoe looked at Eleanor, still showing no signs of grief over the loss of her brother. She seemed too calm. But even still, Zoe's lack of panic was gradually easing Eleanor out of a full hyperventilation.

"You need to go to Tinz?" Zoe asked.

"You've heard of Tinz?" Eleanor asked, shocked.

"Of course," Zoe replied with a benevolent smile. "And I can get you there."

"How?"

"We can fly," Zoe said.

"But, the ship . . . ," Eleanor said, pointing up into the empty space where Zoe's ship had been just minutes before. But something was happening to Zoe that silenced Eleanor completely.

Small cracks slivered across Zoe's face like broken glass. It was happening to her hands and neck as well. Then her space suit cracked, until eventually she looked like a shattered human vase that had been hastily glued back together. Slowly the shards began to fall away. There was something underneath, something she recognized all too well.

As the last jagged piece of Zoe's exterior fell away, all Eleanor could do was scream.

"Did you miss me?" the Wind Witch asked.

CHAPTER

71

Eleanor shook her head in disbelief. She almost retched in revulsion.

"Oh, come now, I don't look that bad, do I?" the Wind Witch taunted.

The truth was, she did. She looked worse than ever. Her skin was so thin and ragged that Eleanor could make out every ridge and curve of her eye sockets and cheekbones. Her pallor was an unimaginable mixture of rot and gloss. When the old hag smiled, her brown teeth looked sharp and nasty.

"How?" was all Eleanor managed to say.

"Don't you remember?" the Wind Witch said. "I told you some time ago that I have many aliases in the book worlds."

Eleanor wanted to run away. She wanted to run right toward the approaching UWOs and let herself be melted down into a steaming puddle of Eleanor. But *something* stopped her. She didn't understand why or how, but part of her was secretly happy to see the Wind Witch. Part of her wanted to stay with the Wind Witch—it would certainly be better than being left completely alone again. The realization made her want to puke. Had her stomach not been so empty, she might have.

"You feel it, don't you?" the Wind Witch asked with a crooked smile. "You feel the pull of family, of our *connection*."

Eleanor nodded weakly.

"That's because I *chose* you, Nell," the Wind Witch said. "You're the most reasonable, the smartest Walker. You've always been my favorite. Even though you're the youngest, wasn't it you who was clever enough to wish away *The Book of Doom and Desire* forever so I couldn't get my hands on it? And yet, what thanks did that get you? Your brother and sister stranded you here on the most dangerous planet, with a murderous outlaw. They left you all alone. To die. How is that fair?"

Eleanor shook her head. She didn't have an answer, because there wasn't one. The Wind Witch was right; her siblings did treat her badly. They never gave her any credit and assumed she was useless. Even when they first got here and she saved them from the Wind Witch's onslaught, they hadn't believed her. They were nice to her, sure, but they didn't truly respect her intelligence. They didn't respect her as an equal. Cordelia was just a smug know-it-all and Brendan a glory hog.

"I respect you, Nell," the Wind Witch said. "To me, you are my equal, maybe even destined to be greater than I am. We both know it was you who blasted me out of the fireplace a few days ago. Now is the time for you to fulfill your destiny, to become as powerful as we both know you are. Help rule the book world with me, and I promise I can even bring your dear friend Fat Jagger back to life. I can make all your wishes and dreams come true."

The Wind Witch held out her gnarled old hand.

Eleanor looked at it and hesitated. But she knew that she was pointlessly fighting the inevitable. The Wind Witch had been right about everything. She may as well give in and stop worrying so much.

It could be argued that there were many reasons why Eleanor did what she did next. Insecurity. The fear of being alone. An attempt to get closer to her enemy only to betray her in the end. But none of those would be accurate. The reality was that much of what the Wind Witch had said was, indeed, true. And perhaps with a complete soul, Eleanor still could have resisted. But, as her brother Brendan had already suspected after reading much of Denver's *Journal*, Eleanor's soul was not complete. It had been severely

corrupted. Such was the power of *The Book of Doom and Desire.*

And so Eleanor reached out and grabbed the Wind Witch's hand.

CHAPTER
72

Just a few miles away, a clear submarine drifted listlessly through a seemingly endless ocean, its two occupants wholly unaware of Eleanor's transformation and new allegiance. The only thing on their minds was the bleak reality of their current situation.

"What are we going to do?" Adie asked as tears streamed down her face.

She was normally so calm and optimistic, but Cordelia had messed up so badly now that even Adie couldn't put a positive spin on it.

Adie was so upset that she didn't even notice that Cordelia's eyes had turned icy blue. It didn't even occur to Adie to use the black scarf Brendan had given them to prevent the Wind Witch from seeing what was happening to them.

They had drifted so far away from Atlantis that the massive city was nothing but a small, hazy dot of blue light somewhere in the distance behind them. Cordelia still hadn't figured out where the Eternal Abyss was located. And she couldn't navigate the submarine. They were basically drifting away into the depths of the ocean to die a slow death in a tomb of darkness.

"I was hoping we'd see some sign of the Eternal Abyss, or the Forbidden Zone, but . . . ," Cordelia said, putting her face into her hands. "I'm so sorry."

She was just about ready to let the dam break and start bawling, when movement outside caught her eye. Adie saw it too, and they both stepped closer to the rear of the clear vessel to get a better look.

There was a second light off in the distance, back toward Atlantis. But this light was growing larger. It was getting closer to them.

"They sent someone to save us!" Adie said, wiping away tears.

"Somehow I doubt that," Cordelia said, the icy blue once again fading from her eyes.

She had seen the look on Democritus's face pretty clearly: She was going to allow them to leave. But that was all. From then on, their friendship would be severed. Cordelia had understood that, but had followed through anyway, like a fool.

"Then who is it?" Adie asked. "Or . . . what is it?"

Cordelia didn't have an answer, so they just stood there and waited for the approaching light to reach them.

It didn't take long to figure out that it was another ship from Atlantis. It pulled up alongside them. The pilot was a young woman in her late teens or early twenties (at least in human years—Cordelia had no idea how time worked down there).

The Atlantisan waved at them.

The two ships drifted together. Instead of a collision, they linked up, as if each one had been slathered in waterproof superglue. A doorway appeared, officially merging the two vessels together as one.

"You look like you need help," the girl said as she crossed over into their vessel.

"We're saved!" Adie said.

The visitor smiled at Adie. For a moment her expression faltered, almost as if she recognized the small girl from somewhere. But then the smile returned in full and she faced Cordelia.

"My name is Anapos," she said.

"I'm Adie." Adie waved. "This is Cordelia. She's a little speechless, I guess."

Anapos laughed. It sounded almost musical to Cordelia, and it caused the worry and uneasiness of their visitor's sudden appearance to drain out of her and into the floor like liquid.

"I know who you are!" Anapos said. "I've been watching you very closely. Everyone in Atlantis was—we don't get many visitors there, believe it or not. But I sensed something unique about you right away. And when I heard that you stole a ship and drifted out into the ocean to find the Eternal Abyss, I knew that my instincts were correct. There was something very special about you, Cordelia."

"So you've come to stop us?" Cordelia asked.

"No," Anapos said. "I've come to take you to the Eternal Abyss."

"Really?" Cordelia asked. "Why are you helping us? Democritus said it was a horrible place where nobody ever leaves alive. Why would you risk your life for strangers? Aren't you afraid like everyone else?"

Anapos grinned.

"Is everyone where you're from exactly the same as one another?" Anapos asked, before stepping back into her own submarine.

Adie and Cordelia exchanged a glance before following her. They watched the door close behind them, and then they detached from the submarine they'd stolen and it drifted away into the darkness.

"The truth is, I'm helping you because I relate to you," Anapos said as she pressed several buttons. The vessel began accelerating through the black water. "My people, they've become too comfortable. We live in what is arguably one of the most beautiful places in the universe. But we don't aspire to *become* anything greater. We just live our lives trapped in the beauty of our surroundings, but it holds us back! I have spent my entire life yearning for something more. And I see that you aspire to do great things as well, Cordelia. That's why I want to help you; I want to get out of here. I want to go on and explore the world."

There was a long pause before Cordelia responded. The accuracy of Anapos's response nearly knocked Cordelia off her feet. Hearing someone tell her exactly how she'd always felt about the world was as eye-opening as a whiff of smelling salts . . . or Brendan's dirty lacrosse socks. It was true, back at school she was teased and taunted for being a know-it-all, for trying too hard. For being an overachiever and teacher's pet. She'd even been called *arrogant* in class by her own seventh-grade history teacher because she'd corrected his mistakes several times during his lectures. But if she didn't believe in herself and demand more, then how would she ever get to where she wanted in life—to be a great scientist, or a world leader, or one of the preeminent academics of her time? She wouldn't, and Anapos totally understood that.

"That's how I've always felt," Cordelia said. "But it's rare that I meet other people who feel the same way."

"I know, me too," Anapos said. "But, I do need to ask you this: Why in the holy name of his greatness, Poseidon himself, do you want to go to the Eternal Abyss?"

"We're searching for something," Adie said.

"What?" Anapos asked, a mischievous gleam in her eyes. Or maybe it was just reflecting water from the hull lights?

"Something called a Worldkeeper," Cordelia said slowly. "Have you heard of it?"

"I'm afraid not," Anapos said. "But it sounds important."

"It is," Cordelia said. "It has the ability to save my world, my home. My family."

"Then I shall help you find it," Anapos said.

"Have you ever been to the Eternal Abyss?" Adie asked.

"No, no one is allowed to go since it's in the Forbidden Zone," Anapos said. "Nobody has ever returned from there alive. But I've always wanted to go. To me, a Forbidden Zone is exactly where I want to be. Because it's certain to be exciting and adventurous."

Cordelia looked out into the dark sea where the ship's lights illuminated only about twenty feet of visibility. The water contained more silt than ever. She soon realized she could see the ocean floor.

"Are we there?" Adie asked.

"No, but we're getting very close," Anapos said quietly, fear genuinely creeping into her voice now.

"How deep are we?" Cordelia asked.

"Eight thousand four hundred sixty meters," Anapos said.

There wasn't an appropriate reply so the three of them remained silent, their eyes scanning the flat seafloor in front of them. There were no signs of life. Then the sandy seabed was gone and they were hovering over a vast ravine with rocky sides that plunged down into nothingness.

Anapos hit a few buttons on the console and then they were descending into the depths of the Eternal Abyss. It widened slightly as they got deeper, and Cordelia could barely make out the walls of the canyon on either side of them.

"How will we find it?" Adie asked, pulling out the papers Brendan had given them. They just said that the World-keeper was somewhere within the Eternal Abyss. Nothing else. No other clues.

Cordelia shook her head.

"I'm less worried about that, and more concerned with the Iku-Turso," Anapos said quietly.

Adie's sudden scream caused all three of them to jump.

"It's okay," Anapos said, holding a hand over her heart. "It's just a nine-gill shark."

"That's a shark?" Cordelia asked.

"Yes, and they're perfectly harmless," Anapos said. "As long as we stay inside the vessel."

Harmless? Cordelia and Adie thought, as they nervously

watched the large shark, larger than any great white Cordelia had seen on Shark Week before, pass lazily over their submarine. It had a rounded head, nine gills, and a long, swishing tail fin. It passed them slowly and was maybe fifteen feet ahead when a huge pair of jaws containing hundreds of razor-sharp teeth, each as large as Adie, shot up from the black depths below them and clamped down onto the shark's midsection.

The jaws were gnarled and bare and belonged to a massive creature that resembled a crocodile—a crocodile the size of two city buses. It held on to the shark and began shaking it from side to side, sending blood spiraling away in all directions.

Anapos stopped the vessel, as Adie's screams became weak whimpers. They could see the entire creature now, and it looked remarkably like a crocodile with fins instead of feet.

"Is that the Iku-Turso?" Cordelia asked.

"No," Anapos said.

As if on cue, a third creature, this one larger than any animal Cordelia had ever seen before, zoomed up from the depths of the abyss. It was large enough to swallow their entire submarine like a piece of popcorn. It looked like a spiky-finned whale with a human head full of jagged and long black teeth, a massive rack of antlers, and a beard made of electrified blue tentacles. It was the most horrific and bizarre creature she'd ever seen, and it was so massive that she was convinced it could have easily gobbled up a colossus like Fat Jagger in just a few bites. As if to prove the point, it gracefully and swiftly swooped in and bit off the entire lower half of the giant swimming crocodile in one quick chomp.

"*That's* the Iku-Turso," Anapos said.

CHAPTER

73

Deep within a hillside just outside of Aswan, Egypt, Brendan struggled to free himself from a mummy's death hug.

"A mummy!" Brendan shouted, fighting against the dead skeleton's surprisingly strong arms. "And he smells like my sister's gym socks!"

"Why would you know what your sister's socks smell like?" Jumbo asked as he rushed over to help, Sir Ed right behind him.

Brendan didn't have time to answer. Instead he took a step back and tried to crush the mummy against the wall, but the mummy didn't budge. For something that weighed probably eighty pounds of literal skin and bones, it felt like pressing up against a semitruck.

Jumbo pulled at the mummy's arms, but couldn't dislodge them. It was squeezing so hard that Brendan couldn't breathe at all, rendering him unable to cry out for help or even wheeze. He was silently suffocating.

That's when he saw the knife. Sir Ed pulled a sharp dagger from his bag and plunged it deep into the middle of the mummy's face, causing its head to explode into a shower of dust, bone, and tattered scraps of cloth. The mummy's grip went limp, and the body crumpled to the ground.

Brendan screamed in pain and covered his right ear with his hand, dropping to the ground next to the mummy's body. The dagger had grazed Brendan's ear. He pulled back his hand and saw blood on his fingertips.

And the bottom of his severed earlobe, which he had already lost once before during their previous adventures.

"Not again!" he shouted, climbing to his feet.

Blood dripped onto his shirt. Sir Ed and Jumbo stepped in front of him. They were shouting but Brendan couldn't hear anything since he was in shock. Their faces were panicked and they pulled at his arm.

All of the sarcophaguses were open and black and gray and brown mummies started staggering toward them from all directions. The tomb in the center slid open and another mummy sat up, wearing an ornate gold-and-jade mask. The eyes glowed red, and it pointed a long, bony finger right at them.

It was King Wazner. And he wanted his revenge. For what, Brendan wasn't sure. But he doubted that the undead pharaoh would take the time to sort out who was actually responsible for whatever it was he was so angry about.

So when Sir Ed and Jumbo took off running, Brendan followed them.

Sir Ed pulled out a pistol and shot several mummies as he ran. One was hit in the torso. It didn't even slow it down. The other took a hit to the neck, blasting it to pieces. The head rolled off and landed at Brendan's feet. He hurtled it easily and followed Sir Ed and Jumbo through an opening adjacent to the one they'd entered.

The mummies were in close pursuit behind them in the corridor. Wazner was among them, the eyes of the mask still glowing in the darkness beyond the reach of Sir Ed's torch. Brendan heard muffled shouting and looked forward again.

A mummy had seemingly come out of nowhere and grabbed Jumbo's shirt. He screamed for help as the mummy pulled him closer. It raised its other arm, but Sir Ed pounded the mummy over the head with his torch, knocking the creature away.

In his panic and rush to save Jumbo, Brendan stumbled and fell, tripping over a mummified cat which was now trying to claw his ankle to shreds through its wrapping, which tickled more than hurt.

The mummy that had grabbed Jumbo was now in flames and stumbling down an adjacent corridor ablaze, lighting the path like a moving torch.

Another mummy suddenly grabbed Brendan's head with two strong hands, stopping him from climbing to his feet. It began to twist Brendan's head violently.

"*Heeeelp!*" Brendan screamed, desperately trying to keep his head attached to his body.

Sir Ed narrowed his eyes and fired off several rounds into the mummy's face, decimating its dusty and ancient head. The mummy fell to the ground, its lifeless arms releasing the grip on Brendan's skull.

A hand grabbed Brendan's shirt and hauled him to his feet. He was vaguely aware that Sir Ed seemed to be growing increasingly annoyed with his total incompetence. And Brendan supposed he had a right to be—he was embarrassed. He had portrayed himself as this great leader, yet some dandy college professor kept rescuing him. Sir Ed was the real hero. This was how you were supposed to take charge. Brendan was like a double-A pinch runner compared to Sir Ed's major league ace of the pitching staff.

But there wasn't really time to mope about it right then, since countless more mummies were still coming after them, now running like Olympic sprinters, and screaming in high-pitched, unearthly voices. They were out for revenge and blood. And they were gaining on them quickly.

Sir Ed shoved Brendan down the hall toward Jumbo, who was already sprinting ahead and diving out of the grasp of a passing mummy. Determined to finally rise up and be the hero he knew he could be, Brendan shoulder-checked it into the wall. The ancient mummy practically disintegrated on impact. It was more satisfying than any lacrosse hit he'd ever delivered.

At the end of a passageway, Sir Ed began kicking a loosened stone in the wall. Brendan and Jumbo joined him until a small opening was created. They clambered through it, seconds ahead of the mummies. As the mummies tried to make their way through, Sir Ed rolled a huge stone in front of it, keeping the undead Egyptians out. For now.

Finally able to catch their breaths, Sir Ed, Jumbo, and Brendan continued down the newly discovered secret passage. It was a short hallway that ended at a massive wooden door. Sir Ed pressed it open, and the three of them stepped into a large chamber.

Their faces were lit up with reflected golden light.

"We did it!" Sir Ed cried, setting the torch in a crevice on the wall.

The chamber was fairly large, perhaps as big as a standard school classroom. And it was filled with all sorts of treasures. Old paintings that Brendan could only assume were stolen from museums across Nazi-occupied France, and were likely worth a fortune. Treasure chests full of old bonds, cash, and jewelry. Stacks and stacks of gold bars covered in dust lined the back wall.

Brendan had no idea how he was going to sort through all of it to find the Worldkeeper. Jumbo and Sir Ed were already wrist-deep inside several chests full of coins and jewels. As much as he wanted to join them, he knew that this was one of those moments that counted . . . where he needed to do the right thing as opposed to what he wanted to do, which was stuff his own pockets with gold and jewels and lost treasures like Jumbo and Sir Ed.

But the *right* thing was to forget all of that and simply find the Worldkeeper. Brendan started by discreetly pulling out Denver's *Journal* from his back pocket. He reread the description of the Worldkeeper inside *Wazner's Revenge*.

No mortally made substance can withstand it's wicked edges.

He reread this sentence several times. It was essentially the only line that even remotely described what the item was. At first he was frustrated that it was so vague, but then he took a deep breath and reminded himself what was on the line. Even if it didn't say what it was, he could use it to figure out what it definitely *wasn't*. The process of elimination—his best friend when taking multiple-choice exams he hadn't studied for in class.

The Worldkeeper was infinitely powerful and had wicked

edges. Based on that, Brendan could already eliminate half the things in sight, including the paintings, gold coins, bonds, cash, and stacks of silver and gold bars. He glanced over at Sir Ed and Jumbo, who were digging through piles of treasure with enough glee to remind him of the Christmas when he was eight years old and got his first Xbox. He'd been so excited, he ran up and down the stairs holding the machine, still in the box, over his head and screaming like the lead singer in an all-female metal band. His mom had recorded the whole thing and made extended family watch it every few years to his increasing horror and embarrassment. It had been one of his life's biggest goals to keep the video off of YouTube.

"Jumbo, look at this!" Sir Ed said, holding up a chalice encrusted with jewels.

But Jumbo barely looked up. He seemed to be on a mission to find something specific. He dug through a pile of old crystal and china with reckless abandon, tossing most of the items to the side as if they were junk instead of invaluable dinnerware.

Brendan had a weird feeling that Jumbo might be looking for exactly the same thing he was, which meant he needed to stop standing there like a frozen mime and get back to work.

He dropped to his knees and pried open an old trunk near him. The undead mummies and vengeful pharaoh still lurking somewhere inside the vast network of pyramid chambers and passages were nearly forgotten at the moment.

The chest was mostly full of old garments: clothes and robes that looked as if they might have been worn by ancient French royalty. Garments that were no doubt worth more than a whole fleet of Maseratis. Brendan tossed most of them aside, but snatched a silk handkerchief to tie around his ear like a headband to stop the bleeding. He moved on to a smaller treasure chest behind the large trunk.

The box contained a mixture of old jewels, a crown, several jewel-encrusted scepters and something so striking that it nearly stopped his heart. Not just due to its appearance, which was magnificent, but mostly because as soon as he saw it, he *knew* it was the Worldkeeper. It was almost like he could feel its power before he even touched it.

It was a knife. But clearly no ordinary knife. It had a gold handle with several large red gemstones set near the hilt. The blade itself didn't appear to be made of any metal Brendan had ever seen—it was incandescent and clear, almost as if it was constructed entirely of diamond. It sparkled in the light from the torch as if it were glowing, alive, and had its own bioluminescence. It was around ten inches long and curved at the tip, forming a wicked-looking *U*—as if it were designed specifically to savagely rip open the bellies of enemies. *Invictum* was etched into the handle.

Brendan reached out and slowly picked up the knife. The handle was hot in spite of spending years inside a dank and cool chamber underground. It almost felt like it was on fire, and Brendan had to resist the urge to drop it. He quickly reached behind him and grabbed an elaborately patterned, ornate velvet scarf from the huge clothes trunk

and wrapped it around the knife. He stuffed it under his shirt and pinned it to his body with his left arm.

Brendan knew that even if this wasn't what Jumbo was so frantically searching for, it was unlikely they were just going to let him have it. It was clearly the most remarkable item among the treasures. It was obvious just from looking at it. The knife had an actual *presence*.

"I need to use the bathroom," Brendan suddenly announced.

"I'm certain you won't find any modern conveniences in here," Sir Ed said, annoyed at the distraction. He was too busy making a mental inventory of their finds to worry about Brendan.

"I drank too much water back there," said Brendan, hopping up and down on one foot.

"Do what you need to do," Sir Ed said, pointing at the door. "Out there, away from us."

Brendan nodded and then carefully stepped out into the dark hallway, the Invictum still clutched under his arm, inside his shirt. He thought about trying to weave his way back out of the labyrinth of pyramid chambers and corridors in the complete dark with vicious mummies and pools of liquid death still on the prowl.

Clearly not an option.

But where did that leave him? He pulled out the small device Gilbert had given him in case he needed help.

"What's the worst that could happen?" he muttered to himself and then pressed the button.

Several seconds later, he felt the ground rumbling beneath his feet. He grabbed the wall to steady himself and the ceiling above him caved in with a thunderous crash.

CHAPTER

74

Far away, across a vast expanse of the book world, Cordelia also felt like she was being crushed. Not by a collapsed pyramid, however, but instead by the sheer terror of a monster so huge and overwhelming that it seemed to absorb all light nearby, leaving the world around it draped in black.

Cordelia wasn't sure what she had expected the Iku-Turso to be. She'd been so worried about simply finding the Eternal Abyss that she hadn't stopped to actually consider what might be guarding it. But now she was certain that she couldn't have possibly imagined anything half as horrifying as it was in reality.

The Iku-Turso was massive, bigger than a blue whale,

which Cordelia knew was the largest single animal in existence in her own world. And she'd had a sense of the scale ever since fourth grade, when some save-the-whales organization brought in a huge, inflatable replica of a blue whale to their school and all the kids got to walk through it to see how big they actually were.

This beast was easily as large as that, if not larger. It had a body shape similar to a whale's, but that's where all similarities ended. The Iku-Turso had a big head, like a human's head, with a mouth filled with multiple rows of jagged teeth. But it also had a series of massive horns protruding from it like antlers, and thousands of long tentacles coming from the bottom of its jaws like a beard. The tentacles moved on their own and flashed with little jagged lines of blue electricity. Cordelia didn't even need to touch them to guess that they had a paralyzing effect on its victims. Horns and spikes ran down the length of its spine, ending in a tail covered in razor-sharp bones. It had three sets of fins, and swam and dove through the water with surprising speed and grace—almost like it was going through a ballet routine.

It dipped, circled around, and finished off the other half of the massive crocodile sea-creature in one deadly bite. Then it spun around and faced the submarine containing Adie, Anapos, and Cordelia: a light dessert.

"We should probably start trying to get away now," Cordelia said.

"Could not agree more," Anapos said, putting both hands on the control console. "Buckle up."

Two chairs opened up from the floor behind Anapos. Adie and Cordelia ran to them, sat down, and then strapped in using shoulder harnesses made from interlocked and dried seaweeds.

As soon as their buckles clicked into place, the ship immediately began a sharp nosedive deeper into the abyss. Cordelia had been on several roller coasters in her life, and the rush of plunging into the Eternal Abyss made them feel like a simple drive down steep California Avenue in downtown San Francisco.

Adie was screaming next to her. This was, essentially, her first-ever roller-coaster ride as they suddenly pulled up and then began spinning and diving and dipping every which way within the abyss. Several times, Cordelia was convinced they were going to crash into the wall of the trench ridges, but Anapos always pulled up or spun away at the last possible moment. It didn't take long for Cordelia to be screaming right alongside Adie.

She craned her head around and saw a glimpse of the horrible, spiny beast in close pursuit. Each time it snapped its massive jaws at the ship, it came closer and closer to crushing it between its teeth.

Then it did finally manage to clamp its jaws around the ship, and for a moment they were looking at the back side of its teeth from inside its mouth. But Anapos managed to spin them right through a small gap in its teeth and back out into the open water a few seconds later.

Cordelia had to mentally will herself to breathe again.

"I can't keep this thing off us," Anapos yelled. "It's too quick!"

"What's that, down there?" Cordelia asked, pointing at a faint light deep below them.

"No idea," Anapos said.

"It might be our only hope," Adie said, looking back and seeing the Iku-Turso gaining on them.

Anapos pressed the throttle forward and the ship rocketed deeper into the abyss toward the strange light. Cordelia had no idea what sort of technology the Atlantisans had developed, but she knew that any human-made vessel would have been crushed down to the size of a soup can by now this deep underwater. It was as if the vessel were completely impervious to any of the pressure effects of the deep ocean.

They gathered more speed as they descended, actually gaining a little bit of ground on the Iku-Turso. Of course, they all knew they'd never have a chance outrunning him back out of the deep trench. But that was a problem for later . . . if there ever was a later.

As they approached the light near the bottom of the abyss, they noticed two things: They were nowhere near the "bottom" of the abyss—the depths below them stretched on seemingly forever, in spite of the fact that they had to have been twice as deep as the Mariana Trench by now—which in the real world would have put them past the boundary of the earth's core. Secondly, the faint blue light was coming from a small opening in the sidewall of the deep abyss. It was an entrance to an underwater cave containing some unknown source of pale blue light.

"Is the cave opening large enough for our ship?" Cordelia asked.

"We're about to find out," Anapos said, dragging a hand across the control panel.

The command sent the submarine spiraling into a right-angled turn at near breakneck speed. As they approached the cave opening, Cordelia realized that it was much larger than it had looked. She panicked and considered the possibility that they were about to drive directly into the Iku-Turso's lair.

But it was too late now—the massive creature was still bearing down on them and approaching so quickly it gave Cordelia motion sickness to look up at its open jaws and electric tentacle beard.

Anapos drove them into the cave. The pale blue light was still visible somewhere up ahead, deeper inside the underwater cavern. Adie looked back, her mouth dropping open in terror.

"Look out!" she screamed.

Cordelia and Anapos spun around and gasped as they found themselves staring directly into one of the beast's glowing red-and-yellow eyes. Nothing existed behind it but malice and death. Its tentacles streamed into the cave toward the vessel, and the three occupants screamed as the ends sizzled with blue arcs of electricity.

75

Back in the pyramid containing Wazner's lost tomb, Brendan stood and blinked uncertainly at the hole in the ceiling that Gilbert had just blasted above him. It ran all the way up to the surface. He could see a dot of pale blue sky at least six or seven hundred feet above, at the end of the long, hollow tunnel that had suddenly appeared.

The ceiling hadn't actually caved in like he first thought. Instead, the rock and dirt and clay simply seemed to incinerate as Gilbert's ship passed right through it.

The tiny door in the sphere opened and Gilbert poked his head out.

"Hello, Brendan," he said.

Brendan never thought in a million years he'd be so

happy to see a pretentious alien.

"What in the name of the queen is that thing?" Sir Ed shouted from the now-open doorway behind him.

The British explorer fumbled for his gun.

Brendan crouched down and dove inside the small spherical spaceship.

"Shall I telepathically vector-force implode that man?" Gilbert asked.

"No, he's a good dude; let's just get out of here!" Brendan said as Sir Ed took aim with his pistol.

Gilbert pressed a button, and the ship fired up into the sky with enough speed to almost knock Brendan unconscious. He sat up once they were up in the clouds and had slowed down. He pulled out the Invictum and grinned. He did it! He'd actually succeeded in getting the Worldkeeper.

He saw Gilbert staring at him with his beady, black eyes.

"I did it, Gilbert!" Brendan said. "I got the Worldkeeper!"

"I knew you would succeed," Gilbert said.

"Really?" Brendan asked, touched at the alien's confidence in him.

"Of course," Gilbert replied. "You may be a most unattractive species, but you are also quite resourceful and resilient for possessing such primitive brains."

"Uh, thanks?" Brendan said.

"Now, where is our ensuing destination?" Gilbert asked.

Brendan smiled and handed his new little friend the map of the book world.

"See that dot labeled Tinz?" Brendan said. "We need to go there. It's time to meet back up with my family!"

CHAPTER

76

Deep inside Wazner's Pyramid, Sir Ed looked up through the huge hole that the strange sphere that had eaten the boy had flown through. He shook his head in disbelief. Animated mummies, duplicate treasure maps, odd spheres with strange little martians inside of them? He lived for adventure, sure, but this was almost too much!

He stumbled back inside the treasure chamber.

"Did you see that?" he asked Jumbo. "It was like something out of an H. G. Wells novel."

Jumbo wasn't paying attention at all, however. He was still frantically tossing things aside inside the chamber. He threw one gold bar so hard that it punched a hole right through three invaluable paintings stacked near the far wall.

"Brendan took it!" Jumbo screamed.

"Took what?" Sir Ed asked. "What are you so upset about? And how do you know the boy's name? I don't believe he ever formally introduced himself . . . typical American . . ."

Jumbo looked up at him, his eyes smoldering in a way Sir Ed had never seen before. This was not his usual assistant anymore. He was someone or *something* else entirely.

"The Invictum!" Jumbo hissed. "You let him get away with it!"

Sir Ed took a frightened step backward, holding up his hands.

"I don't know what you're talking about," Sir Ed said, realizing now that Jumbo was somehow holding his pistol. "Jumbo, my boy, I don't know why you're acting so irrationally . . . but I beg you, put the gun down. . . ."

Jumbo screamed in rage and pulled the trigger.

CHAPTER

77

Deep within a hidden cave inside the Eternal Abyss, Cordelia, Adie, and Anapos's screaming slowly subsided as they realized the Iku-Turso's beard tentacles were going to fall short of the submarine. They were parked well out of the beast's range. And the cave opening, despite being large enough to fit a huge military submarine through, was nowhere near accommodating the impressive girth of the Iku-Turso.

So they watched as the giant beast swam in circles back and forth in front of the cave's opening, apparently content to sit there and wait for their inevitable exit.

"Come on," Anapos said. "Let's find out what that blue light is."

Cordelia nodded and patted Adie's arm.

"How are you doing?"

The girl's eyes were wide and she gripped her seat as if she'd never let go. And then, slowly, her mouth opened and she uttered, "Well, that was sort of fun."

There was a pause, and then suddenly the three of them fell into fits of laughter. The tension was momentarily broken.

As Anapos steered the ship through the massive underwater cave, the blue light ahead of them remained frustratingly faint. But after a few minutes, Cordelia realized that it was, in fact, getting brighter.

Eventually, the light was so bright that it was practically on top of them. But they'd reached the end of the tunnel. They stared straight ahead at nothing but a solid rock wall—there was nowhere else to go.

"What now?" Cordelia asked, looking up at the nearly blinding light.

"I think there's an unflooded cavern above us," Anapos said.

The ship slowly rose and emerged from the water inside a large, dry cave with bright orange-and-green stalactites and stalagmites scattered throughout it like colorful sets of teeth. Ahead of them, sitting on a small boulder with a flat surface was the source of light that had led them there. And instantly Cordelia knew it was the Worldkeeper they'd come there to find.

"That's it . . . ," Cordelia said quietly. "That's what we came here for!"

"It's so beautiful," Adie said.

It was small and round, but glowed blue so brightly that it was hard to look directly at it. The blue almost looked radioactive.

Anapos opened the door of the ship, and a clear walkway extended across the gap over the water to the shore of the dry cave.

Cordelia quickly walked across the clear bridge to the other side. The inside of the cave was cold; she could see her own breath. But she didn't seem to be suffering any effects of the pressure or their depth within the earth's core. Then she remembered that she wasn't really on earth anymore. At least, not her own *real* version of it. The geology of the book world didn't need to make sense; the entire place was nothing but a construct of fiction, after all.

The three of them walked slowly toward the Worldkeeper. It glowed brilliantly, but seemed to have dimmed slightly, as if it were aware of their presence and did not want to blind them with its intense light.

Up close, it simply looked like a medallion, a glowing blue Olympic medal with no ribbon or markings. Except that there was a loop of incandescent fog that remained hovering in a ring above the talisman like a ribbon.

"What now?" Cordelia asked.

She wasn't expecting an answer, but Adie had taken out the papers Brendan had given her and was reading the description of the Worldkeeper for clues.

"I think we can just take it," Adie said.

"No way, it never works like that," Cordelia said. "Remember Harry Potter?"

"Harry *who*?" Adie asked.

Cordelia had completely forgotten that her two new friends existed in a world without the Harry Potter series.

"Harry Potter is this boy wizard in books that exist in my world. Anyway, in one of the stories, he had to watch his mentor, Professor Dumbledore, drink some horrible soul-sucking water to get the Horcrux from a cave. And then, in *Indiana Jones*—"

"Indiana *who*?" Adie asked again, looking increasingly confused.

"He's—oh, forget it," Cordelia said. "The point is, these kinds of things are never easy. I mean, there's always some price to pay, some deadly trap—"

"Uh, Cordelia?" Anapos said. "I hate to interrupt, but, look . . ."

Cordelia stopped ranting and looked down at Adie, who was already holding the glowing blue talisman. She looked fine, her skin wasn't melting off her bones, and there were no deadly spirits rising from the water to devour them. Nothing.

"Here," she said.

Cordelia grabbed the talisman. It felt cold in her hand, like metal. And powerful, yet its presence made her feel completely calm.

That was it? Seriously? Cordelia grinned at their good luck.

"Well, that was easy," she said. "Here, you'd better take it, though."

She handed it back. Adie stuffed the glowing blue talisman and its fog ribbon into the front pocket of her yellow dress.

"Don't celebrate just yet," Anapos said dryly. "We still have to somehow get past the Iku-Turso. It's guarding the cave's only exit."

A few minutes later, the three of them sat inside the submarine at the cave's entrance and peered out into the dark depths of the abyss. There was no sign of the Iku-Turso. But Cordelia wasn't buying it. There was no way they'd get that lucky twice. She knew it was out there lurking. Just waiting for them.

"Maybe the Iku-Turso lost interest in us," Adie suggested hopefully. "Maybe he's off looking for something else to eat."

"Wishful thinking," Anapos said. "But we may as well go for it now, either way."

She slowly eased the vessel out of the cave.

Almost as soon as they emerged, the Iku-Turso came out of nowhere. Just as they were inching outside the cave, the creature's terrible jaws opened and before they knew it, they were swallowed whole by the sea monster.

They somehow managed to avoid getting crushed by any of the monster's teeth, but found themselves deep inside its gullet. The headlights of the submarine shone onto the remains of the huge underwater crocodile slowly dissolving in pools of white stomach bile. The same stomach bile that was already starting to work away on their vessel.

"Can we get out?" Cordelia asked in a panic. "This ship must have weapons!"

Anapos shook her head.

"Unfortunately, our ships are not equipped for battles or destruction," she said. "There's no way we're getting out of here alive."

CHAPTER

78

For someone who was announcing their impending deaths, Anapos sounded oddly calm. But before Cordelia could ask Anapos about her apparent lack of panic, something inside the pocket of Adie's dress diverted her attention.

"Adie, look at your dress!" Cordelia shouted.

Adie looked down and saw a circle of glowing blue light on her midsection where the talisman rested inside the pocket. The glowing intensified, and then rays of pure blue light fired out in all directions.

They seemed to pass right through the living occupants of the vessel without causing any harm. But the light cut right through the Iku-Turso's flesh like blazing-hot knives.

The Iku-Turso was sliced apart from the inside out. Adie, Anapos, and Cordelia could only sit there and watch as large, fleshy chunks of the beast floated all around them. After several moments, the talisman stopped glowing.

Sharks and sea creatures of all kinds swarmed in and started eating the chunks of the evil beast that had terrorized them for generations. They completely ignored the submarine as it slowly drifted away from the feeding frenzy.

"That was really *disgusting*!" Adie said. "But also pretty amazing."

"We have another problem," Anapos said, bringing the celebration to a quick close yet again. "A pretty major one."

"What *now*?" Cordelia asked.

"That creature's stomach juices must be really corrosive," Anapos said. "I think they ruptured the power cell. We're losing fuel quickly. There won't be enough to get out of the abyss."

"What do you mean, *losing fuel?*" Cordelia nearly shouted, not understanding how a machine so high-tech could suffer from such a pedestrian problem. "This thing runs on fuel?"

"What did you think?" Anapos snapped back. "That it was powered by beautiful thoughts and magic potions?"

"Well . . . yeah . . . something like that!" Cordelia said weakly.

Anapos threw up her hands in frustration. It was an oddly human gesture.

"What are we going to do?" Adie asked.

"There is one thing we could try," Anapos said. "It's likely to get us killed even sooner, but there's also a small chance that it could save us."

"Let's hear it," Cordelia said.

"There was an old legend the elders would tell us children at bedtime," Anapos said. "That the Eternal Abyss never ends."

"What do you mean 'never ends'?" Cordelia asked. "I just assumed its name was figurative."

"It doesn't have a bottom," Anapos explained. "Instead, it passes right through the earth to the other side of the great ocean."

"That's ridiculous," Cordelia said. "The center of the earth is made up of mantle rock and molten lava at the core—it's not even possible."

"I didn't say I believed it!" Anapos said defensively. "It's a legend! The sort of story our parents told us for entertainment. Don't you have fake, entertaining stories that you tell each other for enjoyment?"

"The news?" Cordelia said.

"Excuse me?"

"Never mind," Cordelia said, disappointed that Brendan wasn't there to see her cracking a joke in such dire circumstances. "Of course we have fictional stories. But that's all they are. Stories. They aren't real."

"Look, I don't know anything about what's inside the earth," Adie said. "But before today, I didn't think basically *any* of the stuff I've seen in the past twenty-four hours was possible. So if there's even a chance it could work, I say we try."

"That's the spirit, Adie," Anapos said. "Besides, going for it is definitely better than floating around here in the darkness waiting to slowly starve to death. Cordelia?"

Cordelia shrugged, not having any better ideas.

"Let's do it," she said with a sigh.

Anapos nodded, pointed the ship straight down into the abyss, and pushed the throttle all the way forward. As they plunged deeper and deeper into the dark ocean, Cordelia was becoming increasingly convinced they'd all just made the worst mistake of their short lives. The abyss seemed to stretch on forever, with no light or end in sight.

"Power is almost gone," Anapos said somberly after several minutes.

"At least we tried," Adie said softly.

Cordelia admired the girl's high spirits and positive attitude even in the face of death. And was perhaps a little jealous. She certainly wished she could be so calm knowing they were driving a submarine down into the ocean to die cold and alone.

Then the ship began to shudder.

"What's that?" Cordelia asked.

"I don't know," Anapos said. "We're accelerating but I'm not sure how, since we're officially out of fuel."

Suddenly the walls of the abyss were gone, and they were back out in the open ocean. The vessel rocketed toward the surface faster than it could have gone on its own with full power. A trip that should have taken hours or maybe even days took mere minutes, and before long they all saw the glow of the sun above them.

"It worked!" Cordelia yelled. "It's impossible, but it worked."

"Apparently you don't know what the word *impossible* means," Adie said with a grin as the ship broke the surface of the sea and they were met by a clear, bright blue sky.

The ship bobbed up and down in calm waters. They saw a shoreline marked by a small city just several hundred yards away. Dozens of ships were either docked or coming and going from the harbor.

A massive pirate ship pushed past their small, clear submarine. Several drunken pirates were hanging over the side. They saw the three girls in the strange, transparent boat and rubbed at their eyes before taking more pulls from their bottles of freshly pillaged rhum agricole.

"Is we that drunk or am I seeing dis right?" one of the pirates asked his shipmate as they slowly drifted past.

"You see it too?" his companion said. "Arrgh! This

stuff is as potent as me old granddad's homemade bath-tub rum!"

Then Cordelia recognized one of the pirates standing on the bridge. It was Gilliam, the bald pirate with the dolphin tattoo on his face from their first adventure in the book world. He looked down at them, and they locked eyes. He smiled when he recognized her, a gold tooth gleamed in the sun.

"I like your new tattoo, Gilliam!" Cordelia shouted.

"I thought I recognized yez, little girl!" he shouted back down. "Yez really like it? It's a ferocious, man-eating tiger!"

Cordelia didn't want to inform him that the new tattoo where the dolphin on his face used to be was in fact no tiger. Rather, it was a fluffy and adorable orange kitten playing with a ball of yarn. She merely smiled again and nodded.

"It's really scary and cool!" she shouted.

"Arrrrr!" he cried out toward the sky. "Do yez need a tow into town?"

Cordelia looked at the port town nearby. That's when she realized it was Tinz. They were actually there! They had made it. She nodded at Gilliam.

"That'd be lovely!"

He disappeared off the deck for a few moments and then returned with a huge rope in his hands. He grinned at her and tossed one end overboard toward their submarine. Cordelia never would have guessed in a billion years that her search for the Worldkeeper would end with a pirate with a cute kitty-cat tattoo on his face towing them into Tinz.

CHAPTER

79

For Brendan and Gilbert, the trip from *Wazner's Revenge* to the small port town of Tinz within the book *Savage Warriors* passed by surprisingly quickly—in just under an hour. Of course, it helped that they had made the trip inside Gilbert's ridiculously speedy spaceship.

Tinz was just how Brendan remembered it. A relatively small town bustling with activity. The narrow streets were lined with specialty shops and numerous taverns overflowing with pirates, merchants, and sailors. Brendan and Gilbert walked through the streets toward the open-air market at the center of town, filled with tents and tables loaded with wares, food, and various goods from distant lands.

That was where they'd decided to meet up. Of course, he had no idea how long he and Gilbert would have to wait for everyone else to arrive. Maybe they were already there? Or maybe—his throat seized at the thought—they would never show up at all. He had to face the possibility that they hadn't succeeded and that he might be stuck there alone forever.

Gilbert walked next to him, wearing a cloak with a hood pulled down over his face. His arms were also hidden inside the amply flowing robes he'd telepathically created for himself (the same way he'd built the boat for Cordelia and Adie).

To the townsfolk, they simply looked like two children walking the streets. Of course, their strange attire did garner them a few odd stares, but they didn't stand out nearly as much as they would have had Gilbert openly walked around all fully exposed.

"You think they'll be here soon?" Brendan asked as they stood in the center of the busy flea market.

Brendan had to admit that somewhere along the way, the arrogant little alien began growing on him. Plus, he was also starting to enjoy the distraction of Gilbert's soliloquies.

"Yes, we shall locate your siblings quite momentarily," Gilbert said.

"Yeah, how *momentarily?*" Brendan asked with a smirk.

"Right now," Gilbert said.

"Is that so?" Brendan asked. "How do you know that, professor?"

"Because they are standing right over there," Gilbert said, a long, gray finger emerged from one of his loose sleeves. "Also, you should know I presently do not hold the title of professor, nor am I an instructor at any institution of higher education."

Brendan whirled around. Sure enough, standing at the edge of the market were Cordelia, Adie, and a tall girl with dark hair and shimmering blue-tinted skin. They looked around, trying to find a familiar face. His face.

"Deal!" Brendan shouted, a ridiculously huge grin on his face.

Cordelia's eyes found his, and they ran toward each other across the market. It was like a scene from a movie, where the music plays and then the slow motion starts. Except those scenes in movies usually ended with a huge hug and tears of joy. In the marketplace in Tinz, however, when Brendan and Cordelia reached each other they both stopped and smiled while their arms shifted awkwardly, unsure of whether or not to go in for an uncomfortable sibling embrace.

"I'm glad you're okay," Cordelia said.

"Yeah, me too," Brendan said. "I mean, glad *you're* okay. Well, I'm glad I'm okay too, but I think you're getting the point. . . ."

Cordelia nodded and then laughed. There was more urgent business at hand.

"Did you get the Worldkeeper?" Cordelia asked.

Brendan nodded. "You?"

Cordelia nodded at Adie.

The girl pulled the talisman from her dress pocket an inch or two so Brendan could see it. His eyes widened at its glowing blue appearance. Then he smiled as Adie stuffed it back into her pocket.

"And Nell?" Brendan asked.

Cordelia's face drained of all color.

"You haven't seen her?" she asked.

"Maybe she's just running a little behind?" Brendan suggested.

Cordelia shook her head and looked down. It was possible, of course, but something told her that wasn't the case. For starters, Eleanor had already been where she needed to be when they had split up. Plus, of the three locations, Planet 5X was supposedly the closest to Tinz. It shouldn't have taken that long for Eleanor to get there.

Something was wrong. Very wrong.

Cordelia knew it; she could feel it in her bones like the body aches that usually came with having the flu.

"I can embark toward her location in my ship to investigate," Gilbert suggested.

Cordelia nodded gratefully. Before anyone else could say

more, however, a voice called out across the marketplace.

"Brendan, is that you?" a female voice cried out in surprise. "Brendan Walker!"

"You can't even get a girl to talk to you in school," Cordelia said, her eyes wide with surprise. "But you've got a girlfriend in Tinz?"

He shrugged, looking as baffled as she felt.

The whole group whirled around and spotted a young girl with short brown hair and sparkling purple eyes running toward them. She waved, looking relieved to see them. Almost as if she'd been expecting to run into them.

"*Celene?*" Brendan said.

Cordelia recognized her almost as soon as the name left Brendan's mouth. Of course! It was the girl from *Savage Warriors* who had stormed Queen Daphne's castle and helped save all of their lives the first time they'd been trapped inside the book world. It was the girl that Brendan had obviously had a crush on since the moment he first read about her in that book.

"I'm so glad you're here!" Celene said, looking more distracted than happy, not even bothering with the usual pleasantries. "You need to come with me; it's about your little sister, Eleanor. And it's urgent!"

CHAPTER

80

"You know where Eleanor is?" Cordelia nearly shouted as they followed Celene's hurried footsteps through the streets of Tinz. "Tell us!"

"There's no time to explain," Celene shouted back over her shoulder. "It's better that you hear it from the Aged One."

"The Aged One?" Cordelia asked. "Who is that?"

Brendan gave her hand a squeeze as they walked.

"Let's just go!" he said. "The sooner we get there, the sooner we can find out what happened to Nell."

Cordelia nodded and focused on staying right on Celene's heels. She, Brendan, Cordelia, Adie, Anapos, and Gilbert made their way quickly through the streets of Tinz, eventually weaving their way via alleys and narrow paths into a much quieter section of town marked by large buildings that clearly housed multiple families—almost like an old version of a modern-day apartment complex.

As they moved deeper into the slums of Tinz, the scene that greeted them was astonishing. The living conditions were nothing short of squalor. The Walkers observed ravaged and hungry villagers rooting through garbage strewn about the alleys. They looked exactly how you'd expect people to look who lived under a greedy and tyrannical reign like Queen Daphne's. They looked like refugees.

Suddenly, to Cordelia and Brendan, their *cramped* apartment near Fisherman's Wharf didn't seem that bad at all. Both of them were stung by the guilt of their own ignorant privilege. Even at their family's worst moments, they had it better than they had ever realized before.

Nobody spoke as Celene opened a door tucked away in a dark alley. She ushered them all inside and then led the group down a series of dark hallways until they found themselves in a large room with several wooden tables and benches. It looked like a dining hall.

"Wait here," Celene said, and disappeared through a door across the room.

A short time later she returned with an old man. To Brendan, he actually looked less like an old man and more like a walking corpse. He was hunched over a crooked wooden cane and had stringy, thin white hair with a matching beard that covered most of his heavily wrinkled face. His skin was blasted with age spots and it appeared to be a minor miracle that the man was still alive at all, let alone walking and talking.

But even in spite of looking to be nearly 150 years old, behind the folds of skin surrounding his eyes there was still an edge of intelligence and awareness, almost as if the eyes belonged to someone much younger.

"Let me introduce you to the Aged One," Celene said. "In our land, none of the residents get older. Year after year we stay the same. Age does not exist here in our world. Except for this man. Over the years, he has gotten older. And he will be able to explain everything to you."

They gathered around the old man as he slowly sat down on a bench. Something about Celene's comment clicked on a light in Brendan's brain. It was something he'd read in Kristoff's *Journal*—something about the passing of time in the book world. Denver had surmised that time passed differently here, that it moved slower and in some cases never moved at all—that the book characters would never age past what they did in the novel's text, which meant . . .

"If you age . . . ," Brendan said slowly, his voice rising, "then that means you must be from our world! The real world!"

The old man nodded slowly.

"He's been the leader of the Resistance for years now," Celene said.

Brendan remembered Celene explaining that the Resistance was a group of villagers, freedom fighters, constantly working to end Queen Daphne's evil reign over Tinz and the surrounding provinces. He now also remembered something else she had told him back during their first-ever meeting.

"*That's* how you knew!" he said. "That's how you *knew* you were a character in a book! It's how you already knew we were from the outside back then. Because your leader is from the outside too."

Everyone looked at the old man again as Celene nodded. The Aged One smiled thinly at the group. Adie just kept watching Brendan looking at Celene like she was a queen or something, and her face was getting redder and redder.

"Please, Mr. Aged One," Cordelia said. "Can you tell us where our sister, Eleanor, is?"

The old man chuckled under his beard. It seemed an odd reaction, but there was nothing but gentle kindness behind it. And a bit of sadness as well.

"Eleanor is fine. She has not been harmed. For now," he said, his voice sounding as old as he looked. "But, please, don't call me the 'Aged One.' Call me Eugene. Eugene Kristoff."

"*You're* Denver's brother!" Brendan exclaimed. "He told us to find you!"

"He said that you can help us stop the Wind Witch's plans," Cordelia said. "That you can show us how to use the Worldkeepers to seal off the book world forever."

The Aged One nodded slowly while stroking his beard.

"So, it's happened then?" he said.

"What has happened?" Brendan asked.

"The seams between the two worlds must be fraying," Eugene said. "Denver always suspected this was inevitable. He sent me here many, many years ago to help him keep an eye on *The Book of Doom and Desire*, and on this world in general." His gaze passed over Adie, Anapos, and Gilbert in turn as he said this, pausing on each one momentarily. "Unfortunately, I lost track of the book some time ago."

"That's because our little sister wished it out of existence," Brendan said proudly.

"Did she?" Eugene said, using his gnarled old fingers to fiddle with his mustache. "Interesting. Interesting indeed. At a great cost, no doubt. But regardless, probably all for the better. I don't know why Denver didn't just destroy that blasted thing in the first place. . . ."

"I'll tell you why," Cordelia said. "Because he's a greedy old son of a—"

"Can't disagree," Eugene interrupted. "But that's irrelevant, because my main purpose here in this world shifted some time ago, a time well before *The Book of Doom and Desire* was apparently destroyed. Things here, in many of these book worlds, began to go awry and have only gotten worse over the years. . . ."

"Wait a second," Brendan said. "Why would you be willing to give up your whole life to help your selfish older brother guard a book that ruined his life and destroyed his family?"

"Because I was once a selfish man myself," Eugene said. "In a somewhat different way, of course. You see, I cared not for money and power the way my brother did, but I still had no regard for other people. I only cared for myself. I only did what made *me* feel good, however unsuitable those things were for the civilized world. . . . Can you comprehend this selfishness?"

"Yeah," Brendan said, suddenly feeling a tight burn in his stomach as he thought about his own father and his gambling addiction. His thoughts also wandered back to the time he willingly split from his sisters to stay at the Colosseum only to look out for himself and what made him happy. Was he really any better than any of these men?

"It was all about the adrenaline rush of doing something outside the boundaries of the law," Eugene continued. "I spent much of my youth in search of adventures. And it landed me in various prisons over the years. My life was a mess; I could never seem to fulfill my desire for more excitement. And so when Denver offered me the chance to come to a place where the *adventure finds you* . . . I couldn't resist."

"Amazing," Cordelia said. "Every time we're here we do everything in our power to get out. But you chose to stay."

"Oh yes," Eugene said. "And at first I spent several years traveling from book to book, finding my own adventures and excitement—it was spectacular. But after a while, I began to notice another, more disruptive outside presence in many of the books."

"The Wind Witch," Brendan said.

"Yes, my very own niece," Eugene Kristoff confirmed, nodding slowly while shifting his gaze from Brendan to Adie. "Except that it wasn't her anymore. Not the Dahlia I remembered, anyway. She was now ruthless, and she somehow found a way to actually *transform* herself into the characters from Denver's stories. I certainly had my share of fun, but I never interfered with the integrity of the worlds within the novels. Dahlia, however, had other ideas. And she's only grown more ruthless and powerful in recent years, spending most of her time as Queen Daphne, torturing the poor and innocent souls within *Savage Warriors*. Her reign has far exceeded, in the scope of cruelty and savagery, what Denver ever intended. That's why I joined the Resistance. To try and help restore some of the balance. And now, I'm afraid she's somehow recruited or enchanted another outsider into helping her with another, even more terrible scheme."

"Eleanor!" Cordelia nearly yelled, covering her mouth with shaking hands.

"I'm afraid so," Eugene Kristoff said. "Several Resistance spies spotted her inside Castle Corroway with the Wind Witch, preparing a massive invasion—an invasion, I can only assume, of our real world."

Cordelia breathed out heavily and tried to fight back tears. Brendan looked from Eugene to Cordelia and then at all his other new friends.

"We need to go after her!" Cordelia said. "Save her!"

"And I can help you do that," Eugene said.

"But Cordelia needs to leave the room first," Brendan said suddenly. "She can't be here while we talk about this."

"I'm not going anywhere!" Cordelia said, her eyes glowing icy blue. "I don't care about my stupid eyes anymore!"

"You *know* it isn't safe, Deal," Brendan said.

"I've heard enough!" she said, not backing down. "You're just a selfish glory addict! Just like the last time we were here, back at the Roman Colosseum! You don't care about helping other people or doing the right thing at all. . . . All you care about is looking like a hero. You're always thinking of how cool everyone back at school would think you are if they saw you 'saving the world' here in Denver's books. You're self-involved and borderline narcissistic . . . and I'm tired of letting you get away with it!" When she finished, even she looked shocked at what she'd said.

Brendan didn't know how to respond. They'd always squabbled like siblings to a certain degree, but it never involved them saying things so hurtful, so deeply insulting to their very character.

"That's not fair," Brendan said quietly. "You know it's different now. It's not my fault that you're linked to the Wind Witch—"

"Linked to the Wind Witch?" Eugene asked.

Brendan quickly explained how they could sometimes see and hear things through each other. Eugene Kristoff looked increasingly alarmed as Brendan spoke.

"Then I'm afraid young Brendan is correct," Eugene said to Cordelia gently. "It's not safe for you, or for any of us for that matter, including Eleanor, for you to be a part of this. In fact, I think it might be better off if you just remain in Tinz altogether for now."

"Remain in Tinz!" Cordelia shouted.

"Yes," Eugene said. "It's imperative that you do not take part in our next mission."

Cordelia's angry, frosty-blue eyes looked from Eugene to Brendan and then to Adie, Anapos, and Gilbert. They were all looking at her with pity. Because it was clear that they all agreed with Eugene and Brendan—even in spite of them not fully understanding the nature of the situation.

"You turned them all against me!" Cordelia shouted, pointing at Brendan, a sob escaping in between sentences.

"I hate you! I really, really hate you! I'm so ashamed to have to call you my brother!"

Before any of them could say another word, she spun on her heels and marched out of one of the doors of the dinning hall. She slammed it shut behind her. Everyone else looked at one another uneasily.

"Should we go after her?" Adie asked.

"She'll be fine," Brendan said warily, but not really caring one way or another how Cordelia would feel later. He couldn't get over the awful things she'd said to him. Did she really believe they were true?

"I know this is difficult, but we must act quickly," Eugene said. "Did you get the three Worldkeepers?"

"We've got two," Brendan said. "But I don't know if Eleanor managed to find the third one before the Wind Witch kidnapped her."

"Without the third Worldkeeper, going to the Door of Ways would be pointless," Eugene said. "The Door of Ways is the magical portal that allows the two worlds to intermix. And the three Worldkeepers are almost like the notches on its only key. . . ."

"So it can't be locked without *all three* Worldkeepers," Brendan finished for him.

"Precisely," Eugene said. "And to make matters even more troubling, the Wind Witch has formed a massive army along the only mountain passage up to the Door of Ways. When it is time, we will need to find a way past that army to get you there."

"But first we need to get back Eleanor and the third Worldkeeper," Brendan said. "Hopefully she found it before the Wind Witch kidnapped her."

"You misunderstood me, son," Eugene said. "I am not convinced Eleanor was *kidnapped*. My intelligence agents at Castle Corroway have said that Eleanor appears to be there of her own free will. I suspect that she has been enchanted or simply manipulated . . . Dahlia always was good at manipulating people, even back before her soul was corrupted. Either way, I suspect that Eleanor did find the Worldkeeper first."

"What makes you think that?" Adie asked.

"Because the Wind Witch would not have left the *Terror on Planet 5X* world without it," Eugene said.

"Well, there's only one way to find out," Adie said. "We need to go there and rescue her."

"We know a secret entrance into the castle," Celene said. "I can lead you there and get a small squad inside."

"Great!" Brendan said, standing up. "Let's go. I don't want to waste any more time!"

"Patience, Brendan," Eugene said. "You must rest for now."

"*Sleep?*" Brendan asked. "Are you kidding me? I gotta rescue my little sister!"

"I completely understand your passion," Eugene said. "But you're weak from lack of nourishment and rest. You need all your strength to get your sister back safely. I suspect that there will be much bloodshed before the day ends tomorrow. Celene will show you to your rooms. When you wake, we can further discuss our plans over dinner. You will leave for Castle Corroway before daybreak."

They all stood up uncertainly. Brendan did have to admit that a nap didn't sound like the worst thing in the world. He was anxious to go and get Eleanor back—to get the last Worldkeeper and finally end this all. But Eugene was right. He wouldn't do anyone a bit of good in his current state.

"Wait," Adie said suddenly, looking worried. "What was all that talk about characters in a novel . . . and you being in the 'real world' . . . does all of this mean that I'm . . . that I'm just a character in a book? That I'm not *real?*"

"And me?" Anapos asked nervously.

Brendan looked at them sympathetically, remembering how depressed Will Draper was when he found out that he was a character from a novel and not a real person.

"I'll explain on the way to our rooms," Brendan said. "It's complicated."

"When I first found out that I was a book character, I was very sad and confused," Celene said to Gilbert's, Anapos's, and Adie's confused faces. "But I eventually came to terms with it. I know what it's like, so maybe I can come along to help him explain it all?"

She grabbed Brendan's hand while she spoke and gave it a squeeze.

Adie looked at the two of them holding hands and frowned.

"Actually," Adie said. "I'm going to go check on Cordelia instead." She turned and stormed off down the hallway.

"What got into her?" Celene asked, as she watched Adie leave.

"I have no idea," Brendan said, trying to hide his red cheeks.

CHAPTER

81

*C*ordelia Walker sat alone in her small room with a plate of food, and stewed. She'd managed to sleep a little while everyone else napped, but was still furious at the group for cutting her out of the plans, especially Brendan, her own brother.

Not only had they already said she couldn't go with them to Castle Corroway in the morning, but now they insisted that she eat dinner alone in her room while they devised a plan together in the dining hall. It was more than she could bear.

Cordelia was probably the one person who could help them the most in terms of strategizing and organizing. Besides, nobody knew Eleanor quite like she did. If anyone could reason with their little sister it was her. This was the final straw, she decided, throwing down her unfinished plate of food.

Fueled mostly by anger, resentment, and sleep deprivation, Cordelia Walker snuck out of her room. All the guests had been given rooms in the same hallway as one another, as well as a place to store their things and fresh clothes to help fit in with the locals. Cordelia went from room to room, peeking inside each one until she found Brendan's.

She dug through his dirty jeans with the bullet hole in the butt where he'd been shot by Sheriff Abernathy. Just like she'd figured, Brendan had been irresponsible enough to leave Denver's *Journal of Magic and Technology* behind while they all ate and planned their invasion of Castle Corroway. This only further justified her actions.

Cordelia sat on the edge of Brendan's straw bed and read several pages of the *Journal*. The words inside filled her with purpose and seemed to cure her of the pent-up stress and frustration, like some kind of miracle drug. She even found a separate passage about the Invictum and discovered it was more powerful than any of them had realized. She planned to read more eventually, but had other ideas for the moment.

Next, she snuck into Adie's room and found the talisman still stashed away inside her yellow dress. If she stole the talisman, then they would have to take her with them tomorrow, she reasoned. Then they wouldn't be able to just leave her there and pretend she was worthless. It would give her a purpose again.

Cordelia looked down at the glowing blue medallion in her hand. It shimmered as if it were agreeing with her thoughts. She held it up close to her head and slipped the fog tendrils that looked like a translucent ribbon around her neck. In spite of being weightless, the tendrils held. She dropped the talisman into her shirt as it hung from her neck.

She then continued down the hallway until she reached the door to the dining hall. She crouched next to it and listened in on the conversation. They were still discussing the plan. They went over how many people to take, where the secret entrance to the castle was, and when they would likely be arriving.

Slowly, Cordelia inched forward so she could see inside the room. They all sat around the table, eating and drinking and laughing while they discussed the mission. Adie, Brendan, Celene, Gilbert, Eugene Kristoff, and Anapos. As her gaze passed over Anapos, Cordelia's throat clenched like it was trying to strangle her.

Anapos looked different. Cordelia couldn't quite figure out what it was, but she definitely was not imagining things. There was an aura of darkness emanating from her new friend. Something that had not been there before. It almost looked like Cordelia was getting a glimpse into a black soul. And she knew instantly that it was the talisman around her neck—showing her the truth, like Denver said it could do in his *Journal*.

Cordelia backed away suddenly and ran back to Adie's room. She replaced the talisman where she found it and then did the same thing with the *Journal*. Cordelia knew now that she didn't need those things in order to help out. She now had a real and valiant reason to follow them in the morning. There was something deceitful about Anapos. She couldn't tell them now, of course. If she did that, they would know she had spied on them, and then who knows what Brendan and Eugene would do; they might even lock her up. No, telling them now wasn't an option. Instead, she would follow them in the morning to keep an eye on Anapos. And then save the day in the moment of truth, in that moment when Anapos was about to betray them.

A healthy mind might have realized the many flaws of her plan, the inherent danger of hiding what she'd discovered. But Cordelia's mind was far from healthy in that moment. Days of losing control, of being pushed aside, of losing her sense of purpose had worn her down. That, and a lack of food, water, and sleep had completely robbed Cordelia of her normally sound judgment. In her own mind, what she was doing was the best thing for her family.

When the rest of them departed the next morning before sunrise for Castle Corroway, Cordelia would follow. Because she had the one thing she cherished above all else in that moment: knowledge that nobody else possessed.

CHAPTER

82

The first time Brendan had travelled from Tinz to Castle Corroway, it had been in the back of a dirty horse-drawn cart, tied up with his two sisters. They had been prisoners of Slayne and his terrible band of Savage Warriors. The journey had lasted two long days in cramped squalor. And the Savage Warriors had taken their time, stopping often to pointlessly slaughter animals, pillage small farms, and get drunk at wayfarer taverns.

This trip, however, felt much different. For one thing, his sisters were not with him. Cordelia was back in Tinz and Eleanor was already at the castle. And this time the band traveled by horseback at a steady gallop nearly the whole way. It took just four hours compared to the two slogging, terrible days the first time around.

The rescue party consisted of Brendan, Celene, Gilbert, Anapos, and Adie, who had insisted that she get to see this through.

"I've been through so much the past few days," she had said when Brendan protested. "I'll be darned if y'all are just going to leave me behind now."

Brendan hadn't had a good counterargument.

Eugene Kristoff was leading a much larger army several hours behind them, in case things went poorly. Which, the old man had said, they likely would. Eugene fully expected a large-scale battle to break out by the end of the day. Brendan could only hope he was wrong, or that they'd at least get to Eleanor and the last Worldkeeper before it happened.

The five infiltrators dismounted their horses near the edge of the thick forest surrounding Castle Corroway. Celene led them to the hidden entrance of the outer wall surrounding the castle. The sun had only risen part of the way past the mountains to the east, casting much of the royal grounds in relative darkness.

Celene finished breaking into the sewer drainage tunnel, and in a matter of minutes, they had successfully entered the castle through a series of hidden underground passages. They emerged in the castle's wine cellar to find a startled guard just waking from a nap.

Celene had a sling out before Brendan even fully realized

what was happening. A small rock sailed across the room in an instant. There was a soft thump, and the guard slumped down to the stone floor with a huge lump already developing on his forehead.

"You beefed him," Adie said in shock.

"No, he's not dead," Celene said, pointing at the man's chest, still rising slowly with his breaths. "But he'll probably wake up with a terrible headache."

"Right," Brendan said, eyeing the guard's massive forehead welt uneasily, as Celene picked up the stone and put it back in her satchel. "Where to now?"

Celene consulted a map of Castle Corroway that Resistance spies had drawn.

"Queen Daphne's chambers are five floors up," she said.

Brendan nodded, and the group crept up a narrow set of stone steps. They stayed quiet as they stealthily navigated the cold and dark castle. There were very few people around, either due to the early hour or preparations for the invasion of San Francisco.

They had only made it up to the third floor of the castle, when Celene suddenly stopped dead in her tracks at the end of a long hallway. Brendan pushed past her to see what she was gawking at.

It was Eleanor, standing right there in front of them.

CHAPTER

83

Eleanor's panicked eyes found Brendan's and then she smiled. Before he even realized what was happening, she ran forward and wrapped her arms around his waist. The shirt on her back was matted with sweat and she was trembling.

"I'm so glad you came!" Eleanor sobbed. "I don't want to be here anymore."

Brendan was so relieved he couldn't stop the tears from streaming down his face—his usual self-consciousness completely pushed aside by the joy of seeing Eleanor alive and well again. Deep down he'd always known she would never knowingly help the Wind Witch. Sure, they'd all made their mistakes in the past. But none of them would ever actually follow through in helping the Wind Witch, at least not on purpose.

"What happened?" he asked. "Are you okay?"

"No, I'm not . . . I mean, sort of, but . . . not really," Eleanor said. She was a frantic mess, barely able to string her words together. "The Wind Witch . . . she tricked me into coming with her. I almost fell for everything she said . . . but then I saw the sorts of horrible things she's doing here and the awful plans she's making and I came to my senses and escaped."

"What is she planning?" Brendan asked.

"To send an army of Denver Kristoff's most evil and dangerous creatures into San Francisco!"

"So it's what we've always feared," he said, thinking about the sort of devastation those awful alien-piloted robots alone could unleash on downtown. "How can we stop her?"

"I don't know," Eleanor said. "I just want to get out of here before she finds out I escaped!"

Brendan looked at Celene.

"Let's get back to Eugene and the main army," Celene said. "He'll know what to do."

Brendan nodded.

"Did you and Cordelia find your Worldkeepers?" Eleanor asked.

"Yes," he said, patting the Invictum, which was in an awkwardly large sheath attached to his belt. "It's a diamond knife called the Invictum. Did you find yours?"

"Yes . . . well, sort of," Eleanor said, glancing at Gilbert. "I'll explain later! We need to go now!"

"This way!" Celene said.

They started to follow Celene, but Eleanor stopped them.

"No!" she said. "They know you're coming. Cordelia spied on you last night and the Wind Witch saw part of it. They know you're all here. Come on, this way will be safer!"

"Cordelia spied on us?" Brendan asked, shocked that his older, supposedly smarter, sister could do something so careless and dangerous.

"She isn't herself right now," Eleanor said. "She's not thinking clearly!"

Celene, Gilbert, Anapos, Adie, and Brendan followed Eleanor as she led them down a short corridor and then into a curved stairwell. They started descending, step after step, around and around in a spiral. Brendan was actually getting dizzy after the thirtieth or fortieth step.

Finally, at the bottom, they reached a solid wrought-iron door with a huge handle. Eleanor grabbed it, but it wouldn't budge. Celene and Anapos tried to open it together, but it didn't even so much as groan from the pressure.

"It's not moving," Celene said. "There's no way we can cut through iron with our swords. It's a dead end."

"Let's go back up," Anapos suggested.

"We can't!" Adie shouted from the back of the group. "I hear footsteps . . . someone else is coming down!"

"We're trapped!" Anapos shouted. "You led us into a trap, little girl!"

"No," Eleanor said. "There has to be a way to cut through the door! What about that, Bren?" She pointed at the Invictum. "Remember, the *Journal* said it was sharper than anything in the world!"

Brendan nodded. It was worth a try. He drew the Invictum from the sheath, careful not to slice off one of Gilbert's arms in the cramped stairwell. There wasn't room for him to try and squeeze past everyone, and so he passed the sparkling diamond knife forward toward Eleanor.

She grabbed it; the shining diamond blade gleamed in the reflection of her eyes. A smile spread across her face. Then she turned and jammed the blade into the iron door. It passed through it with ease, as if she were cutting into an avocado wedge instead of solid metal. She sliced through the section containing the lock and the door slowly swung open.

The group rushed through it and into the open air. Brendan and Adie were the last two out the door and they slammed it shut behind them. He spun around . . . and then gasped.

They were standing outside, high atop the tallest tower of Castle Corroway, in spite of just having *descended* at least a hundred steps!

"How is this possible?" Brendan yelled. "We just went *down* at least six flights of stairs!"

"It was dark magic," Celene said, her eyes growing wide. "We've been tricked."

Everyone turned toward Eleanor. She stood near the edge of the vast tower and grinned at them. Then she began laughing. But it wasn't her usual laugh, there was something menacing behind it now, and something that didn't sound quite human.

"Eleanor, no," Brendan whimpered.

Eleanor spread her arms like a bird, the Invictum still gripped in her right hand. Then she floated off the ground and hovered in the air above them, smiling and laughing and looking remarkably like a young version of the Wind Witch.

"*Now* you're worried about me?" she spat at Brendan. "You should have thought of that before you left me all alone on that horrible alien planet."

Before Brendan got a chance to reply, the steel door slammed open as the person following them down (or *up*) the staircase burst out onto the tower. It was Cordelia. She tried to make sense of what she was seeing: Her little sister was holding a nasty-looking diamond blade while flying and cackling just like . . . the Wind Witch.

"Cordelia!" Brendan shouted. "Are you here to betray us too? Again?"

"The opposite," Cordelia said. "I'm here to help you."

"Yeah, and how's that?" Brendan asked. "By tipping off the Wind Witch to another one of our secret plans?"

"There's a traitor among you," Cordelia said.

"Besides you?" Brendan taunted, knowing he was laying it on too thick now. But he couldn't help it, he still felt so hurt that she'd spied on them the night before and accidentally tipped off the Wind Witch to the whole plan. It was her fault that this whole thing was heading south after all.

"Anapos," Cordelia said, pointing at her supposed friend.

All eyes turned toward the Atlantisan with shimmering blue skin. She had been mere seconds from shoving Celene over the edge of the tower to certain death. But with Cordelia's warning, Celene was just able to duck away from Anapos's outstretched hands.

Anapos hissed at her, then lunged again. This time, Celene was not able to get away, as the lithe Atlantisan grabbed Celene's short hair with one hand and knocked her dagger away with the other.

Cordelia charged forward and shoved Anapos over the edge of the tower before she could harm Celene.

The stunned group turned and faced Eleanor again, still hovering in the air above them. She didn't seem upset that Cordelia had just killed her spy. In fact, she was still smiling at them smugly.

"You'll have to do better than that," Eleanor said. "If you

want to kill my great-great-*grandmother*."

Behind them Anapos rose up into the air, her blue polished skin cracking like shattered glass. She laughed as she flew over to join Eleanor. They all stared in shock as the pieces of Anapos began to fall away, revealing something far worse inside.

"You fools!" the Wind Witch spat at them. "Without you, I never could have retrieved the Invictum. But not only did you do that for me, you also delivered it right to us!"

Brendan stared in shock at Eleanor and the Wind Witch flying side by side. It was too awful to be true. He felt Cordelia's hand clasped around his and they both looked up at their little sister in anguish.

"What use is the Invictum for you?" Brendan asked, fighting tears. "You've already beaten us. Besides, we don't even have the third Worldkeeper."

"That's where you're wrong, Brendan," the Wind Witch said. "The third Worldkeeper was with you all along. It's standing right beside you."

Brendan looked to his right. Gilbert looked at him, his small frame belying his great power. Fear and uncertainty reflected back from all seven of his unblinking black eyes. It made sense that the alien would have no idea that he apparently *was* the third Worldkeeper. . . . Before they'd met, he hadn't even known he was a fictional character.

"But it doesn't even matter," the Wind Witch said

smugly. "Because I never cared to have all three World-keepers, I only wanted the Invictum. But you, *the tough guy*, somehow managed to get it before me, even after you led me right to it."

"Wait," Brendan said. "*You* were Jumbo!"

The Wind Witch nodded, her ugly smile growing even wider and more menacing and arrogant.

Brendan suddenly felt disgusted with himself that he let Jumbo's fake admiration flatter him.

"I didn't know where I'd find the Invictum, and so I tracked all three of you, hoping one of you would lead me right to it," the Wind Witch said. "But after you escaped the pyramid with it, I formulated a new plan to get my hands on it by using something you love . . . something that is your greatest weakness: your loyalty to your family."

"Our love for Eleanor is not a weakness!" Cordelia shouted.

"No?" the Wind Witch asked smugly. "Then why did my plan work like a charm? I knew your blind love for Eleanor would lead you directly to me, along with the Invictum. And also a special thanks to you, Cordelia, for helping to make the whole thing even easier."

Cordelia stood there and shook her head slowly, fighting at the tears stinging her eyes.

"Oh yes," the Wind Witch said with delight. "You cannot deny the pivotal role you played in me succeeding. The envy and uncertainty you felt led me right to your friends' little plan."

"You old troll, it was you!" shouted Cordelia. "You made me betray my own friends and family; you made me spy on them! You got into my head."

"That's where you're wrong, my dear," the Wind Witch said. "Those feelings which betrayed your family were all your own—I had nothing to do with what you did. I merely used my link to you to benefit from your own errors. You're really still just a silly teenager, Cordelia. You may think you're more mature and smarter and better than all your peers back at school, but in the end, you're just like them: an insecure little brat who lets her emotions trump her better judgment."

"No . . . ," Cordelia said softly, still shaking her head. She wasn't sure what hurt worse, the reality of what she'd done, or the fact that the Wind Witch was right about everything she was saying.

Cordelia was too hurt in that moment to realize that the Wind Witch hadn't actually needed Cordelia at all to complete her plan—since she was already there disguised as Anapos. But the Wind Witch didn't point that out since she was enjoying Cordelia's pain far too much.

She knew she couldn't physically harm the Walkers, which is why she'd concocted a more complicated plan to hurt them in the only way she could: the emotional pain and agony of family betrayal. A pain she knew all too well.

"Still, I don't understand how a simple knife can be so important to you," Cordelia said, deep down still harboring hope that she could somehow save them.

"My dear, beautiful granddaughter," the Wind Witch said to Eleanor. "Will you show them the power of this *simple knife?*"

Eleanor smiled and soared up into the sky even higher. The Invictum in her right hand was no longer the sparkling color of diamonds—it was now glowing red. And it also appeared to be growing, the blade almost twice as long, with the curved U on the end nearly the size of Eleanor's head.

Finally, Eleanor stopped ascending just short of the lowest clouds in the sky. Her laughter and delight was chilling.

She raised the glowing red blade of the Invictum into the air, with glee in her eyes, and stabbed it into the deep blue sky like it was nothing but a piece of flimsy canvas. She dove back down toward the castle tower, dragging the Invictum across the sky.

Large sections of the sky fell away and dissolved into nothing.

Behind it lay modern-day San Francisco. It was a view of the city from the center of the bay. And it was no optical illusion. A passing tourist ferry headed toward Alcatraz packed with people slowed to a halt in front of them, just on the other side of the hole in the universe.

The passengers screamed. Several took out phones and started recording. The realization of what had just happened hit Brendan and Cordelia at the same time and their knees buckled.

Eleanor had just used the Invictum to rip open the barrier between the two worlds. And not only had they failed to prevent it, but they had been the ones who'd inadvertently helped make it happen. They had delivered the Invictum right to the Wind Witch!

"Now it is finally time!" the Wind Witch screamed, raising her arms and spreading them apart like she was tearing open a curtain. As she did this, the rest of the sky fell away and the two worlds were now joined together, almost like the book world was a new sunroom attached to the front porch of a house. "Let my new reign begin! Let the city of San Francisco experience a tragedy and horror unlike anything they have ever seen! Residents of San Francisco . . . please welcome your new neighbors . . . *FROM THE BOOKS OF DENVER KRISTOFF!*"

84

A vast array of creatures from Denver's novels appeared below them from within the castle walls. Some seemed to manifest from out of nowhere as if summoned by magic. Others had been there in hiding all along, waiting for this very moment.

A whole squadron of Nazi World War II planes streamed from the book world into the skies above San Francisco. They flew straight toward the piers beside the bay, firing their high-caliber weapons indiscriminately at the sailboats and massive cruise ships that peppered the water.

Krom and his band of Savage Warriors had already pulled alongside the Alcatraz ferry in a smaller boat and were boarding it with their weapons drawn. They began to mercilessly attack and rob the unarmed, innocent tourists.

From the forest outside of Castle Corroway, Eugene Kristoff waited with his entire army of Resistance fighters. He saw the chaos erupting behind the castle and gave the order for his soldiers to charge. He knew they were out-numbered, outmanned, and outgunned. There was nothing left to do but fight.

From the top of the tower, all Cordelia and Brendan Walker could do at first was helplessly watch the chaos and destruction around them. More and more of Denver's evil creations spilled into San Francisco.

Nazi tanks and cyborgs were moving onto the Presidio, firing cannons and blasting away at the buildings. Fright-ened residents ran screaming in terror. But with more creatures and villains streaming into the city, there was truly nowhere safe to run or hide.

Meanwhile, hordes of white frost beasts were attack-ing Eugene's Resistance fighters on the outside of the castle walls. There were more fighter planes in the sky now, some newer, likely from a Cold War–era novel. Brendan and Cordelia noticed that several US and Allied planes from Denver's novels had joined the fray, but it appeared to be far too little, too late.

Legions of Roman soldiers stormed across the Golden Gate Bridge, tipping over cars and throwing people over the sides.

Behind the mountains to the east of Castle Corroway, Brendan saw several huge UWOs and a family of mean-looking colossi approaching. He knew once they arrived, it would definitely be all over.

A few fighter planes and divisions of medieval-era Resistance fighters would be no match for them. But then another sickening realization dawned on him: The battle likely wouldn't even last that long. From the look of it, Kristoff's villains and creatures were going to destroy San Francisco in minutes, and there was nothing he could do to stop it.

The Wind Witch was finally going to win.

CHAPTER

85

Gilbert was the first of the stunned spectators on the castle tower to act. He had somehow managed to summon his spaceship. He climbed inside the sphere and beckoned Adie, Cordelia, Brendan, and Celene to join him. It was a cramped fit, but they were just able to squeeze inside.

The sphere zoomed away, seconds before a cannonball from a nearby pirate ship slammed into the base of the tower, sending stone bricks flying. The tower teetered and then collapsed into the San Francisco Bay with a thunderous splash.

From Gilbert's ship, Cordelia saw Eleanor and the Wind Witch flying over the city, watching the destruction and chaos. The most gut-wrenching part of it was seeing Eleanor laughing, enjoying the devastation of her beloved city. It was like some awful nightmare that couldn't possibly be real.

But it was.

Cordelia turned toward the alien.

"Start shooting at the bad guys, Gilbert!" she yelled.

"I can't reach the controls," Gilbert replied. "There are too many people in here."

"Then land this thing and unload us!" Celene yelled.

Gilbert put the tiny sphere down in a small clearing next to the castle. The bloody remains of a whole platoon of Resistance fighters were scattered across the opening. Brendan, Adie, Celene, and Cordelia exited the ship.

As soon as they set foot outside, three frost beasts charged out of the nearby forest. Adie screamed and ducked for cover. Brendan shielded her, but there was no need.

Blue lightning erupted from Gilbert's sphere and incinerated all three frost beasts.

"I guess their fontanels aren't their only weakness after all," Brendan said.

"Good job, Gilbert," Cordelia shouted at the sphere. "But you have to get back up in the sky, you're needed most up there."

"I should not vacate your presence," Gilbert said. "You are my companions, I must protect you."

"We can handle ourselves down here," Brendan assured him. "Now go!"

Gilbert nodded and the sphere's door closed moments before the ship ascended, zooming brazenly into the middle of a fighter-plane dogfight. Gilbert's sphere quickly destroyed several World War I–era German biplanes with ease.

"It's not going to be enough," Brendan said, looking across the clearing and into San Francisco, where smoke rose up from the city in thick plumes. "Gilbert can't win this battle alone."

"He won't have to," a voice said.

They looked up. The Storm King hovered above them, smiling wickedly.

"Oh great," Cordelia said. "Now we're definitely finished."

"I'm here to *help* you," the Storm King said. "Don't be so cynical. I have already summoned the assistance of several characters from my other novels. This battle isn't over yet. It's just beginning!"

CHAPTER

86

The arrival of the Storm King and his reinforcements brought with it a little hope as the battle raged on around Castle Corroway and San Francisco. If nothing else, his presence extended and expanded the battle to where the destruction now seemed endless.

Three massive colossi were slugging it out inside AT&T Park, where the Giants played (or, more likely now, *used* to play). One was Fat Jagger's cousin, summoned by the Storm King and fighting on behalf of the Resistance; the other two were bloodthirsty colossus thugs fighting for the Wind Witch. The colossus fight broke out during the fifth inning of a sold-out Giants game, the stands filled with fans. The players of both teams huddled in their respective dugouts.

Everyone watched the colossi battle as if it were the seventh game of the World Series. On the field, every punch exchanged between the three giants sounded like a clap of thunder. And each time a blow landed hard enough to send one sprawling to the ground, it demolished entire sections of the legendary baseball stadium. Before long, the colossi leaped over the ballpark's walls and into the surrounding streets. They were plucking up cars and hurling them at one another like rocks. But the two evil colossi were too much for Fat Jagger's cousin to fight on his own. They pelted him with vehicles until he collapsed into the bay and didn't get back up again.

Gilbert and his sphere were still in the air, looping and diving through a massive mess of aircraft. On the Wind Witch's side, several dozen squadrons of World War I–, World War II–, and Vietnam War–era fighter planes and jets zipped and whirled, blasting machine guns and firing missiles everywhere. They far outnumbered the Allied aircraft from the same novels. And further tipping the scales was the arrival of six flying saucers from *Invasion Apocalypse*, one of Denver Kristoff's many pulpy science-fiction novels. Their red laser beams were nearly as devastating as Gilbert's blue lightning, and with six of them, it completely neutralized the effect he'd been having.

Two massive UWOs from *The Terror on the Planet 5X* stood waist-deep near the rocky shore of Alcatraz Island, blasting green flames up onto the historic compound. The huge mass of legendary buildings melted under the green, alien substance as if they were made of marshmallows instead of concrete. After melting down the entire island into nothing but a puddle of gray goop, the UWOs turned and headed toward the mainland.

As they approached, US army tanks from one of Denver's World War II novels and current National Guard tanks worked together and began firing their huge guns at the invading UWO robots. The large-caliber shells repelled the invading robots for a few minutes, but ultimately, the artillery rounds could not pierce the highly advanced, fictional metals that made up the robots' armor.

Before long, the two UWOs were stepping out of the water and onto the Marina, home to tens of thousands of people. The UWOs coated the nearby buildings with their green fire, destroying countless historical and prominent buildings throughout the Marina. The Palace of Fine Arts, one of the city's most stunning locations that had stood since the 1915 Pan Pacific International Exposition, was completely destroyed in a matter of seconds—vanquished into a pile of goo, as if it had never existed at all.

San Francisco would soon be nothing but a memory.

And the creatures would move on from there. Across the country's Midwestern and Mountain states, eventually all the way to the East Coast, laying waste to America and eventually the world.

There were other creatures and monsters among the battle of San Francisco that appeared to harbor no affiliation with either side. They merely acted on behalf of their own predatory instincts. A *Tyrannosaurus rex* from *Dinosaur Island* ran down Taylor Street and into the Tenderloin, stopping every few steps to snap its jaws at many of the area's homeless people.

In the Financial District, packs of giant lions, bloodthirsty from years of being trained to eat Roman gladiators, roamed the streets, attacking bankers, lawyers, and accountants, running down the slowest of them like gazelles. A flock of giant black dragons perched on all sides of the Transamerica Pyramid downtown, occasionally swooping down and snapping up a poor bicyclist or jogger in their long, wicked talons.

Meanwhile, on the Golden Gate Bridge, an all-out battle had erupted. On the San Francisco side of the bridge, a small army of Resistance fighters, along with Wangchuk and several of his monk warriors, joined a group of local police and SWAT officers in an effort to hold off an opposing army of Roman soldiers, Nazi cyborgs, aliens and undead mummies led by a vengeful pharaoh with glowing red eyes.

Wangchuk and his monks attempted to use magic against Wazner's evil army, but they were simply outnumbered. Monks and SWAT team members continued to fall. Soon,

Wangchuk was the last man standing. And, after a valiant battle for his own life and for the sake of a city he did not know, he was finally taken down by a cluster of vengeful mummies.

The Golden Gate Bridge was lost.

Wazner's evil army, packs of malicious aliens, Roman soldiers, and Nazi cyborgs moved into San Francisco, where they would soon overtake the entire city.

And then, in time, the rest of the world.

CHAPTER

87

Brendan, Cordelia, Celene, and Adie hadn't made it very far once Gilbert dropped them off at the perimeter of Castle Corroway's exterior wall. Just as his sphere departed to rejoin the air battle, a band of forty Savage Warriors led by Krom was behind them. Within seconds, they had surrounded the four kids.

"Kill them all," Krom said to his men. They raised their weapons to attack.

Suddenly, Eugene Kristoff arrived, leading a small squad of Resistance fighters and a platoon of Union Civil War troops.

"Step away from those children," Eugene commanded.

Krom and his men turned to face Eugene and his men.

With a loud roar, they charged at the troops—axes, swords, spears, and blunt weapons swinging wildly.

"What do we do?" Adie shouted.

"We need to help," Brendan said, snatching a small crossbow from the cold grip of a dead Resistance fighter.

"No, I mean about those things," Adie said, pointing in the opposite direction.

A pack of angry frost beasts was marching right toward them.

"Okay, Adie," Cordelia said, picking up a sword from the ground. "Me and you will fight those things. Brendan, you and Celene help the others!"

Brendan nodded as he and Celene ran into the madness of the battle. He fired his crossbow once at Krom, missed badly, and then realized he had no idea how to reload it. So he dove for cover, searching the ground desperately for other weapons. Krom growled and charged at him with his ax swinging right toward Brendan's head.

A Union Civil War solider stepped in front of Brendan and lunged with his bayonet. Krom evaded him easily and dispatched the soldier in one quick motion. But it had bought Brendan just enough time to get to his feet and run for safety.

Celene was the most in her element of the four of them, as she twirled and slashed with two small daggers, slicing Savage Warriors on their arms, calves, faces, wherever she could get her blades to land. She danced and twirled like an artist, always managing to stay one step ahead of the incoming swords and axes.

Meanwhile, Cordelia was wildly swinging her sword from side to side, trying to fend off a frost beast that had her cornered. Adie picked up a fallen Union soldier's rifle. She worked to reload it as quickly as possible, just as her daddy had taught her several summers ago. First the powder, then the ball, then packing, mash it all down with the rod. Put the firing cap on the hammer.

Cock. Aim. Fire.

The bullet from the old Civil War musket embedded into the back of the frost beast's neck.

It spun around, its eyes burning with hatred and rage. They weren't intelligent animals, but this one had just enough brains to identify the small, trembling girl holding the musket as its attacker. It charged at Adie.

Cordelia climbed to her feet again and quickly recognized that Adie had just saved her life. She knew she couldn't let the little girl sacrifice herself, fictional character or not.

The frost beast was just a few steps away from Adie.

Cordelia took three steps forward and launched her sword like a spear. It spiraled upward, spun around in midair, and headed back down toward the ground, right at the top of the frost beast's head. The sword fell short and instead thumped into the back of its thigh with a soft *thwack*!

The creature led out a blood-chilling roar. He spun around again and charged at Cordelia, who was still cornered by the outer wall of Castle Corroway. There was nowhere to run or hide. She was trapped.

CHAPTER

88

Above the battle, hovering somewhere between Castle Corroway and Fisherman's Wharf, the Wind Witch and Eleanor watched the chaos with glee. It was obvious that their army was going to win. There was nothing the puny Resistance army or the confused modern-day military could do to stop them. Even when more reinforcements showed up, the Wind Witch would still outnumber them with her vast array of terrifying characters.

She turned to Eleanor.

"Isn't life so much richer, so much more meaningful, when you possess such great power?" the Wind Witch asked.

"Oh yes," Eleanor said, still holding the glowing red Invictum.

The Wind Witch shrieked with delight and dipped down toward the ground, incinerating a few Resistance fighters with lightning, before rejoining Eleanor in the sky.

Across the bay, the Storm King was locked in a heated battle with a UWO. For most of the battle, the Storm King had been flying around the giant robots, hitting them with every form of powerful magic he could muster. But it had no effect. They were virtually indestructible—and he only had himself to blame since he was the one who'd written them that way. The Storm King was desperate to stop the robots, since they were causing the most significant damage to the city, melting everything in their path.

But then a chillingly familiar sound diverted his attention.

His daughter's evil laughter.

She and Eleanor were still hovering above the action, enjoying the view of the destruction. That's when he saw it: the glowing red blade of the Invictum in Eleanor's hand.

For the first time during the battle, the Storm King was hopeful.

He knew the Worldkeeper was their only shot at victory. He needed to get it back. It was his only chance of stopping the UWOs and all the other horrific creatures obliterating San Francisco. The Storm King loved his characters. . . . He had created them after all. But the last thing he wanted to see was them destroying the city he loved. Even in death,

San Francisco was still his home.

He disengaged from his futile battle with the UWO and immediately launched himself at the Wind Witch and Eleanor.

Eleanor saw him approaching first.

"Watch out!" she yelled, swooping left.

But it was too late. Blue lightning erupted from the tips of the Storm King's fingers. The Wind Witch was able to avoid the bulk of the blast, but the lightning still struck the lower half of her body, sending her tumbling down toward the bay.

Eleanor's knowledge of the magic that the Wind Witch had been teaching her was still raw, in its experimental stage. She knew she didn't stand a chance against the more powerful and experienced Storm King. Instead of fighting a useless battle, Eleanor used that moment to flee.

She swooped down toward Castle Corroway, hoping to find somewhere inside to hide. The Storm King dove after her and easily closed the distance between them. By the time they reached the castle, the Storm King was fewer than twenty feet behind Eleanor. He couldn't miss. He uttered a quick spell and fired more lightning from his hands. This was a more concentrated attack, aimed at Eleanor's right hand still tightly clutching the Invictum.

The lightning wrapped around her wrist like handcuffs. Eleanor screamed in pain and released the Invictum. The knife plummeted toward the ground. The Storm King's eyes gleamed as he raced after it.

But Eleanor was young and recovered from the lightning strike much faster than expected. As the Storm King tried to fly past her, Eleanor let out a scream of pure rage and charged at him, sending a forceful blast of wind at his body. The Storm King flew backward, tumbling head over heels before slamming into the castle's outer wall with a sickening crunch.

His body went limp and fell toward the hard ground below.

89

As Brendan scampered across the battlefield, searching for a weapon, he saw Cordelia throw her sword at a frost beast. The roar that followed caused the hairs on Brendan's neck to stand up on end. He knew in an instant that if he didn't do something to intervene, Cordelia would be killed.

He leaped to his feet and sprinted toward a dead Union soldier with an ax lying near him. Brendan grabbed the ax handle and then he spun back around to go save Cordelia when a *thump* to his left caught his attention.

It was the Invictum; it had fallen from the sky and lodged partially into the ground. The diamond blade sparkled invitingly in the sunlight.

Brendan looked up and saw Eleanor attacking the Storm King. He knew this was his only chance to possibly regain control of the battle. He knew how powerful the Invictum was. He had felt its strength the few times he'd held it. And most important, he'd seen it slice open the magical portal between two worlds.

Brendan needed to get it. They needed it to save their world.

But someone else had also spotted the Invictum. Just ten feet away, Krom held a bloody sword in his hand and stared at the powerful knife. His eyes trailed over toward Brendan, and he sneered.

Brendan gripped the ax and looked back at Cordelia. The frost beast was still approaching her. She was backed into a corner. Brendan knew there would only be time for one course of action.

He could either get to the Invictum and allow his sister Cordelia to die. Or he could save Cordelia's life and let Krom get possession of the Invictum, which would be sealing all their fates.

In a moment of true panic, Brendan froze. He hesitated for several seconds longer than needed to make a split-second decision. The gravity of the situation absolutely paralyzed him.

But then he snapped himself out of it. He just needed to get the Invictum first—then he could save Cordelia.

Without the Invictum, all was lost. Everyone in San Francisco, maybe everyone on the planet, would die. If he didn't get to that knife first, then Cordelia would eventually die anyway, along with everyone else, including him. More important, he reasoned, it's what Cordelia would want him to do.

Brendan ran toward the Invictum, dirt kicking up behind him.

90

Krom and Brendan lunged for the Invictum simultaneously. In the first few seconds of his mad dash toward the knife, Brendan realized that Krom would get there first. And so going directly for the knife would virtually ensure his own bloody death.

He saw Krom's eyes, however, and realized that the big Savage Warrior didn't even register Brendan as a physical threat. All that mattered to Krom was getting the magical knife.

So as Brendan approached, he slowed and steadied himself, allowing Krom to wrap his thick sausage fingers around the handle of the Invictum. In that moment of victory, as Krom grinned and stared at the knife's sparkling blade, Brendan reared the ax backward and swung it like a baseball bat.

The blade sailed through the air and passed right by Krom's head without any resistance.

Brendan had missed!

He had planned it perfectly, had his shot, and missed! And now he was going to die right along with everyone else. Krom had a ridiculous victory grin on his face. He was savoring the moment as he held up the Invictum in celebratory arrogance.

"Stop gloating and get it over with already," Brendan said.

"If you insist," Krom said with a sickening smile as he reared back the blade to slice up Brendan like deli meat.

But a thunderous explosion above them caused Krom to hesitate. They both looked up and saw a flaming World War II plane spiraling toward them at hundreds of miles per hour. Brendan only had enough time to duck and then was knocked by the force of the crashing plane impacting the ground.

He sat up again, dazed. Krom was no longer standing in front of him. The Invictum lay on the ground where he had stood moments ago. Behind it was a streak of burned ground and plane wreckage that carved a fifty-foot path into the dirt. Brendan saw what was left of Krom in the burning heap of metal.

"Gross!" Brendan said to no one in particular, before quickly jumping to his feet and grabbing the Invictum.

He spun around, hoping that Cordelia was somehow still okay.

But he was too late.

Brendan had turned just in time to see Cordelia staring straight at him, her mouth forming a scream. Then the frost beast leaned in, roaring savagely. Brendan felt his body go numb.

91

Brendan let the Invictum fall from his hand and clatter to the ground. None of it mattered anymore; he was already defeated. As tears streamed down his face, Brendan remembered Cordelia teaching him how to read when he was in preschool. He remembered how she always saved the last cookie or bit of dessert for him. He could only remember the good things—the times she was the best older sister a kid could imagine. And he had let her die because he'd hesitated just a moment too long. He had been preoccupied with being the hero instead of just acting.

And now it was all over for him. He knew he would not be able to get his legs working again.

Brendan was still too dazed and torn apart by what he

had just let happen to notice the bright liquid metal sphere floating down toward him from the sky. Gilbert's ship's sensors had picked up on powerful energy readings from the ongoing battle between the Storm King and Eleanor. Once his attention had been diverted, he'd witnessed the entire struggle for the Invictum.

He landed the sphere, stepped out, and stood next to Brendan.

"I let her die," Brendan said quietly, not looking up. "I could have saved her, but instead I just let her die. And the worst part is, she looked right at me. I was the last thing she saw before . . ."

A sob escaped his mouth then and he hunched over farther. Despite being half his size, Gilbert bent over, grabbed Brendan's shirt, and hauled him to his feet with surprising ease.

"Do you know what you need to save your sister?" Gilbert asked.

"Save her?" Brendan asked frantically. "She's already dead. There's no way to bring her back . . ."

"There is one way," Gilbert said.

Brendan looked at him, his eyes red and drained. He shook his head, assuming this was just more of the little alien's arrogant bluster. Gilbert pointed at his own chest.

"This is where my heart is located," Gilbert said.

"Yeah, that's usually where hearts are located," Brendan

said. "You're not making any sense, Gilbert."

Gilbert just looked back at him calmly.

And that's when it all clicked into place for Brendan. Of course! The Wind Witch had hinted that Gilbert was the last Worldkeeper. And Denver's *Journal* had indicated that the third Worldkeeper had its own special power. It had the power to reverse time.

"Your heart is the last Worldkeeper," Brendan said slowly.

"I do not know . . . ," Gilbert said, the first time he had ever uttered those words. "But I do know that my heart is supremely valuable. Powerful beyond imagination. I have expended my entire life avoiding intergalactic bounty hunters and poachers who tracked me for my heart. Because I have spent my life running, I have never known what it is like to have a home or a family. At least, not until I met you and the supplementary members of the Walker familial unit."

"Your heart . . . ," Brendan said, tears already biting at the corners of his eyes. "It can save Cordelia."

"Affirmative," Gilbert said, nodding his tiny head. "Whoever possesses my heart can transverse time and correct their most prevalent error."

Brendan looked down at the bloody battlefield and then back near the wall, where the frost beast had killed Cordelia.

"I don't think I can do it," Brendan said. "Even if it means saving Cordelia . . . I don't think I can kill my friend."

"Your . . . friend?" Gilbert asked, his voice somewhat shocked, softer than ever. "You regard me . . . with the title *friend?*"

Brendan smiled sadly and nodded.

"No one has ever labeled me with the title of friend before," Gilbert said. "Is it because I am so supremely handsome?"

Brendan let out a choked sob and laugh as he nodded and wiped at the tears that were now streaming from his eyes.

"That, and because you're selfless and loyal," Brendan said. "Like all great friends are."

"Then it has to be done," Gilbert assured him. "This moment was inevitable since the beginning. You require my heart to remedy this." He motioned at the entirety of the battle around them. "Furthermore, you already possess the only device in existence that can perforate my skin."

Brendan nodded again, picking up the Invictum at his feet.

"Very well then," Gilbert said, moving his arms so his small torso was completely exposed. "Proceed. After all, I know now that I am not real. I am only a character in a book, a trifling fragment of Denver Kristoff's imagination. My entire existence is an invention anyway."

Brendan held up the Invictum. He pressed the blade to Gilbert's chest but then hesitated.

"I can't do it," he said.

"I will assist," Gilbert said.

He reached out, grabbed the knife and made a small cut in his torso. He removed a small, bright green organ the size of a golf ball and held it up to Brendan.

Gilbert's eyes gleamed. He looked at Brendan one last time and smiled as Brendan took the heart in his hand.

"Optimal luck and fortune in your continued efforts, my friend," Gilbert said.

Then his lifeless body slumped down to the ground as Brendan sobbed.

CHAPTER

92

Brendan forced himself to look away from Gilbert's lifeless alien body. He reminded himself that if they were somehow successful, he might still be able to save his friend's life. Denver had said that bringing the Worldkeepers through the Door of Ways would not only seal off the two worlds from each other forever, but that it would undo all the damage caused.

As Brendan stood there, holding Gilbert's bright green heart, trying to stem the flow of his tears, he suddenly found himself surrounded by swirling purple-and-yellow lights. The bright colors began to spread and dim. They fused together, forming a psychedelic tunnel of light.

At the end of it stood Cordelia. She was alive, but was

frightened and cowering, covering her head as if she were about to be attacked. Brendan realized that was precisely what was about to happen. Again.

This was his chance to fix things.

Brendan sprinted down the light tunnel. The frost beast stepped into his view now, hovering over Cordelia, her sword still sticking out of its leg. Cordelia looked up, and again looked into Brendan's eyes. The frost beast let out a vicious roar and lunged.

Brendan's stomach churned. He'd waited too long to act and now he was about to blow his only chance to save his older sister. He leaped into the air from a dead sprint, whirling the Invictum over the top of his head. The blade came down onto the back of the frost beast's skull and its furry white body crumpled to the ground.

"Brendan!" Cordelia said, her eyes wide and her mouth hanging open.

He climbed to his feet, grinning.

"Hey, Deal," he said, wiping away the last of his tears.

"How did you get over here so fast?" she asked. "I mean, I just saw you way over there, fighting Krom, and I thought for sure I was dead, and . . . and, what are you holding in your hand?" She pointed at Gilbert's fluorescent-green heart.

Brendan looked at it somberly and frowned.

"It's the third Worldkeeper," he said. "I'll explain later.

But from the look of it, our side is still losing badly."

They both stood there and stared beyond Castle Corroway, where they saw San Francisco in ruins. Many of the skyline's most iconic buildings were either in shambles, on fire, or completely gone. Thick black smoke intermingled with the once-magical, famous San Francisco fog. Countless police and fire engine sirens tore through the air.

"What are we going to do?" Cordelia asked.

"We have all of the Worldkeepers now," Brendan said.

"Yeah, but I'm not leaving without Nell," Cordelia said.

"I'm with you," Brendan agreed.

They looked up as someone floated down next to them. It was the Storm King, and he looked like he'd seen better days. Blood dripped down his gray and wrinkled face.

"You retrieved the Invictum," he said. "Well done, Brendan. We will need it to win this battle."

"We need to save our sister," Cordelia said. "And then we can take the three Worldkeepers to the Door of Ways and fix this."

"We'll never get there," the Storm King said, shaking his head.

"Why not?" Brendan asked.

"The Wind Witch has an even larger army waiting at the entrance," the Storm King said. "Even with the Invictum, we won't be able to break through."

"So what do we do?" Brendan asked.

"We need to stop the Wind Witch," the Storm King said. "Right here. Right now. It's the Wind Witch who is controlling the characters, forcing them to destroy your city. Just like she's controlling the army at the Door of Ways. But if she is defeated, the characters will disperse on their own, back to their own book worlds, where they belong."

"So, if we stop her," Brendan said, "we can end this whole battle and clear a path to the Door of Ways?"

"Exactly," the Storm King said. "Now, let me take you to where you can do some real damage with the Invictum. Climb onto my back."

He crouched down. Brendan wrapped his arms around the Storm King's shoulders tentatively and grimaced, like he'd just been asked to hug a corpse.

"I'm not *that* disgusting," the Storm King said.

"If we win this thing, you should think about investing in some deodorant," Brendan said, trying not to gag. He turned back toward Cordelia as they slowly lifted off the ground. "Stay safe!"

Cordelia nodded at him, watching the Storm King and her brother soar high into the air and then back toward the city.

The Storm King clearly had a plan in mind, so Brendan just held on for dear life as the old man flew right toward Fisherman's Wharf. There, several UWO robots were in the process of melting all the buildings and boats docked at Pier 39. Fishermen and tourists leaped into the water to avoid the deadly green flames. The Storm King flew directly above one of the giant robots, above the cockpit at the front of their heads. From this vantage point, Brendan saw a tiny purple alien with tentacle arms inside, controlling the UWO's motions.

"Jump," the Storm King said.

"What!" Brendan shouted. "Are you insane?"

"I wrote those robots to be virtually indestructible," he said. "The only thing that can penetrate their armor is the Invictum. Now stop wasting precious time. Jump down there and take control of that thing. You always wanted to be a hero, right? Well, it's not just going to fall into your lap!"

Brendan looked down at the massive robot. They were still a good ten feet above the cockpit. But he had to do this. If he wanted to save the world, he had to find the courage within himself. It was time to do the right thing when the right thing counted.

Brendan took a deep breath.

And then he jumped.

He landed on the robot's metal shoulder with a metallic thud. He fell to his knees, twisting his ankle badly. He gasped in pain, but knew he likely had very little time to lie there and feel sorry for himself. So he rolled to his left and into a crouch.

He stared directly into the cockpit housing the alien pilot. Up close, the thing was even more hideous. It was purple, but not a pretty, vibrant purple. It looked more like someone drank a seven-week-old grape slushie and then puked all over an octopus. Its mouth was filled with terrifying yellow daggers for teeth and its seven tentacle arms slithered through the air like worms.

The alien saw Brendan, screeched, and immediately pulled a lever. The robot raised his claw hand, moving toward Brendan with surprising speed and dexterity. Brendan had nowhere to run—and couldn't run with a broken ankle even if he had somewhere to go.

Instead he lifted the Invictum.

As the claw was just about to crush him, Brendan rolled to the side and whipped the diamond blade across his body like a backhanded tennis stroke. The Invictum cut through the top pincer of the claw with amazingly little resistance. It folded away and dangled like a hangnail.

Brendan sprang into a hobbling and awkward run. He bit down on his lip to keep from crying out in pain, and in six uneven, bounding steps, he reached the glass cockpit on top of the robot's shoulders.

He stabbed the Invictum into the glass dome and dragged it in a rough circle. A thick hunk of glass fell away inside the cockpit.

The alien, who had spent his existence assuming that the

robot he was controlling was indestructible, was now screaming in shock. The creature's shrieks were ear-piercingly loud, so awful that Brendan covered his head with his arms. He'd just let his guard down, and the alien could have torn him apart with its tentacles.

But it didn't. Instead, it sat there shrieking louder and louder as its yellow eyes bulged. Its flailing became even more desperate.

And then it exploded.

Green and purple chunks of alien guts and flesh rained down on Brendan.

The earth's atmosphere clearly wasn't suited for the aliens outside of their pressurized cockpit. Brendan clambered inside the ship and sat down in a warm gooey puddle of alien slime and guts.

It didn't take long to figure out how to operate the robot. There were six levers and a primitive illustration detailing how each worked. Two controlled the feet, two controlled the arms, and the final two operated the pincers on the claw hand. There was a huge green button on the dashboard. Beside it was an illustration of a fireball. Brendan assumed that this was the trigger for the green flames.

The problem, of course, was that with just two arms, Brendan wouldn't be able to pilot the robot nearly as seamlessly as the aliens with seven tentacles. But he would do the best he could. Slowly, he maneuvered the massive robot toward the other UWO, which was currently shooting showers of green flames over many of the pier's restaurants, gift shops, and tourists.

Brendan managed to stop just short of the other robot. He pulled a lever and raised the green flamethrower arm so it was pointed directly at the robot's back. Brendan took a deep breath and pressed the button.

Green flames flowed from his robot's right arm. They completely engulfed the other robot. At first, nothing happened. Then the other robot slowly turned around, still engulfed in the liquid green flames. Within a few moments, the green flames subsided and the UWO remained standing, unharmed. The alien saw Brendan and screeched, raising its robot's right arm toward Brendan.

Obviously the metal exteriors were designed to withstand the power of their own weapons. Brendan breathed a sigh of relief, realizing that he too would be able to withstand a blast of deadly green flame. But then an awful realization hit him.

His cockpit had a massive hole in it.

And Brendan was sitting directly in front of it.

There was nothing to protect him from the green flames!

Brendan sat there in alien guts and watched in horror as the other UWO took a step toward him, flamethrower raised and poised to melt him into Brendan stew.

CHAPTER

93

Brendan was sure he was about to die. His only hope was that getting melted by green fire was less painful than it sounded. He hit the red button again in desperation and then something astonishing happened. As the other UWO took a step forward, getting ready to fire, the green flames from Brendan's robot licked up against its glass dome.

It melted a huge hole in the side of the glass cockpit. The purple alien squealed in shock and pain and then exploded all over the inside of the glass like a bug the size of a raccoon hitting a car windshield.

"Ewww," Brendan said to himself, forgetting momentarily that he was still sitting in a mound of stinking alien guts.

Brendan pivoted the robot slowly until he was facing the two colossi, still standing inside the remains of AT&T Park. The colossi were taking turns picking up National Guard troops off the ground and flicking them out into McCovey Cove like rolled-up boogers.

Brendan pushed the levers, forcing his robot into a run. He kept the robot's right arm raised, ready to fire. But as Brendan neared what was left of the stadium and saw the size of the National Guard force inside, he realized he couldn't use the green flames. If he did, he'd probably end up melting hundreds of innocent troops in the process.

And so Brendan kept pushing and pulling the robot's two leg levers in tandem, increasing his speed. The UWO lumbered toward the two colossi standing inside the half-demolished park. The first one never saw him coming.

Brendan kept pumping the leg levers as the robot slammed into the colossus's stomach. The half-naked, balding giant belched in surprise as it went sprawling out into McCovey Cove. It landed headfirst, cracking its skull on the concrete pier across the inlet.

The colossus did not move or try to get back up. It just lay facedown and motionless in a pile of smashed concrete, its body sprawled out across the cove. Brendan rotated the robot to face the other colossus. This one was slightly younger and far more muscular than Fat Jagger or the giant Brendan had just bodychecked with his robot. It had a square jaw and head and looked remarkably like a young version of Arnold Schwarzenegger.

Big Arnold let out a yell of rage and slammed the National Guard jeep he'd been holding into the outfield like he was spiking a football. It exploded into a million pieces. Brendan raised the robot's two arms into a fistfighting stance.

Arnold charged at him, flailing his massive fists wildly. Brendan waited, knowing he needed to be patient. As soon as Arnold got close enough, he thrust the right-arm lever forward as quickly as he could.

The robot's right arm landed squarely inside Big Arnold's enormous mouth. The colossus's eyes went wide with surprise as it tried to figure out what had just happened. Brendan knew it was now or never to safely take out the bloodthirsty and brutal colossus with minimal collateral damage.

He stared right into Big Arnold's wide and huge eyes and then pressed the button. Flames fired from the end of the robot's right arm, directly into Big Arnold's mouth. It was the most disgusting thing Brendan had ever seen, and the past year had been filled with enough horrors to give the entire population of Norway nightmares for life.

Brendan rotated the robot back toward the huge opening out in the bay, where the two worlds had merged together. It was clear that the battle was far from over. And the Wind

Witch and Eleanor had now joined the fight. He saw them engaged with a third flying figure that appeared to be the Storm King.

And it was clear who was winning that fight. Brendan watched in horror as the Wind Witch and Eleanor hit the old man simultaneously with a blistering column of intensely freezing air containing a battalion of sharp icicles. The old man didn't stand a chance under their barrage of attacks.

Brendan watched, stunned, as the dual attacks hit the Storm King with enough force to kill a bear and sent him spiraling toward the ground.

CHAPTER 94

Cordelia, Adie, and Celene watched from the grounds outside of Castle Corroway as the Storm King plunged down toward the front gate.

Cordelia still could hardly believe what Eleanor was doing. It was incomprehensible that it was her little sister, flying around and using dark magic to harm other people.

Adie, Celene, and Cordelia ran toward where the Storm King had fallen. They found his crumpled body lying in the dirt near the castle's front gate.

"Oh no," Cordelia said as she knelt next to the Storm King. Adie and Celene were right behind her.

She wasn't sure what was more shocking: the fact that she had just seen her own sister take down the Storm King, or that she was actually saddened by his demise. Cordelia knew that the Storm King had been their only hope to survive the battle. They were no match for the power of the Wind Witch alone, especially now that she had an apprentice by her side.

The Storm King groaned and rolled over. Dozens of icicles had pierced his ancient, decrepit body. His blood drained onto the ground around him, mixing with the melting icicles.

"You must go," he said. "Protect the Worldkeepers. There is still hope."

Cordelia didn't get a chance to reply because a steady rumble under her knees caused her to look up. It was one of the huge robots from *The Terror on Planet 5X*. At least, she reasoned morbidly as the UWO aimed its flamethrower at them, they wouldn't be suffering much longer.

But then her fear faded when she realized the robot was being piloted by her brother!

Brendan waved at her from the cockpit. Then he looked up toward the Wind Witch and Eleanor hovering above them.

"I'm going to finish you!" Brendan shouted through the hole in the cockpit glass.

The Wind Witch laughed in his face.

"I'm serious," Brendan shouted. "Release my sister or I'll melt you like a s'more!"

"I'm not forcing your little sister to do anything against her will," the Wind Witch said calmly. "Your family has never treated her with respect. She is by my side because I recognize her intelligence and power."

The Wind Witch turned to Eleanor.

"Go on, granddaughter," the Wind Witch said. "Show them just how powerful you've become."

Eleanor smiled as she raised her hands and fired a funneling burst of wind directly at Brendan's robot. The miniature tornado impacted the robot's chest, sending the UWO flying backward. They all watched in horror as it flipped end over end in midair, and then crashed facedown onto the grounds of Castle Corroway.

95

Brendan opened his eyes and looked around. Luckily, the inside of the cockpit was equipped with a futuristic version of an air bag. Upon release, it cushioned Brendan's fall and saved his life. He didn't get away completely unscathed, however. His bones and joints ached, blood ran down his face from a deep cut on his head, and he was covered in bruises.

Brendan squeezed his way out of the wreckage. He stumbled outside and saw Cordelia, Adie, and Celene cowering near the lifeless body of the Storm King. The Wind Witch and Eleanor hovered over them menacingly.

Brendan limped over to rejoin his older sister. The only sister he had left, apparently. They embraced briefly and silently. It was over. Even with the Invictum still clutched in Brendan's left hand, the battle was lost.

He knew the Wind Witch's magic could disarm him easily before he could do much of anything with the powerful weapon. And so, he stood next to Cordelia and Adie and Celene and looked up at the Wind Witch's smiling face in defeat. He had no more jokes to offer.

The demolished ruins of San Francisco smoked behind the Wind Witch and Eleanor like a smoldering campfire.

The Wind Witch smiled and said, "Well, it appears that I have *finally won*."

96

The Wind Witch could hardly believe it herself. She was finally going to get everything she wanted: to rule over both worlds, to replace all the love and family she had lost in her life with absolute power.

Even her sorry, pathetic excuse for a father couldn't stop her now, as he lay dying on the ground beneath her feet.

"It is time to complete your transformation, my dear granddaughter," she said, turning to Eleanor.

"How will I do that?" Eleanor asked.

"By killing your siblings," the Wind Witch said.

Cordelia and Brendan exchanged a shocked glance.

"You actually want me to kill them?" Eleanor asked.

"Why not?" the Wind Witch said. "These are the siblings

who always held you back, who always thought they were better than you, smarter than you, stronger than you. They could never love you the way I do."

Eleanor looked down at Cordelia and Brendan. Adie stood next to them and shook her head slowly in shock—as if what she was about to witness were impossible. For a moment, Eleanor's intent appeared to waver. Deep down, Cordelia, Adie, and Brendan truly believed Eleanor wouldn't, *couldn't* go through with it.

But once a soul had been touched by *The Book of Doom and Desire*, there would be no fighting its deepest wishes. The Wind Witch knew that better than anyone. And Eleanor had used the book twice, more than enough to irreversibly damage the core of whatever it was that made her human. The Wind Witch leaned close to Eleanor and whispered softly into her ear.

"Do what I cannot," she prodded. "Finish off your brother and sister. Once and for all."

Any doubt that lingered on Eleanor's face disappeared. She turned and looked at her siblings. Her face was cold. It was as if her eyes were now made of glass.

The Wind Witch watched with pleasure as Brendan's and Cordelia's faces changed from hopeful to a sort of devastated acceptance as they realized that their sweet little sister *did* have it in her.

She was going to kill them.

97

Eleanor moved in for the kill. Nothing was going to stop her; she could feel that deep down where her healthy soul had once breathed life into her. But that part of her was gone. All that remained was darkness. And anger. And resentment.

The two people she stared at weren't her *siblings* anymore. They were no longer her brother and sister, but just a pair of arrogant brats. They deserved this. They deserved it after the way they'd always treated her—the way they'd held themselves up on a pedestal over her and everyone else around them.

Eleanor raised her hands and prepared to cast the wicked spell that the Wind Witch had taught her. It would lead to a horrible, painful death.

"*Hostibus meis pessima—*" Eleanor began.

But then suddenly the words caught in her throat as Adie stepped in front of Brendan and Cordelia, attempting to shield them.

"Stop!" Adie shouted with tears in her eyes. "Or you'll have to kill me too!"

Eleanor hesitated as the doubt rushed back all at once.

"What's the fuss?" the Wind Witch asked, clearly annoyed at the delay. "Just kill her as well."

Eleanor gritted her teeth. "Move aside," she said.

"No. You can't do this," Adie said softly. "They're your family. Your bond runs deeper than anything else. Deeper than magic or some ancient book. Family is the only thing of value any of us are born with. I won't let you destroy your own. They love you too much, Eleanor. Believe me when I tell you . . . they love you *more than anything*! And I won't let that kind of love die. You'll have to kill me first!"

This simple act of kindness and sacrifice sapped the hatred right out of Eleanor.

All at once, she saw how petty the quest for power and money and things really was. The very things the Wind Witch had promised her.

None of those things mattered—not really. Eleanor realized that now. The ten million dollars she had wished for on their first adventure had only brought pain to their family. Eleanor would be happier living in a cardboard box with her family and friends than living without them in a huge mansion filled with everything she'd ever want, including a stable of horses.

For the first time in Eleanor's life, she understood the true nature of compassion and love. It required a sacrifice, giving up a piece of your own happiness and well-being in order to improve the lives of others.

Slowly she flew down to the earth. She landed and dropped to her knees in front of Adie, Brendan, and Cordelia.

"I'm so sorry," she said as tears streamed down her face.

Cordelia rushed forward and wrapped her arms around her little sister. As soon as they embraced, Eleanor felt herself become whole again. They probably would have stayed there and hugged for hours had the Wind Witch not interrupted them with a howl of fury.

"If I can't kill you," the Wind Witch spat, "then I will make you feel the most intense pain of your young lives!"

Before any of them could respond, she let loose a powerful ball of red fire that slammed into Adie's chest. The girl flew backward and landed in the dirt with a soft thump. Her eyes were still open, but there was no life left behind them.

98

The Walkers stood there and stared at Adie's lifeless body in shock. They were stunned at how the little girl they'd just met a few days before had sacrificed herself for them. And also at just how easily and carelessly the Wind Witch had disposed of her. But perhaps the most terrifying part of all was the cry of anguish that escaped from the throat of the dying Storm King.

Even in spite of his fatal injuries, he crawled over toward Adie's body leaving a trail of blood behind him. His sobbing wails of grief were so shocking that they had even stunned the Wind Witch into silence.

She watched along with everyone else as the Storm King cradled Adie's body and wept. She had never seen her father act like this, even before he had corrupted his own soul with *The Book of Doom and Desire.*

"Why?" she eventually demanded, floating down toward him. "Why are you mourning a meaningless character from your book?"

The Storm King shook his head, still crying, unable to speak.

"You fight me at every turn, working against me to make me unhappy!" she screamed, her anger returning. Except it was different now. The cold, empty fury was gone. "Yet you mourn a character as if she were your *own daughter?*"

Finally he looked up, his face streaked with a mixture of tears and his own blood.

"But she is my daughter," he said quietly. "Don't you even recognize yourself? What you used to be?"

The Wind Witch was standing on the ground now and took a step backward, shaking her head.

"No," she whispered.

"Yes, it's you," Denver said, stroking Adie's hair. "I created this character in one of my books to try and preserve the best of my young daughter, my sweet Dahlia. I wrote her exactly as you were when you were her age, just the way I remembered you before that terrible book stole you away from me. It was the only way to preserve the good in you. You were once so kind, generous, strong, and sweet. And now . . . now you've just killed the last bit of good left in you.

You've become so twisted you didn't even recognize yourself."

The Wind Witch stood there shaking her head. But she looked different somehow. More human. The magical, murderous rage she'd held onto for so many years seemed to have faded.

Cordelia suddenly saw an opportunity. Maybe she could connect with the old Dahlia, maybe she could somehow reach her, if the old Dahlia was still somewhere inside of the twisted old witch before them.

"Do you see the power of family love now?" Cordelia asked, stepping forward. "This is why you've been so evil and confused ever since we met you. It's because you lost your father, your true family, at too young an age. Once he started using *The Book of Doom and Desire*, he ceased to be himself. But now your father is back.

"You can be with him again. You spend your life searching for power. . . . What has it gotten you so far? Only more misery, pain, and defeat. Even we're guilty of the same thing to some extent." She motioned at Brendan. "Brendan has long been obsessed with his own self-image rather than just being the person he truly is. Heroism isn't something you can *try* to be. Those are things you just *are*. And they ultimately don't even matter as long as you simply stay true to yourself.

"And I realize now I was guilty of that too. True intelligence is realizing and recognizing not what you know . . . but what you *don't* know. That my sister and brother can each have amazing ideas that I could never dream of. We're all flawed, but together we're at our best."

She was crying now, and so was Brendan in spite of his best efforts to hide it. They all watched the Wind Witch silently.

They watched her expression soften. She suddenly appeared twenty years younger, free from all the tension and anger. Her eyes filled with tears for the first time in decades. She stepped forward and gently knelt down, tenderly embracing her dying father, who was still cradling Adie's body.

It was the first time they had been at peace since *The Book of Doom and Desire* had entered their lives all those years ago. And as they held each other, something shocking happened. The Wind Witch started to transform.

The Walkers and Celene watched in awe as she changed back into the little girl she had been when she had first used *The Book of Doom and Desire*. The father and daughter in front of them were no longer the Storm King and Wind Witch.

They were Denver and Dahlia Kristoff.

Together again, at last.

CHAPTER

99

"Once the Wind Witch changed, the evil characters and creatures from Denver's books lost their purpose. As if coming out of a trance, they all stopped attacking the city. They turned and headed back to the portal between the two worlds, back to their own book worlds.

But the city of San Francisco was still in ruins. There was no celebrating the end of this battle. There was still work to be done.

"You can fix all of this," Denver Kristoff said to the Walkers weakly. "Take the Worldkeepers to the Door of Ways. It can undo this madness. If all three pass through the door at the same time, it will reverse the magic, returning the city to its normal state and severing the link between the two worlds forever."

"But how will we get there?" Eleanor asked.

"I've summoned some friends of yours," Denver said. "They'll take you there."

Just then, two P-51 Mustangs came soaring in and landed in the clearing behind them. The two pilots hopped out of their planes and walked over.

"I heard you Yanks need a lift," Will Draper said.

"Will!" Cordelia yelled, running over to him and giving him a huge hug.

He laughed and hugged her back.

"What about your ex-husband?" Felix asked, holding open his arms, pretending to be hurt.

Cordelia laughed and gave him a hug as well.

"Go now, you must hurry," Denver said. "The battle may be over for my book characters, but I can do nothing to stop the real US military reinforcements that are on their way here—they may not know who is friend or foe and ultimately do more harm than good."

Brendan spun around and faced Celene. He wanted to send her off with a legendary and epic speech that would be repeated and retold in Tinz for years to come. But the words that came out of his mouth were certainly not something for the history books.

"You are . . . um . . . I like . . . you know . . ."

And then she stunned him by moving in and pressing her lips to his. His eyes widened.

It was his first kiss. And he definitely would not be forgetting it anytime soon. She pulled away from him several seconds later and smiled. He opened his mouth to talk, but she shook her head.

"Don't say it, Brendan," she said, smiling. "Sometimes it's better to just *not talk*. Good-bye. I'll never forget you."

He nodded in a daze and then allowed Cordelia to pull him toward the waiting P-51 Mustangs. She grinned at him, and he blushed.

"Eleanor, come on!" Cordelia yelled.

The youngest Walker stood in front of a twelve-year-old Dahlia, who looked remarkably like Adie. She smiled at her and then the two embraced. They had been through a lot together the past few days, even if it was as slightly different people. They saw Dahlia whisper something into Eleanor's ear, and Eleanor responded. Then she broke away and ran over to join her brother and sister.

"What did she say to you?" Cordelia asked.

Eleanor grinned. "Can't tell you that."

"Oh great," Brendan said, still a little dazed. "I hope you didn't ask her for ten million bucks again."

"Did you really just say that you hope we *don't* get ten million dollars?" Cordelia asked, shocked.

Brendan paused. Then he nodded.

"Yeah, I guess I did," he said. "And I actually meant it."

"Come on, then. Let's go," Will said with a grin. "You haven't actually saved the world just yet!"

CHAPTER
100

B rendan, Eleanor, and Cordelia Walker stood in front of the Door of Ways. The talisman dangled from Cordelia's neck. The Invictum was secured to one of the belt loops on Eleanor's jeans. Gilbert's heart was cradled in Brendan's hand.

Together, they took a deep breath inside the cave as they faced the shimmering waterfall of light that was the Door of Ways.

"I just realized something," Cordelia said suddenly, breaking the silence.

"What's that?" Brendan asked.

"Well, you had a crush on Adie, right?" Cordelia asked.

"Noooo . . ."

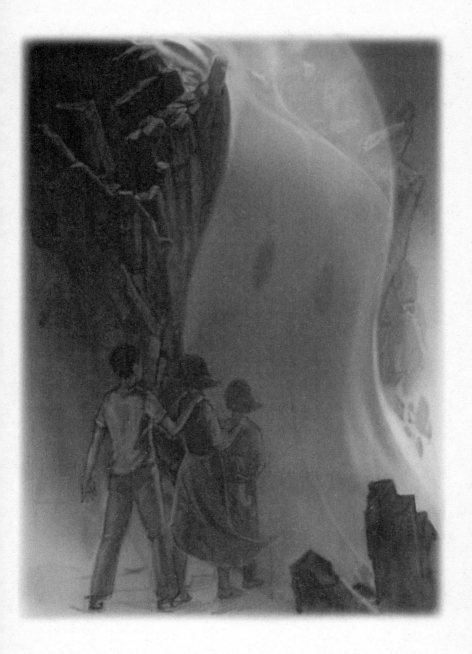

"Brendan, admit it."

"Okay, yeah," Brendan said. "Maybe I had a small, tiny, infinitesimal crush on her . . . before we ran into Celene, that is."

"You know what that means right?" Cordelia said.

"What?"

"That you technically had a crush on the Wind Witch!"

"On your own great-great-grandmother!" Eleanor added, laughing. "Gross!"

Brendan shook his head, but then he couldn't help himself from bursting out laughing. Then they went quiet again as they looked at the shimmering Door of Ways. The last time they had stepped through the doorway, it had challenged them. They had no idea what to expect this time.

"Are you guys really ready for this to be over?" Cordelia asked.

"That's supposed to be a joke, right?" Brendan said.

"No, I mean it," Cordelia said. "Think about it . . . once we walk through these doors, we can never come back here again. Ever. All the friends we've made here will be gone forever. . . ."

Brendan didn't say anything, actually considering her question this time.

"Plus," Eleanor added, "even in spite of all the dangers and terrible things we went through, you have to admit that part of you had fun, right?"

"Somehow, this crazy world actually made us all better people," Brendan added, nodding.

"And made us all a lot closer in the end," Cordelia said.

The three of them stood there for several minutes and let their words linger. They reveled in the moment as they stared at the magical Door of Ways.

"Okay, it was a pretty cool experience overall, and I'll never forget it," Brendan finally said, breaking the silence. "But I think it's definitely time to save the world and get out of here now, right?"

"Let's do it," Cordelia and Eleanor said in tandem, which caused them all to grin.

And then, the three Walker children, still holding hands, took several steps forward and entered the light.

CHAPTER

101

"There you are!" Mrs. Walker shouted. "You're always running off. Come on, we need your help."

The three Walker kids opened their eyes and stared at the sunlit Kristoff House from the front driveway. There was no hole in the ceiling where Fat Jagger had spat them inside. His dead body was no longer draped on the front lawn. Everything in San Francisco looked to be back to normal, just as the Storm King had promised.

"What are we doing back here?" Cordelia asked, too overcome by the relief and joy of seeing San Francisco in one piece again to notice the moving truck sitting in the driveway.

"What's the matter with you three?" their mom said.

"Don't you remember? The estate lawyer found an updated version of Denver Kristoff's last will and testament in a safe-deposit box downtown. It turns out that he left the house in the care of his next of kin. And since Dahlia Kristoff passed away last week, that made your father the next in line."

"So the house is officially ours?" Eleanor asked, hardly daring to believe it was true.

"Yes, honey," Mrs. Walker said. "It's our new home . . . for good this time."

"So we can finally stop moving every week?" Eleanor asked.

"Definitely," Mrs. Walker said with a laugh. "Now, come on, let's all pitch in. I want us to have everything moved in when your father gets back from treatment . . . which could be any moment now! Who's up for some pizza and *The Three Stooges* tonight?"

She didn't wait for them this time as she walked toward the large moving truck to grab another box to carry inside.

"Dad's coming home?" Eleanor asked hopefully.

"It sounds like it!" Brendan said. "Let's go help."

He headed toward the truck, passing by one of the movers. It was the same guy Brendan had remembered talking to the other two times they'd moved recently.

"Wow, kid, your family sure has some commitment issues," the guy said as he lugged a box up the walkway.

Brendan shrugged but couldn't keep a grin off his face.

He boarded the moving truck and happily grabbed a box to carry. Before, Brendan probably would have complained about having to help carry boxes, but at that moment it sounded like the most fun (and safe) activity in the world.

Meanwhile, at the end of the driveway, Eleanor stood and stared at a small boy slowly skateboarding his way toward her. Her jaw dropped open as he smiled and waved. He continued rolling down the slight incline and then pulled up just short of her, kicking the board into his hand.

She knew it was impossible. It couldn't be him, even in spite of what Dahlia had told her before they left.

"Do I know you?" he asked. "You look familiar."

"M-my name's Eleanor," she stammered. "We're just moving in. I mean . . . we already lived here once before. But now we're coming back and . . . well, it's complicated."

"Sounds like it," he said, smiling at her.

And then she *knew* it was him. It may not have actually been him, but it was in a way.

"My name is Michael," he said. "We just moved in down the street. Just yesterday. All my friends call me Mick. You know, because of that old singer, Mick Jagger. My parents and their friends all say I look just like him."

CHAPTER

102

Eleanor nearly passed out. When Dahlia had asked her what was the one thing she wanted most in the world aside from her family, she had said a real, human friend like Fat Jagger. She hadn't expected anything to come from it, and she certainly hadn't expected to find a colossus waiting for her when she got back home. But this was the best option of them all.

"Can I call you Mick?" she asked.

He cocked his head to the side.

"Yeah, I don't see why not," he said. "I do feel like we're friends already for some reason. . . ."

Eleanor could only manage to smile in response.

"Well, I gotta go," he said. "But I'll see you around, I hope?"

She nodded and he hopped back onto his skateboard and rolled away. Eleanor walked back up toward the moving van to help unload the boxes. Cordelia was standing next to it gaping at her little sister.

"Was that who I think it was?" she asked.

"I think so," Eleanor said, grinning ear to ear.

"Will the Kristoffs ever stop surprising us?" Cordelia asked.

Eleanor shrugged and grabbed a box. Cordelia paused, then grabbed her sister and hugged her. She squeezed so hard Eleanor almost couldn't breathe.

"Come on," Cordelia said, finally releasing her. "Let's help get unpacked so the house will be all ready for dad when he comes home."

As if on cue, a cab pulled up the long driveway. The three Walker children turned and watched eagerly as the back passenger door opened and their father stepped out into the sunlight.

The three children dropped their boxes and rushed forward, engulfing Dr. Walker in a series of hugs. It was the ultimate Walker Hugwich.

"Wow, I was only gone for a few days," Mr. Walker said as he hugged them back, stunned and delighted at the same time. "I guess I should leave more often. . . ."

"No," Eleanor said, nearly in tears. "Please don't."

"Don't worry, I won't," Dr. Walker promised. "I'm here

to stay this time, I promise. Now, let's get settled, shall we?"

As the three Walker children headed back toward the house, Eleanor looked up at her older siblings hopefully.

"You really think it's finally all over?" she asked.

"Actually, no," Cordelia said, but she was smiling. "Somehow, I think this is just the start. The Walker family's new beginning."

Epilogue

It took the Walker children several weeks to realize that Kristoff House had several new residents besides their family. It had started with small things, such as items disappearing, only to be found weeks later, and the house cleaning itself while the kids were at school and Dr. and Mrs. Walker at work during the day.

Then, over time, the kids would swear they heard voices whispering to them at night. It frightened them at first, but slowly the voices became more distinct, clearer. And it became obvious that they were friendly voices.

Three weeks after moving back in, Brendan was the first to actually see one of the house's new *residents*. He'd been up in his room, trying on a new hat he'd bought for himself using birthday money. It was a San Francisco 49ers hat: the kind with a perfectly straight brim and all the stickers still on it. He was checking himself out in the mirror, adjusting the hat so it was slightly off to one side, when a face suddenly appeared behind him.

Denver Kristoff's face.

"That hat looks ridiculous, Brendan," Denver said.

His face wasn't as ragged and gaunt and horrific as it had been when he was the Storm King. Instead he looked just like any ordinary, writerly old guy with a large, gray beard. Even still, Denver Kristoff was dead and gone. And so no matter what he looked like, seeing him in the mirror was still terrifying.

Brendan screamed and spun around.

Nobody was there.

His sister Cordelia poked her head up into the attic, looking panicked.

"Are you okay?" she asked. "I heard you screaming!"

"I'm fine," Brendan said, sure he was going crazy. "I'm just . . . seeing stuff, I guess."

"Okay," she said slowly as if she didn't believe him. "But take off that hat; you look ridiculous."

Brendan wasn't seeing things, however. Several nights later, Cordelia sat in her room, writing in her journal, struggling over whether or not to tell a boy in her English class that she liked him. Not just liked him, but *really* liked him. She was even debating asking him to the homecoming dance. She looked up into the mirror on her vanity and nearly screamed when she saw Dahlia Walker's twelve-year-old face staring back at her.

"You should definitely tell him," Dahlia said.

Cordelia whirled around but saw only an empty bedroom.

It didn't take long for the three Walker children to conclude that the ghosts of Dahlia and Denver Kristoff were now living alongside them in Kristoff House.

One night, they brought a Ouija board to the attic at three a.m., the hour of the dead, and staged a séance. Dahlia and Denver made their presence known almost immediately by flicking Brendan's twice-severed earlobe, which he didn't find very funny. He'd become very sensitive about his earlobe since his adventures inside Denver's books.

But the ghosts of Denver and Dahlia eventually appeared before them as translucent, smiling figures that dimmed with the lights. They assured the Walker children that they meant no harm. They merely wished to live with their last remaining family members. To watch them grow and help out whenever possible.

And the three Walker children believed their promise.

Well, mostly. Because with the Kristoffs, you never really could be sure of anything.

CHRIS COLUMBUS has written, directed, and produced some of the most successful box-office hits in Hollywood history. He first made his name by writing several original scripts produced by Steven Spielberg, including the back-to-back hits *Gremlins* and *The Goonies*. As a director, Columbus has been at the helm of such iconic projects as *Harry Potter and the Sorcerer's Stone*, *Harry Potter and the Chamber of Secrets*, *Home Alone*, *Stepmom*, and *Mrs. Doubtfire*. As a producer, Columbus was also behind the hit films *Night at the Museum* and *The Help*.

NED VIZZINI (1981–2013) began writing for the *New York Press* at the age of fifteen. At nineteen, he published *Teen Angst? Naaah . . .*, his autobiography of his years at Stuyvesant High School. His debut teen novel, *Be More Chill*, was named a Best Book of the Year by *Entertainment Weekly* and was selected for the *Today* Show Book Club by Judy Blume. *It's Kind of a Funny Story*, a cult classic, was adapted into a feature film and was named one of the 100 Best-Ever Teen Novels by National Public Radio. *The Other Normals*, his third novel, was a Junior Library Guild selection. He also wrote for television, including MTV's hit show *Teen Wolf*.

CHRIS RYLANDER is the author of the Codename Conspiracy series and the Fourth Stall saga. A fan of chocolate, chips, and chocolate chips, he lives in Chicago. You can visit him online at www.chrisrylander.com.